For Simon
for loving my books when he hates historical fiction.

Prologue

Raphael's house, Rome, April 1520

The heavens opened and the rain poured down, making the streets of Rome look like streams. I was standing outside the studio I'd been working in for days, trying to dry off before entering, an ever-increasing puddle forming around my feet. I shuddered, wet and cold. The light was gloomy. I looked around. Outside, the clouds were dark, loud, threatening; inside, a sense of foreboding enveloped me like a cape. I never did like this weather. It always filled the air with sorrow, and now it gave me the uneasy feeling that I'd done the wrong thing.

The clouds clapped thunderously in agreement.

The door I was about to open was blown suddenly ajar by the wind. I stood still. Inside I could hear Cardinal Bibbiena, the man who, with flattery, had persuaded me to paint over my late master's most precious work. He was talking to somebody. I waited. Listened.

'The woman in the painting, who is she?' The voice was accusing, the accent northern European.

'Some whore he paid for.' I winced at the Cardinal's answer. 'Look here. He's even added a ribbon with his name on as proof of purchase.' He laughed. His guest did not.

'His reputation as the most . . .' The stranger paused, looking for the right word. '. . . *amorous* artist in all of Rome was no idle boast then.' The flames of his northern disapproval licked around the door.

'No, indeed it was not. His nature was ever thus.' The Cardinal adjusted his tone.

I hovered, afraid to enter, reluctant to retreat. The Cardinal's fleshy ringed hand slipped round the side of the door, pulling it to, shutting me out. I put my ear up close to listen some more.

'That must have been trying,' the cold, faceless voice said. 'For you. And your niece.'

'No. All this—' I imagined the Cardinal gesturing towards the painting, as I'd seen him do so many times before '—was nothing but lust, not love. Love. That was something Raphael shared with my dear Maria.' The Cardinal sniffed loudly as if fighting back the tears. 'He never recovered after she left this world. However, I have made plans to bury him in the Pantheon, in the same tomb as my beloved niece. They will be together at last.'

I reeled at the news and put a hand against the stone doorway to steady myself.

'Fitting,' came the reply.

'Yes, they were perf—' But before the Cardinal could finish the lie his guest cut him off. He had not come here to listen to how Raphael and the Cardinal's niece were perfect for each other, or some other made-up story.

'The world grieves to lose such a rare talent.' The northerner's voice now softened. I imagined him moved by the beauty of my deceased maestro's work on the easel before him, admiration warming his eyes. I'd recently added the finishing touches to it, painting over the tell-tale foliage and ruby ring. 'Even this rendition of a whore shows the scope of the artist,' he said. My chest dared to swell a little with pride, my ear suddenly forgiving of his harsh northern consonants, strangely deaf to his slur on the model. But he hadn't finished. 'Though it is not as flawless as

2

many of his other works. The background is . . .' He paused to find the right word. 'Clumsy.'

My hand shot up to my mouth in time to silence the splutter of surprise provoked by this foreigner's damning summation of the changes I myself had made to the painting. The Cardinal had told me he found them sublime. I held on to that. What did this man with the guttural accent know of beauty?

'And this hand,' he went on, 'it's . . .' He paused again. This time I wasn't hopeful. 'This hand, well, it's so . . . unnatural.' Though expecting the slight, I still flinched at the injury. Unnatural? The Cardinal had assured me the now ringless hand was so well executed as to be indistinguishable from any done by Raphael himself. But it made no difference; the stranger's words cut too deep for me to be able to heal the wound they had inflicted on me. My chest hurt as if punctured, and my mind conjured up a vision of claw-like hands stab, stab, stabbing at the parts of the painting I had worked on with such devotion. That northern European accent was beginning to grate.

But not as much as the Cardinal's deep, throaty laugh that followed. And not as much as the words that came after that.

'Yes,' he answered when he'd composed himself, 'sadly those elements do detract from the rest of the work. It's almost as if he'd allowed his least talented apprentice loose on it. That aside, Raphael was peerless – a prince among painters, brought down by this lowborn wench. That must surely be the reason for the angel tears falling from heaven down in the streets outside.'

It was still raining heavily – and ordinarily I would have wondered at the Cardinal's quickness of wit in using the elements to convey his own sorrow. But the revelation that he thought me the *least talented* of Raphael's apprentices came as a shock. My whole body shook and shivered, with cold, loss, then shame. Yes, an overwhelming sense of shame ran through me. I was drenched with it. It flushed out my vanity and ambition and presented them to me for what they were – ugly sins that had turned my head and seduced me into betraying one of the kindest people I had ever known.

'So the woman in the painting,' the grating voice started up again, 'she is the one who killed Raphael? She is the baker's daughter of whom everyone is talking?'

'Yes. Base. Immoral,' the Cardinal replied, the deep laugh now a lascivious sneer. 'This is the woman who brought down one of the finest artists the world has ever known with her wantonness. This is *La Fornarina*.'

I lifted my ear away from the door. I'd heard enough. My mind searched wildly for a borrowed dignity with which to disguise the tatters of my own. I scraped together some well-woven deceits with which to cloak myself made up of my righteous indignation at the Cardinal's undeniable duplicity. But it was no use. Thunder clapped outside once more. Yes, I had done the wrong thing and I did not need the elements to tell me so.

Chapter 1

Twelve years earlier

Rome, January 1508

The year was 1508, the month January, and it was a Friday. I remember it all too clearly. I was still innocent then. 'Pietro! Get that weak arse of yours up now!' My father's rough hands dragged me from my sleep. He threw open the shutters, exposing me to the bright glare of the early morning sun. 'If the Venetian throws you out too, I'll . . .'

My body tensed as he bellowed at me. 'S-s-s-s-sorry,' I stuttered, waiting for the blow.

It didn't come. Instead, my father looked out of the window, distracted by a commotion that had broken out down in the street below. 'The lads have pulled something out of the Tiber!' a voice called up to him. More voices joined in, urgent, excited.

My father looked back at me for a second, his eyes distressed at my attire. His knuckles twitched but they stayed at his sides; the sounds of men running towards the river was too great a lure even for him. He left the room, though his disgust remained.

I looked down at myself, at the white shirt and the yellow hose

I still had on from the day before and that I loved so well. My legs hurt, my eyes felt swollen, my head ached. Yesterday.

Yesterday my father was proud of me; I was an apprentice in the workshop of the great artist Michelangelo. This morning I was not.

Artists. They weren't popes or cardinals, kings or princes; in Rome they were better than that. At least in the eyes of people like my father – the common man. And that was because they walked among us, drank with us, sang with us, painted us. They even took us on as apprentices making our fathers proud.

Gifted, feted, popular, they enjoyed all the dishes at the rich man's table without having to torture or kill for them. Though Michelangelo had seemed no less ruthless to me.

It's true that most artists sang their happy song like a bird within its gilded cage, wings clipped, without the freedom to sing as they chose, fly where they might or most importantly paint what they liked. But one or two, whenever their patrons left the cage door wide open, soared high above and up into the heavens. And there they dazzled us.

Michelangelo was one such painter, though his temper was as brutish as his work was divine. And yesterday, talk in his workshop had turned to another: Raphael Sanzio. Though I'd not yet seen a single one of his paintings (he'd been working in Florence), I knew that as an artist he shone so brightly that nothing could subdue his brilliance, nor eclipse his perfection. *Perfetto, ottimo, squisito, meraviglioso, eccellente, superior, divino*. It was claimed that there weren't enough superlatives in the whole of the Italian language to express how exceptional Raphael was. And rumour had it that as a man he was as sublime as his work, in both character and appearance.

And now he was coming to Rome. The prospect of his imminent arrival was causing the already full cups of the rich and powerful to bubble over. Lists were being drawn up in fortified palazzos around the city of all the artworks they would have

Raphael paint for them. Of altarpieces, frescoes, birth trays, tondi, even going so far as to ponder which jewels and garments each family member should wear for that most essential object for the aristocrat hoping to dazzle with a show of wealth – the portrait. Prosperous families were coming to blows over whom Raphael would paint first.

And Michelangelo hated him for it.

That was why two starry-eyed apprentices, caught with Raphael's name in their mouths, were beaten and dismissed with nowhere to go. Luigi and Federico had promise. They would never fulfil it now, the fools. Those of us suspected of the lesser crime of listening to them had received a good kicking but were not completely discarded. Michelangelo had handed us over to another artist who had recently arrived in Rome, this time from Venice.

'That artist you've been passed on to, Sebastiano Luciani, he's got a good reputation. But be careful. They say he's another moody bastard.' My brother Giacomo's voice, deep with sleep, pulled me back to the present. He had still to get up. 'So keep your head down, otherwise Father will have it.' He yawned. 'And don't speak unless you have to. That stammer of yours can get you into trouble.' Giacomo's eyes studied my attire as I left the room. 'And try not to draw too much attention to yourself,' he called after me as I stooped down to pick my jacket up from the floor. I left, closing the door behind me.

I'd recently started grinding pigments at Michelangelo's. I'd enjoyed it. I walked in disgrace to the workshop of my new maestro, Sebastiano Luciani. A great colourist, he would surely have pigment grinders of his own. So what of me? Only the idea of Raphael Sanzio, an artist beautiful in mind and body, or so it was said, prevented me from feeling like a condemned man. By the time I stepped over the threshold of my new maestro's workshop I knew what I had to do – not say a word and try my best. I took off my jacket and ran a hand over my hose for luck before pulling on a white tunic and tying my leather apron at the back.

I had much to learn, from watching more advanced apprentices as well as observing Sebastiano himself. Yet as I and the other boys were taken round the workshop that first morning to admire our new maestro's work, I for one saw nothing superior in it. Though I knew better than to share my opinion. With every flick of Sebastiano's self-satisfied wrist as he presented another of his paintings to us, my face expressed wonder while my mind felt nothing but disappointment. The artist from Venice had some way to go before he even came close to deserving the reputation bestowed upon him.

It was said he had trained under the great Giorgione. If that was true he disguised it well.

'And this,' he said, standing in front of an unfinished work depicting a young, dark-haired woman, a fur-lined cape draped over her shoulder, 'is a piece I call *La Fornarina* – The Baker's Daughter – because she is the woman in the painting.' He clapped his hands together with delight and gave a little laugh as though sharing a secret joke with someone. No one laughed back.

'Note the composition . . . and the tones here . . . and here . . . And I say again, it's of . . .' He paused like an actor waiting for the crowd to finish his line. The silent horseshoe of apprentices grew bigger as each boy, bar one, breathed in. They wiped the palms of their hands on the leather aprons that protected their belted white tunics while taking a step back. Their wide eyes shouted respect and fear but not a peep came out of their mouths. Only Giulio Romano, standing at one end, an apprentice I'd known quite well at Michelangelo's, seemed calm and composed enough to say anything. I was surprised to see him here. Giulio was older than me and more skilful than the rest of us, the equal of Giovanni da Udine, who wasn't here; Michelangelo must have kept him on. Giulio appeared decidedly unimpressed as he looked at the unfinished painting before him. I caught his eye, distracting him from his silent assessment. He raised an eyebrow, mouthed: *'You tell him what it's called.'* I looked at him with foolish, trusting eyes and began.

'*La F-f-forn, f-forn . . .*' My mind swam, my face felt hot, and my eyes asked Giulio for guidance.

He mouthed: '*La F-f-fornicatora.*' Desperate and horrified that I'd stammered, I took Giulio's lifeline without caring to see what it was. Without thinking I threw it back out as quickly as I could.

'*La F-f-fornicatora.*'

The moment I said it I knew. And the squeal of delighted horror that pierced my left ear made by the young boy standing next to me confirmed it. But it was too late to take it back. The new apprentices fizzed and frothed, unable to suppress their mirth, and as I searched Giulio's face for an explanation I saw that his treacherous eyes had disappeared behind tears. Of laughter.

'Stupid boy!' It was Sebastiano who spoke.

Something ungovernable had been unleashed and the maestro of the workshop, the great Sebastiano Luciani, held me responsible for unleashing it.

He stood and waited, holding his head high like the grand *maestro* that he was. He coughed first, glowered second, and on the third count he attempted to beat the horseshoe of apprentices back into shape.

'It's called *La Fornarina. FOR-NA-RI-NA!*'

Squeaks and titters escaped from behind hands. The damage had been done. Sebastiano ranted and railed like a bad choir-master unable to keep control. Squeaks became shrieks, the titters guffaws. Eventually, beaten, a pained expression settled on his face and his nose twitched as if displeased by a bad odour. 'Let's to work!' he exclaimed with a clap of his hands. And then he walked away.

That was the end of our introduction to the workshop, and my first meeting with *la fornarina*, the woman in the painting. I did not like her.

Chapter 2

A flurry of prospective patrons with a penchant for portraits patrolled the workshop over the following days and weeks. Now there's a sentence I couldn't have said at the time. I kept my head down and worked hard. My father's ire was – for the moment – appeased. And though, after that first day at Sebastiano's, I'd been demoted to mopper-upper (all because I'd got the name of a painting wrong), I very quickly worked my way up to brush cleaner. Giulio said I was the best. The best brush cleaner he'd ever seen. And, very recently, I had been called on to grind pigments. At last. The job I'd had when I was at Michelangelo's was mine once more. Giulio had seen to that.

Giulio had a very special talent when it came to drawing that was in great demand. And the guilt he'd felt at the humiliation he'd caused me had prompted him to use his particular drawing skills to help me out. He had an excellent hand and eye when it came to drawing the human form, and Taddeo, in charge of assigning jobs in the studio, had a greedy interest in Giulio's particular line of work. He was so hungry to accept Giulio's latest drawing of a young woman, undressed, that he overlooked the fact that I might need training for one of the jobs I was soon going to be called upon to do. That I was managing to grind Verona green, umber, sienna, until I could hide behind their undulating hills of colour, must have misled him. But for now, we had no idea what disaster lurked up ahead. For both of us.

It was a Tuesday, the day that wretched girl came. Or was supposed to. I'd seen her once or twice. She was more graceful than in Sebastiano's, admittedly unfinished, portrait of her, her features less lumpen. She'd been unreliable of late, and her blatant lack of respect for the maestro divided the apprentices, shocking some (Taddeo and myself), entertaining others (Giulio and everyone else). Out of all the people to pass through the studio, she was the only one who'd ever said *buongiorno* to me. But I still didn't like her.

And now Sebastiano was waiting for her to arrive. He paced the studio floor, starting each time a would-be patron came through the door. His face forced a smile as noble after noble looked round the studio with a view to securing a portrait of themselves. The rich and the vain of Rome, unlike the girl with the floury skirt, were queuing up to be painted. They had bags of money with which to pay, while *la fornarina* clearly paid in other ways. As I peered over my impressive mounds of ground pigment, I observed Sebastiano. His eyes smouldered like hot coals sparking angrily to life every time they caught an apprentice chatting, smiling, looking up from his work. I slumped further down behind my pigment piles. I could only imagine that the girl in the unfinished painting was late with her payment.

A common baker's daughter, immortalised in paint by one of the finest painters in all Europe. At least, that was the reputation Sebastiano had. She did not realise her good fortune.

I looked on while the nobility of Rome jostled with each other to enjoy the same privilege, bombarding the maestro with questions.

'Who have you painted?'

'*Him*? Have you really?'

'*Her*? Well I never.'

11

'*Them*? How marvellous.'

'Could I possibly *see them*?'

'When can you start?'

'When can you finish?'

'How long must I wait?'

Interest was overwhelming. Portraits were easier and evidently more profitable than painting an elaborate fresco cycle for a church or a monastery, they needed less planning and were relatively quick to complete. Sebastiano must have been pleased when he'd turned his hand to them. But as I noticed the colour in Sebastiano's face rising, caught the flames flickering in his eyes, it was clear portraits were not uppermost in his mind this Tuesday. I kept my head down. He could go off at any second.

'Have you seen her?' He drew close to Giulio, his eyes pulled to the door by invisible strings.

I clapped a pigment-covered hand over my mouth as I watched an interested patron reach out to touch a just-finished portrait left to dry on an easel in the corner. 'The hair, it looks so real,' he trilled with enthusiasm.

Sebastiano turned. The invisible strings snapped.

'DON'T TOUCH!'

The nobleman jumped back. When the shock had subsided he glared at the artist.

'*Signore*, it's best you don't touch it . . . *per favore!*' Sebastiano added quickly, his good sense returning. It was one thing to shout at one's apprentices and quite something else to shout at one's patrons.

'One drawback with portraits,' he explained, his tone somewhere between apologetic and grovelling, 'is the drying time of the oil paint . . . *signore* . . . and it's a devil to get off one's fingers.'

Still, portraits were durable (when ready), and easy to display. And fashionable. That made them desirable at any price. That's why, shouted at or otherwise, this nobleman couldn't hand his ducats over fast enough in order to seal the deal.

For the next few hours Sebastiano occupied himself with business matters. He needed to simmer down. He sat in a quiet corner with interested patrons, and in a special book he recorded names, measurements, family mottoes, interests, estimated completion times, costs.

But when the business had been settled, and the last of the noblemen had been shown out, it was clear that the maestro still had that girl on his mind.

'Is she here yet?'

He stood before his painting of her and shouted. 'Taddeo! I need— Fetch me— Don't forget— Give me that—'

Sebastiano's demands spread out across the studio like molten lava and not even my mountains of ground colour could stem the flow.

'Here, boy. Pietro!' Taddeo had found me. 'The maestro needs lamp black.'

'But I don't know how to m-m-m . . .'

With consummate care and attention Taddeo trained me dutifully in the preparation of lamp black by considerately pointing to Cennini's handbook, *il libro dell'arte*. Every artist's workshop had a copy as it told you how to make pens, paper, brushes, work on frescoes, grind pigments – you name it, Cennini's handbook could tell you how to do it.

'Chapter th-th-thirty-seven,' he yelled at me, with the stammer a cruel and unnecessary addition, I thought. There was no need to make fun of me. 'Everything you n-n-n-need to know is in there.'

Sebastiano mixed lamp black with lead white to form the *imprimatura* for his paintings, the base for his portrait work. And so he needed it. Lots of it, as portraits were fast becoming his stock in trade. In itself lamp black was comparatively simple to make. And it was quick. The easiest way, according to Cennini, was to burn linseed oil in a lamp and collect the soot created by the process. It needed no grinding, and, once burned, the soot was as fine as powder. Even a fool could make it. 'Lamp black. Sebastiano needs more lamp black!' Taddeo shouted at me.

'Is she here yet?' the maestro's plaintive cry reverberated around the studio like an echo. Giulio raised an eyebrow.

*

The following Tuesday the atmosphere in the workshop was even more tense.

'The takings are down,' Giulio whispered in my ear as he passed by.

'B-b-but the p-p-portraits—'

'I know,' he said, cutting me off. 'If he would only allow me to do them.'

I sniffed at Giulio's arrogance. But he had a point. All Sebastiano had to do was work on the designs, start the drawings. The more experienced apprentices – Giulio among them – could do the rest. But the maestro would not entertain the possibility. Unfortunate, as he was experiencing artistic paralysis, the cure for which was that common girl. I willed her to appear.

'That commission, the one from Pope Julius,' Sebastiano barked at Taddeo, 'is it here yet?' That a papal commission Sebastiano had been promised had yet to turn up also did nothing to lighten the mood. 'It should be here by now,' the maestro muttered. Though apprentices nodded, they kept their eyes on their work, afraid to look up. Still, we all expected instructions from the Vatican to arrive at any moment.

'Is she here yet?' Sebastiano paced the studio. 'Is she not here yet?'

A red velvet curtain divided the workshop in two: one area, closest to the entrance, for the apprentices; and the other, at the far end, for the maestro and his baker's daughter. He had already pulled it up in anticipation of her arrival, ready to let it fall dramatically the instant she crossed from one side to the other.

14

He had yet to finish his painting of her. Tongues had, initially, wagged with wanton excitement as to why that was. The maestro, it was said, was too busy fornicating with the *fornarina* during their sessions together to find the time to plunge his paintbrush in his paints and get the work done. But that wasn't it, even though many of the younger apprentices held on to this illusion and even though, I suspected, the maestro would have wanted it so.

No, the reason he hadn't finished his painting of her was down to the fact that she rarely turned up. And many of the apprentices were now beginning to lose interest in the girl, the maestro, their supposed relationship, and the painting.

Giulio was taking a break from grinding lapis lazuli to make pens, some fine, some broad. He'd been instructed to make six of each. I was tempted then to ask why he had twenty quills ready instead of twelve. But I already knew the answer. He was stealing them. Out of defiance. But also because he needed them. I'd seen him slip charcoal into his pockets before, that he'd used to pursue his sideline in unsavoury drawings. I wondered that his pockets weren't bulging. I looked at them and saw that they were.

'Where is she?' Meanwhile Sebastiano's frustration spread out over the studio like a barbed net, causing apprentices to jump and writhe and pray that the girl would arrive soon and put them all out of their misery.

Giulio breathed in deeply. Both eyebrows rose. He glanced at me. He'd had enough. Mischief danced across his features.

He rummaged round his bag and pulled out a miniature portrait – a copy, no doubt, that he had made himself. It was of a young man, handsome, and clothed. Giulio passed it round the squirming apprentices as if it had soothing powers.

'Look. This is a portrait of Raphael of Urbino, the artist. He's recently arrived here in Rome.'

At the mention of Raphael's name, I felt the pain in my leg where Michelangelo had kicked me, imagined my father's knuckles as they twitched at his sides. I kept well away. Taddeo's

15

beady eyes were everywhere and I could not afford to get into any further trouble. Giulio on the other hand seemed to laugh in the face of fate. And fortune seemed to favour him.

'Giulio! You need to be quicker.' Taddeo's voice was all authority. Giulio's face was all scorn. You couldn't rush Giulio Romano and to do so made him slow down intentionally. He put down the quills he'd been working on, stretched out his arms high above his head then gave a yawn. Taddeo scuttled back to his place.

Meanwhile, the miniature portrait had made its way around nearly every workbench, dazzling the eye and mind of each apprentice and elevating them above Sebastiano's net of barbs. Raphael. Quite the hero, and to see his likeness confirmed it. The apprentices at the workbench nearest to Taddeo had put down their tools in anticipation. Unable to resist, they huddled round the boy currently looking at it.

'Is that him? Is that Raphael?'

It did not matter that the words were whispered, barely audible to the human ear. Sebastiano had heard them. Like a hunting dog, and Michelangelo before him, he sniffed the air.

'That's Raphael?' 'Is that Raphael?' 'Raph—?' Excitement had rendered the apprentices oblivious.

Sebastiano threw his paintbrush to the floor and roared.

'I never, NEVER, want to hear that name in here again. Understand?' The voices of the young apprentices died instantly; the miniature was hastily pushed under a pile of sketches.

'What's the time?' Sebastiano asked.

'Half past ten.'

'I know it is, Taddeo. I know what the time is, you halfwit!' Sebastiano said. 'But where is she? That's what I want to know, you oaf. Where is she?'

The maestro stormed off, wearing his bad mood like an aura around his head. He stood before his portrait of the baker's daughter, as if willing her to step out of the picture.

The apprentices pulled out the miniature again, the urge to

see this now forbidden young artist more irresistible than ever. 'Nature made him then broke the mould,' one of them said with appreciation, taking care not to mention the artist by name. I was sure I'd heard that phrase somewhere before, but, while I struggled to place it, Taddeo, with eyes cruel and greedy as a tyrant's, marched over to see what was going on.

That tyranny begets tyranny was never borne out so clearly. Within seconds he had prised the portrait from their hands and was holding it up. He shot a look of victory in Giulio's direction. His mouth was open, about to chastise the apprentices for wasting time. Then he heard the cry.

'Taddeo!'

Sebastiano's faithful assistant glanced up at the portrait in his hand. He lowered his eyes. They met the maestro's, recognised what was coming next. Taddeo's eyelids flapped wildly, as if by blinking alone he could become airborne and escape. Beads of sweat broke out across his forehead.

'It wasn't me . . . It was them . . . They had it . . . I . . .' He mumbled his excuses. A spurt of pleasure shot through me as I watched his suffering. At once unfair and so deserved.

Sebastiano thundered over and snatched the offensive image out of the faithful Taddeo's hands.

He looked at it.

If the mention of the young artist's name had irked him already, the sight of Raphael's image up close put him in the foulest of tempers. Dark clouds marred Sebastiano's features like flies on rotting flesh. I glanced over at Giulio. He had a knowing look upon his face. It gave me a secret thrill to see it.

Sebastiano, miniature in hand, went over to the far side of the workshop to where his easel was set up. He smashed the perfect image down on a nearby table. 'Damn that wastrel from Urbino!'

He returned to pacing. This time we all hid behind our work.

'Have we no letter from the Vatican yet?' he shouted, pushing the miniature away. We'd heard a workshop was being set up for

Raphael. He had wealthy patrons, said to be friends of the Pope. 'Look at him!' Sebastiano said to himself, glowering at the likeness as if it were alive, 'as beardless as a young girl!' Several of the apprentices came out of hiding. They dragged strange sounds from their mouths and nodded, thinking they'd been called on to agree. They had not.

'Who asked you?' Sebastiano growled at their forced laughter and nodding heads. 'Go back to your work. Now!'

I looked towards the entrance, attracted by a sudden movement. And there, framed in the doorway with her eyebrows raised in mockery at the commotion, stood the girl. The girl the maestro had been waiting for. Here. In the studio. At last. Knowing I'd seen her, she glided in.

Sebastiano, his face blanching at the sight of her, ran to pull the heavy red velvet drape down, an action he had been waiting to perform for such a long time. She made her way to the table, intrigued no doubt to see the face of the man who had provoked the scene she'd just caught the tail of. She picked up the small portrait and gave an approving smile. Her face opened up like a flower in the sunshine at the sight of it.

Sebastiano noticed. His already cloud-eaten face turned blacker still. He tugged on the curtain repeatedly. It resisted his pull.

'Damn! Damn!'

The atmosphere in the studio cranked up to thunderous; in an instant the velvet curtain had crashed to the floor.

'Take it to the side, for heaven's sake!' At the flick of his wrist he conjured up two apprentices. They scuttled over and made the curtain disappear.

The girl was still waiting. Still amused. Still unperturbed.

'It's too warm to be wearing this,' she said, as she picked up the fur-lined cape hanging over the back of her chair. She draped it over her left shoulder nevertheless, while stooping over to pick up a laurel wreath from her basket. She wore it on her head like a green crown. I watched her, grateful for the patches of light and pockets of calm she had brought in with her. The maestro's bad temper, like a poison-tipped arrow, breached the walls of almost every other person in the studio, while she remained inviolate.

We had never observed Sebastiano paint this model before, though we'd occasionally heard them behind the velvet. We liked to imagine the scene, full of lust and desire. But today, with no curtain to shield our eyes, nor fuel our imaginations, we would get the opportunity to see Sebastiano and his model in the flesh. There was a sufficient whiff of excitement at the prospect to cut through the dark clouds of the morning.

We buried our heads in cleaning, grinding, planning, sketching. Every apprentice made the workshop seem busy. The noises of wooden brushes dropping on floors, paper tearing, knives cutting, chair legs scraping, had the space filled with life so that Sebastiano and his model would soon believe that no one was interested in what they were doing or saying.

But we were.

Whenever we looked something up in the Cennini, or asked a fellow apprentice for some help, we watched out of the corners of our eyes. Our maestro performed his role much as we'd envisaged, with the wandering hands of an attentive paramour. Yet his model seemed to have forgotten the yielding lines our heads had written for her, replacing them with some feisty ones of her own. She sat, her back straight, on a chair on a raised platform, bathed in the light that flooded in through the window.

Sebastiano went to hang a pearl drop from her ear.

'Please don't. I can do this myself,' she told him, with a shrug. No, Sebastiano's model was not responding in the way we'd expected at all. Sebastiano's fingers dropped from her ear to stroke her face; she reeled her head back like an untamed horse. The maestro attempted to smooth down her dress; she brushed his hand away. He caught her hand in his; she withdrew it, a delicate hand from a coarse, ill-fitting glove.

'I am the great Sebastiano!' he said, smoothing his own dark hair back with disappointed fingers. His widow's peak and pointed beard made his face look, in that moment, like a heart. Vulnerable, he cast his eye around the studio. Had we witnessed his humiliation as the girl rejected him? Overheard the girl's insolence as she refused his help? Our studied concentration on the jobs in front of us, and our louder-than-usual discussions regarding work-related matters, reassured him. 'The great Sebastiano!' he repeated, as he returned to the task in hand: the painting of the girl.

'Your hand needs to be pointing towards your heart,' he said. Afraid to touch her now, he modelled the pose for this lowborn girl himself.

I stole a glance at Giulio. His eyes twinkled with tears of mirth. To see the power this model wielded over the maestro entertained him.

'Now turn to the left and look at me. Look at me. Yes, that's right.'

I too was amused.

Yet something niggled at the back of my mind. Who was this worthless girl to treat the 'great Sebastiano' so? And how could he let her?

There was no money in it. And, from appearances today, no profit of the sort Sebastiano was interested in either. Whatever he was hoping to get from her it was apparent that he wasn't getting it. Nor ever would. I did not know whether to applaud or curse her but one thing was clear – she was not the girl we'd all assumed she was.

'When can you come again?' The sitting had come to an end and the maestro's voice was little, beseeching.

'I don't want to sit for you again. You've finished.'

'I haven't. The hand, pointing to your heart. It's not quite right.'

'You are *the great Sebastiano*,' she said, her voice mocking, 'you don't need *me* to finish your painting.'

'You can't stop coming. I forbid—'

The girl raised her hand. She looked around the workshop. It was silent. Conspicuously so.

'Sebastiano!' Her voice rang out like a warning bell. If she'd intended to bring the maestro to his senses, she hadn't succeeded.

Lust and pride, a heady concoction, had got the better of Sebastiano the great. And it made for the most unedifying of sights.

'You WILL come back . . . Powerful Romans pay a lot for a portrait by Sebastiano Luciani . . .' Bitterness twisted itself around his words. 'I have noble families queuing up for the privilege . . . yes, it's a privilege . . . I paint you and receive nothing in return. Girls like you . . .'

She threw her head back and lifted her shoulders. She'd heard enough. 'Remember, I did not ask to be painted.' She was strong, proud.

'I have an agreement with your father. I have paid him . . .'

'To PAINT me,' she said, giving way momentarily to exasperation. 'And now you have. But as for—' She broke off, aware that she had an audience. 'As for all the rest, believe me when I say that I will not be bought.'

We silent apprentices listened on. Excitement crackled in the air.

'Besides, my father needs me. There's a grain shortage going on. It might not affect you, but times are hard for ordinary working Romans.' She paused. 'And you made a promise you'd be finished by now. A promise.'

'Margarita. I can gi—'

'Ssh!' she hissed, trying to silence him. 'It's not about the money. All right, I will stay, for a little while longer, if you need to paint my hand. But trust me when I say I am deaf to all other entreaties.' We waited.

But as maestro painted model, they said nothing more to each other. Pockets of chat and the sounds of work built up again. The show was over. For the moment.

Chapter 3

Giulio was the first to retake the floor. He had finished with the quills and was now back on the lapis lazuli. His eyes twinkled with mischief. 'They found another body in the Tiber this morning, wearing nothing but a pendant of St Stefano.' He waited for the gasp. Instead, just when Giulio thought it was over, the disagreement between Sebastiano and his feisty model bubbled up again. Apprentices' eyes shot to the warring pair but Giulio drew them back again. He would not be outdone. He'd found the maestro's humiliation as amusing as the rest of us, but what was a lovers' tiff compared to the gruesome tale he had to tell? Lovers' tiff? It wasn't even that. No, Giulio had had his fill of listening to the desperate bleating of a lovesick fool chasing some girl the like of which he could pick up easily in one of Rome's many brothels.

He clicked his fingers, gave a dismissive shrug of his shoulders to show his disappointment at the master's performance, and carried on with his own story. He beckoned us closer. 'Man. Young,' he clarified. 'Found with the remains of his hose wrapped around an ankle, a coin in his throat with a huge stone wedged in his mouth to keep it there, and a pendant of St Stefano wound one time too many around his neck.'

For a second Giulio looked straight at me, a knowing look on his face. I told myself I was imagining it.

'He was a pretty boy, if you get my meaning,' he added. I knew then I was not. My stomach lurched. My skin prickled. I felt threatened. But the other apprentices noticed nothing of the tacit communication that had passed between Giulio and myself. All they wanted was for him to go on with his grisly story and they strained their ears to listen some more.

'Nose cut off.' No longer interested in me, he threw himself into the performance, slicing the air with the side of his hand. While his audience made noises of pity for the pain of losing one body part, he hit them with another. He thrust his hips forward and slapped his two hands between his legs. 'Cock too.' This time he grinned like a fool. Smothered titters and horrified howls rippled around him. 'I even heard that they cut off his . . .'

'LAMP BLACK!' Sebastiano's roar, followed by the sound of something clattering to the floor, put an end to the morning news as told by Giulio. The maestro's disagreement with his model was over, again, and the one with us was about to start.

My heart was still thumping against the prison of my ribcage, my mind imagining the dead body. But Giulio had been silenced. For now. And I was glad of it.

I looked over to discover what had brought about this change. A messenger from the Vatican had finished talking with a disgruntled Sebastiano. The messenger made apologetic gestures; Sebastiano exuded disappointment. The workshop had not secured the large commission after all. I watched him as he returned to his model. He whispered what I deduced from the look on her face was a question. It caused her to pick up the miniature of the artist Raphael that had been thrown down on the table earlier on while the maestro himself moved his head round the workshop like a lit torch in the dark. We looked down at our work.

'You shouldn't ask a question when you have no desire to know the answer,' his model's even voice replied. 'I am no flatterer, nor will I ever be.' What could Sebastiano have asked? My mind worked hard to fill in the gaps; all I could come up with were the vain enquiries of a self-deluding madman.

Sebastiano puffed up his chest. This could only end one way. The girl gave her answer. Sebastiano let out a roar.

We worked hard, harder than ever. Lamp black, lamp black, lamp black, I told myself. The pressure was palpable. The maestro's roar told us his model's answer had not been the sweet consolation he was seeking after the papal disappointment. He was going to be taking his frustration out on us for the rest of the day. As I struggled to keep up with the demand for lamp black, the girl who was responsible for Sebastiano's latest show of anger walked by. She passed in front of the bench I was working at, swinging her basket. She displayed none of the outward signs of a lover spurned or model chastised. If she was quaking with fear, she didn't show it.

I looked up all the better to see what the attraction was now that she was so close to me. Though the clothes she had on now were not as fine as the ones she had been dressed up in by Sebastiano for the painting, and the pearl earrings were no longer hanging from her ears, and a single laurel leaf was all that was left of the wreath sitting on her head, the colour and style of her hair were the same, as was the shape of her face and the deep brown eyes.

I thought about the portrait. Close though the Venetian was in capturing this young woman's likeness, I could not say that his art had in any way improved upon nature. The girl, though not of noble birth, as was clear from the way she dressed, was a beauty, her skin soft and plump, the light in her eyes warm and radiant. The light in the studio was good and to see her movements swathed in it made me question Sebastiano's rendition. He acted like a man bewitched but there was no hint of this in his work. What he had produced was a lacklustre imitation, competent in that it was recognisable, but without expressing the life and energy of this bewitching creature who danced past me, skirts swaying, hair bouncing, and whose flesh, I couldn't help but notice, quivered ever so slightly with every up and down sweep of her arm.

Not that I found this jiggling of flesh attractive myself, not even at fourteen, but I could see, in that moment, why many men would. She moved the way she spoke. There was something to be learned from her. She was rebellious yet not aggressive, confident yet not brash. Strength, grace and gentleness radiated from every step and turn of her head. Qualities I'd thought of as quite disparate harmonised within her. I was in awe and could do nothing to resist. Sebastiano, in the same moment, had noticed her movements too. They elicited an altogether different response in him. And it wasn't the one we'd seen when he'd been painting her earlier.

'Stop swinging your basket!'

He was cross with the girl. No longer the amorous artist. It must have been something she'd said.

Though usually changeable in temper, events of the morning had made his humour worse than ever. I looked over to see him push the miniature of the artist from Urbino across the table in a fit of rage. It scraped across the surface, flew off the end, and crashed to the floor.

Not satisfied the miniature was on the floor, he kicked hard at it, pushing it away still further. Giulio sucked the air in through his teeth. The girl with the basket reddened. For the first time she appeared vulnerable. I was surprised.

Then I understood.

Sebastiano was jealous.

I looked at his blotchy face. His nose was an angry red and his eyes were incandescent with a rage so strong it threatened to consume him.

As for the girl's cheeks, they returned from flush red to a warm pink the nearer she got to the door. She sprang by, determined not to be cowed by Sebastiano's display of bad temper. She gave me a wink.

'STOP . . . SWINGING . . . THE BASKET!'

Sebastiano's voice boomed across the workshop like a clap of thunder.

In my shock I jumped. I have no idea what the dancing girl without the pearl earrings did because I froze. It was my heart that now lurched into my mouth – preferable to the contents of my stomach that had threatened to make a reappearance in response to something Giulio had said earlier.

I'd knocked over the lamp and I watched in horror as hot linseed oil surged from it to create the most perfect of arcs. It slipped through the air and landed in the uncovered lapis lazuli dust on the neighbouring bench. Its globular heaviness made the precious pigment puff up. Thousands of specks of exquisite colour cascaded before my eyes. It was as if time had slowed down as I watched this disaster unfold. When I'd looked back up from the now settled ultramarine powder the girl was nowhere to be seen. The main door slammed shut. She'd gone.

I turned to look at Giulio. Mockery had vanished from his eyes. Arrogance had abandoned him. He was looking behind me. His mouth opened as if to speak but it was as if the deluge of the shock within had flooded him so completely that no sound came out.

Then I felt it. Sebastiano's heavy palm, slap, on the back of my head.

I stumbled forward, gasped for air. I sneezed, my nostrils irritated by the dust Giulio had produced after hours of grinding. Celestial dust. Colour of the heavens and the Madonna's sacred robe. The most expensive pigment in all the world. And now it lay over the bench like a fine covering of newly fallen snow. The hand that had struck me wrapped itself around my upper arm and squeezed hard. I felt the gold ring on one of his fingers dig into me. I sneezed some more, unable to stop. I watched, appalled, as moisture now clung to the lapis dust to form dark, wet dots. The same hand that squeezed me shook me. Pain and

26

shock rendered me breathless. Sebastiano had achieved his aim: I stopped sneezing. But by then it was too late.

I looked at Giulio. In my naivety I hoped that he might be able to do something, say something, that would save me: it was clear he could not. Invisible ropes had already started to pull him back to his place of work. His eyes looked on me with sympathy but his work-worn hands were securely tied. He had no choice but to watch as Sebastiano dragged me to the heavy oak door of the workshop and cast me outside. He threw my jacket after me.

'Think yourself lucky I don't get you locked up for this. The money you've lost me! Now clear off! Talentless dog that you are!'

As the door slammed shut behind me, I imagined my father's knuckles cracking.

Chapter 4

I could not believe what had just happened. The injustice of it burned the backs of my eyes. What would Father say? What would he do to me? I lay there sprawled across the street, too afraid to move.

Passers-by walked round my fourteen-year-old body as I allowed Sebastiano's taunts (preferable to those I anticipated from my father) to still ring in my ears. Some walked over me, tripping as they went. But I remained there, eyes shut tight, not knowing what to do next.

I must have been lying there for ages by the time someone gave in to temptation and decided to have some sport at my expense. A full-blown hammer foot made its way into my side. Winded, my eyes shot open. I spluttered, gasping for air and feeling like a pig's bladder. 'Look at you in your yellow hose!' a cruel voice mocked. 'You look like a g—' But before he could finish someone had pulled him back, causing him to thud, backside first, on the ground. Laughter rippled all around. The disturbance was attracting quite a crowd.

'Get off him! What are you doing, you filthy worm-head? Leave the poor devil alone!' It was the girl in the painting, the one with the basket, she of the flour-hemmed skirt, and she was yelling and pushing my attacker away. 'Get off with you! Get away! Kicking a lad when he's down. Some brave man you are!' People's sympathies changed direction like ears of wheat as this feisty girl vented her rage towards my attacker. Shouts of agreement came from people in the street. The *brave man* who'd kicked me when I was down scrambled to his feet.

'If you was a man and not a girl you would not be able to speak to me so,' he snarled, half standing and wiping his nose with the back of his hand.

'Well I am a girl,' my saviour announced, 'and I will shame you all the same!'

Sounds of approval rustled all around.

The man who'd used me as a kickball looked at the angry faces. The fear that what he had done to me might be done to him was etched deeply on his face. He turned heel and took flight.

The girl stooped down.

'Thought I'd come back and make sure you were all right. Lucky I did! Here, let me help you.' Careful not to let her basket out of sight she dragged me up to sitting. I reached out for my jacket and pulled it to me. 'Feeling better?'

I nodded that I was, though that I couldn't bring myself to speak told her that I wasn't. I felt as though I'd received a stunning blow to the head and a crippling kick in the ribs, probably because I had. And I was now in shock, unable to comprehend what had befallen me. Yet my faithful, unwanted friend, humiliation, was slowly spreading across my body like a rash as the whole sorry experience came back to me. I hoped she hadn't seen everything. Her hand on my shoulder, gentle and caring, told me she had.

'You're not like all them – them inside.' She gestured to Sebastiano's workshop with a tilt of her head.

The girl with the soft brown eyes had a soft, sweet voice, and although she intended for her words to comfort me, instead they thrust the knife in, gave it a turn. 'You belong out here in the real world.' I rubbed my side, a reminder of how painful the real world could be. Understanding flickered across the girl's face. 'Oh, that's not what I meant!' She laughed. I winced. 'No! It's just, well, I could tell when I saw you in there. You're well, you're more like, well, more like me, I suppose.' I looked at her. She was pretty enough, certainly prettier than Sebastiano's portrait of her, but her clothes, I saw for the second time that day, gave away her rank; no matter how clean they were, no amount of care could stop flour from clinging to the edge of her skirt, and patching only drew one's attention to well-worn cloth. My hand went to brush some of the dust off my brightly coloured hose.

'It's better to be honest and have your self-respect intact than allow another person to treat you like an animal.' She patted me on the arm as she chatted on about the virtues of being what I could only presume was *like her*. This repelled me at the time. But in my defence, upbringing had a large part to play in how I was thinking that day. As well as fear. I had been brought up by a father who constantly told me how he had married beneath himself and had lived to regret it. He'd got married for love, to a lowborn woman who had gone and died. She'd brought him no dowry, given him seven sons. 'And then she died, giving birth to you!' My father had shouted this at me often enough to make me realise he'd never forgiven either of us for that. My mother for leaving him, and me for staying alive.

I looked at this girl with the passably pretty face and the dress that she'd made good and kept washed. And I imagined my mother. I quickly pushed the thought away. That way danger lay. The woman was dead. No good would come of softening towards a memory, nor towards a girl with little to her name.

But she had saved me from the ruffians; that much was true. 'Thank you . . . for chasing off those thugs.'

'Oh, that was nothing. And there was only one of them. Besides, did you not see how we all came together to support you?' The crowd had now dispersed but with a flourish of her hand this girl presented every passer-by to me as if each one of them was a saint or an avenging angel. 'It's the likes of *Signor Importante* in there that we both need to be wary of. The great *maestro*.'

An old woman walked by, and, overhearing our conversation, shouted out, '*Si, ragazzo*, no shame in being one of us. The people of Rome are the best in the world.'

Then, as if to prove it, a man with a donkey smiled at me, his weather-beaten face as brown and shiny as well-used leather. I waited for him to offer himself up as one of the self-righteous rabble. He did not disappoint. '*Si, ragazzo*, plebeian.' He chuckled. 'That's what we are.' His voice was as gravelly as the dirt roads he walked along, albeit streaked with a pride that, in my newly fallen state, I was far from understanding. For me it was as if I had been expelled from the Garden of Eden, while plebeian was a word my father used when describing my dead mother – and he didn't mean it as a compliment.

I stared with longing at the large oak doors, now firmly shut behind me. The thought that Paradise was on the other side and that there was no longer any place for me there bored a hole in my heart. That Sebastiano should be cast as God was one of life's little ironies – earthbound paradises had their drawbacks.

I shuddered.

The girl's hand, still on my shoulder, felt the tremor within. 'Artists! Who do they think they are? Gods?' she cried, as if reading my thoughts. 'Look at you, with your bright eyes!'

I lowered my eyelids to stop her from seeing any more. I looked down at my lamp-black-stained hands, the soot in and around my fingernails. As I hid them in the folds of my shirt I discovered the holes at the elbows of my tattered sleeves. My fingers slipped through to the bones. They stung to the touch, felt wet and sticky. I guessed they were bleeding. My eyes drifted up towards the hands and attire of the proud plebeian leading away his trusty steed that was no more a steed than I was now an artist's apprentice, never mind an artist.

What was that saying my father liked so well? Something about every ass thinking himself worthy to stand with the nobleman's horses? Well, I was the ass. The man's clothes were no worse than my own, and, in many ways better, I realised, as my fingers now covered the recently made tears in my sleeves. But I still couldn't think of myself as a plebeian, no matter what I looked like, no matter that I'd been cast out. Ass, yes. Plebeian, never. I rubbed my shoulder blades, half hoping to raise angel wings from beneath the skin, for in that moment to be a fallen angel far outshone life as a common man.

'All right! Take it easy! I only wanted to make sure they hadn't hurt you.' I'd brushed the girl's hand off my shoulder a little too brusquely while checking for feathers. The indignation in her voice pulled me back to myself.

'Thank you. For stopping,' I said again, remembering the tens of Rome's finest who hadn't.

'It was nothing,' she said, her voice soft once more.

'My name is Pietro,' I told her.

'Margarita,' she replied. Although I already knew that.

She held out a hand, helped me to my feet, then led me to the side of the street. I staggered slightly and leant against the wall to steady myself. To hope she hadn't noticed was too much to ask for, that I knew already, but I had hoped for a little sensitivity in the way she addressed it. Instead she went for the blunt approach. 'You've had the wind knocked out of you right enough,' she said. 'Your eyes look like cockroaches on a bedsheet. Your hair's gone grey with the dust and your . . .' but then she stopped mid-flow. And for that I was truly grateful.

My eyes, screwed up and looking for the ground beneath to gape open and swallow me whole, lifted to see what or who had caused this direct-talking girl to desist. Striding towards us was a papal party, as intimidating as an invading army, and there, at the head of the group, was a fierce-faced Cardinal, red robes flowing, his band of mercenaries marching behind him. The Cardinal's eyes swivelled left and right, sweeping all before him. The disgust they registered as he looked upon me turned to desire as they fell upon Margarita. I thought I saw recognition cross his face. But if I did, it vanished as quickly as it had arrived.

Besides, by the time he looked at her again she had turned her back towards him, a gesture of defiance so flagrant I expected one of his thuggish entourage to drag her away by the hair. I was relieved when they didn't. She was uncouth and lowborn, and to accept charity from such a person did kindle some sparks of resentment, but I was starting to appreciate her kindness and recognise its value – despite her unchecked tongue – in this city that to me seemed now full of hostility and danger.

'That was Bibbiena.' She almost spat the words out. That she had failed to say 'Cardinal Bibbiena' did not surprise me. I was beginning to get the measure of the girl. 'The man's a worm-head,' she continued as she arched her neck after Bibbiena and his men. 'Good. The piece of filth has gone. Time I was going too. You'll be all right?' she asked.

'Of course,' I lied, strangely invigorated by her use of the local vernacular. 'I'll take myself home and I'll be fine.'

She put one hand on my shoulder again. I did not recoil. She nodded, satisfied with my answer. 'Look after yourself, Pietro, and if you ever happen to be in Trastevere, come and say hello. My father runs a bakery there, on Via Santa Dorotea. His name's Francesco Luti.'

'Many thanks . . . Margarita. And you too . . . l-l-l . . .' I could not say 'look after yourself'. I satisfied myself with a repeated 'many thanks.' She smiled. She'd touched me and she knew it and she plunged her fingers in my dust-coated hair to acknowledge the fact, giving it a vigorous, sisterly ruffle before setting on her way. And with that she was gone, dancing her way along the street, head bobbing and dark brown hair rippling behind like a stream as she swung her basket up and down, all thoughts of Cardinal Bibbiena gone.

It was in my mind that I would probably never see this girl

again, and, for the briefest of moments, this saddened me. I was rubbing at my eyes with the back of my hand, when I noticed a growing din coming from an exuberant group of young men. You had to be careful in Rome, even in the daytime. A cardinal and his followers was one thing, the arrival of noisy groups of men charging along the street was something else. It could herald danger for a boy on his own, a boy like me, no matter what Margarita believed.

Margarita. For a moment I hoped she would come back; she seemed more than capable of handling thugs. But as the sounds grew clearer it was evident that the approaching group did not have violence on their minds. Artists and apprentices, wielding nothing more dangerous than paintbrushes, paint, and paper, were heading towards me. Relief and trepidation flooded my senses in equal measure.

I put a hand up to shade my eyes for fear of being recognised and to hide their tell-tale puffiness. I needn't have worried. Not a head turned my way. Every boy in the group had eyes only for their leader and they jostled with one another to get close to him.

As heads parted I saw him for myself. Even from afar, I understood why these young men were leaping like spring hares. There he was, a handsome young man, surrounded by excited young men dressed in the latest fashions, with him the most fashionable of them all. His brilliant white shirt billowed like a dazzling sail, his black velvet jacket was slung over his shoulder as if that was the way it was meant to be; his perfect hose were well tailored and, as my eyes fought to find a break lower down in the wall of bodies around him, I caught sight of well-sculpted calves. As for his hair, topped by a black velvet cap, he wore it longer than most young men of Rome at the time but it looked all the more attractive for that. Long, dark, and neat, it framed the most luminous of faces out of which shone the most beguiling of smiles. I watched him, transfixed.

And the closer he got the more I felt sure I knew him. Who

was this beautiful man? I racked my brains. I'd seen him very recently. But where? At one of the studios? Had I happened across a likeness of him? That was it: the miniature portrait, the one Giulio had passed round only that morning. 'Likes to pose more than paint! Look at him! Steals the ideas of others. No originality. The man's a pretty-faced apprentice. *Nothing else.*' I recalled the fierce red patches of resentment on Sebastiano's face as he raged against the likeness of the clear-faced person here before me. Yes, I knew this man: it was the artist Raphael Sanzio.

Awe, warm and comforting, flooded my soul as Sebastiano's 'pretty-faced apprentice' drew near, rapidly followed by an unpleasant chill; I recognised two of the boys vying to get close to him. A sense of shame lapped all around me with its icy waves. Luigi and Federico had been kicked out of Michelangelo's workshop the same time as me. They'd had nowhere to go. The memory of my having sneered at them stung like a newly opened wound. They would have the last laugh now, if they saw me. I averted my eyes.

'Pietro? It's Pietro!'

Too late. Luigi had spotted me.

I looked at him with a weak smile, a nod of the head, and a feeling akin to gratitude that he seemed to have no intention of breaking away from the group to talk to me further. But then . . .

'Is this man one of your friends?' The dazzling figure at the centre of the group stopped dead some distance away from me, his voice cutting across the street. His followers stopped too, squashed in a huddle. I made to get away but my foot had gone to sleep, causing me to trip up. I fell. My nose was in the dirt. When I turned around Raphael was looking down on me.

Then I understood.

I saw for myself why the fools jostled to get close. Yes, to my fourteen-year-old mind it was as if all the virtues radiated from him. He was grace, truth, and beauty. The smile he gave me was unwavering, and so bright that I had to lower my eyes.

'So this is Pietro, you say? It's a pleasure to make your acquaintance, Pietro. My name is Raphael. From Urbino.'

I blinked up at him. Luigi, the boy who'd spotted me, nodded enthusiastically and pulled me up to sitting. Urbino. One word can evoke a whole world. Reputed to have the most civilised court in all of Europe, Urbino was where, it was said, manners, appearance, philosophy, and art had all combined to create this most perfect of artists. And here he was standing before me, the idea of perfection in human form. The white of his shirt dazzled me once more. I looked down upon my own apparel and saw the sorry tale it told. I had no need to say what I'd done, where I'd been, my dishevelled appearance said it all. I had tell-tale paint splashes all over, I was outside Sebastiano Luciani's studio, I was covered in the dust and dirt of the street, and although I'd tried hard to swallow them back, tears had insisted on drawing lines down my face. I winced and wondered how this perfect courtier would manage to withdraw friendly overtures without the whole affair seeming awkward.

Instead he pressed me for my story. His followers listened attentively.

'Your father is a potter? How interesting.'

'Yes. And I-I-I . . .' I felt the fire of embarrassment burn behind my cheeks. My infernal stammer!

'He's been apprentice to Michelangelo and Sebastiano.' Luigi saved me.

'Fine artists,' Raphael said. 'Two of the finest in all of Rome. The best, in fact,' he continued, somewhat generously, I thought, as I knew both well enough to be certain that neither one of them would ever have said the same of him.

He placed a hand on my shoulder before retreating to confer with Luigi and Federico. I could not make out the words but their tone was gentle. When Raphael looked back at me, his eyes bore no trace of ridicule.

Their discussion was over.

'It has been an honour and a privilege to make the acquaintance of such an experienced apprentice, Pietro. I hope—' he placed a hand on my dust-stained shirt once again '—you might consider continuing your apprenticeship with me. With us.'

I smiled my gratitude as I knew words would fail me.

'Now we'll be off,' Raphael said. 'We will meet again very soon I hope, Pietro.'

I nodded – I could do nothing else – and I watched him as he led his followers away. When the last one of them had disappeared through the arch at the end of the street I noticed that the sky was clouding over. I'd better get home before the weather breaks, I thought to myself, and tell my father the good news.

Chapter 5

Most times you will hate me when I tell you my secrets and confess to the lies I have told, but once or twice, when I tell you what I have told no one else, you might find it in your hearts to pity me. What I'm about to tell you is one such time.

I should never have told him the truth, when I returned home, of what had happened to me that day. Or at least I should have told him the good news first. Either way, my story might have been very different, a tale of a potter father laughing, back-slapping and congratulating his talented son on being newly apprenticed to Rome's most shining star. We would have celebrated carnival together, watched the processions trail past, and I could have pointed Raphael out to my father in the crowd. He would have showered me with paternal pride. I would have reciprocated with filial affection.

Instead, all that rained down on me was this.

'You're like her, like she used to be – weak! Useless! You take everything, give nothing.' That was my father. I told you he'd never forgiven my mother for leaving him with seven sons to bring up. He went on. And on. I covered my ears to keep his brutal words at a muffled distance. But still his face contorted before my eyes. I closed them tight, turned them inwards desperately searching for somewhere to hide. But my father wouldn't let me.

'No more! You're out! I'll not have you here anymore.' He screamed the words into my ears, causing a fire to rampage within. My eyes shot open.

'Shut up!' I wanted to scream in his face. 'Shut up! Shut up! Shut up!' Instead I begged my father not to cast me out. 'P-p-p-please. Please d-d-d-don't! I'm sorry, Father. Forgive me. Please. Father!' But his clay-stained hand was already grasped tight around my arm, ready to throw me away and see me smash to the floor like a misshapen pot.

I'd told him how Sebastiano had treated me. His vice-like grip as his fingers pressed themselves into my flesh confirmed this had been a mistake. But if I told him about my good fortune in encountering Raphael from Urbino, I reasoned with myself, I could prevent the worst from happening. A threat to throw me out was, after all, just a threat.

'But something g-g-g . . .' I stumbled over my words again. I had a habit of doing so at times like this. It irritated me. But not as much as it irritated my father.

I dared not try to explain again. My only hope was to submit to his tirade and pray that he wouldn't follow through and banish me from home completely.

'Useless!'

My arm still in his grip, he shook me before releasing me with a savage push. Searing pain ran through my upper arm, across my shoulder and up my neck. I staggered forward. My instinct was to cry out but I knew I shouldn't. I bit my tongue. Reined myself back in. I could hide my feelings, conceal how and who I was. I'd had to do so ever since I was small. And on the rare occasion when I'd failed to dissemble, silence had come to my aid. I prayed it would do so now.

This will pass, I told myself. *This will be over soon.*

I had no choice but to watch and wait. My father wiped at his palms repeatedly. It seemed as if, by touching me, he believed he'd sullied himself. He studied his hands with horror. I was unclean, a contagion. He went over to the water butt, thrust his arms in as deep as they would go, then tried to wash the imagined taint away. Water sloshed around, cascaded over the sides, formed pools on the floor.

I hurried to mop it up. I shouldn't have.

'Should have weighed you down with stones when you were a baby and thrown you in the Tiber!'

My father got hold of my hair. He plunged my head into the butt. It was no Tiber but he was going to have a good go at weighing me down in the next best thing.

My nostrils stung. My eyes screamed. My lungs burst. My arms were splashing, thrashing, now crashing against the sides. Heavy hands pinned me down, under the water. Every muscle in my body fought for survival as I bucked and bolted against the blackness. Heavy hands gave way. My head reeled backwards. I spluttered and gulped at the air greedily. Dirty-tasting water gushed out of my nostrils, got pushed up at the back of my throat. I collapsed on the newly sodden floor, gasping.

My father was wiping his hands on his dirty overalls by the time I looked up. His nose wrinkled as if at a bad smell. He picked up a jug full of wine and slugged it back before pointing a finger at me in condemnation. Hope, rekindled in my soul by the meeting with Raphael, was all but extinguished as I sat in the pool of clay water on the floor. My hair dripped. My nose ran. And my father hadn't finished with me yet. He put the jug to his lips once more. Red wine trickled down his chin until it could trickle no more. He slammed the jug down, angry it was empty.

He turned to face me and snarled.

'I cast you out upon the Burning Plain.' This thinly veiled reference to Sodom made me shiver. I'd been with my father when we'd heard street preachers speak out against sodomy enough times to know what his opinions were on the matter. And also to know what he'd do if he ever found one of his own sons was a sodomite. But who could have told him? Giacomo. My brother

Giacomo must have told him. My encounter with an older boy last summer came back to me, bringing with it feelings both happy and sad. It had seemed so right until Giacomo caught me and tarnished what I'd done with ugly words. I dragged myself up, opened my mouth to speak but no sound came out.

It wasn't Giacomo.

Father put a hand in the pocket of his leather apron and pulled out . . . no. It couldn't be. It was. 'I'll have none of Sodom under my roof.' Father had my precious book in his hands, the one where I wrote down all my hopes . . . and secrets. He waved it around, nodding, his features ugly with disgust. It was *my* words Father had read. I had given myself away. I froze. He spat on the book before tearing it apart, scrunching page after page, then stamping each one into the filthy floor.

Outward silence belied my inner turmoil. Anguish raged and roared within my head, along with the watery memory of a story I'd heard (could it only have been that morning?) of a young, pretty boy and his gruesome demise. He'd been of Sodom too. Mutilated faces swam towards me. I pushed them away. But I could do nothing to stem the flow of tears that scorched my cheeks with searing rivulets of shame-coated anger. My father knew, knew what I was. I saw it in his eyes that burned into my flesh like hot needles. And I was the one who had told him by writing about it in my diary.

'And now you can't pay for your keep. When I found this last year . . .'

My heart missed a beat. He'd known about this last year and had said nothing. Until now. Why now? It was the money. It had to be. He didn't care what I was as long as I could carry on putting coins into the family coffers. I should have told him about Raphael first. I still wanted to tell him. There was still a way back for me.

'I-I-I . . . Pl-pl-pl . . . Y-y-y . . .' But try as I might the words wouldn't come. My senses had been flushed away, deaf to his

41

cruel words though they continued to flow out of him like vitriol, blind to his hateful looks though he still tried to stab me with wild eyes. And though bony fingers seized me once more I could feel no pain.

I came back to myself some time later. I was sitting in the filthy street. Cast out, again. My head waterlogged, my soul crushed. My jacket had been flung out after me. The clouds had moved in and were lying heavy over Rome. And I had nowhere to go.

Chapter 6

I stumbled through the narrow streets, holding my jacket with its four metal buttons close to my chest. Traders hawked their wares, donkeys dragged their fat carts through narrow alleyways and street boys chased round stray goats and chickens, throwing the occasional stone at me. Men loitered. Prostitutes laughed. And dogs barked at people slumped in the shadows. I had nowhere to go. After walking round and round I slumped in the shadows too. I had arrived at my destination: this was nowhere.

I sat against a wall, my legs under me. I stared blankly into space for some time. Discordant thoughts ricocheted violently off the walls of my mind. Though seated, they made me dizzy. I closed my eyes.

I must have fallen asleep. I don't know for how long but it must have been for a good few hours because by the time I woke up night had started to paint the street a darker shade of evening. It had also lured out a different sort of Roman. When my eyes had adapted to the lack of light I recoiled. Men still loitered, though more numerous than before, and several of them eyed me with interest. And now more desperate prostitutes laughed, forced and raucous, hoping to catch one of the many bawdy soldiers as they thundered past looking for another tavern to frequent.

Everything seemed louder and more lurid than before. I'd woken up to a nightmare.

It was also starting to get cold. I put my jacket on.

A torch was lit a little further down the street. It drew my eye. And it was then I noticed a boy, propped up diagonally opposite. He hadn't seen me yet. He was probably not much older than me though he looked as if he'd been suffering for all eternity. Even in the dull light he looked drawn. Sunken eyes, hollow cheeks, his entire body sucked in, his skin shrunken cloth on a skeleton, stick-thin legs splayed out before him like the roots of a tree. He was filthy – the torchlight could not disguise it – and his clothes were all rags.

I rubbed my face as if to clean it, dropped my hand to cover the bloodstained rip of my shirt so as to hide it. Knots of wealthy men and women threaded their way through and around, the strange, the louche, the destitute, and the desperate. Rapt by and wrapped in conversation, they chatted about some diversion they wanted to see or some person of note a friend of theirs once saw. They were oblivious to the loitering men and the excited prostitutes with their high heels, ribbons and bells. And I watched as one after the other, they stepped or tripped over the poor boy slumped against the wall. No one turned, stopped, or looked at him. Not one of them. The boy with the sunken eyes was invisible. Fitting, I thought to myself. A nobody. In nowhere. Just like me.

As tempestuous thoughts clouded my mind once more, I didn't see the dark, short man slide past me. I wasn't supposed to. He wore a black cloak, the hood pulled far over his head, obscuring his features. Only when I heard the invisible boy cry with fear as a wide column of black towered over him did I register the hooded man's ominous presence. A chill ran through my already cooling blood. I felt the threat. People continued to walk past, unaware or uncaring, it was hard to say; even a person like me, whose mind was shouting 'No,' found myself unable to act.

I watched as the sinister figure crouched down. My body was numb with the icy coldness, though my mind still raced.

'No! No! No!' it was screaming. A man dressed in dark hose and patterned tights tripped over me. I waited for the rebuke or apology. Neither came. Only a laugh interrupted the flow of his conversation as he regained his footing. I watched as he walked away, the sight of his legs blocking my view of the hooded figure and the bag-of-bones boy.

The legs moved on. Now when I looked for the boy all I could see was the shifting hem of a black cloak. The sinister figure still had his back to me but was now standing erect, the voluminous folds of his garment drawn like a curtain around his prey. The hem slithered suggestively though the air was still.

I sensed evil was afoot. I wanted to stop it. But . . .

I looked around. There were so many people, all blind to what was happening in plain sight. They did nothing. Why should I? The memory of Margarita came into my mind unbidden, how she'd come to my aid. Then I realised. This boy could be me. If not tonight, then tomorrow, or the day after.

An instinct as quick and flaming as lightning scorched through me. It freed my ice-bound limbs, melted my snow-packed voice.

'W-w-w- . . . LEAVE HIM!' I failed to say one thing, managed to say another. It was the black cloak that froze now. I got to my feet.

The people walking by flowed away from me, on the whole undistracted from their conversations, though aware something was amiss. I'd attempted to throw a great boulder into the centre of their consciences; I'd succeeded in creating only the most imperceptible of ripples. But as the dark column turned his hooded head in my direction it seemed I had done enough.

Cruel eyes burned out of a shrouded face and stared at me. My heart went cold once more. I waited for the devil to come over and rip it out. Instead he placed something around the boy's neck, and seemed to force something into his mouth. Then he swept around, the edge of his cloak flying up like wings.

I watched as he disappeared into the night.

*

'Come.'

His name was Luca and I would never have befriended a boy like him. But I was on the streets. My circumstances had changed. And for these few hours at least I had a heightened sense of life. And death. Desperation was settling in my veins as well as the cold.

Sometimes vile events can make the good seem insubstantial and trivial. Or so it seemed to me then. My good fortune on meeting Raphael seemed ludicrous. No longer real. Terrible things had happened to me since then. My father had disowned me, and my descent into the underworld of Rome had been rapid. Absurdly so. Until that evening, I'd only known of its existence through a series of cautionary tales, not unlike the one Giulio had told us that morning in Sebastiano's studio. Far-fetched fictions to frighten, about those who'd strayed from the right path.

I dragged my feet along Rome's bloodstained gutters and dark passages. I was damned. The world inhabited by Raphael no longer existed for me. I followed Luca. It was my only choice. What's right and wrong never really changes, I know. But I was learning fast that the colours often run between the two in an all too imperfect world.

*

Luca didn't speak much. I walked behind him through labyrinthine lanes, accepted the food scraps he offered me that he picked up from outside rowdy taverns. I did not care about colour or taste; I snatched them from him and forced them down my gullet, thankful to be eating. We passed a man selling cooked rabbit. My insides ached at the smell of it. I was still hungry. To my surprise Luca stopped and held out his hand to the vendor. He exchanged a coin for the meat. I looked at him but, like a guilty man, he would not look me in the eye and he placed his free hand on top of his shirt as if he didn't want me to see what was under it.

When the transaction was over the vendor walked one way and we walked another, Luca the proud owner of a cooked rabbit.

'Wh-wh-wh-where did you . . .?' My stuttering voice was accusing.

'You're on the streets now,' he said, as if that was answer enough.

'B-b-but . . .' I pushed.

'Don't you go giving me any fine words and fancy morality,' he snapped, cutting me dead. 'Keep 'em. I don't want 'em.'

We carried on in silence.

'We are nearly there,' he said.

'Where?' I asked, but he did not answer.

Up ahead I saw an arch. It was as if Luca could see our destination beyond it while all I could make out was night as black as pitch. I walked carefully over uneven ground. A line of moonlight had traced its way around a dark cloud. It caught ripple tips as feral boys threw stones into water, tiny twinkles of light cascading out. We were near the river – a place I would never usually visit after dark. It smelt dank, dangerous.

The talk of that morning came back to me of a mutilated body that had been recently pulled from the tangle of riverweed. With that in my already gloomy mind, I jumped at every rustle of a leaf, every lapping of the water, every snapping of a twig underfoot, even when it was my foot the twig was under. I would have jumped at my own shadow if I'd had one. Thankfully Luca had the good sense to walk away from the feral stone-throwers. I followed him. He stopped near some bushes. We sat and ate the rabbit.

The sound of an animal scurrying towards us gave me a shock.

'Throw the bones in the river,' Luca said. The animal ran over my feet. It made me start. It plunged into the water. My hand rummaged through the dark to find Luca's. I heard another animal run and jump. Then another. And another. 'A rat,' he whispered. 'Only a rat.' I clung on to his thin hand. It was cold. I took off my jacket, wrapped it around his shoulders, and moved so close

47

to him that I could feel his breath on me. I rubbed his hands in mine, stroked his face with my fingers, put my hand inside his tattered shirt. My fingers found a pendant hanging down upon his soft, hairless chest. He raised it up to show me. In the moonlight I could make out the image of St Bartolomeo. So that was what the dark figure had placed around his neck.

'I didn't want it,' Luca said, taking the pendant from around his neck and offering it to me, a sudden tremor in his voice. 'He forced it on me. Take it, please!'

My instinct was to accept it and hurl it in the river along with the rabbit bones. But as I went to do so Luca caught my hand in his and guided my palm to his heart. To be this close to another human being strengthened my soul. Fear at the sight of the pendant had disappeared. I moved my fingers to a nipple. He didn't pull away. I didn't want him to.

Chapter 7

I was awoken by the cold the following morning. I opened my eyes, wondered where I was, looked around. I was on the banks of the Tiber. My jacket had been placed over me like a blanket. I pulled it on. A solitary silver button was hanging by a thread. Three were missing. Luca. Bit by bit the events of the day before came back to me. I breathed in sharply. Strange to think the skeletal waif of yesterday was the same boy who had made me feel so alive last night and was the same boy who had stolen three of my four silver buttons. And now he had gone.

But so had the clouds of the day before, and the bright light made me want to hide myself away. I moved out of the spring morning sun, into the shade of a nearby bridge. I sat down, legs pulled up, chin resting on my knees. I felt despair as I looked at the mud-coloured water of the river. I imagined myself lost in its depths, and as I did so green tendrils rose up to greet me, waving back and forth across the liquid surface. They looked enticing as they beckoned me, over and over. I closed my eyes, but there my father's words tormented me as I pictured Luca's face.

I forced my eyelids open. But there was to be no escape. Watery arms were still there calling me to them. I thought of the cool release they might provide. A cessation of this agony. No more worries about money. No more guilt about family. No more shame, no more fears about who I was.

'This is it,' a comforting voice whispered inside my head, 'this is where you're going to die.' A physical urge pushed me to the river's edge. This would be my choice. Soon I would be free, wrapped in loving green arms in a soothing watery bed.

I walked into the shallows. The bottom of the river was slippery. I proceeded carefully. The water lapped around my ankles, my calves, my knees. I welcomed its coldness as it took my breath away. I remembered Luca. He too had made me breathless for a few precious moments. I walked further in. I longed for the river to wash away the memory of his touch. Soon the agony of the burning plain would be extinguished forever. Sodom would be no more a part of me.

Slowly the fire raging within my head subsided and Luca's face receded the deeper I went in. But the voices still plagued me. 'You don't belong here!' 'You're not one of them.' Voices. They swam round in my head. Familiar. Harsh. But then, a kind voice broke its way through.

'Pietro! It's Pietro, isn't it? What are you doing down here?'

I heard the voice again. 'Pietro! You're in far enough. Don't go any deeper. What are you doing?' For a moment I thought it too was inside my head. But then a hand grabbed at my shirt. It pulled me back. The voice came again. 'Do you have a wish to die, you fool of a boy? What are you playing at?'

I turned around to see the cross face of Margarita Luti. The feisty girl from the workshop, the gentle girl who had come to my aid. When was it? The previous day? It seemed a lifetime ago. Margarita Luti. A good person. Perhaps the only one who would be pleased to hear about my chance meeting with Raphael. But did I even care about that anymore? I'd been through so much. I couldn't imagine how I would ever get back to what I'd thought of as my life. I fell back into the water. My head went under. I floundered for a while, splashing and spluttering, until this time my saviour threw an arm around my neck and dragged me to the riverbank. I crawled out and lay panting on the ground.

'Lucky for you I came up here to wash!' she said. 'Most people like to go further down where it's not so dangerous. But it's too public for me there. Near the bridge, it's more private.' She went silent for the briefest of moments. She pulled down her sleeves, brushed down her skirt to make sure her ankles were covered. 'You daft bugger!'

I cringed at the word but saw from her face that she meant nothing by it. She sat herself next to me, not caring if she soiled her skirt. She pulled me to her. Though my heart thumped in my chest I allowed her to cradle my head in her lap like a baby's. I started to cry like one. I owed my life to her. 'You daft little sod!' she said.

*

When I woke up the blue of the sky had deepened but there was a chill in the air. My head was still in Margarita's lap and despite my clothes and hair now being dry my bones felt damp. I gave a little shiver. I pulled myself up to sitting and mumbled an apology. 'You should have woken me.'

'I couldn't. You were so peaceful. And I reckoned you needed the sleep.'

I twitched uncomfortably, my eyes staring down at the damp earth upon which we were sitting. 'Well, thank you. Thank you again.' I looked up at her. Kind eyes met mine.

She ruffled my hair like she'd done before.

'So what happened?'

'I . . . I . . . I . . ?'

'There's no need to say a word,' she said. 'I can see you're not made of the same clay as other men.' I had a vague memory that she'd said I was like her only the day before, which I preferred.

The mention of clay made me think of my father. It made me feel uneasy. Exposed. Unloved. 'Now come with me.'

I pushed myself to my feet and followed her. I had nowhere else to go.

*

We went back up on the road. The sight of a band of men stopping well-dressed nobles caused me to clutch my one remaining silver button tightly in my grimy palm. Margarita laughed. 'We've got no need to be frightened of them. Look at us. We've got nothing to detract from the glory of God. Not a bauble, bead or shiny buckle between us. My, you've even lost most of the buttons from your jacket.'

It was the sumptuary police, and they were having a word with a well-dressed woman. Margarita was right. We had nothing on her. The three rows of pearls and one gold chain that she wore around the fleshy cushion of her neck were impossible to miss. I looked at her clothes – a black velvet gown with an embroidered edge. Expensive. From her belt hung a large purse of crimson velvet embellished with tiny pearls. The sumptuary laws were strict – a citizen could not wear clothes or jewels that were overly ostentatious and that might be seen to distract the human eye from what should be its sole purpose: the contemplation of God. This woman was clearly flouting them.

We crept past. Not a soul, sumptuary or otherwise, turned to look at us.

'Pass that necklace over to us. It will help feed the poor.'

'But this is an outrage.'

'As is your wearing such shows of wealth around your neck.'

'You cannot take it.'

'We can and we will . . .'

'Being poor is not without its benefits,' Margarita whispered. 'Dressing like this,' she said, taking her clean but well-worn skirt

52

into her hands, 'always grants us safe passage. And don't worry about her.' Margarita had mistaken my expression of alarm for concern. 'Somebody will come by and pay off her fine soon enough. And think how she'll have swelled the coffers of the Vatican in the process so that the Pope and his humble cardinals can carry on living like kings and princes. Sumptuary laws indeed! Out of one pot and into another.'

I followed Margarita over the Ponte Sisto, glancing down at the Tiber with relief. Life was drawing itself back into me as I breathed in the air. It tasted pleasant and sweet. I prayed it would stay that way. We trailed our way around winding lanes, full of pedlars, traders, carts, mules and assorted livestock. Stone-faced women barged into us, who, on contact with Margarita, changed from grumpy, old harridans to warm-hearted mothers. They gathered her to them and smothered her with their fulsome bosoms before rushing off in pursuit of their real offspring, who were weaving around the ankles of all and sundry.

This world was opening itself up, welcoming her in. She grabbed hold of my arm. She was taking me in with her. The smell was of spices, raw meat, cooked meat, cheese, unwashed bodies: a heady concoction. Sounds came from within buildings as well as without. Shouts, cries, laughter, singing, braying, tweeting, lutes playing.

'Look out!' At the sudden call from above, a space cleared in the street below. Margarita grabbed me by the arm and pulled me away just in time. Slop! The contents of a chamber pot steamed in the hastily made clearing. I glanced up to see an unkempt woman retreating from the balcony, offending chamber pot, now empty, in hand. 'That's mad Lavinia,' Margarita explained. All human life was here. We were in Trastevere.

We made our way along Via Santa Dorotea. Progress was slow. This was Margarita's neighbourhood – that much was clear. Everyone greeted her and wanted to find out how she was, where she'd been, and what she was doing with me. 'I saved him from drowning in the river.' She laughed, patting me on the shoulder. 'Who would believe it?' Certainly not them. They laughed back, shaking their heads. We carried on.

The sun was sinking in the sky and my stomach was empty. It was a long time since I'd had the rabbit. Margarita stopped under a wooden sign that swung ever so slightly in the evening air. Close by a cart had pulled up, sacks piled up on the back of it. A stocky man with a round belly was standing as if on guard, arms crossed, before his precious cargo. He pulled up his belt. It slipped back down.

I nodded at the portly fellow. He smiled at Margarita. He looked me up and down. I'd been expecting deference from this working man. As I followed his eyes over my ripped, bloody shirt, my mud-stained hose and my wild hair I understood why on this occasion I hadn't got it. I looked as if I'd been dragged along the bed of the river, rolled along its bank, then given a good beating. His eyes lingered on the button dangling by a thread from my jacket that I held in my arms. He wouldn't be describing me any time soon as a fancy man, though he was attracted by my one remaining shiny button.

'We're here,' Margarita said to me. We were at her father's bakery.

Chapter 8

'Tell him he needs to come and get it himself. I got extra sacks for Easter for him and I did my back in while I was loading them onto the cart. I can't afford to make it any worse. Have to be careful how I move. And if he doesn't come out soon I'll take it elsewhere. It's as valuable as gold these days, tell him, and if yer father doesn't want it, I knows of a hundred other bakers who do. And the rest. So he'd better be quick. The fancy man's gone now and so he's got no excuse.'

'Good day, Giorgio.' Margarita breezed up to him with a wave of her hand and a long-suffering smile – she'd heard his complaints before.

'Come, let me do it.' She wrapped her arms around a large sack and propped it on her hip before struggling with it to the doorway.

I followed suit while the gallant Giorgio said to her, from a seated position, 'Stop! It's no job for a girl like you.' She breathed heavily and carried on. Giorgio didn't move. Margarita didn't moan. And I barely managed, dragging two sacks to Margarita's four. I was relieved when we'd lugged all six sacks off the back of the cart. But we'd created a pile two sacks wide and three high and if the intention had been to go inside the bakery we'd scuppered our chances by blocking the way.

'Thank you, Giorgio. You've performed miracles, getting us this much flour. These are hard times, but my father appreciates all you've done for him.'

'He hasn't paid me.'

'He's just coming.'

Margarita smiled patiently and turned. 'Father? Father?' she shouted. 'Giorgio needs paying.'

A cross voice with a Roman accent as rough as Giorgio's boomed loud from the other side. 'How can I when his flour is blocking the way?'

Margarita went on tiptoes and peered over the top of the sacks. She issued instructions to a small red-faced group of men congregated inside. Within minutes the sacks had been taken in and stored away. Her father had no choice but to come and settle up with the sedentary Giorgio. He sniffed and waved a purse around. It looked expensive: black velvet and decorated with fine pearls. It also happened to be bulging.

'There!' The baker hurled some coins into the back of the cart. 'You've been paid.' His churlish tone gave the impression that he could barely afford to settle his debt; the black velvet purse told a different story. Giorgio's mouth opened, and not to say thank you. He gave me one last cursory glance before looking back at Margarita.

'Goodbye, girl. You're a good'un.'

Her father humphed.

'He's gone, boys,' he said, returning to his friends.

I stood behind Margarita near the entrance. I swept back my hair anticipating an introduction. Instead, Margarita went to fetch me something to eat.

I peered inside the baker's shop. The space was small and cramped, the ceiling low. There, squashed inside, Margarita's father was deep in the conversation he had been pulled away from.

'That poor sinner who got pulled from the river. You've got to feel sorry for the lad,' he said, now cradling the fat purse like a distended stomach.

My hand felt for my nose, a body memory of what Giulio had told us at Sebastiano's studio.

'What?' an indignant voice cried. 'Sorry for a lad who likes to plunge his *uccello* in arseholes?'

'Messy business!' Margarita's father replied. The group erupted into fits of raucous laughter. 'That's not what I meant, you dirty bastards. It's hard . . . no, that's not what I mean. Calm down, calm down . . . when you gets your extremities cut off for preferring peaches to figs, it don't seem fair. It's all fruit after all!'

'Yes. Our Orlando,' one of them continued, 'found the poor bugger—' titters bubbled up again '—not two hours since.'

So there had been another killing.

''Orrible, 'e said it was. Worse than before. This time the murderer had tried to flay the unlucky lad.'

I played with the silver button on my jacket. When I let it go it dangled by its thread.

'Orlando said that whoever had done it couldn't have wanted to rob him as the boy still wore some flashy pendant around his neck, I think of St Bartolomeo, if I remembers right.' The man paused for the briefest of moments but it was enough to make me miss a breath. 'And clutched in his hand,' he continued, 'he had hold of three silver buttons.'

My hand went to my chest, enveloping the only button I had left. My blood ran cold. It flooded my mind. Luca! For a while he was all I could think of. It had to be him. I turned and twisted the button over and over again. Luca had been murdered. The thread broke. The button fell to the floor and spun round and round like a coin. I picked it up to stop it. But it was too late. Suspicious eyes had already turned towards me.

'Here. Something for you to eat and drink.' Margarita was back.

'Who's this?' her father asked, not waiting for a reply. 'Who would leave a pendant?' he continued, his fascination in the murder outlasting his short-lived interest in me. 'They could have got decent money for it.'

The baker's eyes grew round and greedy. Until they met the critical gaze of his daughter.

'Stop your staring now, girl.' He shifted the purse up level to his heart.

All faces were now set on the baker's daughter.

'Where did you get that?' Margarita pointed to the bulging purse.

'Now don't you go all accusing on me, my girl.'

'Where did you get that?' she repeated.

'This is from him.' He stroked the velvet. 'Came today. Has a right high opinion of you, he does.' I wondered at what I was hearing. Rome was full of prostitutes, and the better ones came from almost illustrious dynasties. I'd heard of mothers training their daughters in music, poetry, and in some cases philosophy, as well as other essential womanly skills to please the eye, heart and body. Then they rented out their girls to men. Wealthy ones. Even cardinals sought solace in their arms. This girl knew Cardinal Bibbiena – that much I knew already. Was this what the baker had done? Accepted the purse of money to rent out his daughter?

Margarita's father lifted the velvet purse in front of him and dropped it on the table. It made a dull, heavy thud.

'What have you done, Father? I told him I didn't want to do it anymore.'

'Well, you won't agree to accepting any of your suitors, and I can't keep on looking after you forever . . .'

At this a low titter burned through the room; mutters of 'you look after her?' and 'more like the other way around' smouldered away at the edges.

Margarita clenched her fists. 'Father!'

'Lawless daughter!' He banged his own fists on the counter in retaliation. He would not be shamed; flour flew up to prove it.

'Isn't she the most lawless daughter?' he appealed to those present, his palms held high, his head cocked to one side. No one replied. 'Where's your respect for your old father?' His voice wavered in the air, the bullish confidence gone.

'Did he come here himself?' she asked.

Her father looked sheepish.

'He didn't, did he? He thinks himself so high and mighty that he couldn't bear to sully his fine clothes by coming here and asking for me in person.' She was accusing.

'He sent the money.' Her father would not be deterred.

Margarita inhaled deeply. She closed her eyes and opened them on the outward breath, staring at her father with the most uncomprehending of expressions.

'The lad he sent,' he blustered, his eyes wandering over to me, 'he was well dressed. Very well dressed.'

'I will not be bought.'

Ah. The moment the words fell from her lips I remembered where I'd heard her use them before. And to whom: Sebastiano Luciani. So it was his messenger who had delivered the purse of money.

A tut of exasperation gave way to a sigh of the deepest disappointment.

'But, Marg . . .'

'Father, don't you see? He sends someone as his errand boy because he sees it as beneath him to come and barter with someone . . . like you . . . like *us*. For pity's sake. He may be able to afford to buy up whatever he pleases but it matters little to me how rich he is. He will never be able to buy me. Nor will anyone else for that matter.' She looked deep into her father's eyes. He ran flour-tipped fingers through flour-covered hair. White powder fell like snow on his shoulders.

'There are more important things in this life than money. You taught me that. Or have you now forgotten?'

'You'll be the death of me,' her father tutted as the look of shame that passed across his face showed he accepted the rebuke. No one said a word, though disturbing noises emanated from deep within each of them. Whether caused by hunger or emotion it was difficult to tell. Although as they belched, farted, and whistled their thoughts through sucked-in cheeks I deduced it was most likely a combination of the two.

'Do virtue and good name count for nothing? Self-respect? Honour?'

Human once more, now that I'd let the pain back in, I was a confusion of emotions. Part of me was moved by the force of feeling in her voice and inspired by her beautiful words. But the greater part of me envied her deep sense of self because, after my long night of the soul spent down by the banks of the Tiber, I wondered if I still had one.

I played with my button some more. Thought about Luca. Remembered his words about fine clothes and fancy morality.

I possessed nothing other than the rags I was dressed in. The velvet purse was bulging and plush. My stomach rumbled like loose cartwheels over stony ground. What was the point in feeding my soul with words when my stomach cried out for food? I was starting to tire of my saviour's show of self-satisfaction. I shook my head, dragged my thoughts to a better place. What was I thinking? I owed this girl my life. I coughed.

Margarita gave me a pat on the arm. Her father grimaced. He could not say of me that I was well dressed. He pulled his daughter to him and whispered something in her ear.

'Fine!' she said as she reared back like a wild horse. 'I'll do it. I'll let him finish his painting of me. But when he's done there will be no further transactions between us.'

The rumbling stomachs in the baker's shop, mine included, breathed out as one, relieved at this compromise. Margarita pulled me after her. 'I'll light the candles,' she said.

She sat me down on a stool and hummed a pretty tune while she poured me some watered-down wine.

'Over here, girl!'

She shared it round as she lit the tallow candles. Their gentle light lifted her beauty from the natural to the heavenly; it made her father's flour-dipped appearance seem soft, and refined.

'You've made your father a happy man.' He pulled Margarita to him and gave her a hug. His eyes were dancing with delight. Her father was not like mine.

'Who've you dragged home now?' I gave a start. It was time for introductions at last. I swept my hand over my hair again – it was still gritty but I hoped the candlelight would be forgiving.

'My father, Francesco Luti. Baker,' Margarita said to me. I stood up and bowed.

'Pietro . . . Aaartist's apprentice,' I replied, managing to sink my stammer in one deep sound. The warmth from the ovens was starting to envelop me like a comforting blanket. The candlelit room felt inviting. I was glad to be here.

'My Margarita's brought home with her an artist's apprentice,' the baker said to his friends.

'A young one, Margarita,' he said to his daughter.

'Are you shaving, boy?'

His friends laughed.

I fiddled with the button in my hand. The candlelight caught it. Margarita's father scrutinised me as if calculating the weight of an invisible purse. His eyes ran over what I was wearing: dark green velvet jacket, white shirt and once brightly coloured hose. Creased, stained, ripped, and smelling of the river maybe, but in the gentle light some quality was still discernible. As I looked around at the attire of *Signore* Luti's local customers I hoped that, even dishevelled, he might see me as a cut above. He did. I glimpsed a squint of appreciation in his eyes.

'These two loaves are for you,' he said to me.

I sensed hackles rise all around.

Sensing it too, Margarita intervened. 'There's enough bread for all of you. Take it and get yourselves home to your families.' Her voice was authoritative but not unfeeling.

'But I've not finished my . . .' one of them started to say but the baker's daughter was having none of it.

'Come, Alessandro,' she said, taking the cup from the man's

hand and replacing it with a loaf. 'Olivia won't thank me for letting you return home smelling of the grape, but she'll be happy when you've come back with the grain. It's as precious as gold in the city these days and you know it. Here.'

'But they haven't paid.'

Margarita went over and tapped the black velvet purse, immediately silencing her father.

'Now isn't this nice,' he said, throwing a warm arm around my shoulder when the last of his friends had gone. 'Just the three of us. No special woman in your life?' Margarita glowered a warning at her father. I cast my eyes to the floury floor.

Chapter 9

'She'll make a good wife,' her father told me as she cleaned the jugs of wine away and disappeared out the back.

'God, it's disgusting out here, Father,' her voice shouted through. 'You'll kill us all off if you're not careful!'

'Place wouldn't work if it wasn't for our Margarita,' the short, round baker with red cheeks told me. That he was Margarita's father was hard to see. The years had not been kind to him.

'Of course, I can't leave it to her. All this.' My heavy eyes followed his hand as it showed me his kingdom. 'Not unless she's married. I keep telling her. I won't be able to hold on to it forever. I could go at any second, feeling a bit strange now as a matter of fact,' and with that he sat on a bag full of flour propped up against the wall. 'And then what would she do?' I had no need to answer. The man rambled on, his voice strangely comforting after the horrors of the day. 'I've got two girls. A blessing and a curse for a father. Her sister's married. To a barrel maker. The man has a trade, can look after her. He's no interest in taking over all this. Our Alicia got married at fourteen. Good age for a girl to get wed. Our Margi'll be too old soon. I keep telling her that. Oh, she's had suitors. That girl's a pearl. Always was. Our precious pearl. Who wouldn't want to be married to that? But that lustre won't last forever. Oh no! Thinks she's clever. But it doesn't do to be clever for a girl. And she needs to be careful because she's too clever. Soon she'll be too old and too clever. Then what's she going to do? A man doesn't want a clever shrew for a wife. Though her mother was a bit of a shrew, God rest her soul, and I married her soon enough . . .'

Margarita shook me. I must have fallen asleep. She placed one plate of food in my hand and another in her father's. We both followed her through to a small room situated at the back of the main bakery where we sat at a wooden table. In the middle was another candle that flickered as we breathed, so close were we to it. We ate in appreciative silence. I was back asleep within the hour, slumped over the table.

*

It was just before sunrise when Margarita woke me the following morning. My bleary eyes looked up to see her smiling down at me, her hair cascading in waves around her face. The ends tickled the tip of my nose. I swept them away and rubbed my eyes. I got up, surrounded by warmth and the smell of baking bread. I looked over towards the oven. It glimmered and bathed the entire room in a deep orange glow. I felt a thin layer of flour beneath my hands. I'd slept on the floor curled up like a cat in the corner of the kitchen. And I could hear singing. It was her father. It was neither sweet nor melodious. But it was confident and heartfelt, which gave it a charm that brought a smile to my face. He pulled a tray of freshly baked bread out of the gaping mouth of the furnace and slid another one in. I inhaled deeply and felt myself transported away on the wings of delight. And the pangs of hunger.

Margarita wrapped the small loaf my eyes had settled on in a cloth she'd taken off a hook. 'Come!' She grabbed my hand. 'I'll be back in time to help,' she called back to her father as she stepped outside, pulling me after her. The street was silent and bathed in the deep blue-purple light that was somewhere between night and day. The air was fresh and alive. It licked my face with promise and I lapped it up. That morning was the closest I'd come to heaven. Lost in the moment, memories far away, the responsibilities of life set aside. The world seemed good and I was good in it.

And it was spring.

Spring in Rome is the prettiest season, a time for new beginnings, and so it was for me that April morning. As I walked past sleeping houses, hope surged in my heart.

'Come! This way!' Margarita led me down side streets. The countryside all around Rome was so rich and abundant at that time of year that farmers and peasants were already trickling into the city, their heavy carts laden with the season's bounty. One such cart laden with the most magnificent blooms pushed us to the side. The colours dazzled; the fragrance made me dizzy. I followed on, drinking in the early morning, and watching the sky as it changed to a radiant purple canvas now streaked with flashes of deep pink and orange.

We passed merchants setting up their stalls, boys making deliveries to the taverns. Nobody noticed us as we floated by. It was as if the incidents of yesterday had never been.

When we came to the city walls, the trickle of traders and peasants had turned into a flood. Gateways bulged, not just with carts and beasts of burden laden with every imaginable commodity, but also with monks, pilgrims, adventurers. This was Rome after all. Soon all the streets of the city would be heaving with life. Margarita made her way along the wall's perimeter. It was ancient and dilapidated, running to only several stones high in places. It was at one of these places that she stopped and clambered over. I did the same, falling into a shaded thicket on the other side. I did not know where we were, nor where we were going, but I did not care.

I looked up at the now blue sky above through wavering leaves and marvelled at the music of the birds. Gold-lined streaks of white now replaced the pink and orange of the breaking dawn.

We proceeded on our way through the trees, dancing over twigs and raised roots as the morning sun dappled the ground beneath. We said nothing. Margarita was lost in her own thoughts while my mind was empty of thoughts and memories of any sort. An overwhelming feeling of peace came over me as I tramped my way behind her through the glowing greenery. We wound our way round and up and over and up some more until she disappeared through an opening. I tumbled after her. New-born into the light.

We'd made it to the top of a hill. Out of the city. Into the countryside. Margarita threw herself down. I did the same. The ground beneath our hands was cool and damp, the air fresh. And there we sat and gazed in wonder at the view before us. A delicate mist lay over the fields that stretched out below, concealing the life burgeoning beneath. We watched, waited, in silent wonder.

The sun's rays became stronger, the mist finer. Soon we could make out the water in the streams flowing fast, and, as the cover thinned still further, the earth, pulsating with new life after winter, gave itself up to our eyes. Juicy green leaves and blossom as heavenly as angels' wings burst forth on the trees. They throbbed with life and filled the air with heavenly music. The mist had all but disappeared and the world was now vibrating with hope, life, and colour. So much so that it seemed to me that even the peasants, admittedly no bigger than ants in the distance, were happy. How could they not be?

'One day, when I'm older, I'm going to live on a big estate in the country. Perhaps I'll have a vineyard, and space for chickens, and I'll have dogs to take hunting, and a horse.'

'That's a fine dream, Pietro,' Margarita said to me. Dream? Yes. It was. A beautiful, beautiful dream, I realised. Hope had come back into my life. My winter was over. Spring had arrived.

*

'You must go.'

When I'd told Margarita about the opportunity to work at Raphael's studio she was pleased. For me. It was a new experience, to have someone care what I did for my sake. Not theirs. No one had ever wanted me to succeed before without bringing with it untold benefit to themselves. But this girl was selfless, different.

And it hadn't taken me long to work out that she was not a prostitute, lowborn or otherwise, not even a woman of easy virtue. Indeed, she was a much-loved daughter, and, that most rare of jewels, a clever and beautiful woman much admired by men and women alike. I, by contrast, was an unloved son, and little admired by anyone. Giulio liked me, I told myself. But then, did he? I remembered how he'd tricked me into saying *fornicatora* . . . how I'd stammered, how he'd laughed, and then there was that knowing look he'd given me. Then there was Luca. I'd been touched in more ways than one by him. I'd truly believed that something meaningful had passed between us – until I'd woken up the next morning to find him gone, along with most of my silver buttons.

Fate had been kind to her, cruel to me.

The reasons for me not to get on with Margarita were all there at the start.

But against my stronger, if not better, judgement, part of me grudgingly liked her. And besides, I needed her – to feed me, put a roof over my head, and give me the confidence to walk into Raphael's studio.

Chapter 10

I was fourteen, Raphael was twenty-five, when I walked into his workshop. Yes, you know already that I had Margarita to thank for that. She'd looked after me like the little brother she'd never had, much to her father's disappointment. He'd wanted her to show a very different type of interest in me, one that would lead to marriage, babies, a secure future. But that was the last thing on Margarita's mind when it came to me. Instead of blushing every time I entered a room, she took me to a barber's, patched up my clothes, and, to put a stop to her father's constant innuendoes once and for all, she got me a room in a nearby boarding house. And on the day I moved in she sent someone to pick up my belongings from my father's house.

I would never have seen Federico's message if it hadn't been for Margarita because I was never going to go back there. Delivered to my father's house and marked as important, the message had been thrown on top of a small pile of my possessions.

'Here. You'll want to read this,' she said as she handed it to me. I trembled as I took it. I looked at her, my heart flipping between hope and despair. She placed a gentle hand on my shoulder, beamed at me, then nodded. 'New home, new start,' she said. I unfolded the message, my breath becoming easier as I read each wonderful word.

Dear Pietro,
My maestro has asked me to discuss terms of apprenticeship
with you. Please be at Hostaria dell'Orso next Thursday, at 7.
  Federico

But it was Thursday already. Panic replaced my newfound relief. What was I going to wear? What was I going to say? How? Where? Who? When? I walked back and forth, my mind racing. 'Stop this.' I looked at Margarita, saw her outstretched arms. I melted into her embrace. I shook. She calmed me. 'There now. Everything is going to be all right.'

*

It was six o'clock when I heard the knock on the door. I sat up, bleary-eyed. I must have fallen asleep.

'Time to wake up, sleepy head. Time to leave for the hostaria.' It was Margarita. I opened the door and she took my arm. She'd come to take me to my meeting.

'I-I-I-I c-c-c-can't. It's t-t-t-too late.' Her hand tightened. She pulled me after her; she said nothing. She was taking me to the tavern. I ran my fingers through my hair, straightened my clothes. The sun disappeared, taking the warmth of the day with it. I was soon wide awake.

The tavern was down one of the streets where I'd met Luca. I shuddered at the memory of the sinister figure who had crouched over him. 'Not far now,' Margarita said, her voice reassuring. Her hand squeezed mine.

When we got inside, groups of men were playing cards and dice, roaring with every round and roll, while wine sloshed over jugs transported by big-armed men and round-cheeked women. A small band of musicians played in the corner, while lovers, the worse for wear, groped each other greedily, not caring who saw them. Laughter and loud voices filled the air while fat-stinking candles and flickering oil lamps kept the darkness at bay. I thought of the cloaked figure, of Luca, of Death. All outside. Life spilt over all around me. I gave Margarita a little smile.

'Pietro! Over here!' There in the corner stood Federico, waving at me. Luigi at his side.

Margarita pushed me towards them.

'It was hell tracking you down,' he said. 'Spoke to your father.' The background noise in the tavern masked my silence.

'You've found him now,' Margarita said. 'When can he start?' I was surprised at her audacious intervention and when Federico opened up to her, his mouth as round and red as a poppy in the morning sun, I was grateful too. And she continued to fire questions at the two apprentices in rapid succession, which revealed more to me than I'd ever thought possible about Raphael and his studio. 'What is he like?'

He was *talented*, *courteous*, *just*, and *good-natured*.

'What of the education you receive?'

The training both boys received was *appropriate* and *thorough*. They glowed like disciples as they regaled us with tales of the care Raphael took in teaching them. Margarita made sounds of appreciation.

'This artist sounds perfect indeed,' she mused. 'There must be some catch.' She laughed. 'Don't tell me that he's hideously ugly with the body of a barrel and the jowly face of an old cockerel?' This time the boys laughed. Luigi dug deep into his pocket and pulled out his own miniature portrait of Raphael – a copy of a copy, no doubt. Seemed to be a lot of them about. He presented it to Margarita. I watched her, knowing that she'd seen something similar before. She said nothing and raised her eyebrows in mock delight. But what she had seen had wiped the smile off her face.

'Portraits tend to embellish,' she added. 'They often improve on nature.'

'L-l-like Sebastiano's of you?' I'd found my tongue at last.

She laughed and struck me playfully about the ear.

'He's beautiful,' Luigi added with a blush. 'The most beautiful man you'll ever see. And though this portrait is beautiful, the person is yet more so.'

'We think that's he's perfection,' Federico whispered. I had seen the artist and knew the words of his apprentices to be true. I sipped my wine, deep in thought. But the notion of perfection was too much for Margarita.

'Please, boys. Stop this nonsense. You had me going there for a while with this fairy story. But you've gone too far. Perfection, indeed! Here, let me look at that likeness of him again.'

Luigi held it out to her. She studied it carefully.

'He's probably a vain, ridiculous creature, like all artists.'

Federico and Luigi looked crestfallen.

'Sorry, I'm not talking about you,' she said. 'But you know what I mean.' They didn't.

At that moment a handsome young man, well-built and with thick, dark hair, caught my eye.

'Margarita?' He knew her. His eyes flicked from her to the rest of our group. Anger thrust him towards us.

'Oh no,' she whispered. 'Come. Let us talk,' she said, addressing the attractive fellow. She led him away. His large, manly hand caught her elbow. She pulled away. Her eyes flashed a warning. 'I've never pretended,' I heard her say to him, 'I've never deceived you.' Honesty. She unleashed it upon this would-be suitor and it wounded him. I looked on for a while but I soon lost interest.

'Raphael . . .' It was Luigi. 'His only weakness is women.'

The two apprentices poured lively talk into my ears as keenly as I poured red wine down my throat. By the time the candles had burned to their bases I was happy, and completely intoxicated. Fear had released my soul from its ugly claws. I would soon be resuming my artistic training at the most exciting workshop in Rome.

I looked around. Margarita's young man had long gone. 'It's time I got you home,' she said to me, her arm now holding me upright.

'Fortune favours the brave,' I slurred, satisfied with myself.

'Yes. It takes a man of exceptional valour to put away more wine than he can handle, and seize an opportunity when it's handed to him on a platter,' she said.

*

During the following days my skin tingled and my breath quickened every time I thought of Raphael. I would be there in his workshop soon. Luigi and Federico had told such marvellous tales about him. While I believed them, Margarita did not. She sniffed around like a hungry hound seeking to tear the meat from the bones of the apprentices' extravagant claims. She was in a strange mood. Jealous, I told myself, of my good fortune.

She hunted around. Though she knew few people who mixed in artistic circles she knew a few who loitered around the edges. A servant friend of hers who worked for Cardinal Bibbiena was one of them. 'She says there's not a woman who hasn't desired him,' Margarita reported back to me, 'nor, if she's been lucky enough to get it, who hasn't been satisfied more than by any other man before.' This news seemed to appal her, though it thrilled me. 'He's a philanderer! Woe betide any woman who trusts him,' she added, waving her finger up and down in my face.

'And what's worse is that Cardinal Bibbiena is one of the artist's patrons.'

She paused to cough. She found the information unpalatable. 'There. Your artist's a bought man,' she persisted with the finger wagging. 'And when you're a bought man you're trapped. Only as good as the man who pays you. And believe me, Bibbiena is not a good man.'

Her words confused me. One minute she had a hand on my back pushing me towards him, the next she was doing all she could to keep me away from him. Raphael aroused strong passions. Even in Margarita. I hardened myself to her words.

Her desire to besmirch Raphael's reputation was starting to look a lot like need. 'According to Sebastiano, he copies,' she said, quoting the words of a man she despised, '. . . has no ideas of his own . . . is not serious . . .' To be on the side of someone who bleated like a jealous rival did not sit comfortably on Margarita's shoulders but she said it anyway. I decided she was desperate to keep hold of me and feared she would use any means possible to do so.

But I was wrong about that.

When the day came to go to Raphael's workshop, she called for me at the boarding house, as she'd promised she would.

'You look magnificent.' She laughed as I opened the door. My hair was clean and neat, thanks to Margarita's barber friend; my green jacket was fresh and stain-free, after she'd soaked it, scrubbed it, then scented it with lavender; and my shirt looked like new, whiter than when I'd first bought it, with the tears in the sleeves invisible after she'd spent hours sewing them up. I was wearing yellow hose. She cast her eyes over them quickly but looked away before I could see what she thought.

'Now stand up straight and walk tall.'

I shuffled, my stomach churned, my head felt heavy. As I set off on the journey that would change the course of my life faces queued up within my head to torment me: Michelangelo's, Sebastiano's, my father's. They tried to hold me back, but it was Margarita who pushed me forward. If she did not want me to go, she did not show it. Pilgrims, priests and monks flowed around us, buffeting us this way and that. I was all at sea within and without. But Margarita kept going, taking me with her.

'I don't want to go.'

'Oh yes you do.'

'No. I don't.'

'I've had a week of you telling me what an opportunity this is going to be. It was me, can't you remember, who spoke against it.'

Margarita was right. I'd been the one overjoyed at the prospect, determined to succeed. But now my resolve had gone. My fear of failure had returned. I couldn't face it. Not again.

'I don't understand why it means so much to you, to work there. But I know that it does. And I cannot deny that this Raphael sounds better than any other artist I've come across.'

I still resisted.

'Now come on, Pietro. I'm not going to let your weakness cripple you.'

I was weak; I knew it. The scapular accuracy of her words left me exposed and wounded. I could say nothing back. I seethed.

'Artists in my experience – granted it's not wide – are parasites. They flatter the rich and powerful and are prepared to sway in any direction for the right price in the hope that one day they too will become rich.' She stopped to apologise to a Dominican dressed in white whom she'd bumped into. 'That's not to say there's no talent involved,' she continued, 'but I've not come across one who I think worthy of my respect.'

I felt nauseous. Did she know what she was saying? I lurched to the side; she dragged me on.

'Want to buy a relic?' A wizened old man placed his bony fingers on me, thrusting a red cross into my face. He sensed my despair. 'I have no money,' I told him as Margarita steered me out of his path. He came at me a second time.

'A relic? Where is it from, this relic? Genuine, is it? Along with the tens of copies you have of it in that basket of yours?' she challenged him. He did not try to sell me one a third time.

'Come on, Pietro,' she said, not to be put off. 'You have to do what your heart tells you to do and I accept that you're resisting it at the moment but that's because you're decent. You're not like them. That's what's good about you. And who knows, when you're a famous artist, you can be the first one I respect.'

The baker's daughter from Trastevere gave my hand a sudden pull.

'I think we're nearly there.'

We were at the end of the street. The sight of apprentices filing into the workshop made my feet feel like blocks of marble. We watched, waited.

'Look! Look! There's Giulio. Giulio Romano.' Margarita hit me in the arm at the sight of him. Joy and trepidation enveloped me. I had no idea why he was at Raphael's but I was glad to see him. The power of a familiar face, no doubt.

'Now go. Oh, and my father says there's always a job for you at the bakery if this doesn't work out. And come and let me know how you get on either way. As soon as you can.'

She shoved me in the back and I started to walk. She was calling after me, her voice loud and encouraging, but I no longer heard what she was saying. What she'd said earlier about weakness came to mind; it was a weakness that I should want to give in to the urge to return to her. I would conquer this feeling. I would need her no more. My back was now turned on this girl from Trastevere and although I felt sick at the thought of it I had my ambitions set on the glamorous world of art again. There I would envelop myself in the folds of its power, and power, I well knew, brought with it its own immunity.

I'd not been born into good fortune; the only way for me, and men like me, to climb high in the world, was to be prepared to sever ties with those who by association would tether me to the ground. If that meant doing bad things then so be it. All Margarita's kindness, much like the kind words she was hurling after me, would soon become as insubstantial as a windswept cloud trailing across a clear sky. There. Then gone. Forgotten forever.

As I stood outside the workshop door I imagined my future. I was about to re-create myself.

Chapter 11

Summoning to mind my meeting with Raphael, as well as the portrait of him Giulio had circulated round Sebastiano's studio, I armed myself with knowledge. Everything I knew, or had ever heard about him, I called on to support me now, to give me the strength to step over the threshold. Whereas Sebastiano had shouted, and the ferocious Michelangelo had growled, I already knew from my one encounter with Raphael that his voice was kind and sweet. Even in speech he belonged to a different breed. His tone and refined choice of language was a far cry from the coarse discourse engaged in throughout Rome. I entered the workshop of the painter who threatened my former masters more than any other in the whole of the city: I felt no guilt.

I'd promised Margarita that I would let her know if everything everyone had said about Raphael – all the stories of his goodness, virtue, character, and talent – were true. I'd said, with the utmost conviction, that I would. But she belonged to my past now.

I hovered outside the workshop, my hand shaking as it tried to grab hold of the handle.

I failed, instead only managing to paw away at the wood behind it. Raphael from Urbino. The thought of him overwhelmed me. Full of fear, I fell against the door. It opened.

Once inside, the sound of buzzing buoyed me instantly, lifting me upwards. Industry and purpose filled the air. And there was the sound of something more, a sound I'd never experienced in either of the workshops I'd been in before, the unmistakable sound of joy. I belonged here. Happy voices reverberated off walls, quiet laughter ebbed and flowed around tables of apprentices. I breathed it in deeply, felt dizzy with the excess of it. I was about to fall when a firm hand lifted me up by the arm. It made me gasp. I hoped its owner hadn't noticed. I smoothed my hair with a finger.

'You're here, Pietro. Welcome.' I looked up and saw Raphael's kind, brown eyes smiling at me, their warmth as comforting as the sun.

Everything changed in that moment.

From then on I was to have a new focus for my dreams. Strange and wonderful to think how something as insubstantial as a look had the power to navigate the course of my life forever. As for his touch, the magic of it thrilled me to the core, arousing sensations so profound as to take my breath away.

'Shall I prepare the panel now?' an apprentice called out, causing Raphael to release me from his grasp. When he did so, it was as if he took part of me with him. For a moment I wanted to close my eyes and imagine his fingers still there, touching me, their tips pressing into my muscles. Instead I cast them around the room, looking to see where the intruding voice had come from. As I did so I saw a sea of people, preparing paints, making paper, covering canvases with size to seal them, mixing gesso, sketching, colouring, cutting goose quills, cleaning brushes. All familiar sights to me. I had experience in the most important workshops in Rome after all. But this one, with its joyous laughter was a revelation.

Certainly, in Michelangelo's workshop you would never have heard such levity, and in Sebastiano's there was laughter but usually only his when he was tearing into the work of one of his apprentices as he humiliated him for sport. Here, in this space, apprentices were enjoying their work, moving around, joking with one another. And while a few seemed deep in concentration, clearly engaged in those parts of the artistic process that required focus, not one appeared miserable in his work.

Then I saw him, the owner of the intruding voice, now also in possession of two equally intruding arms that he waved like flags at the start of a chariot race. I noticed that he had hair styled like Raphael's. My instinct was to sneer but then quickly remembered where I was. Suffice to say that although imitation is reputed to be the sincerest form of flattery (and I have no doubt this young apprentice wore his hair thus in homage to his master), it was apparent that this poor dolt could never be anything other than a pale imitation of the refined, beautiful Raphael.

I watched the boy with hair so very nearly but not quite like his master's. It was the same length and pulled down to frame the face in the same way. It was even the same rich brown colour. The only difference lay in the tufts that protruded either side of his head, no doubt caused by all the jumping up and down he was currently doing in order to catch Raphael's attention. And the apprentice's face seemed unnaturally red, even from a distance. I swung my head towards the maestro. Calm, composed, in mind and in body, skin unblemished. And no tufts disturbed the surface of his hair. I cast my eyes back towards his imitator. More court jester than refined courtier, I thought to myself. Dress him in pointy slippers and attach some tinkling bells and the look would be complete.

'Please, forgive me.'

I'd rarely been spoken to in so solicitous a manner and I could have sworn Raphael almost bowed as he made his apologies to go and deal with this fool. In response to this courtly gesture I felt my cheeks flush hot. I lowered my eyes, willing his to do the same, then raised my hands as if to push back my hair, all the while hoping I was covering the high colour beneath. 'Yes, of course.' I forced my eyes open and attempted to respond in similar courtly fashion, stepping back and lowering my head slightly as Raphael had done. A smile danced across his face at the sight of me, though not in mockery.

'Good lad!' Raphael's hand came softly across the back of my head to touch me for the second time but though it was gentle I flinched all the same. Sebastiano's whack from only a week before had left its mark and I smarted with the memory of it. The young artist responded to my reaction and dropped his hand quickly to my shoulder. He gave it a little shake. A sigh of pleasure escaped from my lips.

'Andrea?'

The apprentice gesturing to Raphael from the other side of the workshop bounded over like a puppy, exuberant and self-conscious at the same time as his hands moved before his face, pulling his hair into place over and over again. Yet the tufts I'd spotted from across the room remained. Pigment-stained hands pulled on what I now saw were pigment-tipped locks, to no avail. As he approached, his eyes kept throwing themselves to the floor. I recognised the habit. I did the same thing myself whenever I wished to hide something.

I wanted to tell him that looking down no more hid the erupting pustules on his skin than it had stopped my cheeks from blazing moments before. Raphael didn't seem to mind as he moved his flawless skin impossibly close to Andrea's thankfully pustule-free ear and whispered in it gently. As silken words worked their way inside so Andrea nodded, dark lashes blinking in agreement. Raphael touched him on the shoulder, as he'd done to me only moments earlier.

I tried not to glower as he asked this apprentice to take me under what I maliciously surmised was his scabby wing. Raphael had passed on responsibility for me to this self-conscious boy with bad skin. 'I know you'll do a good job of introducing Pietro to what we do here at our workshop.' I looked on as he made his way to the far right of the room, talking to his apprentices as he went. Kind. Thoughtful.

And then, as if Andrea had read my mind, he leant up close to me and said, 'Raphael is not like every other artist.'

I watched the back of my new maestro's head as he turned this way and that, making sounds of appreciation to each of his apprentices as he did so. 'I know,' I told Andrea, 'he is not.'

My eyes followed him with wonder, and longing.

'Pietro?' I jumped as Andrea's high-pitched voice pulled me out of my reverie. I was now in the tender charge of the Spotty One. My eyes tried to look into his to prove my concentration, but they strayed to the pustule-encrusted landscape on his forehead that I could see quite clearly now that he was next to me. I instinctively ran a finger across my own, anticipating a sympathetic outburst.

'I've worked in Michelangelo's workshop.' Although I had no great love for the curmudgeonly old bull I wasn't blind to the awe his name aroused. To know the skill of the artist, be aware of his renown, was to be impressed by the apprentice who had worked under him. I knew better than to admit that he'd seen me as a waste of space. My father had been so proud when he'd secured me a place there. Initially I'd been proud too. But any sense of pride was soon beaten out of me by the violence of the great artist's outbursts. No one could do things as well as him and he could never forgive them for it.

A body can carry so many memories with it, every body part, even, as in my case, a body part as mundane as the little toe on my right foot. And as I boasted of having learned, somewhat ironically, at the feet of the great master, so my toe throbbed with the memory of the time he'd thrown down his chisel. It hadn't even been my work that had provoked the tirade.

'Michelangelo? That must have been an education indeed. But they do say he has an ugly temper on him.'

He did. But I had no intention of diminishing my own thunder by telling the truth to this grinning halfwit. I sniffed and said nothing.

'The maestro has many sketches of your old maestro's work,' Andrea continued, his attempt to draw me on Michelangelo's foul moods abandoned. 'Of work he saw in Florence. Values it highly. It has taught him a great deal. Believes it has saved him from becoming stale like his old teacher Perugino.'

The great Perugino. I'd heard rumours that he had fallen out of favour. It was said that he was stuck in the heady days of his past, and that would never do in these fast-paced times.

'Never wanted to learn from others, unlike Master Raphael. That's why he keeps your old maestro's work over there, with the work of another master he came across while in the fair city of Florence. A certain Master Leonardo da Vinci.'

I bristled at the mention of the artist's name.

'Maestro Raphael believes him to be the equal of Michelangelo. Equally magnificent . . . when he finishes a piece,' he whispered mischievously. 'But then, that is the issue with Master Leonardo, because he rarely finishes anything.'

I knew that Michelangelo, though fully in agreement that Master Leonardo did not have an extensive body of artistic work, did not share Raphael's opinion as to the legendary artist's merit. Neither did I. Master Leonardo, indeed! That procrastinating horse-modeller. He still hadn't cast the equestrian statue for the Duke of Milan. It seemed that I had inherited something from my former master after all, even if it was only his poor regard for fellow artists. I sniffed again.

An awkward silence filled the space between us, accentuating the hum of joyful industry all around. Andrea gave a nervous laugh, followed by a cough and a stammering, 'A-a-a . . . yes! F-f-f-follow me, P-P-P-Pietro.' My sympathy went out to him, fleetingly. He smiled while looking at the floor, and moved to an older boy who had a desk in front of a bookcase. 'Alberto,' he told me, scarcely raising his head. 'He does the accounts.' Alberto turned around and reached up to one of the shelves, running his fingers over a series of bound leather books and bringing down the one marked *'il salariati'*.

'Name?'

'Pietro.'

'Age?'

'Fourteen.'

'Job?' Alberto addressed this question to Andrea.

Andrea glanced at me quickly. 'A-a-a-apprentice,' he stated. 'K-k-k-k-k-key task: the mixing of p-p-p-paints.' He glanced at me, nervous. He pulled his eyes quickly away.

'Commissions to work on?' Alberto enquired.

'The V-V-Vatican: v-v-various,' Andrea replied.

I swallowed hard and screwed up my eyes. I watched Alberto as he wrote in the book. He then turned and took down another, thicker one. Its size alone told me that whatever was written within the covers of this one was important, weighty. I scanned it as closely as I could. Much of what was written in it I could only guess at as it was in Latin, but even I could make out the name of Pope Julius II. So, this was where Sebastiano's papal commissions had ended up. What my old maestro would have done to get his hands on these.

Chapter 12

I would be working at the Vatican for Pope Julius II. A tingle of excitement ran from the tips of my fingers to the ends of my toes. It didn't seem real.

I recalled the day he became Pope even though I was but a small child way back in 1503.

After an unsettling spell of papal deaths (Pope Alexander VI, the fattest of God's representatives on earth, had succumbed to malaria, while his successor, Pope Pius III, had lasted but a few weeks), the cries of *habemus papa* – *we have a pope* – were as music to every Roman's ear. Pope Julius II had arrived.

'He's said to have the soul of a Caesar.'

'He wants to make Rome great again.'

And he did. In the years he had been Pope he had overcome our enemies and brought a smile to every artist's face with his ambitious plans to save ancient treasures and create new works of art fitting for a legacy. This was our golden age.

Pope Julius II. Emperor-pope. Leader of a Latin-Christian empire. Patron of the arts. Not long ago I had stood in Sebastiano's studio, disappointed when His Holiness had not chosen to commission the studio to work on the Vatican palace.

But now . . . My heart swelled with pride as I looked at the book used exclusively for papal commissions, here, in Raphael's workshop. I found it hard to suppress a huge smile at my good fortune. This was where Sebastiano's hoped-for requests for work had gone. How he would fume when he found out the truth. My skin prickled with fear at the thought of it. My eyes raced round the studio, the calm, productive studio I now found myself in, desperate to fix an eye on my new maestro. When I found him I sighed with relief.

I looked back at the Vatican order book. I watched with pride as Alberto added my name to a list of apprentices taken on specifically to fulfil the demand for artistic works. There would be no running back to Sebastiano for me.

A hand rubbed me on the back. An affectionate, fatherly rub. 'Fourteen?' Raphael was right behind me looking down over my shoulder. My body melted at his touch. He was so close I felt the warmth of his breath on my neck.

'That's the age I was when I went to Perugino's studio. A wonderful artist in his day. Treated me as one of the family.'

There was no mention that his old maestro had fallen from grace. All Raphael talked of were Perugino's qualities, as an artist and a man. And the way he behaved that day, to me, and to others, I would soon learn, was typical of the man. Always positive and generous. I soon learned how he had lost his mother, then his father, when still a boy. Yet no darkness furrowed his brow, no shadows clouded his bright eyes. Joy radiated from him.

I've often asked myself how some men seem unable to let go of the chains that tied them once, clinging on to the rusty links as if they were a part of them, allowing them to weigh their minds and bodies down for all eternity; whereas others manage to shake them off and fly away high into the heavens. I've pondered the problem much but I still cannot fathom it. I've often asked myself too how some men can be generous-spirited even to those who would act against them while others bear a grudge that they can never let go. That too will always remain a puzzle to me. Suffice to say that very first day I met him in his workshop I knew the type of man Raphael was. Brim full of generosity, even towards Sebastiano and towards those who would see him flounder. He was a shining star.

That is not to say he was without mischief. His desire to know of a rival's failings knew no bounds. 'If you haven't got anything nice to say about Sebastiano,' he would say with a rare glint in his eyes, 'come sit next to me and tell me about it.' To begin with I was too embarrassed to say one bad word. I knew what these artists could be. One minute enemies, the next the best of friends. But as I basked in the warmth of Raphael's attention – touching my arm, showing me how to hold my brushes, how to stand, what to look at when drawing – my heart became lighter, my tongue looser. And I stoked the flames of jealousy with gay abandon.

'Michelangelo did what?'

Over the coming weeks I discovered that Raphael had a particular interest in listening to stories about the bear-like curmudgeon. And he had a few stories of his own he liked to share with his apprentices. 'He ruffles feathers, you know. Leonardo had to flee to France to get away from him. Perugino tried to take him to court.' But it soon became apparent that these tales were about the man only. Raphael held him in the highest of regard as an artist and sculptor. I once made a detrimental comment about a painting Michelangelo had been working on. I never made the same mistake again.

'Magnificent. Monumental. When in Florence I took the opportunity to sketch many of his works, as well as those of that other giant, Leonardo da Vinci. The man is a genius. They both are. Staggering. So much to teach the world.'

And as time went by it became apparent that Raphael had so much to teach me.

Chapter 13

A growing number of girls had started to attach themselves to the studio. Racy types in the main, and loose with their favours. Most of them tried their chances with Raphael; many succeeded. Raphael liked to change his girls more regularly than his shirt. But I had only seen a few girls lucky enough to leave with him more than once and not one of them meant a thing to him. I was his friend. I trusted him. He trusted me. I was happy. Work was good. And before I knew what had happened weeks and months had passed.

How is it that when times are good you can never think of much to say about them?

But one morning I came into Raphael's workshop to discover that something had changed.

Giulio and Raphael were huddled together over the table covered in antique busts. Giulio was talented; it hadn't taken Raphael long to find this out. That was why he liked to work closely with him. And so, when I found the two men discussing a new project, I should not have been surprised. But to see their heads touching was unbearable for me. I watched in horror as Raphael rested his hand on Giulio's shoulder. The sight distressed me more than talk of any girl in my dear friend's bed.

I walked up to the table, pretending to study a figure with a broken nose.

'Commissions aren't coming in at the rate they were before.' Raphael's voice was small, bewildered.

'I don't understand it,' Giulio replied. 'The quality of the work we produce far exceeds that coming out of any other studio in Rome.'

'Perhaps, perhaps not, good Giulio. Either way, we are sinking, and so I thank you for introducing me to your friend. We need exceptional individuals like him to pull ourselves out of these choppy waters. He will be joining us within the week.' Raphael ruffled Giulio's hair. Giulio ruffled the maestro's hair in return. I pressed my thumb against the jagged edge of the broken nose and felt my skin split.

'In the meantime, try to keep the others positive,' Raphael said. 'Don't worry them about the drop in commissions. There's no point in distressing them too.'

Raphael noticed me as I quickly tried to stem the flow of blood from my thumb. 'Ah! Pietro! Are you hurt?' I was, but not in the way he imagined. I mastered my expression with a mask of inscrutability. 'Such an innocent face!' he cried, his voice suddenly upbeat. 'Doesn't he have an innocent face, Giulio?'

I had no idea who Raphael and Giulio had been talking about but over the following days I noted that commissions continued to fall. I also noted Raphael listening to Giulio more attentively than ever before. Half-dressed girls covering the maestro's neck in kisses were as nothing to me when compared to this. I mentioned the lack of orders to the other apprentices, spreading disquiet. I wanted to hurt them, Raphael and Giulio, make Raphael believe that Giulio had betrayed him with his loose tongue. I succeeded in whipping up an uneasy atmosphere in the workshop. I failed to implicate Giulio. Raphael and he were as tight as ever.

'He's coming in tomorrow. It's all been arranged.' The maestro's hand touched Giulio's back. I couldn't bear it.

'You'll see,' I heard Giulio reassure him, 'our fortunes will pick back up soon.'

'Coming?' One of the girls looped her arm through Raphael's. It was Clarice, a familiar face around the workshop.

'Things are looking up already,' Giulio said, with a lascivious wink.

The next morning I arrived early. Raphael and Giulio had arrived earlier still. They were in the office. The door was closed. Laughter was coming from the other side. I could make out Raphael's voice, calm and good-natured, Giulio's, rough and mocking, and another voice that I couldn't yet place. I watched the door, willing it to open. Then it did.

One hour later, when most of the apprentices had made it in, Raphael gathered us to him. '*Garzoni!* Let me introduce Giovanni da Udine to you.'

When Giulio and I had been sent to Sebastiano's workshop, Giovanni da Udine was the only apprentice Michelangelo had chosen to keep on. No wonder Raphael wanted him to join us. Raphael's words of welcome filled the studio with their warmth. 'Now let's get to work!' he cried, when he'd finished. 'We have a reputation to maintain. And surpass.'

Giovanni greeted me with a nod, without breaking the thread of his conversation. I took the nod as an invitation to draw closer. I stood, listened. 'It's Michelangelo. He's been helping Sebastiano secure private commissions, for portraits and fresco work, all over Rome.' Giovanni was older than most of the apprentices at Raphael's studio and had survived longer than most at Michelangelo's. That was because he was highly skilled: he had a reputation for being able to draw birds that were so lifelike you expected them to fly out of the picture frame and flap around the room. It was also because he was quiet. That's why it was a surprise to hear him; gossip was flowing from his mouth faster than piss from a chamber pot when thrown from Mad Lavinia's first-floor window.

Apprentices' heads waved like ears of barley in the wind as Giovanni exposed the underhand machinations of his now former maestro. We understood why commissions weren't coming in; we knew where they'd been diverted.

Raphael laughed and shrugged. 'Why would he not?' But when the laugh had melted from his face I could see that the information troubled him. Michelangelo was not a popular man but he was a popular artist and his recommendations, when it came to other artists, went a very long way, especially when it was generally accepted that he held very few of his peers in high regard.

Giovanni caught my eye. He'd said enough for the moment. I watched him as he gravitated towards the ancient Roman artefacts. Raphael was rapidly accumulating an extensive collection of statues, feet, hands, and various architectural pieces that he'd salvaged from sites around the city – Giovanni was fascinated. He became the Giovanni of old. Quiet, reflective, whose eyes fixed on an object and wouldn't let it go until it had given up its secrets.

He looked first at the trace of blood I'd left on the noseless bust, then at my bound thumb. 'We'll talk later. Discuss plans,' Raphael said. When he'd gone Giovanni looked me in the eye. I averted my gaze. He would be extracting no secrets from me.

*

It was in the weeks following Giovanni's revelation that his old master had been securing commissions for Sebastiano that Raphael eventually cracked. The laugh and the shrug and the 'Why would he not?' had all but disappeared, and the requests for work were still not coming in. Raphael had always had enough work of his own without having to worry about losing out to Sebastiano. And he usually found it amusing when he got word that Michelangelo and Sebastiano had made some disparaging remark about him. But that was before, when their seeds of malice bore little fruit.

The workshop still had several important commissions to work on for the Vatican. These were substantial and Raphael was currently working on plans that, if taken up, would be more substantial still. But it was the amount of work coming in from private individuals, which made up a huge part of the market, that was disappearing. It would not affect the workshop financially in the short term, but if Michelangelo continued to put his not inconsiderable weight behind Sebastiano then there would be a problem. And it was how he was securing the work that was even more alarming.

'It's like a poison,' Raphael said, 'killing off our good name.' And he was right. Spiteful rumours, cruel slurs, especially coming from an artist as great as Michelangelo, these could seriously damage Raphael's reputation in Roman aristocratic society. There had been talk of taking on more apprentices. That would have to be postponed for now. It was a worrying state of affairs.

Raphael was starting to lose confidence.

But he'd been asked to submit plans by a very minor dignitary to design and complete a fresco as well as to put forward ideas for a series of family portraits. It was not a glory project but it was work and it would keep us ticking over until demand from private clients picked up. The maestro was just waiting for the word.

*

'I can't believe it.' The maestro had recently returned from one of his archaeological visits in the city. Usually he was in fine form when he came back from one of these outings. *Such wonders, such learning, such perfection.* His enthusiasm would reverberate around the room. But this morning, his brow furrowed and jaw clenched, it was evident that the only thing he'd come back with was *such bad news.* He forced a smile as he passed his apprentices but it convinced no one. The news, whatever it was, was not good. For any of us.

He patted me on the back, muttered, 'Good work.' He was going to stop. Talk. I was sure of it. My breath quickened. 'Giovanni!' he called out, and kept on walking.

Giovanni. He had not been in the workshop for five minutes and already he was the maestro's new confidant.

'The commission's been given to Sebastiano . . .' Raphael told him, incredulity in his voice. 'All of it.'

Giovanni said nothing. The room was devastated. I was not the only person listening.

'He's a great painter. I have no right to be offended,' the maestro continued. Splutters of disagreement burst up like fountains around the room.

'But he's nothing compared to you.' This was bold for Giovanni.

'Giovanni!' Raphael raised his voice in warning.

'You're too generous, maestro. All of Rome knows that he's less than fulsome in his praise of you.'

'That may be so but the fact remains, he is a great artist. A mean-spirited, impossibly petty human being,' Raphael added with a laugh, 'but, a great artist nevertheless. Now, on a more serious note, work is drying up and we need to do something about it. If we were the best we would have been awarded the commission. That's the plain truth. And so that's what we will be.'

Raphael said no more. The sound of hard work filled the room. I too had been inspired by his rallying words. I'd been allowed to paint the sky in one of the Madonna portraits and I was taking the utmost care over it. However, the thought that Raphael could believe that Sebastiano was better than him was torturing me and I could not let it go. Then it struck me: the composition of the portrait I was working on reminded me of that of Sebastiano's *La Fornarina*, his portrait of Margarita. Had Sebastiano ever finished it? A smile tripped across my lips as I remembered the day he'd pulled down the curtain. That seemed so long ago. Sadness pierced my heart like a thorn at the memory of Margarita but I removed it quickly, little realising that in so doing I would be leaving myself wide open to guilt. But it was too late. It flooded in and clouded my mind. It would not be so easily chased away.

I looked at the woman in the painting before me as I added white to my sky. I marvelled at how Raphael had captured the essence of the girl who'd modelled for it. I remembered when she'd walked into the studio earlier in the week. Her hair was fair and her features neat. But in all she seemed unexceptional. Yet as I looked at the canvas the face upon it dazzled me. It was the girl, yet so much more than the girl. I compared it with the portrait Sebastiano had done of Margarita Luti. His had been of the girl, yet so much less than the girl.

For Sebastiano's workshop to be chosen over Raphael's, for any commission, seemed an injustice indeed.

Raphael had been doing the rounds, encouraging, advising, helping, reassuring the apprentices. At last he was with me. I wanted to tell him that he was the best, but I didn't. He picked up a paintbrush and tapped it against the side of his head. He looked perturbed. Was there something in the way I was colouring the sky that bothered him? 'Beautiful brushstrokes, Pietro,' he murmured. 'Exquisite tones.' It couldn't be that. He tapped his head some more, as if by doing so he might dislodge the answer to the problem he saw before him. I braced myself; it was time for me to speak out. But I couldn't.

I looked over at Giulio, drawing the face of a young man over at the left of the studio. Not here five minutes and he'd made his mark. Everybody knew who he was. Then there was Giovanni, confidant to Raphael, and here for even less time. I doubted if many of the other apprentices even knew my name. But Raphael did, and that was all that mattered to me.

'M-m-master . . .' I'd forgotten about that. Perhaps that's why I'd not chosen to speak out before. So much easier to imagine what you would have said rather than to try and fail. Giulio's eyes jumped towards me then jumped back to his subject. I looked at Raphael, waiting for an impatient sigh. It did not come.

'Yes, Pietro? Continue.'

'If . . . if . . . if you don't mind me saying so, this painting is beautiful.'

'Thank you, Pietro. But there's something not beautiful enough about it.'

'B-b-but you have improved on nature herself,' I said, pushing the words out. 'The woman is l-l-lovely and your p-p-painting more so.'

'I'm not sure. I think I need to find a woman of even greater beauty than the one who modelled for this. I have a certain ideal in mind . . .' He looked deep in thought. 'Now all I need to do is find her.'

He'd spoken to me, not to Giulio, not to Giovanni, or to any of his other assistants, but to me. This was something that was dear to his heart and it had been to me that he'd revealed his thoughts.

I knew how I could help him.

'When I look at this,' he pointed to his Madonna, 'it makes me see that I still have so much to learn.' He smiled at me before going back to Giovanni.

'Perhaps next time we should try a different composition. Or a different girl. Or possibly several and combine the best qualities of each to form one perfect, harmonious vision of heavenly beauty. What do you think?' Giovanni nodded while I continued with my little patch of sky. I could help him, but, for the moment, I'd said enough.

I listened as the maestro discussed skills that needed to be improved upon, techniques still to be learned, compositions to be attempted. He would work himself harder than ever before. But for all his enthusiasm, doubts plagued him. He had to learn from the best. If only Michelangelo would help him the way he helped Sebastiano. Perhaps that was why Sebastiano's work was better?

Giovanni had heard enough. The brooding mountain of a man exploded. 'It's not in your nature to speak ill of others but I cannot stand by and say nothing while you deceive yourself

93

like this. It was no accident the new private commission went to Sebastiano. Michelangelo had his large hand on Sebastiano's back and pushed him forward. Sebastiano is Michelangelo's puppet. And together they are malicious. They are infected with a jealousy towards you so virulent that they want to see you wither on the vine. Their attack on you is most deliberate.'

Raphael put a hand on his heart as if someone had pierced it.

'My sincerest wish is that Sebastiano will drown in the work he has stolen from you. He has taken on more commitments than he can cope with,' Giovanni added. 'He won't be able to deliver on them.' I too knew this to be true. Raphael's approach to work was meticulous, well organised. Sebastiano's was not. A deadening silence descended.

'What you say wounds me,' Raphael said at last. 'But part of me knows you speak the truth and I thank you for it. But I have never scorned another's talent, and I won't start now. What you have told me makes me more determined than ever to be the best. Talent and hard work will out. Truth and beauty in art will trump deceit. I will make this workshop the most celebrated in Rome. I will make this workshop the most sought after in all the world. Envy is no part of me and I will not allow my art to be destroyed by it or my soul to be corrupted by it.'

Passion shook the studio. I watched him, entranced.

'And believe me, *garzoni*,' he added, addressing every apprentice in the studio, 'if you think we fail today, do not allow yourselves to despair, as it will be this very failure that will add such sweetness to our success. I will strive, you see. We will strive, together. We will succeed.'

He leant over me to study the gentle face and cascading hair of the blond Madonna on my easel. I breathed in the scent of him, bathing in the heat of his blood. His chest swept the edge of my ear. I did not move.

'I need to find beauty,' he sighed. 'Michelangelo is talented beyond measure . . . I need to put my efforts into getting better, not in maligning others. No good will come of petty jealousy. The solution lies in beauty – I know it. And I have a certain ideal in my mind.'

The maestro picked up a miniver brush and added light to his Madonna's face. 'But this isn't it.'

He stood back. My heart beat fast. I had a plan. Desperate for me to be the one who could help him, I opened my mouth and let the words tumble out.

'S-S-S-Sebastiano has a painting very similar to this.'

An expression of incredulity swept across Raphael's face, a hint that he might not be as full of humility as I'd supposed. He twitched his nose, gave a sniff, then said, 'In what way precisely?'

'The s-s-s-subjects stand slightly to the side, their eyes l-l-look back at us . . . the c-c-c-composition is the s-s-sa . . .'

'The colours?' Raphael cut me off; he did not like to hear the paintings were 'the same'. 'And the light?' he continued, 'and the texture? The spirituality? Surely they must be different?'

I'd failed to make my point. I tried again. 'S-S-S-S-Sebastiano has r-r-r-rendered the model less b-b-b-beautiful than in life. He's th-th-thickened her n-n-neck . . .'

Giulio laughed. 'But apart from that, the painting is the same in every particular.' His tongue was so sharp I wondered that he didn't cut himself with it. I hadn't seen him come across the room, but there he was bending over the bench and showing Giovanni what I guessed was another of his 'erotic' drawings. Then he turned to me to carry on with his sneering. 'Sounds masculine. Your type, Pietro!' I reddened at the jibe but Raphael hadn't noticed it. He was waiting for me to say more about Sebastiano's piece.

'If you were to p-p-paint her p-p-portrait, the w-w-w-w-woman in his p-p-painting, you would make her . . .' I paused, willing myself not to stutter '. . . the model of . . . perfection.'

Giulio nodded with silent approval.

'And?' Raphael said, pushing me to say more.

'Sebastiano's p-portrait makes the girl look w-worse than she does in real life. I kn-kn-know her, you see. She's . . .' I glanced hastily at Giulio whose lips were already starting to curl up. I turned quickly towards Raphael for reassurance. The sight of him calmed me. I would not stutter. 'She's beautiful,' I said, looking straight at him. 'Hair like skeins of silk, deep, brown eyes that sparkle in the light like jewels, dark eyelashes that brush against skin that glows and beautiful lips, deep pink, and as juicy as ripe fruit.' I blushed as I realised I was describing Raphael's face, though in my defence, he and Margarita Luti did look very similar. I shot a look at Giulio again. He held his chin between forefinger and thumb. He was listening and watching most intently.

'Who is she?'

I told Raphael her name. '. . . *la fornarina*,' I added, not daring to look at Giulio for fear of getting put off. 'That's what we called her in Sebastiano's workshop. That was what he called his painting of her.'

'*La fornarina*,' Raphael repeated as ideas rippled in the pools of his eyes. 'I must paint her.'

'Ay, that you must,' Giulio said. 'And as for you, little Pietro, I must draw you. You really do have an interesting face.'

Chapter 14

I'd seen Margarita Luti several times after the day she'd walked with me to my new life as an apprentice at Raphael's workshop. But I'd made sure she'd not seen me. Whenever I'd passed her on my way to the Vatican, transporting drawings and painting materials back and forth, I would disappear down a side road, or conceal myself on the other side of a cart. One day, I had told myself, I would stop and tell her how I was getting on. But not yet. I was too busy.

But the truth of it was that I was turning out to be my father's son. Ambitious, selfish, I'd wanted to distance myself from the poor of the city in general and Margarita Luti in particular. Yes, she had shown me compassion, and it would have been the noble thing to have acknowledged her, gone to see her. She'd saved me in oh so many ways after all: she'd been strong that day outside Sebastiano's, chasing people off me; she'd been heroic when she'd rescued me from the Tiber; she'd been kind; she'd been generous; she'd been warm and good and loving. But she was also extremely common, and boasted about the fact as if it was something to be proud of. Then there was her unsettling assumption that I was common too. No, I had not wanted to see her at all. The father that I feared and had every good reason to hate had taught me if not well then thoroughly. His values were the blood in my veins and the blackness in my heart.

But now Raphael needed to see her. I'd told him about her. I would face her for him.

'If we walk along by here, along the banks of the Tiber, we'll come across her, I'm sure,' I called back to Raphael. We made a dazzling sight, Raphael, Giovanni, Giulio, and myself, walking along with our bags full of rolled-up paper and drawing implements, our clothes colourful and well cut, our hair combed and faces shaven on the way to the Vatican to discuss work plans with Bramante for Pope Julius II. Bramante was a friend and most fervent supporter of Raphael. As the Pope's architect, he was in charge of many important civic works, including the construction of St Peter's, and wanted his young friend to be part of the rebuilding of the eternal city that was Rome. Ancient monuments pushed up through its soil like the bones of a giant. It was said that the Pope wanted Bramante to bring that giant back to life.

As we made our way through the maze of narrow streets and overcrowded hovels that lined the Tiber I could see why. This Rome was squalid. Still, after we'd found Margarita, we would soon be at the Vatican. My skin prickled with excitement. Heads turned in admiration as we made our way there. I felt proud to be part of this group.

We were getting close to the bridge where I remembered Margarita liked to bathe. It was more private here as a rule but as we passed, I noticed there were more Romans than usual washing away the dirt and dust of the day. One or two looked up at us and the news that we were artists spread across the surface of the water like oil. Stories of the lowborn being snapped up by artists and immortalised in art were becoming less fable, more fact, and the hopefuls, women as well as men, started to display their wares with flair if not decorum. I glimpsed an arm here, an ankle there, and in some cases, a whole lot more.

I noticed the lascivious smile bare flesh brought to Giulio's face. 'Why should the eyes be denied what delights them most?' He shrugged.

I well knew how he longed to capture sexual pleasure in his drawings. And I'd heard many of the workshop models complaining because his requirements were so physically exacting and morally compromising. From the strained poses of the girls in the water, thrusting their bodies towards us and flashing themselves with a promise of post-painting rapture it was clear these girls, if chosen, wouldn't show the same reticence.

But there would be no choosing models today. Giulio would have to come back on his own another time. We walked on, abuse, a sign of their disappointment, ringing in our ears. 'Pretty boys! Off to flash your arses at the Vatican, are you?' Uncouth street girls. Their words made me feel uncomfortable and I looked at Raphael for guidance. He was laughing.

'You're not normal, red-blooded men,' the girls continued. 'Wouldn't know what to do with this if it was sitting on your face.'

At this Giulio looked around quickly to catch a look. He gave the girl who gave the challenge a leer and did something disgusting with his tongue to say that he would. 'Are you going to get a surprise,' he mumbled to himself. We were subjected to no further name-calling.

But of Margarita there was no sign.

As we made our way along the riverbank I carried on scouring the Tiber. Solitary figures scooped up water to pour over themselves, stopping immediately at the sight of us. Many let their skirts, up until then pulled up around their waists, drop into the water rather than show their bodies to passers-by. They weren't looking to make it into a painting. Old women and old men washed themselves here. One or two of them helped each other in and out of the shallows for fear of falling over and not being able to get themselves back up.

'Magnificent,' Raphael said, 'age.'

'But you wouldn't want it on your wall,' Giulio quipped. I was of Giulio's opinion but said nothing.

Raphael did not agree. 'That depends. If the face is one of a life well lived, then that is surely something worthy of contemplation. Would that I might live to a ripe old age, with a face that tells the story of my years.'

'Ay, and perhaps then you'll see that the only vision worth contemplating is not your own but that of the young girl you'll have in your arms, and that it's not old age that's ripe but the juicy peach that you'll be squeezing to see if she's in season and ready for the picking, plucking and . . .'

'Giulio.' Raphael laughed, raising a hand to ask for silence. 'You're making young Pietro blush here. And perhaps you're right. Age is probably better to listen to, enjoy its wisdom, more than it is to behold.'

'Yes, give me a hot, tight, young body to hold – and behold – over one that's wrinkled and stre—'

'Enough, I say.' Raphael smiled. 'The boy is blushing.'

I put a hand to my hot cheek.

'For me, beauty, because that is, I assume, Giulio, what you are talking about, is so much more than that. For me it's what inspires, reveals goodness, leads to goodness, is goodness.'

Giulio shrugged, unconvinced. I was surprised at his lack of deference to Raphael but our master didn't seem to mind. In fact, he seemed to value Giulio's outspoken character, respecting him all the more for it. And it was true that you couldn't call Giulio a sycophant. He was ever sincere.

'I don't know. I've seen many a beauty who's been as evil as sin, and I've enjoyed every minute. That's what women are. Evil.' Giulio then pulled at my sleeve. 'You've been quiet, Pietro. What do you have to say on it?'

I had very little experience of women. My mother had died when I was born. I had no sisters. I'd observed girls who worked as models, couldn't fail to notice the ones who carried bells and wore high heels down the backstreets of the city. But they held no interest for me. The only time I had had any interaction with a woman was when Margarita Luti had rescued me from a beating. She'd shown me kindness, which had surprised me. But I didn't like to dwell on that.

'And does that apply to your own mother?' Raphael was back on the subject of women and Giulio's assertion that they were all evil. He was having sport with him.

'Keep my old mother out of it!' said Giulio. 'But you know what I'm saying, Raphael. You're full of courtly tales and manners after your time spent in Urbino, but you have to admit, even the Bible says Eve's the sinner who corrupts man. The holy book is full of them. Sinful women. Take Delilah. She can cut my hair any day.'

'You haven't got that much of it to lose. You don't have much strength for her to sap either,' Raphael teased. 'Pietro's bag is heavier than yours!'

'That's where you're wrong. I am strong. In a special way. A way that ladies love. Staying power, that's what I've got, when it comes to . . .' Raphael nudged him. Giulio nudged me. Laughed at his own joke. I tripped a little. 'What would Delilah sap you of, young Pietro?' Giulio asked. I said nothing. He didn't seem to mind. 'Whereas you, Raphael. Imagine what she could sap you of! She could lure you into her den, cut your hair, keep you in bondage, and drain you of your life force. And with your life force she'd rob you of your God-given power to paint.'

Giovanni had distanced himself from the group and was walking ahead. I contemplated joining him but found the conversation strangely mesmerising.

Giulio continued. 'When the Pope says, "Bring Raphael. He's got to paint my wrinkly face and immortalise it for posterity," I'd have to reply, "Papa, dearest, highest, holiest, Raphael can't because he's fallen into a little known circle of hell, one that Dante shares with only his closest of friends, and that's the one where he's got to suffer that most exquisite of punishments, a living death in the eternal service of Venus." Making love! What a way to go! And I'd have to tell *il papa*, "No, you can't join him," because he'd want to.'

I let out a muffled giggle as I clamped a hand across my mouth. Giulio! Talking about the Pope in such a way.

'But I can't see you going for it myself,' Giulio sighed. 'Not even saucy Delilah could bewitch you, Raphael. She sounds a beauty to me but your beauty – your ideal of beauty – she's something completely different. The woman to ensnare you would need more than a pair of shiny scissors and an eternally plump, wet, juicy . . .'

'Enough, Giulio, enough!'

As I walked and listened, a strange joy filled my soul. I laughed quietly away at Giulio's ribald remarks, watching the afternoon sun dance on the surface of the Tiber where it fragmented into a thousand jewels of light with my every step. My eye followed each one as they echoed out to form myriad glinting ripples, and there, at the edge, stood the greatest, rarest jewel of all. The one we'd all been looking for. The one I'd promised we would find. She stood there, ankle-deep in the river, shining as brightly as the sun. Moving facets of water lapped around her and spangled like stars.

I tried to look straight at her but she dazzled me. I stumbled. Raphael and Giulio helped me up. Margarita's presence dragged my eyes towards her once more. Raphael's hand, already loosely around my forearm, locked around it, tight. He stopped moving. He had seen her. Even Giulio was transfixed at the sight of her. Unaware of us, she splashed herself joyfully and then paddled over to an old woman standing not far away who was struggling to get to the riverbank. Margarita clambered out first and extended a strong arm, sleeves rolled up, taking hold of the frail woman by the wrist. She helped her out of the river, guiding her to a large stone that looked as if it might have once been the base of a Roman pillar. Smiling, she knelt down, taking the cloth of her skirt that she had kept out of the water to dry the old woman's feet. She rubbed them gently as her hair, rich and dark, cascaded around her shoulders and fell over her eyes in heavy coils.

We moved closer so that soon we could hear the sunshine in her voice as she warmed the old woman's soul. She stood up, tossed her hair back and thrust strong hands on her hips. Her figure was there for all to see, poorly disguised beneath a lightweight frock. She leant over to help her friend up. Her soft, round breasts quivered with the effort. Raphael gasped. The old woman frowned; she had seen us. 'I'll be fine,' Margarita said, giving the woman a loving push in the direction of the bridge. 'This one's a friend of mine,' she called out, pointing to me with what I was relieved to see was genuine delight. The old woman looked at me and made a face that caused her skin to crease and droop like fold upon fold of excess silk. She was not convinced but went anyway.

After I'd made the introductions nobody spoke for a while.

Raphael stood before Margarita. His fingers trembled as he lifted them to his hair. His mouth opened but no sound came out. She looked at him. Her eyes looked directly into his.

'I would like to paint you.'

He'd said it. She did not reply.

'I would like to paint you.'

He'd said it again. She did not reply.

'Would you allow me to paint you?'

His voice was tremulous, vulnerable.

'I know who you are,' she said. 'Of your reputation. I won't pretend that I don't, and I hear you're better, and by that I mean kinder than most. I don't care how good you are as an artist as I'll never have any of your work. But I do care what you're like as a man. A human being.' She paused for a moment. Her eyes strayed over to me, then returned to Raphael. For a moment I believed she was going to say *yes*. Then it came. That word. The word that, as soon as you hear it, tells you all your hopes are about to come crashing down.

'But . . . But it makes no difference how kind you are, I'll not be a model for you. Not now. Not ever. I'm done with that.'

Raphael was speechless.

'Had more than enough with that Venetian,' she explained. 'And so, I thank you for your . . . interest . . . and I'll be on my way. Good day sir. Sir.' She nodded to Giulio. 'Pietro.' She looked at me with a piercing gaze as if I understood. Giovanni was nowhere to be seen. We suspected that he was at the doors of the Vatican already.

As Margarita walked away I was sad. My plan had come to nothing. But then she stopped. She turned and looked at Raphael. I hoped she was going to change her mind. She lowered her dark lashes. By the time she had raised them my hope had changed to dread. With horror I saw how she touched his soul with her eyes; and, equally disturbing, he touched her soul with his. No matter that they'd never met before this day; they recognised one another. It was as if they had known each other for all eternity. My insides ran cold. Something profound had passed between them and I was the person who had brought it to pass.

All this time I'd wasted my time feeling jealous of Giulio, then Giovanni, when all the time the person I should have been worried about was Margarita. She was The One. I couldn't bear it. And I, yes, I had been the fool fate had chosen to bring them together. I looked at her, appalled. And to think I was beginning to feel guilty about not keeping in touch with her. What had I done? Margarita. I wanted to destroy her.

'Margarita!' It was the old woman. She'd been watching down from the bridge all along. Margarita looked startled as if she'd been given a good dose of the salts. Her eyes now had fear in them. She turned away from Raphael. The spell was broken.

Giulio put a hand on his friend's shoulder to steady him. Even he knew this was not the time for jokes and crude remarks after what he'd just witnessed. Margarita ran off, her hair undulating down her back, her feet running as quickly as they could to take her away from what she sensed would be captivity. She'd weakened, and now she had to get away.

'Raphael. We'll be late for Bramante.' Giulio spoke up at last.

'Bramante can wait. I have to go after her.'

Giulio tried to bring Raphael back to the path of reason but the master's desire was a wall too thick and high for him to breach directly. Retreating from the battle, the quick-witted Giulio immediately circumvented the obstacle by gesturing in my direction as if I were the key. 'We can find the girl later,' he said. 'We can't be late for Pope Julius.'

At the mention of the Pope's name, Raphael came to.

'Let's go to the Vatican. We have papal commissions to secure,' he declared, before taking me to one side asking, 'Pietro, you do know where she lives, don't you?'

Chapter 15

We had now caught up with Giovanni and were all waiting for Bramante in a small room in the Vatican. We were late. He was later. 'She's fond of you. I saw that, Pietro. You do know where she lives?' The maestro's attention warmed my soul. Ordinarily my eyes would have been running over the ceilings and walls, taking in the statues, the tapestries, the gilded ornaments, the upholstered chairs. But I noticed none of these material things. I sensed the urgency in Raphael's voice and luxuriated in the knowledge that only I could help him. I so wanted to please him that I would have told him I knew where to find her even if I didn't.

But the truth of it was that I didn't need to lie. Not this time. I could make the difference, help Raphael where others could not. I looked at Giovanni and Giulio. Their heads were locked together, discussing one of their many secret projects. I moved closer to Raphael, expecting him to pull me to him and ask me more questions about Margarita. Instead, he joined the other two. The pain of rejection howled through my heart like a wounded wolf.

When I look back on this moment I sometimes tell myself I had a choice: that I could have easily obstructed the path fate had set out for Raphael and Margarita with a lie, but, instead, I chose to help him to find her. Yet no higher impulse drove me.

No. Desperation did that, urging me on to do anything, anything, to please Raphael, to make him notice me, to need me. Even if it meant bringing Raphael and Margarita together. Besides, it would never last, this feeling he had for her, I told myself. She was a baker's daughter, lowborn. He would soon tire of her. And until that time Raphael could paint her and tell himself he was searching for beauty when all the while he would be asserting his superiority over a rival who wished him ill and looking for revenge.

'I-I-I-I know who she is,' I blurted out like fate's unwitting puppet. Raphael pulled himself away from Giulio and Giovanni. I had his attention. 'Wh-wh-where she lives. I know. I met her at S-S-S-Sebastiano's. And I was the one who went to p-p-p-pay her father when she first came to model for him. He's a b-b-baker, in Trastevere. I can t-t-t-take you to him.'

I don't know why I lied but I did. Not even the stammering could stop me. As lies go it was fairly harmless, if not pointless. Although now, when I think about it, it did save me from having to dredge up the whole sorry story of how Margarita rescued me, and from catapulting her up onto an even higher pedestal.

'Bramante!' The door opened and my master turned to embrace a grizzled man of advancing years. Bramante, though old, was a bear of a man and he hugged each of us in turn. I myself was slight of build and he smothered my face in his luxurious velvet cape.

'Come.' He had assistants in tow. They carried drawings too. We followed them along the grand corridors. My eyes now wandered in awe over the riches adorning this palace.

Bramante turned off into a side room. We shuffled in after him, taking care not to damage our plans and drawings for the various projects we'd been asked to do.

'I'm late because I've already had the meeting with Pope Julius,' he explained, talking quickly like a man who didn't have much time. '*Il Papa* insisted on conducting it in the garden,' he added with a furrowing of his brow. 'And I have *good* news . . . as well as *bad*.'

Raphael nodded. He wanted to hear it all, the sooner the better. 'Pope Julius wants his rooms redecorated.'

'But they were finished not so long ago by some of the most daring and accomplished artists of all time. Giovanni Antonio Bazzi, Bernardino di Betto, our beloved Pinturicchio . . .' Raphael read out a long list of past and present masters. 'I have seen their work and it's magnificent . . . sublime . . . Pope Julius can't mean for us to paint over it?'

Bramante pulled his lips back in a scowl. His face said he was in pain. That was precisely what Pope Julius had in mind. So this was the bad news. I went over the names of the artists whose work would soon be painted over. Bazzi had a remarkable reputation as an artist (though equally renowned for his predilection for young boys; he wasn't known as *il sodoma* for nothing), and he was still making his mark in the art world. Then there was Pinturicchio, much admired by the late Spanish pope. His work was hugely popular.

'This would secure work for the studio for many months, possibly years. And it would leave you a legacy.' Bramante placed a sympathetic hand on Raphael's shoulder, in a rather-you-than-me way.

Raphael shook his head. 'I refuse to do it. You can't expect me to destroy the work of such great artists.'

'There is nothing to be done about it,' Bramante said. 'Pope Julius has made it clear that all paintings made of, or for, the Borgias must be covered up. He wants no trace of them about the Vatican, no sign that there ever was a Borgia pope. He needs you to paint Alexander VI out of existence.'

'I will talk to *il Papa* myself,' Raphael insisted.

'Ha!' Bramante's laugh was cynical. 'Believe me, it will do no good. If he is prepared to sacrifice his own daughter to distance himself from the Borgia papacy he will have no care to preserve art done in its name.'

Raphael could not disagree. Pope Julius II took great pains to spell out to the people that he would not indulge in the excesses of his predecessor. His daughter Felice della Rovere would be no Lucrezia Borgia. She would be treated no better than any other lady of the court (and we all knew that in many cases she had been treated worse).

'We'll talk about this later,' Raphael said with a sad smile, 'but now let us hear the good news.'

His friend looked to the side and bit his fleshy lower lip.

'No!' Raphael said, shock in his voice. 'You can't say that was it?'

Bramante paused before inhaling deeply.

'There is also another commission on the table. Undoubtedly more challenging than the repainting of Pope Julius's rooms. Possibly for you.' He spluttered. 'The Pope is keen for you to do it, though I've told him it would be impossible for you to do both.'

'To do what exactly?'

Bramante took Raphael to one side. Both men huddled together. Fingers ran through hair, sighs erupted from whispers, faces grimaced. After much ringing of hands the pair came back. Raphael had the look of the damned about him.

'So . . . the painting of the Sistine Chapel . . . and the ceiling . . . of the Sistine Chapel . . . It will take years.'

'Pope Julius wants the best,' Bramante said, 'for his own legacy.' Architect and artist looked crestfallen. Ceilings. Difficult to paint at the best of times, but to have to design and execute a ceiling of the magnitude of the Sistine Chapel seemed like a prison sentence. I for one wanted no part of it. I searched every labyrinthine passage of my brain again and again. And then I found it. A way out. It occurred to me that for two gifted men, Bramante, and even Raphael, were decidedly dim-witted. They could see no escape. I could.

I thrust myself forward in the most beguiling of ways.

'M-M-Michelangelo?' I asked, my voice unsure, my face innocent, not minding that I was stammering as it could only add to the impression of naivety I wished to convey. 'M-M-M-Michelangelo? Could he not p-p-p-paint the ceiling?' Giulio rubbed his chin between thumb and forefinger in that disconcerting way of his; he observed me with interest.

Bramante swept his hand before him, brushing my suggestion away. But Raphael paused. He revered Michelangelo's ferocious talent – that I knew – if not the man. Michelangelo was the best and that was what the Pope wanted. To use this to get out of a lifetime of artistic hard labour was worth considering.

'Yes, if any artist could do it, it would be him. He's more driven than any other artist alive. He could do it justice more than I ever could.'

'But it is out of the question,' Bramante insisted. 'He's working on the Pope's tomb. It's a monumental undertaking. He's been working on it for years already and it's said that he'll be working on it for years to come. You know how he is.'

'He could finish it after the Sistine Chapel,' Raphael reasoned. 'Our pope is a warrior and won't be departing this world any time soon. Imagine how sublime the ceiling would be executed by a master of Michelangelo's enormous talent. The designs of his that I've seen most recently show that he is at the height of his considerable talents.'

Raphael had taken my lead and was running with it. He did not mention that these designs were the ones Michelangelo had been drawing up for Sebastiano so that the Venetian could steal away commissions from Raphael himself. But he had no need to.

Raphael did not want the poisoned chalice that was the Sistine Chapel. He would do all that he could to pass it on to Michelangelo. That would keep his talented hands busy and his creative mind fully occupied. He would have neither the time nor the inclination to draw up compositions for his friend Sebastiano the Venetian anymore.

'Pietro?' Giulio called me over to him. 'I would love to draw you. Your face, it fascinates me. Those cheeks that no lie will redden, those eyes that hide what lurks in the depths of your soul.

You have the perfect face, an innocent face. Ideal for a biblical character I've had problems finding a model for. Until now.'

'Which biblical character would that be?' I asked, flattered.

'Judas,' came the reply.

*

Bramante had the Pope's ear and a tongue more persuasive than even he himself had realised. It was decided: Michelangelo could finish the tomb after he'd finished painting the ceiling of the Sistine Chapel. The design and execution of the ceiling would suit him because of the scale and ambition of the project. Besides, he'd already started to annoy the Pope with his belligerent ways and so to keep the gifted bear tied up in the chapel for a while would do everyone some good. Far better to employ Michelangelo to express the glory of the papacy while Julius was still alive. The Pope was strong and of a robust constitution. His tomb would not be needed for a good few years yet.

*

The year 1508 was drawing to a close and at last the smaller, more manageable commissions started to arrive in Raphael's workshop once again now the main person responsible for their drying up was grappling with one of the most challenging projects of his artistic life. Meanwhile Raphael had started his project for the Vatican, namely redecorating the Pope's apartments. This, though requiring great planning and being artistically demanding, was not the ordeal we'd all imagined it to be. In fact, this period in our lives proved fruitful and exciting. I accompanied Raphael's group to the Vatican most days. We measured, sketched, and worked hard, Raphael the hardest of all. It was a joy.

*

'Giovanni, Giulio . . . you too, Pietro. I want you to make copies of the paintings before we start work on top of them. They must be meticulous, done with the utmost respect.' Before we could even touch the walls and the ceilings Raphael instructed us to make faithful reproductions of the work we were about to replace. At first I could not understand why he was bothering, but I did as I was told regardless.

I dutifully made faithful imitations of the works of *Il Sodoma* and Pinturicchio, which was at times compromising as they and many other artists whose work we were soon to paint over, were still involved in other commissions for various cardinals dotted around the Vatican palace. Many of these wronged artists prowled by on a regular basis. I awaited their rebukes as they dreaded what we had in store for the work they must have one time thought would last forever. Raphael was charming with them when he caught them passing by. He engaged them individually in quiet discussions, showing them drawings, asking for their help with his cartoons, soliciting their advice.

Then, one morning he appeared, accompanied by *Il Sodoma*.

'Listen now, my men. It is with the greatest joy that I introduce the maestro Giovanni Antonio Bazzi to you. You will all know of the excellence of his work.' Giulio winked at me and stroked his own thigh suggestively. 'He has done us the great honour of agreeing to collaborate with us so that together, with the aid of his extensive experience, we can achieve the highest and most perfect results here in these papal rooms.'

Il Sodoma's chest swelled a little at the fair praise an otherwise usurper was showering down upon him. That the same man would soon be painting over the evidence of his extensive experience did not seem to concern him at that particular moment. I'd always known a man was fair game to flattery. Every man underneath is a proud peacock and there was none so proud or peacock-like as *Il Sodoma*.

But as I observed Raphael I sensed that this was not the

self-serving sycophancy I'd been used to seeing bandied around between rival artists. He meant every word of praise and respect he uttered. It wasn't the swelling chest of a man well flattered that I was seeing before me as *Il Sodoma* breathed in with deep satisfaction, it was that of a man grateful that a peer could see the value of his art. Trust twinkled in his eyes as he looked Raphael in the face.

One by one the artists whose work we were about to conceal were treated with similar solicitude and respect. Several accepted Raphael's offer to collaborate with him, others did not, though of the latter group, they went away if not happy then at least with their self-esteem intact. Raphael's reputation was fast becoming one of someone generous, conciliatory, supportive of others. And he was working with a growing number of artists, assistants and apprentices to complete the Vatican commissions with commitment and passion. Artistic circles were awash with tales about him. The harder he worked the more famous he became.

*

It had taken the maestro many months to finish the cartoons for the first room, the *stanza della segnatura*. The *School of Athens* was to be depicted on one wall, with the *Disputation of the Most Holy Sacrament*, the *Cardinal and Theological Virtues*, and the *Parnassus* on the others. Each design was meticulously planned. For the *School of Athens* alone he'd had to confer with modern-day philosophers about who to represent from the ancient world and how to best express their characters. There would be Plato, Aristotle, Socrates, of course, as well as Pythagoras, Euclid, Epicurus, and the like.

Then he would work to give certain figures a matching Christian identity – the fresco was to grace the walls of the Pope's personal apartment after all – while giving each of them a recognisable face taken from our own time. Plato looked like

Leonardo da Vinci, while Aristotle had the distinctive face of Bramante, that sort of thing. Raphael's friend, Count Baldassare Castiglione, was in there too as Aeschines (a Greek orator, soldier, and diplomat, apparently, though if you've heard of him your knowledge of the ancients is better than mine).

Thankfully I could pick out the Count as he often paid us a visit. He had first made Raphael's acquaintance in Urbino and they had been very close friends ever since. He seemed to be as fond of Raphael as I was myself and he was usually accompanied by his friends Pietro Bembo and Fabius Calvus, both humanist philosophers, whose faces too made it into the *School of Athens*. Compositionally it was a work of great detail, where the stance of every figure had significance. I did not envy Raphael the job.

I could now paint well enough, especially when it came to copying, but the composition of complex designs such as the *School of Athens* would have left me confused beyond belief. Raphael on the other hand loved such challenging work. He'd talked to the entire workshop for weeks about how he planned to set it out. And although I already knew some of the famous faces to look out for, he was careful not to reveal the identity of every modern-day figure.

'I promise you, you'll all be in for a treat when I've finished sketching. I'm planning to put one or two surprises into the final drawing for our amusement,' he would tell us with the gentle tapping of his nose with one of his elegant fingers whenever anybody asked him what he had in store. I guessed Pope Julius would be one of those little surprises to make an appearance in the fresco. I had no idea who else Raphael had in there to divert us but I was confident that the final fresco would be a delight for the mind and the aesthetic senses. Satisfying on every level.

The months were passing quickly and before I knew where we were over a year had passed. And I had all but forgotten about Margarita so immersed was I in my artistic endeavours. Raphael seemed to have banished her to the sidelines of his mind too now that he had started on the designs for the Pope's private rooms. The *School of Athens* was only the beginning.

Besides, Margarita would not have stood a chance with Raphael. Greater crowds of women started to hang round doors awaiting his entry and exit at workshop and palace, while would-be apprentices followed him as if he was their spiritual leader. That I was one of the chosen made me feel truly blessed.

I loved working at the Vatican, on the Pope's rooms. Apprentices came and went, helped each other out; the atmosphere was friendly. This was the nearest thing I'd ever had to a proper family and at the head of it all was Raphael, there to guide us. I rarely thought of Michelangelo Buonarroti working some five minutes away: it was too depressing.

But then, one day, Raphael walked along the corridors, away from the Pope's private rooms and went straight into the Sistine Chapel. He'd encountered a tricky problem while drawing up his cartoons. 'Michelangelo will know what to do,' he said.

Bramante had tried to dissuade him from going but Raphael would not be told. If we were his family, Michelangelo was his brother, albeit estranged. They'd been feuding for far too long. It didn't have to be this way. Surely what united them was greater than what divided them. Pure artistic talent flowed in their veins. Raphael would ask for his help and Michelangelo would be there, would jump at the chance to support him, in the spirit of true artistic brotherhood.

Within seconds of peering his trusting face around the door leading into the Sistine Chapel Raphael realised he'd been expecting too much. Michelangelo felt well disposed to a very small number of people. And Raphael was not, nor ever would be, one of them.

His respectful enquiry had not been well received.

Within minutes he was back in the Pope's *stanza*, surrounded by lesser mortals, mortals who did not have the weight of the world on their shoulders and who did not see it as a weakness to smile and laugh.

Raphael whispered something only I caught.

'What's that?' Bramante asked.

'He bellowed at me from the top of the scaffolding,' Raphael answered. 'Told me to get out.'

'You saw how he was getting on, at least?'

'I saw nothing, only the boards he was lying on. The man's an enigma, one I'll never be able to fathom.'

After that encounter Michelangelo took to locking the chapel to keep prying, thieving eyes out, and the prying, thieving eyes of Raphael in particular.

Chapter 16

'Go!'

Raphael's team worked together on the frescoes, occasionally silent, more often jovial, always focused on achieving the best result possible. If one of us had a problem we would ask for advice: there was always someone ready to give it. Another year, maybe two, slipped past in a haze of joy. Raphael worked hard on his art while his reputation as a lover of women was developing nicely. Each girl believed they were special though the fact that he took home a different one every night (sometimes two, on occasion three) reassured me that they were not. Friendship was what counted and whenever the maestro brushed my fingers with his, or let his hair sweep my cheek as he showed me a technique I had yet to master, I knew in my soul that what we had was not infinitely replaceable. He did not mention Margarita in all that time. Not even Giulio and Giovanni worried me anymore.

While I was there with Raphael, training under many of the finest artists in the whole of Italy, not just Rome, I was the happiest I'd ever been in my entire life. Raphael would nod at me approvingly from across the room; Giulio would come up behind me and praise my work; even Giovanni allowed me to work a corner of one of the frescoes.

117

That's why, when one day I saw another of Michelangelo's apprentices pass by where we were, his master's shouts blowing him down the corridor from the Sistine Chapel like a leaf in a hurricane, I breathed a sigh of relief. I had found myself on a calm desert island peopled by beautiful artists. I was lucky indeed. I sensed Raphael had got caught up in some sort of storm of his own with Michelangelo but if anyone could weather it Raphael could.

'And don't bother to come back!'

That was Michelangelo again.

We watched the apprentice fly past, his arms flailing, a look of terror on his face. Go back? He'd be a fool if he did! I thought to myself.

'I think that's the last of them,' Giulio said. 'That's the last of Michelangelo's apprentices. What's he thinking? He's a madman.'

Raphael laughed. He had that rare talent of seeming to agree with everyone while simultaneously letting you know that he had his own opinions. I'd never witnessed anyone disagree so respectfully before. I'd never come across an artist who wasn't ready to stick the knife in a rival when the chance presented itself either. I wondered if this was another example of that which Castiglione was always talking about – *sprezzatura*. According to Raphael's friend from Urbino, this was a quality greatly to be admired. He had explained it to me once in the briefest of terms as a natural ease and spontaneity of expression. It struck me that Raphael had it, *sprezzatura*, but he took it to an even greater level by imbuing it with a virtuous core.

'He's an exceptional talent who finds it frustrating when others aren't as good as he is. He is the sort of artist who works better alone.' Raphael made a habit of standing up for Michelangelo and here he was, doing it again.

'He should train his people more.' Bramante did not agree.

'He should. But that would require him to communicate more. And that, I think we all know, does not come easily to him.' Raphael stood over a set of drawings laid out on the large table in the centre of the room. He bent down, leaning on his elbows. He rubbed the middle finger of his right hand across his left eyebrow and frowned; something about the drawing he was looking at displeased him. 'Pity,' he said, 'as I've encountered some problems only Michelangelo could help me with.'

'You've tried that. You have to accept it's not going to happen,' Bramante said.

Raphael humphed in agreement. The suspicious Michelangelo had already taken to locking the Sistine Chapel at the end of every working day. He worked late but Raphael often worked later and the older artist did not trust his enthusiastic rival to stay away.

Michelangelo was right, of course, to be worried. When Raphael had returned from the chapel after being refused help, he'd seen more through the wooden scaffolding than he'd admitted to. It wasn't much but he'd seen enough to know it was sublime. When he came back to the part of the palace we were working in he was in a state of ecstatic despair. 'To know such beauty exists yet to be exiled from it' were, I believe, the words he used.

'But I still have the problem,' he told Bramante now. 'See here.' He pointed to a drawing of a man. 'I can't seem to make this figure solid. I can't get the angles and proportions right at all. If only Michelangelo wasn't so hostile.'

Bramante did not answer.

'He is a giant of an artist. I could learn so much . . .'

'It's impossible. He's fiercely protective of his work. There's no way he's going to allow you – of all people – to see what he's done,' Bramante snorted.

'One look. Just one look at that ceiling of his. That's all it would take to help me understand what I need to do to get this right,' Raphael said, tapping the outline of the figure with the tip of his index finger.

Bramante was silent for a while. He looked around. I felt his eyes on me. I feigned complete absorption in my work. He drew himself as close to Raphael as he could get and covered his mouth

119

with a hand. I strained my ears but could pull out no words from the muffled whispers.

Giulio was nearby and dropped a brush on the floor. 'Damn!' he cried. Instinctively Bramante's voice rose in order to be heard over the clattering sound as wood hit the floor. 'We can both look at the chapel. I have the KEY,' he said.

We all carried on, seemingly unconcerned. But I for one had heard him. Bramante's voice could drop to the lowest of whispers now and it wouldn't make any difference. I knew. Raphael would be going to look at the Sistine Chapel ceiling to see what he could learn. Not even a locked door could stop him.

Chapter 17

Two days later Sebastiano appeared at the Vatican Palace. He had come to learn from the brushstrokes and compositional methods of his friend and great master. And he had been invited to do so. I imagine, knowing how lacking in drive the artist was, that he'd had to be asked several times before he'd got round to coming to see how Michelangelo's latest masterpiece was coming along, but he was here now and the palace corridors buzzed with the news of his arrival.

He put his head round to see how we were getting on in Raphael's team. He appeared furtive, not wanting to be caught.

Giulio spotted him and surreptitiously leant over and whispered in Raphael's ear. 'Sebastiano's standing in the doorway.'

Raphael was delighted, offering his hand in friendship and beckoning his rival in. 'Enter. What an honour. Let me show you what we're doing.'

'I'm on my way to see Michelangelo,' he said, feigning a lack of interest.

'Please, let the great Michelangelo know that he is most welcome to come and see what we're doing too. At any time. Our door is always open. Never locked.'

Sebastiano disliked Raphael's courtly manners. He gave a

sour smile, which turned into something unpleasantly sweet. Michelangelo would never take himself away from the Sistine Chapel to come and pay a brotherly visit on a fellow artist. Not even for a minute. Well, as Sebastiano had made an effort to come and see Michelangelo he might as well run an appraising eye over a rival's work and report back. Sebastiano entered the *stanza della segnatura*. Raphael welcomed him in with a bow.

'I will observe.'

Sebastiano looked at me. I'd made the mistake of openly watching him and I'd been caught. A cloud descended upon his face as he tried to remember how he knew me. He searched my features until the cloud dispersed. He'd decided that he didn't know me after all. Why would he? It had been nearly three years. I was seventeen years old now. Taller, bigger, my features more defined, my chin not as smooth as it once was. And all he had ever done was yell instructions at me, usually at the back of my head.

Still, I was relieved, though I felt the need to hide in my work. As I mixed paints for Giovanni, my hand trembled slightly as I thought of the lamp black I used to make for Sebastiano all those years ago. But I was safe now.

Raphael was delighted to share everything with Sebastiano: his work methods, techniques, organisation, plans, philosophical concerns, historical references. Everything. Sebastiano accepted them, greed in his voice, spite in his heart. When I felt calm, and brave enough to watch him again, I saw that he was the same weak artist of old. If Raphael expected to move him and ignite within his breast any spark of fellow feeling, which by some miracle he would carry on to Michelangelo, I could tell he would be sorely disappointed. I looked at Raphael, open, generous. Sebastiano was paltry and meagre by comparison.

'Thank you for coming by, Sebastiano. Please know that you are always welcome, here, or at the workshop. Any time.'

'You too,' Sebastiano replied without feeling as he retreated.

'Really? It would be an honour and a privilege to look round the workshop of a great master such as yourself,' Raphael called after him, not a hint of irony in his voice. 'I will drop by soon.'

'I cannot wait,' Sebastiano replied.

The smile on Raphael's face told me he thought the meeting with Sebastiano had gone very well. The sound of feet running in the direction of the Sistine Chapel told me that it hadn't.

'What a stroke of good fortune! Sebastiano will be able to talk to Michelangelo and who knows, put a good word in for us, God willing. I do believe this meeting will bear fruit.'

I didn't know whether to admire or pity Raphael's naivety as he revealed his faith in human nature. An excellent classical education of the sort Raphael had received in Urbino, I saw, had its drawbacks when applied to the real world with its real people.

But the meeting had sown seeds that produced an altogether different type of fruit, fast-growing and poisonous, that took the form of a series of letters penned over the following days.

The first arrived, addressed to Raphael, the very next morning. Work on the Pope's rooms was in full swing and the mood was good as ever. Out of the corner of my eye I saw a messenger hand Raphael a letter.

'Pietro, see here,' he called over to me, jubilant. 'Michelangelo has written—' Raphael had been right when he'd predicted only the day before that his meeting with Sebastiano would prove to bear fruit. But as I watched his eyes run over the words on the page I saw very soon that it was rotten. My maestro's voice crashed to the floor. The excitement in his eyes changed to horror. I moved towards him. He pushed past me as he left the room.

It wasn't until some time later that I discovered Michelangelo had accused Raphael of copying and stealing from him.

The problematic truth for Raphael was he himself would not have disagreed. During the precious years I spent as his apprentice I saw that he admired many artists. He was ever eager to learn from them, and it was true, he did make numerous sketches of their work, but only with a view to improving his own. He had a constant need to perfect his personal output and saw artistic endeavour as an expression of the age and the language of his generation to communicate with the generations to come. He granted responsibility to his apprentices, collaborated with fellow artists, and took what was sublime from others and developed it into a style that was completely his own.

Michelangelo did not share the same spirit. That he seemed to have found an artist friend in Sebastiano was initially a puzzle to me and most other people. But when other letters came to light bearing equally rotten fruit to the one Michelangelo sent to my master the truth came into focus. Michelangelo and Sebastiano's sole purpose in joining forces was to shoot slings and arrows at Raphael: this was the glue that bound the two men together.

Yet Raphael was still working on his *School of Athens* fresco and had a few cards of his own to play. He had yet to paint the face of Heraclitus. He needed someone his contemporaries would recognise. He needed someone sour and curmudgeonly.

Around the same time an apprentice friend with an axe to grind passed on news of another letter, this time written by Sebastiano to Michelangelo.

'So I'm *talentless and derivative*, am I? I possess *no artistic originality of my own*? I *owe everything to others*?' Raphael soon heard of it.

Think, think, think think think. I wanted to help him. He might possess great talent and express himself with *sprezzatura* but such gifts, though infinitely precious, were not going to help him on their own against such underhand attacks. Raphael might have thought there was enough work to go round for all the many artists in Rome, and that his skills would ensure a constant flow of commissions for everyone. But, apart from the dip in commissions shortly after his arrival in Rome, he'd never had to struggle in life, and I was determined to make sure he never did.

Margarita. A germ of an idea was fomenting in my head. Could it work?

I remembered the spark that had passed between her and my master. The thought of it unsettled me. But I quickly dismissed it. I reassured myself I must have imagined it because why else would he not have pursued her straight after? That's what every other man in Rome would have done.

We'd been working at the Vatican for years now and no mention of the girl to whom I owed my life had been made. She'd not been seen hanging round either, unlike so many other girls who had started to hang on and follow us as we walked between studio and workplace.

I thought of Sebastiano's portrait of Margarita, *La Fornarina*, the one he'd been working on when I'd first gone to his studio. My idea to help Raphael gnawed away at me. It had come to nothing before but could it work now?

'M-maestro?'

'Yes, Pietro?'

'Do you still p-plan on going to visit S-S-Sebastiano's workshop?' I asked.

'Hmm. Yes, he did invite me, didn't he?'

'If you decide to go, I would be g-g-g-grateful if you could let me accompany you. To be your g-guide,' I offered. Raphael was still smarting from Sebastiano's insults. He would need a push – I gave it.

'The portrait . . . of . . .' I breathed deeply before I said her name, 'M-M-Margarita, I w-w-w-wonder if it's still there. No p-p-patron commissioned it, as f-f-far as I recall.'

The maestro looked into the distance and said nothing for a while. He smiled, coming back to himself. 'Yes my Pietro, I should be very interested to see that.'

Good. I knew the portrait was still there. I'd bumped into an apprentice I'd known when I was working for Sebastiano and I'd asked. I wanted Raphael to see it. Then he would realise that all he needed to do was paint his own portrait of Margarita to show the world how talented he was and put Sebastiano in his place forever.

I looked around at the near-completed frescoes on the Vatican walls. They were magnificent. Could my plan work? Of course it could. The possible stumbling block was Margarita. But she was a pawn and I convinced myself I knew how to play her.

Chapter 18

'We can go to Trastevere in the morning, maestro.'

'First thing, Pietro.'

My plan for Raphael to paint Margarita had failed once. It could not do so again. Sebastiano had painted her and made a passable attempt, but in Raphael's hands a portrait of the girl would be beauty itself. It seemed perfect – to paint the same girl, give the painting the same name. What greater slight could Raphael make to a peer who had shown his teeth, claws and second face? Sebastiano had revealed himself, again, to be the most cowardly of rivals by using cruel words behind the maestro's back. Raphael could use something far more cutting, and longer-lasting: his art.

I had gone with Raphael to look round Sebastiano's studio the day before. He'd been invited after all. An apprentice had opened the door to us. On seeing Raphael he'd reeled backwards. When he'd steadied himself he greeted my master with wholehearted admiration as well as a terror he could not conceal. He well knew his own master's hostility towards the artist standing before him.

'My m-m-m-master is not here. I'm so s-s-s-sorry Master R-R-R-R-Raphael.' The boy's stammer made me realise that mine had all but gone. I had little to fear anymore.

'Oh. How disappointing,' Raphael said. 'It would have been better if he'd been here to show us round but perhaps you can do it instead. Or indeed my apprentice, Pietro. He was an apprentice here before he came to me, you know.'

Terror now took over the poor boy completely. He shook most violently as his eyes searched for mine. They pleaded with me.

'Let me speak with him,' I said to Raphael, as I took the frightened boy to one side.

'We will not be long. You can tell Sebastiano or keep it secret; it's up to you. But he did invite Raphael here and my master has made a special trip here today.' My words weren't artful or winning but my voice was. The boy nodded as if it would be possible for us to look round. His shake died down to a tremble.

'What did you say your name was?' Raphael asked. 'I shall remember your kindness, young man.'

The boy, called Ludo, showed us round the many portraits, several of which were commissions Raphael had lost out on, along with religious panels and tables of drawings. The paint-making areas were the same as I'd remembered.

'Where are the older portraits?' I asked.

'If they've not gone to private patrons they'll be over here.' He pulled aside the large velvet curtain and we entered Sebastiano's inner sanctum. There, displayed on an easel like a shrine, was the painting we'd come here to see: *La Fornarina*. Raphael looked at it, speechless. A surprisingly playful smile tripped across his lips.

We did not stay long after that. His eyes were blind to all else. 'Thank you, Ludo,' he said. 'You can tell your master that what I have seen here today has proven to be most . . . inspirational.'

When Raphael stepped out into the street I turned to the apprentice and winked. 'Or perhaps you don't need to tell him anything at all.'

*

While I went back home Raphael decided to return to his studio. 'I've been inspired and won't be able to sleep until I put down on paper what's in my mind.' I offered to go with him but he said he liked the quiet sometimes, the girls who waited for him each day would have gone by now. I did not argue the point. I longed to spend time with him but even those who yearn need to sleep. Besides, I'd tried to keep up with Raphael several times before but I'd invariably ended up slumped on a table, softly snoring. I was no match for the master on a physical or artistic level. His stamina was not human, in the same way as his talents were divine.

When I first realised his ability to function highly on little sleep I'd told myself that that was why his work was so good – because he had twice the waking time in which to practise. I now know that such sophistry is nonsense. The truth was that he was a man of exceptional talents who pushed himself to the limits. But he was still very much a man, with a man's mortality and capacity to feel pain and to suffer when he'd not had sufficient rest. As I saw all too clearly the next day.

The following morning Raphael looked puffy-eyed and his hair, though neat, flicked out at the jawline as opposed to flicking in. I had a Madonna to work on for Sigismondo de' Conti, chamberlain to Pope Julius, and Raphael had a meeting arranged with some of the Pope's advisors to discuss a further design for the Pope's private rooms – *The Expulsion of Heliodorus from the Temple*. But before we went to the Vatican together we would go to see Margarita.

It was early, and as we walked along the cobbled streets, shops were opening, and traders pushed by with their carts and animals late for market. Apprehension vied with pride in my head. I had a plan that could work. My heart swelled to think that if it did Raphael would have me to thank.

We turned a corner and there, creaking back and forth in the fresh morning air was Francesco Luti's baker's sign.

'*Buongiorno!*' We called out as we went into the small, dark, warm shop. There was Francesco, his cheeks still flame red, his skin a little clammy, two customers waiting for bread. The minute the baker saw us he wiped his floury hands on his overalls and ignored the two people in front of us.

'Gentlemen!' he said, his eyes running over our well-tailored clothes. Raphael was dressed in a red velvet cape over a deep green velvet waistcoat, his hose dark brown. Upon his head he wore a beautiful black velvet cap with a feather in it. As for me, I was dressed in a more sombre manner, but it was fair to say that I too looked like a man of quality – a gentleman – and not a peasant or lowborn workman. Francesco hadn't recognised me yet. I stood tall, puffed my chest out and coughed. I moved forward. Arms moved to bar me, elbows stuck out.

'We was next!' one of them growled.

'Ah, watcha mouth!' Luti was as pugnacious as ever.

'What are ya gonna do if I don't?'

Francesco was about to show him when the polished metal buttons on the maestro's jacket caught his eye. He let go of his customer's rough tunic and took a deep breath.

'My shop, my rules. Get out. The pair of you! Now!'

Francesco Luti wasn't talking to us.

'Please, *Signore* Luti, do serve these men first.' A look of pleasant surprise appeared on the baker's face. So the man with the shiny buttons knew his name.

He became starry-eyed, but it changed nothing. The two men still had to go. The bakery changed into a riot of colourful language.

'STOP!' A loud shout caused everyone to freeze. Then, one by one, we turned our heads around. There, framed in the doorway, was the beautiful silhouette of a girl, daylight behind her. It was the girl we'd come to find. It was Margarita, more beautiful than ever. I looked at Raphael. I had only ever seen him look at a person the way he looked at Margarita now but once before.

And that person had been Margarita herself when he had first set eyes on her by the river. Instinct told me what I saw in his eyes was love. It ripped up my heart and left it in tatters. Jealousy coursed through my veins like poison. I wanted to turn round and leave but it was too late now.

'Please, there's no need to send these men away without serving them,' Raphael said, 'They speak the truth. They were first. We don't mind waiting, *signore*.'

Margarita stepped inside and made her way towards her father. She looked at Raphael, surprised to see him after such a long time, a hint of grudging respect in her eyes. She went from one side of the counter to the other.

'These men can wait their turn.' She shot me a look of playful defiance before attending to the true customers.

'Only comes 'ere 'cos of you,' one of them said to her.

'You only comes 'ere 'cos of the bread,' Margarita's father corrected him.

When the two men had gone Francesco went to pat his daughter on the shoulder. She shrugged him away.

'I would like your permission to paint your daughter.' Raphael said what he'd come here to say.

I expected Margarita to start protesting. She did not.

'But you must understand, my Margarita . . . she's precious to me . . . *very precious*. Dear to me . . . *very dear*.'

Raphael understood the clumsy code: it was time to untie the strings of his purse.

'Name your price, *Signore* Luti.'

Francesco reeled back under the weight of gold he envisaged as ducat signs flashed before his eyes. He looked at Margarita, at Raphael, then at me. He scrunched up his eyes as he tried to place where he'd seen me before but he couldn't place me, and all the while his face flipped between greed and guilt.

'Name your price, *Signore* Luti,' Raphael repeated. 'How much for you to allow me to paint your daughter?'

My heart was starting to beat with excitement. My plan was going to work. The baker would take the money. I'd always known that he would. And Margarita was not going to protest. This might yet prove to be the purchasing of her services I had hoped for, rather than the love match I had feared at the start of this meeting.

Margarita had changed. She was no longer the haughty young woman with a high opinion of herself. It looked like she could be bought, like a common whore. Raphael went to get some coins out of his purse.

The drumming in my chest and the fanfare of trumpets in my mind turned my body into a musical ensemble. The emotional connection I'd seen, and feared, before was being turned into something far more governable: a business transaction. Margarita would be paid for, and painted. When finished, Raphael's portrait of her would signal his supremacy over Sebastiano, and Margarita would be of no further use. A sound of victory escaped from my mouth, attracting the attention of Francesco Luti. He looked at me as if I was a puzzle he was close to solving. But not for long.

'How much?' Raphael asked.

'*How much? How much?*' Margarita's mocking repetition silenced the music within me. 'Am I to be bought like some chicken? Goat? Cow? Sheep? Loaf of bread?'

She had not changed after all.

'Now now, Margarita! Show me some respect. I would never sell you! Sell you? How can you even think of such a thing?

'Let's take no more than three ducats, shall we?' he whispered to her. 'To pay for flour . . . cover the time you're away. It's only fair.'

'I will NOT be bought. You will NOT sell me. Do you understand, Father?'

Raphael emptied a pile of coins onto the table.

'Make it five ducats and I'll escort her to the studio myself,' her father said to us.

'I won't come,' Margarita said.

'They are for you,' Raphael said to him, 'to do with as you will.

132

I came here to ask for your *permission* to paint your daughter. Nothing more. You have granted me that. I have paid you for it. If Margarita does not wish to be painted that is her choice. I will be deeply disappointed if that should be the case, but be under no illusion that this money is now yours.'

Raphael's eyes wandered towards Margarita as he spoke. She coloured ever so slightly.

She hadn't expected this show of virtue.

'If your daughter should feel disposed to model for me,' he continued to the baker, 'please know that I am to be found at my workshop most Tuesdays and Wednesdays after ten in the morning. On completion of a painting that is satisfactory to her I will pay an additional five ducats.'

''Ere, 'ave this.' Francesco thrust a bread roll into Raphael's hand. 'On the 'ouse. You too, lad. It's Pietro, innit?' I nodded. He'd finally solved the puzzle. 'Thought it was. My, you've scrubbed up well.'

'Good day, *Signore* Luti.' Raphael gave his best courtly bow. 'And my lady,' he said to Margarita. 'I hope we meet again soon.'

*

'The arrogance,' Margarita whispered, though when I looked back I saw that her eyes said something different.

I hurried after Raphael. 'Expensive bread rolls,' he said with a broad smile on his face. I looked up at the sky and swallowed for a moment, wiping away a solitary tear. 'Yes,' I said. 'Very.' I forced a smile. I did not want the person who meant more to me than anyone else in the world to see me cry.

What had I done?

Chapter 19

The *School of Athens* was the first of the frescoes at the Vatican to be finished. Most details had been painted for some time. There was only one figure still to be completed: the misanthrope Heraclitus, the Greek philosopher given to bad moods. Raphael had been struggling to decide whom to base him on. Giulio and I were about to discover that he'd found his man at last.

'I was going to keep this as a surprise, but . . .' he said, clearly buoyed by his visit to Luti's bakery the day before. '*Garzoni*, let me introduce my Heraclitus to you.' He moved aside. We looked on in amazement. Raphael had given that most bad tempered of philosophers the lined, familiar features of . . . Michelangelo.

'What if he sees it?' I said, shocked.

'What if he does?' Giulio interjected, defiant as if he had done it himself.

All the while Raphael's eyes twinkled with good-natured mischief. He'd put all problems with Michelangelo behind him. 'Now, what's next?'

There was still work to do on *The Expulsion of Heliodorus*. It lacked authentic classical details, but not for long. 'Giulio, Giovanni, gather together a group of apprentices to come and join us and learn from our glorious ancients. We have all we need in our very own city.'

Margarita did not come to the workshop. But that did nothing to dampen his mood. We'd been to her father's bakery and, most importantly, seen her. And I was the person who had brought this about, I told myself. Raphael had me to thank. Surely this would secure me a place in his affections? Desperate to please, I offered once or twice to go back to persuade her to come but he said no. 'I won't have her coerced,' he insisted. '*When* she comes it will be of her own free will.'

I did not push him on the matter.

The plans for *The Expulsion of Heliodorus* were finished and the fresco had been started. Raphael had taken his research seriously, going underground and exploring the buried treasures of ancient Rome. He had spent hours on end in cold, damp spaces, measuring, drawing, and observing the symmetry and perfection of the classical world. And Pope Julius, a keen collector of *ars anticas* himself, had, in the meantime, made Raphael responsible for the preservation of all ancient art and artefacts within the city. This was yet another feather in the maestro's cap and it suited him perfectly. He took this responsibility as seriously as he did every other role that had been placed on his shoulders and set about drawing, cataloguing and protecting as much of Ancient Rome as he could.

But every Tuesday and Wednesday after ten he would remain at the workshop. And wait. It reminded me of when Sebastiano would pace his studio, wishing for the girl to appear. Sebastiano was still buzzing around the city, sniping about my master, and Michelangelo was still helping him out so that he could steal commissions away from us. But this seemed to matter less and less. Besides, the endorsements from the Vatican meant that we were beginning to receive more work than we could physically manage. Raphael had expanded the workshop to meet the demand but even that wasn't proving to be sufficient.

Then the banker, Agostino Chigi – reputed to be the wealthiest man in Rome, and possibly the whole of Italy – dropped into the workshop. It was a Tuesday. Raphael knew Chigi socially and Chigi knew everybody else. He surrounded himself with cardinals, artists, and aristocrats. He counted Pope Julius among his closest friends and had known him when he was still Giuliano della Rovere. Chigi had amassed a fortune exploiting the alum mines at Tolfa and as a result was able to help the Holy Father out financially. He was treasurer to the Vatican, allowed to add the oak of the della Rovere family to his own coat of arms. He was a very influential man.

Chigi had just had a villa built for himself overlooking the River Tiber. A magnificent, classically proportioned affair with a garden and water features. (To say 'garden' and 'water features' without embellishment is to do both a great disservice, but, though tempted, I will not digress.) He now wanted the decorators in and had been in talks with Raphael that Tuesday morning for hours. I imagined it was going to be an ambitious project. I wondered how we were going to be able to fit it in given all the other work we had to do. It was madness to accept it.

'It has to be spectacular, classical, a paean to love!' Raphael told us when Chigi had gone. What he didn't tell us, and something that I only found out when we started work inside the villa, was that Chigi had already secured our nemesis Sebastiano to decorate another room and that the wily old fox had used this information to get an already overstretched Raphael to commit to embarking on a project so ambitious that it would push my master to his limits.

It may sound rich, me calling Chigi out on his cunning, but it's important that you know there were several key players in what happened to Raphael in the end. Not just me. Though I admit, I was not blameless.

Chigi knew Sebastiano and Raphael were rivals, even if my master did not want to be. And Chigi used that. I don't know, perhaps coming from the banking world he estimated healthy competition would improve the quality of the work, ensure it was finished. And when you see what the workshops produced you will see that it did. And so you might argue that old Chigi was right. But Raphael gave away more of himself than he could afford to give when he worked on Chigi's frescoes.

Raphael had already started to break; the signs were all there, the day the banker came in to outline his demands. When he'd left, the maestro slumped in a chair. He did not get out of it for hours. His shoulders, usually so strong and upright were rounded as if his energy was slipping away. A few of the girls who liked to hang round tried to pull him to his feet. They looked at him invitingly, swaying and smiling, seduction on their minds. He shook them off, uninterested. I shooed them away and they bustled off.

That evening, as the day was drawing to a close and the apprentices were starting to pack up, I went round and lit the lamps and candles. Against my better judgement I was making the workshop ready so that Raphael could make the most of the quiet and work a few extra hours. I looked at him, my beautiful Raphael: he was exhausted. There were dark shadows under his beautiful eyes and even in the gentle evening light his face showed signs of age. My young heart longed to take care of him.

I watched him, moved and disturbed. His will to create was so great that it was putting a strain on his body. He stretched across the table next to him and picked up a rough sketch. It was of Sebastiano's *La Fornarina* that he must have made from memory after he'd returned from Sebastiano's. He ran his finger delicately across its surface. I closed my eyes, took a deep breath, then put my arm around him. I opened my eyes again when I realised that he did not resist. 'Come, let's take you home to rest. She'll be throwing herself at you soon enough, just like all the others.'

'I think not, Pietro, because she's not like all the others. She's not like any woman that I've ever known.'

I looked down at the sketch of Sebastiano's painting. The

137

painting was nothing special. It hurt a little to think that the girl it depicted was.

'You're a good lad,' Raphael said to me, patting the arm that I'd thrown around him. 'A very good lad.'

As I escorted Raphael home, the poor man barely able to walk because he was so worn out, a girl flew towards us. It was Clarice, one of the girls who hung around the workshop. 'Allow me to join you,' she said to me with a wink as she took over, pushing me out of the way.

Chapter 20

I often wondered why Raphael still did not pursue Margarita. Perhaps because he was more accustomed to being pursued than pursuing? Perhaps because there was a core to him stronger than love? I did not understand it. Most men I knew had made fools of themselves over girls, or boys. But I suppose that was it. No one could ever have accused Raphael of being a fool when it came to affairs of the heart. Young women fluttered around him, many he spent a night or two with, but he never allowed them to distract him from the true purpose of his life – his art. Oh, many believed they had captured his heart, even women from the highest levels of society. He could have married well, very well. But a passion for his work burned deep within his soul and was the essence of the man. No woman ever came close. Until her.

I wonder now if he knew all along that she was his destiny. I think deep down I did, but at the time I pushed this thought away. I saw that he was attracted to her, but he'd been attracted to a great many other women. That's why I urged him on. And I wanted him to paint her. To do so would take the sting out of his rivals' bite. But he would not go to her. It was around this time that he started to give many of the girls who liked to hang around the studio a wide berth.

I wonder now if he was afraid to go and see her. Afraid of the strength of the feelings that were etched on his face. Afraid where those feelings might lead him. He knew, I think, that once engaged on the course of action that was love with Margarita Luti he would never be able to turn away from it. Yet I refused to see it. I braced myself, at most, for a dalliance between master and model, and willed Raphael to get on with it. Soonest started, soonest over. Margarita was a strong girl, she would cope, and if all went to plan she would be immortalised in paint.

And so why, for heaven's sake, did she not present herself at the workshop? Every morning when I came in, I told myself 'this will be the day when Margarita turns up.' And every evening when I left for home I could not believe that she had not. I knew her to be stubborn but I'd never thought of her as stupid. It surprised me greatly that she could not see his genius. This was an opportunity for a poor girl like her to have a legacy. In years, decades, even centuries to come, people would look at Raphael's painting of her and ask, 'Who is she? The woman in the painting?' And as for the present moment, did she not see Raphael's beauty? This prince among painters was a god among men.

Oh Raphael. How it troubled me to witness him suffer so. Margarita was torturing him.

I wanted her to come and put a stop to all this.

One month passed and the painting to eclipse his rival Sebastiano's still had not been painted. It had not been started. And Raphael was not himself. I wanted him back and I was getting the unsettling feeling that Margarita was responsible for his growing malaise. If only she would come he would get better. Giulio and Giovanni made wild guesses as to why the maestro seemed so flat. *He'd had too much sex. He'd not had enough. He had the French disease. His latest lover was a contortionist. He was in love with a prostitute. He was in love.* It was the last one that came closest to having the ring of truth about it.

'Shall I go and talk with her?'

It had come to the point where I no longer had to use her name.

'Let her be. It's enough that I have seen her.' The faraway look in his eyes horrified me. This was obsession. I'd heard from Giulio that the cure for obsession was possession. I had no idea if this was true as I was relatively inexperienced but Giulio assured me that the reason he went round 'possessing' as many women as he did was to keep obsession at bay. And didn't it work for him? I supposed so. If only I could drag Margarita here to the studio. A little light 'possession' – that's what would bring my master out of his lovesick state.

*

It was carnival time again in Rome, that time when the citizens of the city came out in force. Peasants flooded in through the gates and the poor lined the streets to watch the wealthy parade by in their finery and be entertained by the lavish processions.

Agostino Chigi had invited Raphael back to his elegant villa after the main parades had finished and he had insisted Raphael bring along with him assistants and apprentices to capture the opulent occasion in pictures. Some of us would be helping to decorate Chigi's home soon enough and the maestro estimated it would be good for us to enjoy the full Chigi experience all the better to understand the plans he'd drawn up for it. The villa was architecturally ambitious; the maestro's plans for the interior were more ambitious still.

'Love is the theme. Remember that when you're at the party tonight,' Raphael had told us.

Those of us who had been invited to Chigi's agreed to meet up at the studio at the start of the day. Raphael would be there too. He'd told us he wanted a little word with us about something. I was still concerned about him. Clarice had turned up and escorted him home after work once or twice recently, but more often than not he was choosing to stay late, later than ever. Clarice as a diversion was doing nothing to brighten his mood.

As I saw him standing next to a desk full of rolled-up drawings I hoped he might want to join us. 'Now go and have fun at the carnival,' I heard him say to Giulio as he handed him the drawing materials he would need when he arrived at Chigi's. There were several half-finished drawings next to the scrolls. He would be going nowhere for a while.

Many of the other apprentices turned up in fine mood, picked up their materials, then went outside to wait. When the door opened I glimpsed a small group congregating. The girls were there, done up in their fanciest clothes, Clarice among them. Their eyebrows had been plucked most artfully, their hair dressed in the same way, making them all look like members of the same family. They welcomed the exiting young men with open arms and encouraging smiles, all except Clarice who looked in at Raphael, her expectant expression slowly disappearing behind the closing door.

'Pietro!' Raphael beckoned me over. He stood up and whispered in my ear about remembering to take my drawing materials. Nothing of any great import. But I felt the admiring eyes of the waiting group upon me as if whatever it was he was saying to me was something that could be said to me alone. He gave me an affectionate pat on the back. He must have regarded me much as he would his favourite dog but at the time I felt I was his most trusted aide and confidant.

'I have a little finishing off to do and then some research.' He held his copy of Ovid up by way of explanation. 'I'll join you soon. I'll meet you at our meeting point if I don't bump into you before.'

Clarice pushed her way in and swayed over to him with purpose, her lips pouting and a confident smile on her lips. 'How much longer am I going to have to wait for you? Coming?' She got a key out and made as if to wiggle it in some invisible lock. Caught by my confused smile, she hid the key away.

Raphael, the one for whom the charade was intended, was

already buried in the pages of his book. 'Later,' he said, not looking up at her. His voice was not unkind, nor was it full of feeling. She placed her fingers lightly on his shoulder and swept them gently up his neck. He brushed them off, still not looking up. Clarice pulled back a little, gave a nervous giggle as if not sure how to proceed.

'Yes, later,' she said with a languorous drawl, as she bobbed her head side to side for her audience: me and several other apprentices. 'You heard the man promise, didn't you, everyone? Later!' She'd decided to withdraw with dignity, seeing victory in her defeat.

Clarice was a popular girl. She numbered many cardinals on her list of admirers and she was generous to them for the favours they showered upon her. She'd thought herself popular with Raphael. Was her popularity waning? How could he be impervious to her charms, offered up to the artist freely but which many great men were willing to pay a pretty sum for?

Clarice modelled herself on the renowned beauty Simonetta Vespucci, much painted by the Florentine artist Sandro Botticelli, and it was said that she kept miniature copies of some of the artist's finest portraits of the model on her dressing table. Clarice was captivating with her honey-coloured ropes of hair and her milky complexion. She looked good enough to eat and that was all part of the plan. Yet Raphael had lost his appetite and she didn't like it, especially after she'd spent hours applying ash and lemon juice to maintain her golden hair and more ducats than she cared to admit on attar, specially imported, for her skin. It must have hurt her but she was adept at showing that there was plenty of her to go round.

I was the last person she'd seen Raphael talking to and the first person she chose to link up with when she left the studio. 'Take me to the carnival, young man!' she said.

Carnival in Rome was a spectacular affair. There were races, feasts, plays, and the streets teemed with people. Vendors sold tasty treats while pedlars entertained crowds with quicksilver, a stick, and a slate, breaking up the strange substance into tiny, shiny balls, then watching as each one returned to its natural state. The scent of cherry laurels filled the air. The sky made every Roman think of the sea not so very far away. 'I say let's go over to the Circus Agonalis first,' Clarice said with a toss of her head, her eyes glinting.

The Circus Agonalis was where the Pope held races inspired by those held in Ancient Rome. It was also one of the busiest places to be, as well as the rowdiest.

'Let's put a bet on! I want to put a bet on!'

'Let's have a drink! I want to have a drink!'

People pushed and jostled for space while street vendors made the most of the crowds to sell their wares. After her first drink and the realisation that even if I was the betting sort I did not have the money to prove it, Clarice abandoned me for another. Nobody knew who he was but he had a certain gravitas about him, especially in the purse area, which was looking decidedly heavy. Particularly foolish, I thought, in such busy crowds. Yet Clarice knew gravitas when she saw it and the pair disappeared soon after, presumably for her to lighten his load.

I was giddy with the sights, sounds, and smells. The sun shone in the blue sky above and only the occasional push perturbed me. People made way like the Red Sea for the competitors to pass and where they did not soldiers ran up to encourage them.

My eyes followed the parading men, their limbs bare in the warm Roman air ready to run, jump and throw themselves into the games. My heart beat a little faster at the sight of one or two of them.

It must have been two hours after I'd left the studio when a hand patted me on the back. I started as if caught *in flagrante delicto*. 'Isn't this glorious?' My heart beat faster still. It was Raphael. I looked at him. He had on a doublet of black velvet, underneath which he wore a brilliant white shirt. I loved white on him. It made his skin luminous and accentuated the brown of his eyes. He was the happiest I'd seen him in a long while. His beauty dazzled me. I couldn't bear it. I averted my adoring gaze for fear of giving myself away. As I did so I recognised Margarita in the distance. She was dressed nicely, as far as I could tell, and, from the shoulders up, she looked as regal as any lady.

After such a long time and all the hoping she would turn up in the studio you might find it strange but I was willing her away. I was praying she hadn't seen me. I tried to lose my gaze in the crowd. But once seen I couldn't stop my eyes from wandering towards her. They followed her as she pushed through the crowd to get a better view and all the while I felt myself swept in her direction by the waves of people now pushed back by soldiers to make way for the riders on horseback who were trotting past.

I lost my footing for a moment and I spluttered as if swimming against the current of a wild and fast-flowing river. When I bobbed up for air I found myself two people away from Sebastiano Luciani. Everybody was out today it seemed. Fortunately, he had his back to me. He could not know I was there. I tried to pull away and reach solid ground but the island that was Raphael had all but disappeared. Even the feather on the top of his hat was lost to me. I searched for it like a palm tree on a mound of sand only to discover there were lots of them. A feather on a hat was not as distinctive as I'd thought on carnival day. It seemed, annoyingly, that many Romans had decided the event worthy of their finest clothes and accessories. Where were the police when you needed them to confiscate a few hundred feathers? So much for Sumptuary Laws.

All of a sudden, another wave of people pushed into the side of me. It had also pushed Margarita into the path of Sebastiano. 'It's you!' he said.

I was now so close that my breath touched him. My body froze to be so near. I was witness to his disagreement with Margarita without wishing to be.

'You will come back to me, girl.' He grabbed her arm in the confined space.

'Let go of me.' Margarita reared back like a feisty mare, nostrils flaring, eyes searching either side for a good citizen to come to her aid. People tutted and cursed, more concerned that their enjoyment of the entertainments was being disturbed than caring that an older man was tugging at a young girl's arm. I shrank back into the crowd. I had no wish to save her, no wish to be seen. And the crowd, after the tuts and curses had run their course, settled down to watch the to-do between man and girl, which was escalating fast and turning into an entertainment in itself.

'I paid your father good money and I haven't finished with you yet.'

She laughed. 'It's been years!'

'They say he's paid for you too.'

So that was it.

She looked at him, an expression of understanding on her face, the same look she'd had when she skipped out of his studio all those years ago. 'Think what you will.'

'He can't have you.'

'That's up to me,' she said, turning her back on him.

I was starting to enjoy the spat between them myself. My heart raced when he grabbed her by the arm. Cackles and quips swept through the audience. '*She likes it quick,*' '*Can earn more that way,*' '*I can't abide a greedy whore.*' Sebastiano's attack had been mistaken for an altercation between a woman of easy virtue and a dissatisfied client. I cackled myself at this gross misjudgement and now, swept to the side and at a safer distance away, I observed the pair in order to fathom it. Sebastiano's clothes were better cut than hers, the cloth expensive; that much was obvious. He was rich. She was poor. He had to be in the right. Clothes made the man, and the people that Margarita thought so highly of were no better than followers, blinded by the sight of gold thread and a velvet purse. The people. Her people. Fawning and crude. They

146

were at the bottom of society where they deserved to be for their stupidity. Perhaps she would see it now.

I took one last look at her. She did not look or act like a prostitute. She stood there, a proud vision of innocence ensnared. She cast her haughty eyes round accusingly. Too late, I thought, my eyes slits of pity-coated ridicule.

I turned and tried to move away. I listened to a wild cacophony of fanfares and bands heralding the starts and endings of races, parades and mock battles. I had lost Raphael entirely and I was beginning to feel a little giddy with all the activity. My mind fixed on the celebrations at the Chigi villa. I would escape this mad crowd and head to our meeting point. I felt an elbow in my back as someone shoved me aside to get past. I staggered. A rough-looking old man caught my arm and saved me from falling. And then I heard them. Mumblings. Weak at first but growing ever stronger. I'd been swept back towards Margarita and Sebastiano and their quarrel was now drawing in an even bigger audience than before.

'Leave the girl alone,' 'It ain't right, you a grown man and all.' I heard the unfamiliar sound of a conscience sweeping through the crowd behind me like flames through a wheat field. I turned to see Margarita's eyes. They were fanning the fire, urging it on. And then they fell on me.

I thanked the old man who'd broken my fall and stepped forward to help her out. As if I had planned to do so all along.

Chapter 21

'S-S-S-Sebastiano. Maestro. Please,' I began. Encouraging coughs and mutterings of *'Yes,' 'That's right,'* as well as a *'What a fine lad. And him with a stammer too,'* bolstered me up, urged me on.

'M-m-maestro, look around.' I led his eyes around the disapproving glances with a sweep of my hand. 'Think of your good reputation.' The heads of the people shot from me to him, now wondering who he was and what this good reputation was for.

'Your behaviour is unbecoming, sir.'

By now the people all around us had formed a circle, preferring to view an entertainment close up than through a sea of feathered high hats on heads. A few fingers reached out to prod him, and feet twitched ready to give him a kick. Excitement was escalating.

'Let go of the girl,' I said, now warming to my theme, all traces of a stammer gone. 'She is unexceptional and not worthy of your talent.' Offence crept across Margarita's face, quickly replaced by gratitude the moment Sebastiano let go of her arm.

'Talent will out,' he said as he moved away from eager fingers and feet. 'Let him paint you,' he called back to her when a safe distance away. 'See if I care.'

Margarita was inspecting the sleeve of her dress. Sebastiano must have caught a loose stitch when he released her arm. The material was now torn.

A fanfare of trumpets sounded as another procession marched by as if heralding the end of our small diversion. There was movement at last as people pushed and shoved their way on to the next entertainment. Sebastiano disappeared, consumed by the crowd to his left, while I now found myself propelled very near to the front of the throng with Margarita. There was now enough space for me to thread my body through the very definite gaps that had temporarily opened up between people. But not for long. The drums approached and revellers more determined than myself squeezed themselves into every gap and space between me at the front and the buildings at the back. I would very soon be trapped again.

And this time I would be trapped with Margarita. She said little to me, playing with the rip in her sleeve, and soon she couldn't say a word. The next entertainment had arrived, a thundering tumult of horses' hooves and screeching trumpets.

All eyes looked ahead at the parade. Huge black stallions trotted by. This procession was on its way, we all knew, to stage a celebration of our city's great victory over Venice. My eye was caught by a finely dressed lady, riding in the middle. Her family must have fought for us.

'She's a Gonzaga,' Margarita managed to shout over the din, sensing my interest. 'And the gold you see on her dress is nine hundred ducats melted down, and beaten by a goldsmith into thin bands and crimped foils.' I looked at her, this unexpected mine of information. 'I know because I have a friend who helped appliqué it onto the black velvet.'

'She looks beautiful,' I said, amazed.

'She looks hot,' Margarita corrected me with a tut of disapproval. I wondered where Sebastiano was and I concentrated on the procession once more. The crowd roared. People jostled. We fell forward. Soldiers came along and pushed us back. The animals towered above me as they passed. The heady smell as they marched over the cobblestones, their shoes occasionally sliding, filled my nostrils while the shine of their large, muscular haunches bewitched my eye to such an extent that I lost myself in it. My senses were at once heightened, every fibre of my body pulled tight and vibrating to every glorious sight and sound.

The horses passed. A brief interlude followed.

I exhaled deeply. I remembered Margarita next to me. I had returned to the real world.

A hand tapped me on the shoulder. I turned around. It was Giulio.

'It's time.' He pointed his head in the direction of our meeting point with Raphael.

The crowd, no longer one impenetrable mass, had broken up into distinct islands of people of differing sizes that I could now sail around safely. Besides, I had Giulio to follow. He navigated his way to an empty alleyway to take stock. I kept close to him. Margarita kept close to me. I did not have the heart, or the strength, to shake her off.

We stood in the shade, not moving for a while, grateful to be out of the full sun. It was Margarita who broke the silence first. She nodded her head back in the direction we'd come from. 'Sebastiano,' she said to explain why she'd followed us. 'I will go home now.'

I have no idea what Giulio was thinking but out of nowhere he offered to escort her back. She refused. I felt safe to follow his gallant lead. She accepted. Giulio gave a you-win-some-you-lose-some shrug. A young girl walked by with an older man. Giulio looked them both up and down with interest.

'We'll have to walk over towards the Via della Lungara first,' I said to Margarita, 'to explain to the others that I'm walking you back. Then we can turn around and come back over this way.'

I'd hoped that by telling her that we would have to walk in the opposite direction to where she lived that this might make her reconsider my offer.

'Thank you.'

It did not.

'My protector,' she said as she put her arm through mine. I smiled graciously.

'I really must paint that face of yours,' Giulio said with an appreciative nod. I wanted to tell him to be quiet.

We picked our way to the agreed meeting place as best we could. We kept to the roads away from the main squares. Though they were quieter we were still harassed by street sellers trying to get us to buy relics and indulgences, and prostitutes hoping to lure either Giulio or myself down an even quieter alley; then there were the men who'd had too much wine and sun and were looking for a fight before they slumped down to sleep in the shadows for a few hours. The walk would have taken ten minutes on a normal day. But normal day this was not.

We were on the Via della Lungara within the hour.

Stepping out onto the street was like stepping into another world and instantly I loved it.

Elegant ladies went round in groups dressed in colourful clothes; fine gentlemen paraded like peacocks; guards patrolled to protect them. There were no sumptuary police out today and the jewels were on display as never before. We were getting closer to Agostino Chigi's villa.

The meeting place was next to a statue of Jupiter, not far from our final destination.

'You're late.' Giovanni, known for his punctuality was there, waiting. That getting to the statue would take longer than usual was a calculation that Giovanni had factored in.

The four of us, Giovanni, Giulio, Margarita and myself, too hot to force a conversation, watched as a steady flow of important-looking individuals went through the gates of the impressive villa. Some in carriages, a few on horseback, most on foot.

'It looks dreadful,' Margarita said. The rest of us said nothing.

Tired of waiting for the others to turn up, Giulio cracked.

'I'm going in.'

'But what if Ra—?' I started to say.

'I need to draw,' he answered. 'Who knows what sights we've omitted to record already?' He turned to Margarita and gave her his most courtly bow. 'Good day, *Signorina* Luti. I trust our good Pietro will get you home safely.' She humphed with a smile. She knew sarcasm when she saw it.

We accompanied Giulio to the gates to wave him off.

'Stop.' It was a gruff guard and he was addressing Margarita.

He assessed her. His eyes stared into her face before roving over her attire.

The guard's lips curled as he looked at the tear in her sleeve caused by the altercation she'd had with Sebastiano. He held his palm up, a sign for us to stay where we were, while he turned to open the gate to a group of women dripping with pearls and decked with ribbons. One of them was Clarice. She giggled and bowed her head to me as she passed. She had no intention of waiting for Raphael either.

'We've been invited by Imperia,' she told the guard. Giulio moved over to join her, giving a sly grin to us as he did so. The guard did not seem to mind, bowing as he closed the gate after them. Clarice gave me a wave with her handkerchief from the other side.

I grant you we must have looked out of place. I was still quite young and had no gravitas, and though I modelled myself on my master very few people would have thought it to look at me. As for Margarita, and she was the real problem for the guard, she looked like the pretty baker's daughter that she was.

'You are no lady.'

Neither was Clarice but the guard didn't say that to her.

I looked at Margarita in her clothes that made her look like a dull brown-breasted songbird about to be pecked to death in this aviary of brightly feathered creatures. She turned to me and with a sigh said, 'Not again. This is too much.' With a shake of her hair and a loosening of her shoulders she went up to the guard. If she was afraid she did not show it.

'Aye, I grant you that, I am not like the ladies I've seen you allow in just now.' When she'd said her piece she stepped back. The guard looked her up and down with an appraising eye. He liked her feistiness. He leant over to whisper something in her ear. By the time I saw his face again it had upon it a lascivious smirk that went from ear to ear. Margarita's hand was raised ready to remove it. I stopped her. But the guard, now angered by her spirited rejection of his proposition, felt the shame of it.

'The likes of you have no right to enter. You shouldn't even be here. Move along. Go back to your own part of the city,' he snarled at her.

'I am a free citizen of Rome, honest and hardworking, and I'm going nowhere. I have every right to be here.'

The few people who had been watching started to laugh. More people came over to watch.

For a second I thought the guard was about to raise his hand back to her.

'There you are!' a familiar voice called over. I looked round to see Raphael making his way towards us. He pushed his way through the small group of people and shooed them away. 'There's nothing to see here. Thank you. Now go back into the city and enjoy the carnival.'

'Raphael!' 'Was that Raphael?' 'I think that was that artist fellow.' The whispers rippled throughout the disbanded throng.

He turned to the guard. 'I'll be sure to inform *Signore* Chigi you've refused entry to one of his guests. Now open the gate.' Raphael put his arm through Margarita's and led her inside. She let him. She glowered at the guard. I followed, along with Giovanni, stunned, behind.

153

Chapter 22

'I won't stay long,' she said to him, clipped. She looked at me for support even though it was Raphael's arm that was holding her up. 'But thank you all the same.' She forced herself to be polite and made a great show of not looking the maestro in the eye.

But as the heavy villa doors were pulled back by liveried servants her eyes struggled to take in the vision before her. She fell silent as if contemplating a hallowed space. I too was lost for words. If outside was another world, inside was heaven. The vision took my breath away. The rooms though largely unadorned at this stage were grand, self-confident spaces on a scale to equal the Vatican. All were completed I saw according to the classical rules of architecture, and the result was sheer perfection. All symmetry and order. A *palazzo all'antica* where even the columns were proud of themselves, in a self-satisfied sort of way. I'd seen several palazzos going up around the city but this was the first one I'd set foot in. I caught Margarita's open mouth from the corner of my eye.

Then she saw the people, standing round together in cliques, each one as tightly closed as the next. She pulled back as if to run away. At that moment I wanted to run away too. Before us there were wall after wall of satin-, brocade-, and velvet-covered backs with no way of breaching them. Giovanni pulled me to one side. I have no recollection what he said as at the same time Raphael started a conversation up with Margarita. I strained to hear it, catching it only in patches.

'Not a chance,' she was saying in that colourful way she had. 'I'd rather work in a bakery any time. It's honest work and I'm not ashamed of that.'

'Please, I would never deride the virtues inherent in good, honest labour but to work at the Vatican is, for me, a privilege.'

Margarita did not accord him the same respect. A snort of derision escaped from her nose.

As the hirsute Giovanni mumbled on to me, I saw from the corner of my eye that Raphael had a beautiful half-smile on his lips. He was used to people agreeing with him, listening as everyone praised everything he said and did. And now here he was, face to face with this baker's daughter and having to put up with her plebeian views. He seemed to like it.

Her voice grew louder and more confident. Raphael's grew increasingly amused. I wanted to stretch her vocal cords until they snapped. Instead they played on in the same tune.

'I've heard that to work in the Vatican you've got to like having a bottle up your arse and a cock in your mouth.'

'I think the verse you're quoting has it the other way round.' Raphael laughed, remembering the songs he'd heard in the taverns around the city where the bottle and cock had different points of entry. 'And you can believe what you like,' he added, good-naturedly.

'I will,' she said, pulling a face. She did not like being corrected – that I knew.

No one spoke to Raphael like this. Certainly not a girl. And certainly not a girl as lowborn as Margarita. Could he really have enjoyed listening to her crudely expressed candour?

Giovanni eventually stopped talking to me and walked away. I hoped he'd not told me anything I needed to remember.

'Over here! Raphael, I've got something to show you!' The backs turned, flinging out arms like open doors that led in to the closed clique. They appeared as if by magic to welcome my master in. 'Come! Quick Raphael!' He resisted the call. He looked at Margarita hoping for a reason to stay. She pursed her lips and made some pretence of studying the marble floor. Before we knew what had happened Clarice and another girl had come over to drag the maestro off into their little group. He smiled back at Margarita as he allowed himself to be taken away. But she didn't notice.

'Don't go without letting me know,' he called back to her, forcing her to look up from the floor. 'Remember what I said. I'll pay.'

'Remember what I said. I am not the sort of woman that can be bought.' And I'm sure I saw her glower at Clarice as she said so.

I was now alone with Margarita. We stood in silence for some time watching the celebrations happen all around us. It was as if we were invisible.

'I think I'll be going now,' she said.

I looked around the room and felt afraid. She couldn't leave me here. Not now.

'But the guard will be outside,' I said, trying to put her off.

'I thought you'd be coming with me,' she answered.

'Oh,' I said.

From the look on her face I could tell that I was not her protector anymore. Her eyes searched round the room for the man who was, Raphael, and together we watched him.

He was still with Clarice, and though she was laughing and stroking him for everyone to notice, he didn't seem to be responding. Not that it mattered: she was writhing enough for two. I was used to seeing women act like this around Raphael. Margarita was not. Try as she might to keep her face from falling, the frowns fought to trace lines across her forehead, and her lips wavered with disappointment. Then another girl beckoned the maestro to her. He unwound Clarice's arm from around his neck eager to accept the lifeline offered to him.

We watched as he walked up to a fresh, plump girl, dressed in the most exquisite gown. Strangely, it did not sit well on her. I don't know if it was the way she was holding herself or whether the velvet was too harsh against her delicate, soft skin but there was something decidedly ill-fitting about her attire, and, dare I say it, out of place about her. Clarice went to pursue her prey but there must have been something about the girl that prevented her. This too was strange – little got in Clarice's way.

I studied the girl again. Was she interested in Raphael? Her body language, despite the fact that she was whispering in his ear, made me think not. Though her head was close, her body was a respectful distance away. She stretched over her full skirt in an attempt to be heard. It was not a beautiful pose she was making. And she did not seem to care. Raphael glanced over in our direction. So did she. Something gave me the uneasy feeling that they were talking about us. I turned away not wanting to be caught. Margarita shot me a complicitous glance as she did the same.

'Pietro! Margarita!' We jumped. Raphael rushed over to us. 'I would like you to meet someone.'

'I am Francesca. Francesca Ordeaschi. Delighted that you could come.'

Her accent was Northern. Possibly from Venice. I'd heard traders from that city speak in the same way. And I'd heard that name before. But where? I racked my brains. And what she said. It was as if this was her party. The dying rays of the setting sun blinded me for a second. And then I realised. Francesca Ordeaschi – Agostino Chigi's beloved. I looked at her again. She had an earthy freshness about her as if she'd come in from the fields or from milking the cows.

Chigi swept past her, his hand brushing hers ever so fleetingly as he made his way over to the far side of the room. To blink would have been to miss it, yet to see would be to feel the intimacy between them. My eyes followed the banker. Cardinal da Bibbiena was the person he was rushing to greet.

Francesca Ordeaschi. I'd heard her name do the rounds in the taverns when I'd gone there with the older apprentices. The story went that Chigi had picked up the girl in Venice when on banking business and that he was so taken with her that he'd moved her to Rome. She was lowborn, common, and gossip about her overflowed. The rumours had it that she was currently living in a convent where the nuns were paid generously to accommodate the girl and prepare her for her entry into civilised Roman society. The nuns – in the main noblewomen whose families had either failed to find suitable husbands for them, or, when they had, could not afford the dowry to go with them – enjoyed the exotic fruits and fine meats Chigi sent round for them and endeavoured to equip his young love with basic table manners while introducing her to the finer things in life. But it was said that she had peasant tastes, liking farro soup more than any delicacy Chigi had yet sent round for her to try. Still, the nuns were appreciative, so much so that their doors were always open to their generous banker benefactor. At any time of the day, or night.

Yet she was here now. Out in public. My eyes searched for Imperia. I knew she was here too. I wondered how the presence of a rival was going down with her.

The girl I now knew to be Francesca, took Margarita off. They looked right together, despite the luxurious gown of the one and the sack-like vestments of the other. Same age, same natural features, same backgrounds. Margarita seemed to have forgotten her wish to leave for the moment.

Raphael led me towards Giulio and Giovanni. I flew after him, buzzing like a bumblebee after an orchid. 'There's a little artists' table set up for you all,' he told me, 'with paper and drawing materials for sketching. Record the event. I have given Giovanni

the precise instructions. I look forward to seeing what you do.'
We exchanged meaningful glances – that they meant different
things I did not see at the time.

*

To draw is to observe, to pick up details no one else sees but are
always there, to capture truths that most people don't usually have
the time to notice. And that evening I understood that by studying
the present I could see into the future. And it frightened me.

Let me explain. To start with, my eyes got drawn with Giulio's
to where Imperia was. His fascination with her rendered him silent,
made his focus intense. Laughter crashed around her like roaring
waves breaking on the beach. She'd been Chigi's courtesan of choice
for many years. It was said they had a strong bond and her presence here tonight was testament to that. She had a new love too.
But there was something excessive in her behaviour that made me
think she still had feelings for her old paramour. She'd had too much
wine to drink tonight, even before the dinner. As Chigi had walked
past her, she'd grabbed him, a breast showing out of the toga she'd
chosen to wear. Hoots of bawdy guffaws joined embarrassed giggles.

Chigi was cock in his own lavish hen house this evening, and
Imperia intended to have him. She'd had him before.

Imperia was a courtesan of the highest quality. She was physically attractive and expensive in a Rome where prostitutes were
often ten a ducat. Roman prostitutes were plentiful and reputed
to be the best in the world. They paid their taxes in this city and
Imperia paid more than most. The woman was truly exceptional.
Or so I'd heard. And she'd pleased Agostino on many occasions
in the past. She was skilled in the art of lovemaking (Giulio made
sure he told me all about that as we observed her). She played the
lute exquisitely and had the voice of an angel. She had even been
trained to talk about art and philosophy in order to increase her
worth and appeal to the cream of Roman male society.

But it was her physical attractions that went before all else. She was a feast for all the senses. The way she moved was seductive; I saw that even though she'd had too much wine. Even when she staggered she managed to add an alluring curve to her figure. The men still laughed at her but inside you could see them all sighing. How each one of them would like to sit at her table tonight and empty their bursting purses before her feet. As I observed her, bedecked in jewels, she looked like a queen. But Chigi took no heed of her now.

As servants filed past I saw that it was nearly time for us all to sit down for the dinner. One or two were young men, in livery, and they looked at me in such a way as to make me look away, their meaning going far in excess of the hesitant glance I'd given to the maestro not long before. That, I liked to think, was shrouded in virtue, but the ones aimed at me by the young men in uniform were all vice. My heart raced uneasily. I looked for Margarita. I expected she would be going soon – that's if she hadn't gone already.

'Where are we to sit?' I asked Giulio.

'Follow me,' he said.

My father would be proud of me now, I said to myself as I went to my seat. The surroundings were lavish and the table looked like nothing I'd seen before.

We were at the far end of the room, not that far away from Clarice and her friends. She looked over at Raphael, seated at the top, near Chigi and the Cardinal. Imperia was there too as was Francesca Ordeaschi. And just behind her I was shocked to see Margarita. Still here. She was gesturing *no*, crossing her down-turned hands one over the other, back and forth. If she thought I was going to escort her back to Trastevere now she was mad. But then Chigi's sweet young thing grabbed one of Margarita's protesting hands and pulled her forwards to take the place that was being swiftly set up next to her.

Servants rushed back and forth, serving wine, bringing food.

I studied the movements of those who'd made my heart race and wondered if they felt what I did when I saw Francesca and Margarita sitting at the table of one of the wealthiest men in the whole of Italy. To have to treat common girls as ladies must stick in the throat.

But the food was being brought out and set on tables with gold and silver plates. I marvelled at the splendour and wondered how Margarita was getting on with it. She wouldn't have seen anything like it before.

I unfolded my white linen napkin and a songbird flew out of it. I saw three, eight, twenty, no . . . so many songbirds flying around the room and filling the space with birdsong.

I had never witnessed such a spectacle in my life.

Next came the food: animals dressed in their own skins were brought out, as were birds, this time cooked, decorated with ornate feathers. Margarita looked over at me through all the activity with fellow feeling. I smiled back at her with insincerity. I watched as she looked either side to see the best way to eat it, I recognised the action; it was what I was doing myself, though I had Giulio and Giovanni to learn from, not Raphael, and I could see now as meat juices trickled down their chins that they were not the best of teachers.

When the venison in vinegar and cinnamon arrived I'd given up trying to eat with decorum. Conversation ricocheted around the room while servants mixed me strong wine. Loud talk about art, philosophy, and quiet, persistent gossip about Francesca Ordeaschi. *She'll be on the streets by the end of the year. He's got his next woman lined up. I've heard he wants to marry her.* This last juicy morsel made me laugh the most. Marry her? I'd never heard anything so ludicrous. Why would a man as wealthy as Chigi do something so unnecessary as to marry a girl he'd found on the streets? *They say he loves her.* So? Marry her? I drank some more strong wine. That would never happen. I chortled to myself, amused at the foolish absurdity of such a thought.

My head swam in the warm air as the candles grew brighter and night-time fell. I searched the room for my men with vice in their eyes. They were gone. I drank some more wine. I thought of Raphael and was soon lost in a satisfied stupor as my eyes danced with intoxicated pleasure at the thought of him. They came to a standstill when they alighted upon Clarice. She too was lost, she was silent and deep in thought, but I could see that she'd found neither satisfaction nor pleasure in the state. Her eyes were fixed on Margarita. The candlelight flickered and it seemed to me as if the flames of hellfire were raging across Clarice's face.

I blinked and joined her in her contemplation. And so too my own heart hardened as there on the far side of the room I saw Raphael pick up a rare fruit, so rare I did not know its name. He offered it to Margarita. There was a tenderness to the gesture. To watch the pair together was agony for Clarice. I saw her fingers curl on the table. It was agony for me. There was something rapturous in the way he was with Margarita and she with him. A servant came by to top up my goblet. 'Yes, more, thank you.' I told myself it was nothing. Probably the wine.

'The bitch is so plain. Drab in every way. Someone needs to drag her back to her kennel where she belongs.' Clarice leant over to me and drew me into her confidence, unable to keep her malicious thoughts to herself any longer. A tingle of pleasure ran through me at the sound of them. 'Although her hair is quite good,' she added. Yes, Margarita's hair was quite good, I thought, as it shone like waves of rich gold in the flickering torchlight.

But that was all there was.

I felt the wine trickling down my chin, following the well-worn trajectory of the meat juices from earlier. And its effects were beginning to tell on me. Richer, less watered down than what I was accustomed to. I stood up. One foot strayed off in one direction, the other veered back in the other. I told myself to walk in a straight line and made my way, convinced that's what I was doing, to the bathroom. The walls of the room kept shifting. People's faces appeared grotesque, while their bodies seemed to be lurching in my way. I slumped down in a pool of piss. I'd made it to my destination. 'Steady there.' I felt Giulio's arm pull me to standing.

'Raphael,' he said as I felt the wine making its way back up my throat. 'He's not himself tonight.'

I retched. The wine burned my throat. It didn't taste as sweet as it had done when I'd drunk it.

'Clarice would have gobbled up his tongue by now,' Giulio continued while relieving himself. I retched again. Wine-dyed vomit gushed from me like a fountain. It coated my teeth and my tongue. I spat it away and although I couldn't get rid of the taste I felt much better. I wiped my mouth with the back of my hand and noticed the walls for the first time. They were now still. And they were studded with gems. I looked at Giulio. The torchlight caught his jewel-like eyes, making them sparkle. I was surrounded by beauty and I was glad to be alive. I'd never thought of Giulio as beautiful before. I lunged at him and put a hand around his neck. I felt the thickness of his neck, the breadth of his manly shoulders.

'You're drunk,' he said, as he pulled away. 'Let's get back in.'

I walked back, again in as straight a line as I could muster, but I must have veered off to the side as I ended up along a corridor that led off from the dining hall. Giulio was no longer with me. The wine had not given him crab legs that insisted on stepping to the side. He was no doubt back in the dining hall by now. I adjusted my eyes. Definitely no Giulio. Instead, there in front of me I recognised the back of Cardinal da Bibbiena. He was pushing someone into a room. The Cardinal. Why did the sight of him ring a bell? Giovanni had asked me something about him earlier on but my thoughts sloshed around in my wine-filled brain with too much vigour for me to get a hold on it. I would follow him. Perhaps the Cardinal himself would know.

I crab-walked my way to find him, taking three steps to the

right, then three to the left, moving ever so slightly forward each time. I toppled through the now closed door and staggered to the far side of the room. When I looked up I saw the Cardinal, his face as red as his robes, standing close, too close, to Margarita. The sight had a sobering effect on my brain but not my tongue.

'Cardinal? Cardinal? I think I must do something to you.'

He looked at me, more annoyed than ashamed that I'd walked in on him (but that was the way with the men who ruled the city). He had no idea what I was talking about. Neither did I.

Margarita seized her chance. She came towards me, took me by the arm and led me out. She cast a look of triumph Bibbiena's way. He shrugged it off with a mocking smile that said girls like her could never win.

I still could not remember what it was I had to do regarding the Cardinal but that didn't seem to matter as Margarita escorted me back into the dining hall and to my seat. I supposed that she had returned to hers. I had no idea where the Cardinal went.

I wasn't the only one who was intoxicated. And Clarice wasn't the only one driven wild by jealousy this evening. Imperia, who'd been well on her way before the feast had started, was now laughing and gesticulating like never before. She was also on her feet, a precarious place for any over-imbiber to be, and was placing them as seductively as she could one in front (well nearly) of the other. Still, as I said before, if anyone could stagger seductively Imperia could. Her mother had trained her well; walking like a crab became her.

She sat on Chigi's lap. He brushed her off. She leant over and nibbled his ear. He nudged her away. She stroked his neck. He laughed and gave in. Body memory, hard to deny it, easy to bring it back to life.

I sat down myself, remembering to refuse all offers of wine, no matter how appealing the servants were. I looked at the water in front of me. I had a vague recollection that Margarita had ordered me to drink it. I glugged it back. My eyes looked for her. They found Francesca. Full mastery over my bodily senses was still far from returning. The girl now looked like a child, and unsophisticated compared to the glorious Imperia. She sat in silence, demure and hurt. Like a spurned kitten, her pink snub nose glistened as she sniffed back the tears that threatened to pour out of every orifice.

Chigi noticed. He called a man over who I'd not been aware of before but who must have been waiting for just this occasion as he rushed to help Imperia away. Then, with a look here and a word there Chigi gathered Francesca up and cupped her heart shaped face tenderly in his hands. He kissed her on her lids, on her forehead, on the top of her head. He flicked his wrist and clicked his fingers. Within seconds a servant had appeared with a cape for her.

'Pietro.' Margarita was behind me. 'I'm going now,' she said, looking revoltingly pleased with herself. 'I'm going home in a carriage with Francesca.' She stopped suddenly. 'Who is the woman talking to Raphael?' she asked.

I swayed and struggled to get the figure into focus. 'The one with the sloping forehead, and sharp nose and chin?' I asked. Margarita's eyes narrowed. Even though I felt like an overfull barrel of wine I could smell the jealousy on her. But then a cold blast of good sense came and blew it away.

'It doesn't matter,' she said, pulling herself back to why she'd come over to me in the first place. 'I wanted to thank you before I left. For helping me earlier.'

'I-I-I-I was looking to see if you needed me to escort you home,' I lied. I swayed some more and looked back at Raphael. The woman with him was the Pope's daughter and I wondered why she was still bending his ear. I felt a tap on the shoulder.

I turned to see what Margarita wanted now. She was gone. Replaced by Giovanni. 'I can get back on my own. Thoughtful of you to ask,' he said with uncharacteristic good humour. 'However, that's not what I came over for. Bibbiena? Cardinal Bibbiena? Did you do it? Did you sketch him?'

So that was what he'd asked me to do at the start of the evening.

Chapter 23

The morning after carnival and the feast at Chigi's villa we'd been given permission to turn up late. I'd assumed that was because Raphael anticipated a bad head. I'd given little thought to the possibility that I might have one myself.

I woke up to a sun that stung my eyes and birdsong that wrapped itself around my head and pulled tight. I was already up later than usual. I had to get to work. I dragged myself through empty, dirty streets, too in pain to care about the rats having a feast of their own in the cool of the morning shadows. The city had still to come to life.

By the time I made it to the workshop somebody else was already there as some materials had been moved and others taken. I was too fragile to seek whoever it was out and instead I found a seat. I felt a hundred years old. I thought about what I needed to do, remembered that Giovanni hadn't been best pleased with me about something last night, and little by little my mind started to work, albeit very, very slowly. My body was even slower, crying out when I made anything other than the most deliberate and careful of movements.

Boom! The front door opened as if thrust off its hinges by cannon fire. It closed with equally bombastic aplomb.

'You had a good night,' a leering Giulio called out to me. I tensed up at the sight of him; the events of the night before were slowly coming back. But it was clearly business as usual in Giulio's mind as he made a beeline for me, his excited hand outstretched, ready to ruffle my hair. I tensed up some more to withstand the assault.

When I'd discovered I'd survived, I looked up at him and noticed something not quite right about his left eye. 'Where's Raphael?' he asked as he turned his back on me and put his left hand through his hair so that I couldn't see that side of his face anymore.

'He's not here,' I said.

'Then why's his cap here? And who else would have got in before anyone else? He told everyone not to rush up.' He tutted as if he thought I was an unobservant imbecile.

Then, from an anteroom we both made out two voices. One belonged to Raphael and the other I recognised as Margarita's. Alarm and Surprise jumped up and down in my head like demonic twins but I was still feeling fragile. I had to stop them. I found a seat. Told myself: *Why shouldn't she be here? It's about time.*

'Well, well, well! The cheeky devil. Must have come back here with her, late, and spent the night together. What I would have given to be a fly on the wall. What's this?' he asked, distracted for a moment by a sketch the maestro had left hanging around of *The Mass of Bolsena*. *The Mass of Bolsena* was yet another part of the fresco cycle to decorate the Pope's private rooms. 'I thought this was done with,' he mumbled, picking it up. 'Who's this?' he asked, pointing to an extra figure that had been drawn roughly in the left-hand corner.

'I d-d-d . . .' I began, my stammer reappearing.

'Never mind,' he said, placing the drawing back down and returning to what he'd originally intended to tell me. He dropped his voice to a whisper. 'I've told you about my sideline?' (He had. Many times.) 'I spoke with Aretino last night who's interested in writing some juicy words to accompany my drawings, and

Marcantonio, the engraver, is seriously considering producing them as erotic prints. They're both very interested in joining me on my little project.' In his excitement Giulio let his guard down. He'd definitely done something to his eye.

'I'm going to have a peep,' he said, 'see if they're still at it.' That I knew Margarita had left before us last night in a carriage I was loath to say. Not that this excluded them from being *at it* this morning. It was possible the pair could have made their way here last night in secret. But I very much doubted it. I couldn't believe they were up to anything. Giulio got up to see. I did not join him.

Moments later he was back, a look of disbelief on his face. He picked up a stick of charcoal and set to work on adding to the outline of a Christ child.

'He's started. Drawing her,' he said, rubbing the dust around the chin of the son of God to create a shadow. 'He has it all set up. A sketch of Sebastiano's *La Fornarina* on one easel, his base all set up ready on another, and that Luti girl in between the two, mirroring the pose. Not how I would have had her, but still.' Giulio laughed. 'Oh that filthy worm-head, Bartolommeo, is going to go wild when he finds out.'

Bartolommeo? The only Bartolommeo I knew was an apprentice in Sebastiano's workshop.

'Giulio. That mark on your face? What is that?'

Raphael appeared in the room.

Before I say more I need to explain something to you; it will help you understand.

In those days if anyone criticised the work of a maestro, that person criticised the work of everybody who worked under him. We all worked to the same end, no matter how small our role, whether it was grinding the pigments, preparing the size, pouncing the cartoon, colouring the panel. And so, to malign Raphael was to malign each and every one of us. We were Raphael nearly as much as he was himself when it came to the identity of the work.

'There's something on your cheek.'

The maestro advanced to brush what he mistook for charcoal from just under Giulio's eye and down the left-hand side of his face, an easy enough mistake to make as his apprentice was now drawing the outline of a baby's foot.

Giulio moved back and winced as Raphael's finger felt the heat beneath the skin.

'I could not stop myself,' he said. 'Bartolommeo said how you'd copied Michelangelo in Florence and how you're doing the same now – copying him. That you have a fine gift for painting but that your finest skill is for stealing the brilliance of others. I had to take him to task.'

Raphael's face clouded over slightly. 'Giulio! My good, honest Giulio. It was a true slur, I grant you, and Bartolommeo should know better than to stoop so low. His master is a great artist and it becomes him not to display such base behaviour. But if he cannot control himself that does not mean that we should behave in similar fashion. It behoves us to show restraint.' He paused. His lofty sentiments comforted me. I wondered at his example. *Such a fine man,* I thought to myself. But my *fine man* hadn't finished yet. 'Our art is something we work at, we excel at, and we need to put our efforts into that, rather than damaging that which God has given us to execute it.' I watched, captivated, as the maestro placed a finger under Giulio's unshaven chin and lifted it up tenderly to examine the apprentice's face. 'Look at your eye. I see it now is obscured somewhat by the swelling.' An expression of deep concern crossed Raphael's face. 'Let me take a look at your hands.'

Giulio held them up to reveal bruised knuckles and broken skin.

Anger sparked in Raphael's eyes at the sight of them. 'Not too bad,' he said, more to convince himself than anyone else. 'But bad enough.' He cast his eyes down and turned his head to the side. He coughed before continuing and when he did his voice quivered. 'Remember there is more skill and artistry in these hands,' he said, holding them gently in his own, 'than in . . . No. I will not be drawn to make negative comparisons.' Raphael released Giulio's hands, clenching and unclenching his fists repeatedly while fighting against the instinct to hurl insults. He walked away and stood in the window. The sun beamed down on him. His silhouette glimmered like a halo.

'You are exceptional, my dear Giulio. As an artist . . . and as a man.' I wondered myself at this latter assessment but I let it go as to dwell on it too long made my still-raw head hurt. 'And Sebastiano's cheap words cannot change that.' (It was Bartolommeo, but I was in no state to correct him.) Raphael went up to Giulio's sketch and looked closely at the perfectly drawn foot of the Christ child. He smiled. It pleased him. 'This,' he said with a flourish of hand, 'is beyond words.'

Giulio was pleased and ashamed in equal measure. Pleased with Raphael's praise, and ashamed (now) that he'd allowed himself to be drawn into childish conflict the night before.

I was conscious of a figure that had appeared on the left of the room. I looked over slowly to see it was Margarita. I was not the only one to be watching Raphael with soft eyes. Her lips fell open, a look of admiration on her face. My chest swelled with pride, as if in some small way I deserved it too. I'd never been selfless but I felt so then, inspired by Raphael's fine words. And it felt good. Even the ache in my head seemed to fade away.

I'd seen many women look at Raphael with longing – longing to possess his beauty, longing to be seen with him, longing to bask in his fame. But I'd never seen one look at him as Margarita did then. With eyes that lit up her face and gazed at Raphael with wonder; she finally saw his worth as I did.

Crash! The magic disappeared into the air. The main door swung open for the second time that morning and in strode a fierce young woman accompanied by her maid.

'Welcome, *Signora* Felice. I was not expecting to see you so soon.' Raphael turned to look at Margarita. His brow furrowed for the briefest of moments. By the time he turned back to the Pope's daughter it was as smooth as a baby's once more.

'Though it is a great honour,' he said, bowing most courteously and kissing her hand.

'My father has sent me,' the stern, young woman said.

'Come.' Raphael held out his hand, ever solicitous. He now had eyes only for her. 'Let us discuss how best we can accommodate Pope Julius's wishes.' And with that Felice della Rovere pushed Margarita aside while the artist picked up his newly worked drawing of the *Mass of Bolsena* before going into his room and closing the door.

Margarita stood there, confused. She had lost what she thought she'd secured.

'I must go,' she said, her voice urgent, her face crest-fallen. I placed my hand on her arm as she passed by. There was, almost, something touching in the way her eyes welled up like bowls full of raindrops as she made her way out. Though, in my heart of hearts, I was quietly pleased that Raphael had pushed her aside. I was starting to become jealous.

But before Margarita had completely escaped Giulio started to laugh. 'Well, well, well! *Il Papa il terribile* wants his daughter – equally *terribile* – to be painted. The sly old hypocrite. So, she's the new figure in *The Mass of Bolsena*. He'll have his own daughter painted on the walls of the Vatican after all.' Margarita, too far away to be able to make out Giulio's words, must have thought we were making fun of her. Her head drooped as she pulled the main door to.

*

I told myself there was no time to go after her.

'What did you do with the drawing you did of Bibbiena last night?'

171

Giovanni may have come in late but the extra sleep had given him the energy to throw himself into the day. And throw himself at me.

He saw my confused look.

'You didn't do it!' He glowered at me. My memory of the night before was like a thicket. The scythe in my mind swiped back and forth, hacking away at the brambles and thorns. Eventually I found my way to a clearing where I saw the face of Margarita. Though still at some distance away, I sniffed the air with interest like a hound chasing blood. Bibbiena came into view. I remembered now. Margarita had had a heated exchange last night. Though over what I could not say.

'Here. Take this. We've got an appointment with him later this afternoon. You'll make up for lost time then.' Giovanni handed me two notes, one granting me entry to the Vatican, another to the Cardinal's chambers. I knew where I had to go.

Chapter 24

'Are you here to start the *stufetta*?' The Cardinal held out his ring. I bowed, kissed the ring.

'I am P-P-P-Pietro, *Monsignore*. I come from m-m-m-maestro Raphael's w-w-w-workshop, *Monsignore*.' I was nervous. I remembered him from last night.

Bibbiena sniffed. The *stufetta* was the Cardinal's personal bathroom and Raphael's workshop was busy planning a design for it. Giulio and Giovanni were very excited about the project and the drawings I'd seen for it so far – of a naked Venus, a lusty Vulcan, and an aroused Pan – were verging on the indecent. They were not so very far removed from the shocking drawings that Giulio was working on with Marcantonio and Aretino.

'N-n-n . . .'

'Spit it out boy!'

'N-n-no. I-I-I h-h-have a note explaining here.'

He read it. Shrugged a bit and adopted his best face.

'I imagine Raphael did not get off to a slow start this morning. The man's a force of nature,' he said with a low laugh.

'Yes, C-C-Cardinal Bibbiena. He was starting work on a portrait of a young woman.'

'A young woman?' He laughed again.

'Y-y-yes, *Monsignore.*'

I don't know why I told him about Margarita. Perhaps it was because I understood her feelings for Raphael. She loved him as much as he loved her. Did either of them realise that their feelings were reciprocated? I hoped not. And I sensed, when I'd walked in on them last night, that there was no love lost between the Cardinal and the girl.

'Pretty, I'll be bound. And young,' he continued.

'Y-yes, *Monsignore.*'

'Dressed in velvets and pearls?'

'N-n-no, *Monsignore.*' I said no more. The Cardinal waited.

'Then what, boy? What did this young, pretty girl have on? Anything?'

He laughed. I laughed back. Uneasy.

I wanted to say that she wore what she always wore. Instead I said, 'Light brown dress and white blouse.' I noted the Cardinal's red robes. Margarita was so drab, I thought, when compared to this.

He shot up. I dropped my materials on the floor.

'What's her name?'

'M-M-Margarita L-L-Luti, *Monsignore.*'

His eyes narrowed. He started to pace the room.

'Was she at the party last night?'

'I-I-I think so, *Monsignore.*'

'You think so? You think so? Oh, I know so.' He frowned; his eyes became slits as he scrutinised me.

'Don't I know you, boy?'

'I-I-I-I don't think so, *Monsignore.*'

His robes slithered across the floor, back and forth like a serpent's tail.

'Does Raphael seem to like her? This Margarita Luti?'

'I-I-I-I can't really say, *Monsignore.*'

I started to shake. The alcohol in my body wasn't giving up without a fight but the Cardinal's face in mine may have also had something to do with it.

'Listen, Pietro, isn't it? Yes, it is,' he said before I could answer. (He was one of those people who liked to answer their own questions, as is so often the way with people who can't stand the idea of not knowing everything.) He stepped back to play with the ring on his finger. I waited. After last night, the inside of my mouth tasted like the bottom of a birdcage.

'I have something to ask you.' The Cardinal's face was in mine once more. His breath was rank. He too had had a night of excess.

'This portrait of the girl you talk of,' he said, turning his back to me. 'You, Pietro. I want you to tell me how Raphael is getting on with it. I would be very interested to know. Very interested. You will tell me that, won't you, Pietro? How the girl . . . how *the painting* of the girl . . . develops?'

I nodded. This was a question he couldn't answer himself. And he couldn't stand that this was so. He turned towards me, and fear fluttered in my heart just for a moment as his hand lifted to open his robe. My eyes watched with trepidation. A jewel caught the light. It was on a purse attached to his belt. He patted it as he looked me in the eye to check for understanding.

'You're coming back tomorrow,' he told more than asked me, satisfied with my answer, even though I hadn't opened my mouth to give one. 'And I will expect you to tell me all you know.'

I took up my pencil. I would finish my drawing of him today.

'Not now, boy.' Cardinal Bibbiena had different ideas.

*

I did not think I would have much to tell the Cardinal the following day. About the painting. Or Margarita. I was secretly relieved to see that Raphael did not think as much of her as I had feared. He had dropped her for *Signora* Felice in a heartbeat. *Margarita wouldn't like that*, I said to myself. There was every chance she wouldn't be back. Also, if Giulio was right – that Raphael had seen her wares and taken what he fancied – the maestro would not be interested in her even if she was bold enough to set foot over the threshold and tempt him some more.

I still would have liked him to paint Margarita; I wanted him to crush Sebastiano. But I didn't think that would be happening now.

No, I did not think I would have much to tell the Cardinal at all.

*

The man with the perfect hands walked off, the expression on his face sour. I put my charcoal stick down. He had been modelling his upraised right hand with palm facing outward for me for the past three hours. '*Grazie, Signore,*' I called after him.

'Ha!' Giulio came over to inspect my work.

'What's wrong with it?' I asked.

'Nothing,' he said. 'If your intention was to draw a winded pig's bladder flattened under the wheels of a cart.' His laughter boomed around the studio. Raphael raised his head. Oh, how I hated Giulio at times.

Within seconds the maestro was gazing at my work. I waited for the criticism. Instead he placed a hand on my shoulder and said, 'I should very much like us to draw some hands together, you and I. Let us say, this afternoon?' I felt his fingers as they ran gently down my back. I looked him in the eye. He gave me a knowing smile.

My disaster had turned into a miracle.

Afternoon came. I waited. Prepared my charcoal. Hummed. Looked through the window at the blue sky. Brushed down my hose. I even cleaned up my apron as best I could, peeling off dried on paint, wiping off plaster dust. It was nearly time. I had no room in my heart for anything other than to hear him call my name.

'Pietro!' It was Margarita. I was shocked to see her here after being overlooked for the Pope's daughter. Yet here she was, her voice, urgent, unsure. There was a vulnerability, a sense of

176

yearning, that frightened me and forced a stake into my breast. 'I have come.'

I took her, trembling, to Raphael, my head deaf to the words that tumbled from her mouth. *She will soon be gone*, I told myself. *She will be overlooked once more, this time for me.* As we approached, the maestro looked up at Margarita. He put down the knife he had in his hand. It too was trembling. I searched his face and caught the look that flew back and forth between them; it worried me.

I retreated. The maestro had promised that we would shortly be drawing hands together. He was an honourable man, a man of his word. I waited.

No laughter, no languorous sighs, no saucy shrieks or flirtatious flutterings assaulted my ears. Yet each second poisoned my soul with jealousy as I imagined their words of love.

It could only have been minutes they were together, side by side, the skirt of her dress brushing the tips of his fingers, yet it seemed like hours.

Margarita said something to me as she passed by. I had no idea what it was.

I looked at my sticks of charcoal, ready for my session with Raphael. He would call me over when he'd finished whatever it was he was doing. I rearranged my charcoal sticks. I looked over at Raphael. Was he coming yet? I rearranged them some more. Any second now he would beckon me over. I picked up my sticks to save time. I noticed that he was gathering his up too. It wouldn't be long now. I walked towards him.

'Maestro?' I asked, standing before him.

'Not now, Pietro! Not now!'

I watched the back of his head as he walked into his office and closed the door behind him.

Chapter 25

On 21st February 1513, Pope Julius II died, catching us all unawares. Michelangelo was still working on the Sistine Chapel ceiling – he never did finish the Pope's monumental tomb. But Pope Julius had left behind him an astonishing artistic legacy, which his successor, Pope Leo X (himself a Medici) had every intention of adding to. It was business as usual for the artistic workshops of Rome. But the change at the top had made one or two cardinals reflect on their own mortality and so their own bloodline. Many of them wanted to create their own legacy, establish their own dynasty.

That's why, less than one week later, Cardinal Bibbiena dropped into the workshop to make a personal call on Raphael. It was at the time Margarita was usually there, a fact he knew because I had told him.

I had been in the Cardinal's employ ever since the day Giovanni sent me to draw him. And Margarita had been coming to the workshop for Raphael to paint her, one way or another, ever since. I was disappointed when she reappeared the day after the maestro had treated her so badly. Where was her self-respect? But reappear she did. There had been nothing for it but to tell the Cardinal everything from then on.

I had told him, while he was still grieving the passing of Pope Julius, that Margarita would be at the studio at ten the following day. But I was surprised, nevertheless, when he turned up on precisely that day at precisely that time. I had no idea he was coming. Information passed but one way, yet while money passed in the other I could not complain. Fragmented memories of what had happened at the feast at Chigi's all that time ago came back to me. My hand moved to hold my head as if it still hurt.

The red-robed figure marched into the building and walked to the small painting chamber at the back. I went to announce him. He brushed me aside. The element of surprise was his.

I'd already given him all the information I had on Margarita and Raphael. He'd come to see it for himself. He walked past me and opened the door without caring to knock on it.

'So. What is this I see, Raphael? A painting by Sebastiano? Of . . . of her?'

His voice sounded genuinely surprised. This was not what he'd expected to find. I hadn't thought to tell him.

'It's a copy,' Raphael answered. 'And yes, it is of Margarita.'

'As your patron I'm not sure I like this. Please explain to me now what is going on here.'

I moved closer to be able to hear what was said. There was much dragging of wooden legs across the floor – belonging to easels or chairs, possibly both.

'Raphael. Your Grace.' Margarita made her farewells swiftly, anxious to escape the room. The swish of her skirt struck me as she passed. I reached out to touch her but her will to flee rendered her blind to all else, even me, who she now believed more than ever to have her best interests at heart. She had no wish to be ensnared by the Cardinal. Fortunately for her he had no wish to ensnare her. Not this time.

'This copy of a painting by Sebastiano is not why you've come here, dear Cardinal,' Raphael said, his voice warm. 'Now tell me truly? What is the reason for you to honour us with a visit? Is it the *stufetta*?'

I strained to hear the Cardinal's answer, but silence is silence whichever side of the wall you're on and no amount of straining was going to change that. Eventually he let out a laugh, no sooner out than stifled and replaced by the sucking of teeth.

'No, no. Giulio is making great progress. The design is remarkable ... But what are you thinking? What do you mean by having this copy of Sebastiano's painting here in your studio?' The Cardinal, now he'd seen the copy, couldn't let it go.

'Cardinal, you know how we learn. We imitate the great masters do we not?' I heard the scraping sound of one easel then another being turned. The paintings on them were proving far too distracting for Raphael's patron. 'And so if you're not here about the *stufetta*, what are you here for?' Raphael had much work to do. That he wanted to get on with it, I could hear in his voice. 'Cardinal?'

'It is about a matter of the utmost delicacy. One close to my heart.' He cleared his throat. 'As your patron I have grown fond of you.'

'Thank you, Cardinal, as I have of you ... and I am indebted to you for your kind service.'

Again, a pause. My heart beat like a drum in my chest. The blood rushed to my head. My own body deafened me. Speak! I thought.

'Yes,' I heard Bibbiena say as his red Cardinal's robes caught the leg of an easel. 'I've grown exceedingly fond of you.' He coughed (he was preparing to say something momentous, of that he was sure even if nobody else was). 'You are like a son to me.' (Was that it?)

'Tha—' Before Raphael could finish Bibbiena carried on, warming to his theme.

'Like family. Like one of my own.'

There was an awkwardness in the air that seeped out of the room like a bad odour.

'I have devised a way to keep you under my continued protection and to put a stop to idle gossip about you.'

It was Raphael's turn to cough. He shut the door. I could hear no more.

Chapter 26

In the coming days and weeks Raphael did not seem to be himself. The last time I put this down to Margarita and this time, at first, I did so again. Blame the woman. She'd been a constant presence at the workshop for some time now. It had to be her. All the signs were there and that's what I told Cardinal Bibbiena at the many meetings I had with him. I thought he'd want to know.

When Margarita was around the maestro was euphoric. The other apprentices saw this as a cause for celebration. I did not. 'It's not good, the way the maestro is around Margarita,' I whispered slyly in willing ears. 'It's not good for the reputation of the studio.' I said no more, saving that for the Cardinal to do.

Yet while I attempted to sow the seeds of stubborn resentment in the hearts and minds of my fellow apprentices so Nature worked against me. Spring – my favourite season – was coming, permeating everything with its fruitful harmony. The workshop throbbed with excited anticipation. Glum faces at the death of Pope Julius melted with the snow on the mountains, and hearts started to flutter like butterflies in the fields. Even I could not resist its power. There was an abundance of joy all about, with Raphael the most joyful of us all.

I could not deny the change Margarita had wrought over him.

'Look. Plato was right. At a lover's touch everyone does turn into a poet. Read this.' Giulio ushered me over to him one beautiful morning. 'I was looking through the maestro's drawings,' he said, amusement in his voice, 'working out which ones I could make a start on, when I found this.' He gave the smirk I was now very familiar with as his finger drew my eye to what looked like a poem. And it was written in my maestro's hand. I read it.

> *Love, you enticed me with your two lights,*
> *Two beautiful eyes, that make me melt, as does your face*
> *Of snow and roses,*
> *And noble words and maidenly ways.*
> *Now I burn so much that not sea nor river*
> *Can put out the fire. Yet the feeling is not unpleasant,*
> *For my passion makes me feel so good*
> *That, burning, I am consumed by ever-brighter fire.*
> *How sweet was the game and the necklace*
> *Your white arms wrapped around my neck*
> *That without it I feel only pain.*

Giulio was still smirking. 'His sap's been rising there,' he said. 'Wonder how long those maidenly ways are going to last?'

'Quite,' I agreed. I thought they had given up some time ago.

'I saw that,' he said, wearing me down, stabbing the last verse with his finger. 'I saw her putting a chain around his neck only last week. Saw the sparks fly between them then. Must say,' Giulio said, starting to annoy me, 'she's put some paint on the end of his brush if his latest work is anything to go by.'

Though reluctant, I had to agree again. The poem was probably intended for Margarita. It was a fact that Raphael's breast was full to overflowing with an appreciation of beauty the like of which he had never experienced before whenever she was present. It was there in his art. Giulio was right. Such passion. Infectious.

'Good thing he's not a poet,' he added, winking at me. 'His verse is terrible.'

And so it was that, although I conspired against her, I grudgingly liked having Margarita around. The workshop seemed a never-ending spring, always with the promise of a cloudless summer not far ahead whenever she was there. We worked, we laughed, and life was a fountain that constantly replenished itself over and over again in her presence.

But something was bothering the maestro. I didn't notice anything amiss at first; perhaps because his euphoria had reached such dazzling new heights that it eclipsed everything else with its brightness. But soon, on the rare occasions Margarita was not around, I started to catch a look on his face, a look of dread, that said his world was about to end. Of this I said nothing to the Cardinal.

*

I set to working it out. I first looked to Margarita. I was happy to tell the Cardinal she was a problem, and as I've said, he was hungry to hear this. She was around the workshop far too much, I told him. And he told me, judgement in his voice, that he knew why. She might prove to be a distraction for a while, he assured me, but she could never offer an artist like Raphael any lasting sustenance.

I was not so sure.

I watched her. She bounced around the workshop like a spring lamb. Her initial intolerance of artists – which she had sincerely felt and had wanted to feel because it was in keeping with the view of society that she had developed and nurtured over the years – was looking slightly worn to me. I was now very nearly nineteen years old and not far off becoming a fully formed artist myself.

'So artists aren't the vain creatures you once took them for?' I challenged her one morning.

'They are!' she said, with a laugh, glancing at the new yellow hose I had on – a recent purchase made with the money I'd been paid by Bibbiena.

'You no longer seem to dislike everything about them,' I tried again.

'True. Not everything. I suppose my views are getting a little threadbare. Like a winter coat that's seen its best,' she said, hanging her own up by the door and letting her hand run down the fabric.

'You seem not to dislike Raphael,' I said, boldly.

'You know,' she said, looking at her coat, 'I don't think I'll be needing this old thing now that the warmer days are here.' And with that she beamed at me. 'Is he here yet?'

'No,' I said, cross that she'd not answered me, 'he's gone to see Bramante about their plans for the new St Peter's.'

'Oh. He said we'd be working on our painting today.'

I shuddered that she should refer to '*our* painting'.

'I've given up helping at the bakery to be here.'

She was cross. I was exasperated. I turned my back on her in order to look up at the heavens. By the time I looked back at her all traces of irritation had faded away leaving something more delicate in its place. Sadness was in her eyes, and disappointment. And there was a hint of something else. Love. Was this why the maestro seemed to have the look of the damned about him whenever she wasn't around? Did he love her too? Or feel guilty that he didn't? Perhaps he felt pursued by her? And was Cardinal da Bibbiena right? Was the smile on Raphael's face when he was with her the smile of the carnally satisfied?

My mind whirred over, imagining meetings between them, conversations, lovers' tiffs, passionate encounters.

But no. It didn't make sense. I wanted to be rid of her for complicated reasons I found hard to articulate even to myself but I could not see her as a whore. Rather, I was coming to see as well that she was also a woman of great virtue. It would have been easy for her to have thrown herself before the maestro (many

185

had done so and tried to do so still) but Margarita had never given the slightest hint in her behaviour that she had ever offered herself to anyone. And though I thought I recognised the look of love in her eyes I knew she was too respectful of herself to give in to Raphael of all people. He was an artist, and although she'd come to see that the world they inhabited was not all bad, it was still another world. A world where she did not belong.

It pained me to admit it but I knew Margarita. And the more I knew her the greater my respect, and my jealousy, became.

She would look after her sister's child, take food to ailing neighbours, stand up for people bullied in the street (I could testify to that), and she would also give whatever she could spare to beggars. She was moved to do the right thing. At all times. I watched her. What gave her the strength of character to follow her own nose?

And she did not shy away from saying what was in her heart.

'You know, Pietro, I will always be grateful to have found you. You are a true friend.'

'Oh, Margarita,' I sighed. If she only knew I was being paid by the Cardinal to spy on her.

'Why are you crying?' she whispered.

She was a pearl. I was a swine.

<hr />

And she was always around. Raphael's painting of her was making great progress. A deliberate imitation of Sebastiano's portrait of her but infinitely better. I'd seen that even before it was finished. Raphael insisted on painting Margarita in private but that did not stop me and the rest of the apprentices from taking a peek when he was engaged elsewhere in the city. As he learned from Sebastiano and Michelangelo, so we, his apprentices, learned from him.

Raphael made sure his piece was identical in every particular to Sebastiano's – composition, clothes, colours. But when seen side by side Sebastiano's was by far the duller of the two, the model somehow stolid and lumpen, of the soil rather than of the heavens. Sebastiano's was very much a portrait of an ordinary baker's daughter, lacking light, life and beauty. While Raphael's was beauty itself.

I looked on in awe. Raphael was a magician, taking base metal and turning it into gold. No insult Sebastiano could come up with would be able to counter this.

'It's audacious!' Giulio chuckled when he saw Raphael's painting. 'Are you going to call it by the same name too?' he asked the maestro.

'No. This will not be *La Fornarina*. This will be *La Donna Velata*.'

'Apt,' Giulio nodded in appreciation, accompanying the word with a satisfied sound like a cat eating its favourite morsel. 'When are you going to reveal it to the world and rub Sebastiano's nose in it?'

'I'm not,' he said. 'I have learned much from this exercise and for that I am truly grateful. Without Sebastiano there would be no Raphael. I acknowledge freely that I have copied from him, but in doing so, I have come up with a work that is completely my own. That is reward enough.'

I was shocked.

*

'It's done.' Margarita beamed at me. 'The painting.'

'I imagine you're pleased. You can leave now,' I said, before I could stop myself.

'Yes,' she blustered, a little surprised. 'I suppose so. All that sitting. Who would have thought sitting up straight could be such agony? But Raphael has done the painting well.' A plebeian understatement, I said to myself, but I let it pass. She would be gone soon.

'Come,' she said, taking my hand. Giulio watched me. I would have shaken her off but for that. Instead I accompanied her dutifully to observe the picture I'd observed many times already.

I stood before it. My legs quivered. This copy of a copy disturbed me deeply. Now finished I could see the artist loved the girl in the painting. I prayed that Margarita couldn't see it too.

*

But it was how mediocre Sebastiano's version was in comparison that caught the eye of the rest of the workshop. Every person in the studio went into the private space to trail past the two pieces. They marvelled at the perfection of the one while tittering (though not in Raphael's hearing, because he still maintained he had the greatest of respect for Sebastiano) at the other. No one saw what I saw. I took solace in the fact. It was war, and not love, that roused everybody else: war between our maestro and Sebastiano. This painting made up for all the slights and schemes Sebastiano had attacked our workshop with. Raphael might have decided not to show this painting to the public, but it was too late for him to call a truce. The painting existed and its beauty was spear, shield, and irresistible beacon. Sebastiano would know of its existence soon enough, of that I was sure.

Chapter 27

'When will this dalliance end? It should have burned itself out after a few months, yet it's still going on.' Cardinal Bibbiena pushed the money towards me. I picked it up and put it in my purse. He was right. It had been going on a long time. Raphael had asked her to stay on, after *La Donna Velata*. The situation disturbed me too, but, the Cardinal's payments for news about the pair eased my pain. When indulging my taste for flamboyant hose, I convinced myself that the baker's daughter would soon be back at the bakery; when purchasing a shirt of the finest white linen, I assured myself a new girl would soon delight the maestro's eye and distract his brush. I bought a jacket, and a cap, in the softest black velvet, and before I knew it I was out in the taverns, dressing like Raphael, attracting admirers, having liaisons. I could not deny that there was profit to Margarita's ongoing presence at the workshop. I was distracted for a while. It was the Cardinal who was beginning to lose patience with the situation.

Then, on a seeming whim, he took himself off to the Court of Urbino for a few weeks and when he came back his patience had been restored.

The Cardinal had only recently returned when he came looking for Raphael. I was working with about ten other apprentices in the Pope's private rooms at the time.

'So where is he then if he's not here?' he asked. His voice sounded piqued. It was well known that Bibbiena liked to think that he'd helped Raphael secure the commission we were working on, not Bramante. Like all great men he didn't like to share praise or plaudits for anything he had a hand in. There was only room for one on the pedestal – him. And like all great men he never gave anything, never helped anyone, without expecting something in return. He was a man who demanded payment one way or another and the time was fast approaching for Raphael to settle up.

'Where is he?'

I don't know if you're aware but the painting of a fresco is a race against time. You paint onto wet plaster and you have to finish what you've planned before it dries. The day Bibbiena came in we were working on the frescoes in *The Room of Heliodorus*. Raphael had finished the drawings some time ago and they had been transferred to the wall. We'd watched him for days work twelve hours with hardly a pause. Today it was our turn and he'd left Giulio and Giovanni in charge to make sure no mistakes were made. By the time the Cardinal made his entrance we'd been working for four hours. He'd come at the most inconvenient of times.

The Cardinal waited. To have to repeat himself once was understandable. But to have to do so twice, well, he was sure there was some Vatican law that forbade such incivility to a man of the cloth, particularly one of his standing. And so was I.

Giulio and Giovanni continued to work the plaster with love and devotion, so deep in the act of creation that their sense of hearing had been left on the other side of the doors of consciousness. I put my brush down and quickly gestured to a resting apprentice to take over.

'But I've got five more minutes yet,' he grumbled. He took up the brush all the same.

'Well I never!' the Cardinal said, suddenly noticing how Giovanni was working on the eyes of one of the philosophers. 'I've never seen that before. It looks as if he's gouging the man's eyes out! Oh! Look at the eyes of that figure there. They make him look like a thinker. Very clever.' I knew what he was talking about without looking. It was a trick Raphael had shown us yesterday and I was impressed that Bibbiena had even noticed it. He was a complex character.

'C-C-Cardinal B-B-Bibbiena.' My regular meetings with him had done little to allay my fear of him. He rolled his eyes not caring to hide his irritation. 'Wh-wh-what a pleasure to see you. Raphael asked me to thank you for all you've done for the workshop. As you can see, with your intercession we . . .' With the raising of one hand he cut me off. He proffered the other to be kissed.

'So where is he?'

Raphael, in his role as Master of Ancient Rome and its arte-facts, was out with a group of young architects rounded up by Bramante, studying the ruins of an ancient villa.

'Speak, boy!'

'He-he-he-he's . . .' I was on the point of telling him this when he lifted his palm to silence me. Dark lines appeared on his forehead. He lowered his lids. He would have an answer to his question, if not from me, then from the depths of his own mind. When he looked up again he gave a mocking laugh. Ever a man to judge others against his own moral standards, his eyes now oozed sleaze and suspicion. 'I see,' he said. He did not.

'So, he's with that lowborn slut of his!' He gave a nod of satisfaction, with himself.

My mind raced. What if I said nothing? I would not be telling a lie. It was the Cardinal, after all, who had misunderstood the situation. What fault was that of mine?

This misunderstanding could serve me well. If the Cardinal's suspicions intensified, so the amount of silver with which he crossed my palm would increase accordingly.

My lips stayed sealed.

'I see,' he said once more, rubbing his chin. I'd not said a word; my conscience was clear. Until Giulio's brush dropped to the floor with a clatter, reminding me of his presence. My eyes rushed to his, in panic. I'd been caught. Dark clouds appeared in my mind and threatened to drown me in a deluge of guilt if I didn't speak up quickly.

'He-he's not with her,' I said, my voice loud enough for all to hear. I looked at Giulio again. *More. Explain more,* his eyes commanded me.

'H-h-h-he's gone,' I continued, 'g-g-gone to the Villa of Livia to study the r-r-ruins there.'

Giulio, satisfied that I'd told the truth, returned to his work on the fresco. But whatever I said now, truth or otherwise, was too late for the Cardinal. I could tell from the faraway look in his eyes that the seeds of suspicion had already been sown in his fertile mind and that he couldn't wait to get away to tend the poisonous shoots. 'I must go,' he said, placing not one but two coins in my hand.

I shot a look at Giulio. He was now wholly engrossed in the work before him, spouting sweet nothings to the still-wet plaster as he lovingly applied colour to it. 'Come on!' he growled suggestively as if to a woman revealing herself to him. 'That's it. Beautiful.' He too was far away. Not even the echoing sound of the Cardinal's heavy steps as he left the room did anything to disturb Giulio's concentration. And, unless he had eyes in the back of his head, he would have seen nothing of the transaction.

But still I was wary of him. I hid the coins in my pocket, crept away to the far corner of the room, and there I mingled with the group of apprentices sat around a table preparing materials.

'What was that about Margarita and the maestro?' they asked, concerned. They too had overheard some of my conversation with the Cardinal.

'Not good,' I said with a shake of my head. I looked back at Giulio. He was still caressing the wall with his brush. Without his eyes to catch me out my conscience was safe. I thought back to the seeds of discontent I myself had sown in the minds of these young apprentices when I'd first tried to turn them against Margarita. It was time to give those seeds a little water. I moved closer, opened my mouth, and let the lies pour forth. They flowed from me as freely as newly fallen rain over the stones of a mountain stream in springtime. I sat back. Disapproval burst out across the faces of my gullible audience like buds in a meadow. At last, my seeds were starting to flower.

*

The Cardinal held a dinner the following week to celebrate his return from Urbino.

'Strange to have a return celebration when he's already been back for one week,' Raphael said as he laid out his sketches of classical columns, frescoes and stucco work.

'Giovanni! Look! Do you think you could imitate this?' Raphael called his assistant over to look at the sketches of stucco work they'd both admired when they'd gone to the Roman ruins. 'Perhaps we could incorporate some of this into our plans for Chigi's villa.' I watched the master. He had such enthusiasm but I couldn't help but notice that his eyelids were looking heavier than usual and dark rings were beginning to cast a shadow over the radiance of his eyes. Even his hair was starting to look a little less cared for. Raphael had never been one of those courtly types who went around with a comb up his sleeve and a looking glass under his cap, but he had always turned himself out with an effortless perfection.

My poor Raphael. I wanted to tell him he was working too hard but I hesitated to do so. My stammer was much improved but even the most assured of men stumbled over their words when talking of matters close to their heart, and Raphael was very close to mine. As I watched him with concern Giulio arrived.

'You're working too hard, my friend.'

The ground moved beneath my feet as I listened to Giulio speak *my* words. Had he read my mind? Was he mocking me for my cowardice?

When Giulio placed a brotherly arm around Raphael's shoulders my heart lodged in my throat. *I* wanted to hold Raphael. *I* wanted to protect him. *I* wanted *my* arm to be the one that wrapped itself around Raphael's shoulders.

Giulio led Raphael outside. Bibbiena had sent a carriage and it was waiting to take us to his apartment at the Vatican where the dinner to celebrate his return from Urbino was to be held. I followed on behind.

When Raphael peeled Giulio's arm from his neck relief swept over me.

'Please, Giulio, after you.' It did not surprise me that Giulio climbed up into the carriage before Raphael. He never did know his place. If Raphael ushered me in before him too I would refuse, I told myself. Instead, the maestro pulled me to one side. 'I have a favour to ask of you,' he said. My chest swelled with pride. I looked towards Giulio. He was watching and did not take his eyes off us as the maestro whispered in my ear. It was time to be daring.

I nodded to Raphael, placed my hand on his shoulder, gave it a squeeze. Every action was bigger, louder and more obvious than any I'd made before. The maestro had chosen *me* to perform this favour. I looked at Giulio. Still watching. Good. He would see that I was the special one. The maestro smiled at me, he climbed up into the carriage and waved me his thanks.

'Now let's go to Bibbiena's, Giulio,' he said.

*

When I got to Margarita's house she was not in. If the girl could read I would have left a handwritten message but she could not, as far as I knew. The message that I had to pass on to her had to be spoken to her in person; there was no other choice. I liked to imagine she was out sharing her obvious favours with the young men of the neighbourhood or the gentlemen with the money to purchase them. Though I knew that she wasn't.

Either way, I had to wait.

I waited. And waited. And waited.

'Cold this evening!' a passer-by said. But if it was, I felt none of it. My initial glow brought on by the thought that I was the favoured one may have vanished, but it had been replaced by a thick layer of my own resentment. The realisation that I was missing a dinner given by Cardinal Bibbiena was fast dawning on me. If I remembered correctly the Cardinal had a certain page I'd met several times before. He had hair styled long, not wholly dissimilar to maestro Raphael.

While I imagined the delights I was missing, Margarita arrived back home singing and swinging a basket.

'Pietro! How long have you been waiting here?'

'Nearly an hour,' I answered, forcing a smile.

'I must have just gone out,' she said. 'I took two loaves of bread to the convent of San Apollonia. I should have taken it to the nuns earlier but . . .' She stopped mid-sentence.

The thought that I could be reacquainting myself with my page at this very moment instead of listening to Margarita's tediously worthy deeds suddenly broke out across my face. I could contain my exasperation no more.

'Two loaves of bread!' I exploded, thinking of the delights I was missing. And for what?

'It's all I can give,' she said, mistaking my words and the look on my face for judgement. Her eyes – soft, gentle and full of honesty – opened up to reveal the depths of her soul. I lowered mine hastily for fear of exposing the shallows of mine. 'I know I should have taken more,' she said. I should have been moved. But I wasn't.

I wanted to get back to the dinner. I had no time to listen to her good intentions. And because she was late, all for the sake of two loaves of bread, I would have to abandon any embellishment or deliberately deceptive flourish I'd intended to twist round Raphael's message.

I whispered it in her ear, made a pretence of caring about what I was telling her, and went to run off to find my page who was surely waiting for me.

'I must return to Cardinal Bibbiena's.' I let the name slip out. I knew Margarita did not like him for obvious reasons, but he was now one of Raphael's most important patrons and so where was the harm in it?

A dark change came over her. I looked at the door but knew I couldn't leave yet.

'What is it?' I asked her.

'Nothing. There's nothing, I tell you.' Her eyes dropped to the floor so that all I could see of them was a watery crescent that twinkled through dark eyelashes. A single, silver teardrop rolled down her cheek, catching the light as it fell.

'I came across him . . .' She paused; I heard her swallow. '. . . When I was delivering bread to a friend . . . Lucia. I-I-I-I . . . walked in on . . .' She couldn't finish; she wouldn't look up.

'Men like him, like Bibbiena,' she spat the name out, 'take what they want. They like to have their own way.' Her voice wavered. She started to shake.

'Oh,' I said, placing a hand on her shoulder.

'Not me!' she exploded, her eyes blazing straight into mine. 'I wouldn't let those fat, fleshy fingers of his anywhere near me. Oh he tried, but I haven't got to my age without knowing how to fight off bitter, brutish men.'

She'd clearly forgotten about the time at Chigi's when she'd had me to thank for interrupting Bibbiena's attempt on her virtue. Who knows what fun those fat, fleshy fingers would have had with her if I hadn't rescued her then?

'Then why are you still so sad?' I asked, genuinely perplexed.

'As I said,' she replied, still shaking, 'men like him take what they want. And I fear that he wants Raphael.'

I did not know what to say. I went to go.

'But wait, Pietro!' she said, stopping me for a second time. 'Forgive me. I should not have burdened you with my silly fears. It means a lot that you have come here this evening, and please, I trust you to give Raphael my answer.'

Her answer. I'd expected her to need a few days before she came up with that. I looked at her willing her to hurry.

'My answer . . .' she started. The night was going from bad to worse. I hadn't expected to be returning with an answer.

'*Yes*. My answer's *yes*.'

Jealousy struck my heart like lightning, yet still I smiled like a putto in one of Raphael's paintings.

'You will be all right?' she asked. 'I know how you hate the dark.'

I gave a brave laugh. I did not want her concern. She kissed me goodbye. The second she closed the door after me, I flew back to Cardinal Bibbiena's as fast as I could. *Her answer's yes,* I said to myself. *Of course it is! What's a girl as common as her going to say to the most sought-after artist in Rome?* I raged with bitterness as I made my way along the dark backstreets of Rome where every shadow made me jump. *Whore. Beggar. Baker's daughter.* I called her every insult I could think of. But it made no difference. Her answer was still *yes*.

*

'Let's drink a toast to it!' The page was there when I got back, and looking as handsome as I'd remembered. He led me to my place at the table and I waited for Bibbiena to make a pointed remark about my late arrival.

He didn't seem to notice.

Instead he was beaming, his crooked teeth on display as his lips parted in a terrifying smile. His goblet dazzled in the torchlight, held, I noticed, by fat, pink fingers. With his disturbingly long, yellow nails, ridged like shells, he tapped on the side of his drink. I raised mine in response but dared not whisper, *Why the toasting?* Though I thought it.

My eyes looked around the table. There was the usual array of guests. But then I noticed a frail young girl. Highborn from her dress but not thriving. Her clothes hung on her. Her hands like dry, broken twigs protruding out of heavy brocade sleeves, deliberately too long, a sign to onlookers that the wearer of such a dress with such impractical sleeves was too lofty a woman to have to use her hands for anything as unbecoming as work. Usually a wealthy young woman's hands would look exquisite, and delicate, like fine jewels amid the weighty finery. But this girl's fingers looked dull and brittle, as if they might snap. Even her hair lacked the strength to support the weight of the jewels intended to disguise its lack of lustre. I'd never seen gems so unpleasantly heavy. Like rocks weighing her down, they dulled not lightened the girl. She reminded me of a scrawny kitten my father had put in a sack and drowned in the Tiber when I was a small boy.

The only spark of joy about her came from her eyes that sparkled with delight. It struck me that such a girl could not have many things to make her sparkle so. But something had made her happy.

'To Maria and Raphael!' Cardinal Bibbiena boomed with passion. What was I hearing? No. It couldn't be.

'To Maria and Raphael!' came the reply from the assembled guests. Maria?

Margarita! My first thoughts were of her. This news, this terrible news, there was something desperately wrong about it. I wiped my brow. Was this what loyalty felt like? I poured the wine down my throat without it touching the sides. Then did so again. As I looked at Raphael I saw that he was drinking hard too. And from his appearance he'd been doing so for quite some time.

'Raphael is to be married to the Cardinal's niece,' Giulio told me. 'Wants to keep Raphael on the straight and narrow. Protect the hen that lays all those golden eggs.'

'How did Raphael take the news?' I asked.

'Look at him. Does he look like a happy man?' Giulio's eyebrow, already raised, knew the answer.

I downed more wine.

'It's like he's just been told he's a lamb,' Giulio cackled, 'then given the news that he's going to be slaughtered.'

'Did Raphael know before today?' I asked.

'I'm not sure but Bibbiena said he'd discussed it at the Court of Urbino and everyone applauded the idea there. Or so he says.'

The Court of Urbino. That was where Raphael had been brought up. It had the reputation for being the most civilised court in the whole of Christendom and Raphael did nothing to dispel this myth. All virtues resided there and it was where Raphael still thought of as home. He'd received the most enlightened of educations there from the most high-minded people. Urbino had made him who he was. That Bibbiena should have discussed Raphael's future with its Duke and Duchess was a sly move. Clever of him. Cleverer than I'd thought possible.

Of course, they would want their most revered, artistic son to marry one of their own, and to support a marriage connecting their beloved Raphael with Cardinal Bibbiena's niece would secure him a place in courtly circles forever.

Raphael agreed with the Court of Urbino on every particular. *'At the Court of Urbino we did . . . we said . . . we believed . . .'* On art, war, law, civic duty, love, women, and . . . marriage.

He agreed with the Court on everything.

But not on this.

I did not know what to think about the news. I should have felt pleased. His future would be secure; the expectations of society would be appeased. Margarita, that thorn in my side, rival for Raphael's affections, would at last be removed. But somewhere in the back of my mind, a feeling of guilt was rising. Devastation was in Raphael's eyes and it was my fault.

'You are betrothed! My very best wishes,' I said to him, a smile of disbelief on my face.

'It would seem so, friend,' he answered, a gracious smile on his.

For the rest of the evening Raphael went round the assembled company like a somnambulist, not truly seeing, listening, feeling. It was as if he wasn't there. His soul had flown out of him that night, I'm sure of it. For there was no other way he would have been able to endure the shock of the news that he was to marry Maria da Bibbiena. There would be no more Margarita Luti. I thought I would have been glad of it.

'Come, Raphael. You should talk to the Cardinal's niece.' He did not answer, just wandered off and sat between his bride-to-be and the man who had made her so.

Just then one of the Cardinal's men stood up and went to speak with Raphael. He was quite a short man but he stooped over the maestro. That movement. There was something in it that alarmed me. It seemed familiar. But then the man nodded to the Cardinal and was gone, taking my concerns with him. I had more pressing issues to deal with. I studied the face of the Cardinal. It was flushed hot with wine and his eyes were shot through with flickering flames, a reflection from the torchlight. Through my wine-doused eyes I saw something of the devil about him.

I moved on to Raphael. His movements were slow, but next to the Cardinal he appeared radiant, and even though the sadness in his tender eyes was almost palpable it was still a beautiful sight as they gleamed gently in a face made up of the softest skin tones, its surface smooth yet mature. And then I noticed the quiet, slight creature next to him, birdlike in her frailty. Though the light surrounded her, it only served to make her seem no more substantial than a dying ember in the hearth, barely alive. Her hairline and eyebrows had been plucked – a fashion I never did understand as it did few favours to even the most beautiful of women; her eyes fought to twinkle; her skin took on a greenish tinge that reminded me of a cadaver I'd once seen when making sketches for Christ on the cross.

My eyes flashed back instinctively to Raphael, life and beauty blazing within him even in his sadness.

Would such a mismatch go unchallenged?

'My lady, what pastimes do you enjoy?' I heard my master ask.

It seemed that even he, the person whom it would hurt the most, not even he was prepared to resist it.

'I love to play the lute,' the delicate creature said, her voice as brittle as a dry reed left out in the sun then crushed under the heavy wheel of a cart.

'Then it would give me the greatest pleasure to hear you do so.'

I watched as a painful exchange took place. Raphael requested one of the servants to bring over a lute and Maria tried to take it in her hands. Yet she laboured to do so. It was a pitiful sight to see how she battled to hold it. She was as fragile as she looked. Tears lined up in her eyes ready to spill over. Raphael took the lute away from her before the poor girl broke down completely.

'Allow me.' Ever the gallant, Raphael picked up the instrument and started to play. His fingers glided over the strings filling the room with the happiest of tunes. He looked at Maria as he played, the kindest of smiles upon his face. Her embarrassment evaporated as she looked into his reassuring eyes. It did not surprise me. The poor wretched girl probably had no more heart to be here than Raphael. And Raphael was ever the kind soul.

He paid care and attention to the little bird after that. There was not a second all evening when he did not attend to her every wish and whim.

'I suppose I should thank you,' Bibbiena whispered in my ear, pushing a small purse full of coins into my hand. I hid it quickly. 'A token of my appreciation for all that you've told me . . .' he said. Giulio stood some way off with his back to me. He sniffed the air and turned to cast his eyes around the room as though searching for someone. When his eyes met mine he leered with recognition: I was the person he was searching for.

Guilt threatened to get the better of me as I felt the purse of money dig into my side. But there was no way he could know about it; of that I was certain. I took a deep breath and returned his gaze. He looked away, almost bored; I had maintained my mask of innocence. 'A marriage, a respectable marriage,' Bibbiena continued, 'that's what Raphael needs to pull him back from the brink of ruin.'

The brink of ruin? Was that where his love for Margarita was taking him? Perhaps not, but, as I cast my eyes around the room, I wondered if the time for a respectable marriage had come. No one railed against the injustice of what had been announced this evening, apart from me. So, the likes of Giulio had made a few dry remarks, but as I watched Raphael lead the Cardinal's niece back to her seat, his expression kind, his touch gentle, his voice soft, it seemed that even he accepted his betrothal to Maria da Bibbiena.

I forced myself to dwell on the bright side: his union with her would be good for the workshop – it would secure the Cardinal's patronage. Also, I remembered, not two hours hence I too saw Margarita as a danger. My jealousy of her had scorched my soul. No one could feel jealous of Maria, I thought, as I looked upon the frail creature weighted down by the generous drapery of her gown and the ridiculous impracticality of those sleeves.

'It's not her fault,' he said to me in the carriage on the way home. 'She really is a very sweet girl.'

'Yes, she'll make a splendid wife,' I said.

'Yes, she will,' Raphael replied, 'but not mine.'

My fingers tightened around the carriage post.

'What did Margarita say?' he asked me.

It was late, I was shocked, I'd lost the will to pursue my young page, and now, here in the carriage, I had no inclination to dissemble. 'She said yes,' I told him.

Chapter 28

I didn't think it right to follow Raphael on his secret tryst with Margarita but my desire to know what had happened on it wouldn't let me settle. Margarita did not turn up at the workshop the next day and Raphael, no matter how many times I tried to catch his attention, was burrowing himself inside his work.

'Any word from the maestro about what is going on?' I asked Giulio. He raised his hand, signalling for me to wait while he finished delivering some gossip to the group of young apprentices huddled round his bench.

'. . . and so dear boys, the moral of that grisly tale is never accept a pendant from a stranger.' He laughed as he wiped his hands on his apron then turned to me. 'Another of those bodies was pulled out of the river this morning. But this time the body was burned. Like Saint Lorenzo. Now, what was it you asked, Pietro?'

I felt the colour drain from my face as beads of fear dotted my forehead. Another of those killings, where the victim ends up in the Tiber after the poor wretch has been subjected to the same death as the saint hanging down from the pedant around his neck. After all this time. 'You don't have one on, do you?' He laughed, pulling at my shirt.

I rushed off, cries of 'Calm down,' following me out. My breathing was quick and shallow, my heart beat loud, and the blood bubbled through my veins as if it was about to drown me.

I needed to see her: Margarita.

*

She opened her door to me, red rings around her eyes. They pricked at my conscience.

'How are you?' Her tone was solicitous, her reception warm.

I could not answer, because I would stammer. I could not tell her, because I was afraid. She held my hand in hers and rubbed it gently. I was calming down, feeling better. She looked at me as if she understood. Perhaps I could share my secret with her.

'I-I-I've missed you . . . at the workshop.' The effort of starting to open up brought with it tears I had not expected. I wiped them away with my free hand and waited for the emotion to subside.

'It's because of us, isn't it? You are upset because of Raphael. Because of me.'

Ah. She did not understand after all. I pulled my hand away. It quickly stiffened.

I nodded, in response.

'You know, I presume,' she said. 'That he's to marry?'

'Y-y-yes.' It was true: she did not care about me.

'Oh, you dear, sweet friend. Little wonder you're so distressed. I knew something like this would happen,' she said bitterly. I remained silent.

She started to sob softly. My heart went out to her but I dragged it back. She was blind to my suffering and so I would harden myself to hers. I had to, I told myself, drawing on all the arguments I had ever heard Cardinal Bibbiena use against her: *to save the workshop, to protect Raphael's soul, to preserve a society where every citizen knows their proper place.* Yes, she was a baker's daughter from Trastevere; he was artist to the rulers of the world.

It would do no good, no good at all, for me to encourage her to take a path she had no right to be on.

'I think it's a good thing. It will be good for him. Good for the workshop.' she went on. 'The Cardinal . . .' She stopped at the mention of a man I knew she hated. She furrowed her brow and sighed deeply before carrying on. 'That man—' She broke off again. My eyes prompted her to continue. 'He is powerful and can do so much for him, for you all.' That I knew to be true.

'And so w-w-what did you say? About the . . . union?' I asked her.

'I can always tell when you're sad. And angry,' she said. I looked away with embarrassment; we both knew she was referring to my stammer.

'I gave him my blessing,' she said, returning to my question.

Her goodness shone through the veil of tears that shrouded her eyes.

'I shall not be coming to the workshop anymore, Pietro.'

She gave a weak but kind smile.

'I've been very foolish,' she said, looking down, her hair trailing in ringlets like a curtain in front of her bowed head. 'I've never been this foolish before.'

My dislike of her was strong in that moment. I'd tried to tell her my secrets but she had been blind to them, seeing them as something quite different to what they were. But my sight was all too perfect. I saw clearly what her liquid eyes were showing me.

It was love. Though she didn't mention the word, the truth of it radiated from her like a halo. Love. Love had made Margarita foolish. Love had made her weak. But I was delighted to see that, in Margarita's soul, love was also selfless. She would leave Raphael if that's what was best for him, though part of her prayed that it wasn't.

'What do you think I should do?' Her hands wrapped themselves around my fingers. Her questioning eyes searched mine. They pleaded with me to tell her she was wrong to walk away and leave Raphael to marry.

I would not. I breathed in. My words needed to be unbroken.

'You've done the right thing.' I enfolded her in my arms as I said so to hide my face. 'If you love him you have to let him go.'

'I don't know if I can do it.' Her words irritated me with their drama. She'd made up her mind – she should stick to it.

'You can, and you must,' I urged. 'I know you are strong, Margarita. You must be strong . . . for Raphael now.'

'I know,' she said. 'But it hurts Pietro. It hurts so very, very much.'

*

There was no more talk of bodies and pendants around the workshop and nothing more was seen or heard of Margarita there for some time. The Cardinal still paid me for information on her and so I would pop in on her occasionally, to make sure she kept away, and yes, I suppose I'd grown accustomed to her company. The truth was, I would have gone to see her, I think, even if the Cardinal hadn't paid me to. Everybody missed Margarita, even if they were relieved the maestro hadn't thrown himself away on her. (And I'd made sure of the latter.) That's why we could all indulge our fantasies, now that she'd gone, and imagine Margarita and Raphael as the greatest lovers that never were. Sublime yet tragic.

We assumed everything would return to how it had been before. We looked forward to getting our maestro back.

But he seemed more remote than ever.

He no longer joined us when we went to a tavern, and even around the studio he appeared distant. Eye-catching Roman girls he would have once enjoyed flirting with were now invisible to him. His eyes no longer sparkled at the sight of them. It was as if he was elsewhere. We all saw it but we chose not to dwell on it too much. The fact was, he pulled in enough commissions to line the pockets of us all and, while we worried about his well-being, the financial buoyancy of the workshop overrode it all.

The quality of Raphael's work was getting better and better, our studio was afloat. Perhaps the maestro's melancholy was a small price to pay for it.

The truth, we privately acknowledged, was that Margarita had become a dead weight; he'd had to throw her overboard.

Chapter 29

It came as a surprise to everyone when Raphael decided to have a party. He'd been preoccupied ever since Margarita had disappeared from his life and so, when he announced he would like to celebrate, we assumed he was at last over her. It was about time. He was betrothed to Maria da Bibbiena after all, whether he liked it or not. And from the workshop's perspective, there was so much to rejoice about. Things had been going from strength to strength artistically even rendering the jealous jibes of Sebastiano and Michelangelo no more threatening than the rumblings of distant thunder.

And the workshop was awash with commissions, the most important of which was Agostino Chigi's, and we were all excited about that. We had known about it for some time. Chigi had broached the subject back before the carnival dinner. Raphael had been in discussions with him ever since and the time for the studio to start work on it was fast approaching. Then there was Raphael's own villa that he'd recently finished. It was ideally placed for work, we all joked, situated as it was not far from the Vatican. There was, you see, so much to celebrate.

*

I still saw Margarita from time to time. I was happier to see her now and genuinely enjoyed the time I spent in her company now that she no longer had a hold over Raphael. And I happened to visit her the day before the party.

The party. My head was overflowing with joy at the prospect of it – the people I would meet, the food I would eat, the drink I would have, the music I would dance to. But consideration, and perhaps guilt, made me careful not to speak of it to Margarita.

'You are blooming, Margarita!' I was surprised to find her in a state of semi-excitement herself as she looked up at me from behind her sewing. Her eyes told me she was happy, happier than I'd seen her in a long while. As was I. My stammer was under control again and I wasn't as suspicious of people as I used to be.

'I didn't know you were good at embroidery?' I said, admiring the skeins of beautifully dyed thread in a basket on the side. I noticed that it was of the finest quality but thought nothing of it.

'Oh, I'm trying to get better,' she said, placing whatever it was she was working on into the basket. She covered it up with a hessian square.

'But tell me, sweet Pietro, how are you?' She moved towards me and took my hands in hers. She gave them a squeeze then released them.

'Do tell me everything,' she said with a lightness of tone. There was a time when I visited her when she only ever asked after Raphael. Her tone had been heavy then. I was relieved to hear no trace of it in her voice now. Still. I took pains not to speak of the maestro with her, despite fizzing with wonder about his party. I had a heart after all.

But to talk about my life was to talk about his, so dependent was I upon him, and so, even when I tried to avoid talking about him I failed. She didn't seem to mind.

'I'm allowed to do some fresco work at the moment, standing in for Giulio when he gets tired. Raphael was pleased with what I did, I think.'

She nodded as if she knew he was.

'Patrons are delighted with the whole studio and they say the maestro is painting better than ever.'

I thought I shouldn't have said so much. Though it was true. Since Margarita had disappeared out of Raphael's life his work was more confident than ever before. What I'd said was possibly barbed, but I couldn't help myself and Margarita didn't mind. She looked almost proud.

As was I that I'd worked hard to separate the couple. I'd had my doubts that I'd done the right thing but the proof was in his work now. His art was thriving without her, and as I saw the fresh bloom in Margarita's cheeks again, it was clear that she was thriving without him too.

'Well,' she said with a little cough, 'I suppose, now more work is coming in than anyone can handle there will soon be cause for celebration? Surely?'

I hadn't said we couldn't handle it but I took her point.

'What would you wear to a party?' she said with a playful glint in her eye. It did not take much to share what was in my mind's eye.

'If I were fortunate enough to be invited to one, I would wear . . . yellow hose. What do you think?'

'Fetching,' she said, with a smile, or was it a smirk? In my dizzy state about the party I'd lost my usual lucidity and could not tell. Yellow hose – I must have gone through several pairs over the years and they still had not lost their appeal.

She went over to a cupboard and pulled out a finely decorated net, popular with women of fashion.

'Look at this.' She said with obvious delight. There, in her hands she held out the fine hair net sewn with what looked like tiny pearls. It was rather exquisite and it made me think how sophisticated imitation jewels could be these days.

'If I had a party to go to, I would wear this.'

'Do you? Have a party to go to?'

'What do you think?' she asked.

Feeling caught out for being cruel I quickly urged her to adorn her hair with the delicate net. 'Oh, do try it on,' I said.

Her fingers fumbled awkwardly trying to catch her hair up. She tried again, this time with success. She folded her hands and placed them in her lap and she gave the gentlest of smiles. She looked like one of the more recent Raphael Madonnas that I'd seen only last week at the studio.

'Yellow hose?' she said, pulling me back from wondering. 'How splendid! So when is this party going to take place?'

'It's tomorrow.' I blurted it out. I was blind to everything but the party at Raphael's. I wouldn't be so insensitive as to tell her whose party it was but I couldn't stop myself from sharing my excitement with her.

'There must be someone going that has made your heart flutter so,' she said, teasing me.

My beautiful page-boy came to mind. 'Oh no,' I lied.

'Will there be dancing . . . at this party?' she asked.

'Oh, I should think so.'

'Shall we practise?' she asked.

'Yes, let's,' I said, taking her by the hand.

We both fizzed up as I threw her round the room again and again. I must have bubbled over because by the time I had to leave I felt quite flat. I said goodbye to Margarita. I was sad to think she wouldn't be coming to the party too. She would have enjoyed it.

Chapter 30

'Nooooo!' It was Giulio who was the first to tell me that Margarita might be coming to the party. It couldn't be true. *They've not spoken in ages. It's impossible. She would have told me.* And as I stood in the hall of Raphael's new villa, still shocked, there was no sign of her.

A valet opened the door into the function room and ushered me inside. He closed the door behind me leaving me afloat in a sea of people dressed in beautiful attire. There were red robes, velvet waistcoats of every colour, and a wonderful selection of hose on display – plain and patterned. My hand moved instinctively to the yellow hose I'd put on myself especially for the occasion. I did not feel out of place. As for the women, their jewels dazzled in the light making even the richest of brocades seem nothing more than background. I saw no Margarita. Giulio had to be wrong.

There in the corner I saw Clarice. A familiar face, I darted over to her. 'Giulio says she's coming: Margarita.' I didn't believe it yet fear compelled me to say it.

She curled her lips, wound a stray curl round her finger, and glanced over at Raphael standing near the door. She gave me a look of pity before leaning over to me and whispering breathily, 'As long as I know what's boiling in my pot I really don't have the slightest interest in whatever anyone else is heating up in theirs! Yours included.'

With a stroke of my shoulder she left me to stalk her prey. Everything about her became feline as she padded, soft and sly, towards him. She slid her arm through his and purred her intentions into his ear, the occasional predatory laugh sounding out every time Raphael responded. She caught me watching. She beamed back, a glint of triumph in her eyes, defiant and so assured I came to doubt that Raphael had ever had any feelings for Margarita and she for him.

My eyes strayed to the entrance once more. Giulio was most definitely wrong: Margarita was not coming and I should never have mentioned it to Clarice because now she was more determined than ever to take Raphael as her prize tonight. She watched Raphael, the look of a hawk in her eyes, the sound of lust in her throat. She would not waste this opportunity. But the wanton noises she had forced herself to make became less frequent, and her lusty laughs fell away to a tinkle. Clarice's boiling pot was boiling no more. It seemed her meat was looking for a different sauce. And from the newly pained expression on her face she knew it. Though as yet she couldn't work out who in the room had outdone her.

I moved closer.

Steps were heard at the door. Clarice shuffled on the spot and ran her fingers through her hair. 'I hear Michelangelo has been awarded the commission for the Sistine Chapel . . . the ceiling . . .' She tried to engage the maestro in old, old news. So old it had happened years ago. Poor Clarice. No amount of lusty laughing and suggestive talking could conceal her parlous state of mind. Desperation was making her confused.

Raphael made no response. His eyes were fixed on the door handle, the joy in them pushing to get out at the same time the person causing his happiness was pushing to get in. Impatience crackled through the air. Raphael was waiting, excited and

213

nervous, for his love to come in. Clarice sensed it, feared it, yet could do nothing to stop it.

The handle turned. Margarita entered, head held high, eyes ablaze. Clarice tried to extinguish the fire within them with the coldness in her own eyes but she failed to attract her rival's attention no matter how hard she bore into her with her icy gaze. Margarita remained confident, aloof. The only time she faltered was when her eyes met Raphael's. Their intensity was too great, their message too honest. She lowered her lashes quickly in a bid to hide her feelings away.

I had been deceived.

The conversation picked up again.

'They say Agostino Chigi is to marry his young love. Move her out of the nunnery where he's been keeping her and into his bed.' It was Clarice who started it off. She set the tone. Mocking. Dismissive. She glowered at Margarita as she spoke.

'Yes, it's quite decided. The girl is completely in love with him,' Raphael answered, wonder in his voice. 'And it's true that he's also besotted with her.' He now looked at Margarita, hoping that she would turn her head towards him and catch the meaning in his eyes. She did not; instead she grinned at me in a sisterly fashion. I concealed my disdain and I returned to her my most brotherly nod.

'Such an unusual thing, a marriage based on love. Whatever happened to marrying for rank, money, power?' Clarice raised her eyebrows. This time she had Margarita's attention. She gave her a knowing look.

'That Chigi's the most powerful banker in Rome and bankrolls the Pope has got nothing to do with it,' Clarice said, her tone innocent, her words malign. 'No nun's loveless marriage for her, feigning faith to keep a roof over her head.' Her eyes narrowed in devilish delight. 'Love,' she sighed, letting the sound of the word hang in the air. Our small group fell silent. Clarice sniffed. 'So overrated.' She sniffed again. 'When I was young I was in love with my rabbit. Fluffy little thing. All bright-eyed. Almost as delicious as you, Margarita.' She smirked. 'Particularly when it was presented to me on a plate after having been cooked over a fire for several hours.' Clarice licked her fingers and pretended to throw bones over her shoulder. She walked away.

As I looked at Margarita's face, it seemed that Clarice's arrow had hit its target. The fight had gone out of it. The girl had feelings for Raphael, but they were dangerous and Clarice's words would remind her of the fact. But if Clarice had hoped to dampen Raphael's desire she had failed miserably. Margarita, in her sadness, now radiated a most spiritual beauty that even I found unsettling. I couldn't bear to look at her. Raphael couldn't bear not to.

'Come,' he said as he took her by the hand and led her out of the room.

They were gone for some time. I was anxious. Clarice was wild. 'Go and find them. Bring them back.' Her voice was furious and a little loud.

'But I don't know where they've gone . . . or what I'll say.' I made a point of whispering so as not to be overheard.

'Are you really as green as you seem?' She hissed at me.

'B-b-b-but I-I-I-I . . .' I did not know what to say to Clarice, and even if I had done my tongue was not going to let me utter another word. My heart was beating fast. My mind was fragmenting. I looked round the room praying no one was watching us.

'Now you can't tell me you want them to get together any more than I do.' She singed my cheeks with the flames that now raged in her eyes.

'Stop your embarrassment,' she ordered, exasperation creeping into her voice. 'I'm the only one to have noticed your fluttering heart and twitchy cock . . . Oh, he doesn't know. I won't tell. But do something to stop all this. Raphael's mine,' she said. She'd seen his betrothed, the fragile Maria. She was no threat. Loveless, sexless Maria would be wife in name alone. No, Clarice saw that it was Margarita who was her true rival for Raphael's affections, not the woman he was going to marry. 'And I'm not going to let some shiny-eyed pet take him away. Now go!'

I swayed while the ground beneath my feet trembled. My life felt as though it had been sucked out of me. With one strong breath I dragged it back in and ran out of the room, looking up and down the corridor, knocking on doors either side. While I was at one end, a door opened at the other. Raphael and Margarita stepped out, so deep in conversation that they didn't notice me hovering in an ill-lit doorway. They went back into the party. I waited a few moments before I went back in too. My eyes darted around the room. Clarice caught me with hers. If eyes could yell and scream then that's what hers were doing. They also reminded me that she knew about me. Desperation was making her dangerous. I stood near Raphael and Margarita as instructed.

'If you love me,' Margarita whispered, 'leave me in peace. You must set me free.'

'But how can I when you are my whole life? And I know that I am yours. To be apart, how can that give either of us any peace?'

Talk of love and Chigi's wedding had brought things to a head between the two of them and I wondered what they could have talked of in private that had brought such passionate words to their lips. As I listened I was at once moved and jealous, and though the thought that I had been betrayed still stuck in my craw, I willed them on. Their words were glorious. But I also recognised the seeds of destruction within them if scattered in the right direction. My eyes flickered towards Clarice. She nodded at me, sly and knowing. I carried on listening.

'To let you leave me would only bring heartache and despair. You are my inspiration. Just imagine to what heights my art could soar if we were together.'

Margarita smiled.

'Say you don't love me and I will release you,' he said.

She said nothing.

'There. You love me. And you know that to be together would bring us both such great joy.'

'Well hello, Pietro! And what are you up to?' A bare arm had wound itself around me and hot breath was bombarding the area around my ear most aggressively. Fear blazed within me. It was Clarice. She'd got fed up of waiting.

Margarita jumped and turned around.

'Oh, Pietro!' She saw me as one of the few true friends she had in this new world she'd found herself in. 'How long have you been there?'

Clarice placed her hand on Raphael's shoulder and slid her body suggestively between us. She didn't wait for me to answer Margarita, instead saying, 'Why Raphael and the . . . lovely Margarita. You two are quite the talking point in the room, you know. And you, Margarita dear, look simply radiant. But a word of advice . . .' And with that she put her mouth up close to the girl's ear. 'Make sure you don't let his key slip out of your lock.'

*

I retreated for a while, passing on the baton to Clarice who was more than capable I knew of turning fine wine into vinegar with the acid bite of her tongue. But still I watched. Love. I'd heard it. Sensed it as it crackled between Raphael and Margarita and it seemed so much purer than I'd imagined. And its purity made it sting all the more.

'Lost in your thoughts?' Giulio came up to me. 'Better off going for him,' he said, pinching my thigh and nodding in the direction of a pretty-faced young page who I'd seen coming out of a side door up at the Vatican one morning while I was going in. My body prickled in self-defence and my chest swelled to push Giulio's slight away. But I made a mental note of the boy all the same.

'I'm off. Here comes Clarice with a face like thunder. You'd better take cover if you don't want a torrent of abuse to rain down upon you.' And with that he was off. 'But at least you'll know why she's raging,' he called back.

*

It must have been about three o'clock in the morning when I slid out of her bed. I flinched as I remembered her naked and straddling me but a few hours before. I pictured her, hair piled high above her head as she'd tried to ride me. She'd peeked a look at me through half-closed eyes before she'd given up and rolled off.

I shuddered.

Clarice hadn't seemed to care. Either because she'd drunk too much wine or because neither her heart nor my body was in it. I'd tried to show willing with my hands to save hers the effort but she'd fallen asleep. With a little luck she would never remember that I'd failed.

'Pietro?' She called my name as I was leaving and for a moment I feared that she might call me back to try again. Instead she gave a laugh, waved me on my way, and went back to sleep.

Last night had not been a love match for her either. Clarice had seen Margarita wanting to confide in me but I was already marked out as hers. She'd come up and coiled her arms around me, resting her chin on my shoulder. Margarita had taken Raphael. Clarice wasn't going to let her take me. And so, when she dragged me away as her trophy, to try to make Raphael jealous, to irritate Margarita, I let her do it.

Giulio was watching me, surprised. I was surprised too. But here was my chance to kill off the rumours about me. Clarice had called me out on it and I had to put her off the scent. And Giulio was a gossip. That he'd seen me leaving with one of the most popular prostitutes in Rome would be all around the city by next morning. Reputation was all, and who knew when I'd be needing it?

Chapter 31

I held my head increasingly high with every knowing look and congratulatory back slap that I received from the boys who had been at Raphael's party. The party itself may have been a way for the maestro to bring Margarita back into the fold, but it was also a chance for me to improve my standing in the workshop. I now numbered among the men who loved women. And that was a far safer group to be part of.

My new sense of belonging brought with it a feeling of well-being and confidence. That it was grounded in a lie did not matter. Appearance was all. It protected me more than any smooth-tongued man of law could ever do. And this security made me happy for a while. Even the shock of discovering that Raphael and Margarita had been meeting up in secret was a truth I could handle.

The already good times we'd been enjoying became even better. For us all.

We had Margarita to thank for that, now a familiar presence around the workshop. But I could not stop myself from maligning her whenever the opportunity arose as pockets of jealousy sprang up like unwanted weeds within my breast.

I continued to question her influence on the maestro. When Raphael encouraged us to 'Go have a drink, you deserve it!' but wouldn't join us, I would say under my breath, 'He's seeing her'; when he painted her I would whisper, 'She's enslaved him'; when he smiled at her I would tut, 'Passion for her is consuming his soul.' Yes, the words continued to slither from my lips, usually when Giulio and Giovanni were away working on a commission.

The truth of it was that even if Raphael's passion for Margarita was consuming his soul it did not diminish his ability to focus on the ever-increasing demands placed on him by those wishing to have some piece signed by him. And there were an ever-growing number of people clamouring for his work and that was because it was reaching even greater heights of perfection. Whatever feelings Margarita aroused within his heart they inspired him to produce pieces more real than reality. His art had more truth and depth than that produced by any other artist alive or dead. And that translated into fame and wealth for us all.

These were our halcyon days.

During those heady times, Giulio would drink the nights away researching the various sexual positions as practised by the most expensive prostitutes, I would let my eyes study the male anatomy beneath well-cut hose, while Raphael would seek to produce work more sublime than ever before.

Months stretched to years. Friendships were forged, skills developed, art produced. It was a time of great flowering in the garden that was Raphael's studio where abundance and beauty prospered and humanity flourished. The only spot on an otherwise blemish-free existence was Margarita. Her presence marred the paradisiacal landscape for me – although, without her such a world would not have been possible. I knew it but I hated that it was so.

The blooms got bigger, the grass grew higher, and there I hid, amid the rich undergrowth, watching and waiting like a sly-eyed serpent, hoping for a chance to remove her. On the rare occasion Raphael struggled with a commission I would shout about how happy I was to see the maestro spending so much time with his love. When Giulio joked with Margarita and the two of them looked to be getting close I would slither up to him when she'd gone and say something wanton in his ear about her. I knew his weaknesses, and I'd seen him appraising her physical assets often enough to know I could play on them. I did everything I could to get Margarita cast out of Eden, not caring that to get what I wanted would mean expulsion for us all.

But I was not alone in engineering the downfall. Raphael the artist had a hand to play in bringing down Raphael the man. The perfecting of his talent was to prove his curse. Condemned, like Sisyphus damned for all eternity to roll the rock up the hill, Raphael worked and worked, but it was never enough. The more he did the more he had to do. And when he could not produce enough the world would come to turn on him.

But before that happened most people would turn on her: Margarita.

Margarita's reputation had survived longer than that of most common girls around the studio. That was because she'd done nothing to sully it. I would cast aspersions, as you know, and encourage Giulio's fantasies, but there was the small problem of a lack of proof. Still, there was something between them, the maestro and his baker's daughter. We all knew it. But no one seemed greatly bothered by it, not even Cardinal Bibbiena.

'That baker's daughter will be ruined soon enough,' he liked to tell me whenever I went to report to him, 'when Raphael marries my niece.' But when would that be? No date for the wedding had been set, and every time a meeting was suggested to finalise plans Raphael would find a reason to postpone it. Little pressure came from the Cardinal. There were rumours she had health problems that the family were trying to resolve, but if the rumours were true the problems had not been resolved yet. It had been a while, which seemed to suit the maestro very well. Was I the only person who suspected that he had no intention of getting married to Maria da Bibbiena at all?

I had had enough. I was bored with the waiting. Yes, there was something between the maestro and his baker's daughter and I vowed to myself that I would do something about it. Gossip, to damage Margarita, was my first line of attack. The apprentices let my latest slurs sink to the bottom of their memories without a trace. The women who frequented the workshop rather liked them and kept them alive. It was to them I turned next for support in bringing Margarita down.

Ever since my sexual encounter with Clarice, I had given her a wide berth. Thankfully I'd managed to navigate around her reasonably successfully so far. She wasn't at the workshop as often as she used to be. And whenever I had to come face to face with her, she seemed not to want to bring up what had happened between us any more than I did, probably because, consummate professional that she was, she accepted it had been a failure on both our parts. But all that was in the past. I was feeling that I could approach her now with impunity. And besides, her tongue was useful.

Giulio liked to sketch Clarice fairly regularly, and so, one day, not long after she'd arrived, I went up behind her and whispered in her ear. I started with something innocent. 'I like her dress,' I said, looking at Margarita at the far side of the studio. Innocent, as I said.

Clarice sneered. She passed my comment round the rest of the girls. They joined forces, went on the attack. They commenced with a thorough dismantling of her appearance. She dressed 'like a plebeian', wore 'rough cotton dresses', and she powdered herself 'liberally in flour every day'.

Then came the assault on her virtue, something I hadn't expected. This proved to be something they were particularly jealous of, not least because it was a quality they had none of themselves. Margarita '*seemed* virtuous but *women like that* were often the worst'; 'She'll show her true colours soon enough'; 'I've heard she used to be Cardinal Bibbiena's whore.'

'Really?' Salacious gossip. Even I was interested. While I

slithered around on my stomach, head nearer the earth than the sky, I soaked it up. And the girls? They rubbed their hands and gathered together more sticks and stones ready to throw at Margarita at the first whiff of social disgrace.

They expected it to come when Raphael tired of what they liked to call her 'impenetrability', otherwise known as *virtue*. Raphael's interest in her was after all, everyone agreed, a momentary *passion*, and if it wasn't satisfied soon then he would quickly move on. Sometimes she was a whore. At others she was a virgin. But most of all she was a tease. And as a baker's daughter she had no right to be one. 'Oh, how she will fall when he tires of her!' And the women in the workshop couldn't wait.

*

Margarita's descent was all of her own making. That was the problem with having a strong moral sense when those around her were corrupt. She was right. Yet the might of those she dared to oppose would crush her because of it.

Giulio and Giovanni had gone to finish Cardinal Bibbiena's *stufetta* and so it was expected they would be gone for the rest of the day. The rest of the workshop was full of activity with apprentices busy on every part of production. For every delivery dispatched, ten new commissions came in. It was busy. It was mad.

'I am swimming in paint and straining under the weight of canvases and wooden panels.' I had a small role to play yet even I was feeling overwhelmed.

'It's important to say yes to everything,' the maestro picked up on my remark, dealing with it promptly. 'It means we all practise; it means we all improve. Isn't that what Cennini says?' Chastened, I settled to my tasks, though not without first noting the dark shadows under Raphael's eyes again. His cheeks, that I'd thought firm and fresh, looked sunken.

'Shall I bring over today's requests?' Margarita had just come

223

in with bread, meat, fruits and wine for us to take to a Roman ruin. As a baker's daughter she did have her uses. I saw that there was nothing sunken about her cheeks. I would say as much to the other apprentices later in the hope that they, like I, would take this as proof that she was sucking the lifeblood from our poor maestro. Although I doubted that they would. Still, I intended to say it.

She gave me a peck on the cheek.

'This one looks grand!' she said, picking a beautifully written missive from the tumbling pile.

Raphael prised it open with a knife.

The shadows underneath his eyes spread across his face.

'What is it?' Margarita asked him, her voice dropping from light to concerned.

'It's from the Ambassador of Ferrara.'

'And?'

'He is writing on behalf of Alfonso d'Este, Duke of Ferrara, who would like me to paint the following for him.' Raphael described a small work, to depict the Triumph of Bacchus, that in itself was not beyond him. Indeed, there were now very many accomplished assistants in the workshop to whom he could entrust the task. His eyes stared at my face without seeing me. He let his arm drop to his side. He would ask no one: there was something in the letter that bothered him.

He started to read again.

'The ambassador writes that the Duke wants it completed and delivered to him by the end of the month. He cordially reminds me that this is the second time of asking and that a man of the Duke's nobility does not expect to have his patience tested so. He needs it in time to display at a dinner he is hosting.'

There was something little in Raphael's voice. He'd received many requests from ambassadors, counts, cardinals, and dukes but this one was different. Most celebrated his talent, lauded his art. He'd grown accustomed to being treated with respect, as a free-minded artist. But with a 'you will', 'you must,' 'my master commands', 'as befits his nobility and rank', there was a condescension in and between the lines that Raphael could not overlook and as he read the letter out loud we all heard it.

'You are working far too hard,' Margarita said to him, smoothing his brow with a finger. The touch was tender. Raphael breathed in and closed his eyes for a moment.

'I must take the *garzoni* out to the Palace of Titus soon.' It was true. Several times a week he went out now with his devoted group in order to study classical art and architecture – to sketch columns and pediments, assess statues and other early Roman pieces. Whether to preserve and protect the artefacts of ancient Rome or break them down and use in present day building was Raphael's decision, and one he took very seriously. Raphael was committed to the task, though it was a dirty one. And the Palace of Titus was the most rewardingly dirty of them all. The Palace had been discovered by chance some years ago with the renovation of the Basilica di San Pietro in Vincoli nearby.

I had only been down to study the remains once, on the request of Giovanni. Though I remembered the freshness of the colours and the excellence of the designs of the frescoes and stucco work I also recalled the pulleys and wooden planks I had to manoeuvre in order to reach down into the rooms as well as the tunnels we had to crawl along to get from one to the other. It was my job to hold a torch to light the way, then, when in the main underground room, to ensure the flickering flames revealed the splendour of the images we were there to study.

But the toads, frogs, barn owls, civet cats, and bats I met while in the bowels of the earth disturbed me. I could not have been more relieved than when we broke back out into the world above. From dark, dank, cold space to dazzling, warm light. It was as though I was reborn. It took me many days to remove the grime from my clothes and body after that, and many weeks to shift the chill that had gone into my bones while sitting sketching the decorated ceiling in that room we now call the Golden Vault. Raphael had announced how beyond imagination the art was: 'The Ancients have so much to teach us. Their knowledge about art – superior in every way to what we know now. We must copy, copy and copy some more. That's how we learn. That's how we improve. That's how we make it our own.'

Giovanni was also entranced by it going so far as to attempt to replicate the stucco work he'd seen as soon as he returned to the workshop. Buried alive, that's what I felt when I was down there. Apprentices clamoured to accompany them both to study and learn from this art *all'antica*. I was only too happy to stand aside for them to be bearers of the torchlight.

Raphael waved the ambassador's letter around then let it float to the floor. I picked it up and put it back on the pile.

'You can say no,' Margarita said in a low voice. 'You know you deserve to be treated with more respect than this.'

I said nothing.

'You are an artist. You give your soul. I see it every day. That's not something to be bought.'

I admired Margarita's words, applauded her insight.

'I have no interest in the money,' Raphael agreed. 'However, I have never turned down a commission and am not prepared to do so now.' He took the letter and placed it at the bottom of the pile. 'But he will have to wait his turn.' He opened his order book and put a line through an entry. Margarita gave a nod of approval. She would get him into trouble.

'*Garzoni*,' the maestro shouted, 'it's time to discover the wonders of Ancient Rome!'

*

The apprentices were busier than usual and when a person has more to do with his hands and his mind he has less to do with his tongue. The workshop was duly silent, the only sounds coming

226

from artists' tools and materials as they cut, mixed, scraped, painted, or stirred. I was adding white to the wings of a cherub, my strokes light and feathery. I was totally absorbed in the task.

'Pietro!' It was Cardinal Bibbiena. At his bark I jumped to attention.

'Raphael?' He thrust his hand out. I bowed, kissed, stood back up, all in a heartbeat.

'He's not here, my lord.'

'I can see that for myself.'

He lowered his chin, kept his eyes on me. His gaze was disconcerting, as it was meant to be. His eyes moved from one side of the studio to another, taking in religious panels, classical friezes, mythological subjects, half-finished portraits.

'Giovanni da Udine?' he asked, pointing to an area of the workshop that the artist had now made his own. He'd succeeded in recreating the stucco formula based on what he'd observed at the Palace of Titus, and the initial results were now visible in several completed commissions around Rome. Barrels of white travertine lime and powdered white marble were lined up ready to meet the flurry of interest that had followed.

'Yes, Cardinal.'

He nodded, serious, approving, allowing his eye one last look at familiar fragments of ancient statues, bosses and pediments and bases of columns, before sighing and coming to the real point of his unannounced visit.

'Come now, boy. It is truly impressive to see the work of Giovanni and Raphael's apprentices. But what of your maestro himself? Show me, at least, now that I've come all this way, what our esteemed Raphael has been working on of late.'

I escorted the Cardinal through the workshop and past the apprentices so deep in work they barely noticed us. I explained their pieces as we went.

'Very good. Excellent. Yes, all very good . . . but what of *Raphael*'s work?'

This was Raphael's workshop. This was Raphael's work. 'He has some hand in everything, my lord,' I said.

'I know! I know all that! Don't fool around with me, boy. You know me well enough not to. I say again. What is he working on at present? Which commissions are taking up most of his time?'

I sensed pencils and brushes freeze for a moment, waiting to hear my response.

We were approaching the part of the workshop where Raphael was currently working. I picked up my pace. The Cardinal would be able to see for himself soon enough.

There. Light from the windows streamed in, revealing to the Cardinal the answer to his question.

There was a Madonna on an easel. But the sun was behind it making it difficult to see. Instead the Cardinal's eyes were guided to the maestro's workbench where he saw, side by side, sketches of frescoes from the Palace of Titus and designs intended for the Cardinal's *loggetta*. Giovanni and Giulio were still working on the *stufetta* but it was nearing completion, and now the Cardinal was pushing for our workshop to start work on the adjacent room. He smiled, clearly pleased to see that it was a priority. The similarity between the classical frescoes and those Raphael intended for the *loggetta* was striking.

Cardinal Bibbiena laughed. But then he looked up and stopped. There, suspended on the wall, a little to the right, was *La Donna Velata*, Raphael's answer to his rival Sebastiano. I thought he'd seen it before but the alarm that swept across his face at the sight of it told me that he hadn't.

He moved around. He went to look at Raphael's latest Madonna, almost finished. Squinting, he positioned the easel to take the painting from shadow to light. But if it was peace he was searching for in the face of the Blessed Virgin he failed to find it there. His eyes flickered back and forth between *La Donna Velata* and this new work. He had thought Raphael considered Margarita as a girl to service his needs, nothing more. She was

228

good-looking, shapely, young. It was understandable that the artist should want to paint her. But horror now distorted his face as he recognised something else in the images before him, a truth that I had discovered long ago. These paintings captured beauty, but, far more unsettling for the Cardinal, they expressed love. And that would never do. He said nothing but he winced as though the mother of God had squeezed the juice of a lemon into his eyes.

'Where are these from?' the Cardinal asked, his finger stabbing at another set of drawings, neatly piled up, on the left of the maestro's workbench.

'Oh. They're not copies. They're ideas. For *Signore* Chigi.'

He picked several up and studied them one by one. Their subject matter was classical, Ovid's Metamorphoses the inspiration. He made approving noises. His eyes fell on the drawing of a woman's face. It was of the sea nymph, Galatea. Raphael had used several women as inspiration for this beautiful creature, but it shared a spiritual beauty with the two paintings of Margarita.

'And she is?' he asked, his voice accusing, his eyes now crawling all over my features for an answer.

'M-m-m-m-m-m-m-m-many girls,' I said at last.

The Cardinal slammed his hand down on the table. His irritation waiting for me to respond had replaced his need to know about artist and model. There was something in the way he turned his back most deliberately on the two paintings of Margarita that reminded me of the way she'd turned her back on him many years ago. She'd done it to signal that she regarded him as nothing, and now, here he was, mirroring her behaviour to say the same thing about her. He said no more about the paintings; for him they no longer existed.

'I was forgetting the purpose of my visit. Now,' he said, pressing the tips of his fingers together. 'Has Raphael started on the Duke of Ferrara's commission yet?'

'I don't know, sir.'

'The Duke has asked him to complete a commission. Small by all accounts. The Triumph of Bacchus, I believe. Which he has yet to see. It does not do, Pietro, not at all, to keep a nobleman waiting. Why has your maestro not answered his request? It's a question of good manners. Civic pride. The artist represents Rome, for heaven's sake!'

I hurried over to where the order books were kept and opened the most recent. My eyes went straight to the entry Raphael had put a line through earlier on. I looked over the top of the book, my eyes apologetic.

'F-f-f-forgive me, C-C-C-Cardinal, there's no record of having received an order from the D-D-D-Duke of F-F-F-F-Ferrara here.'

Bibbiena rolled his eyes. 'Don't question me, boy. You know me better than that. What am I paying you for?'

I wanted to remind him that he hadn't paid me anything for some months but, seeing the annoyance already on his face, thought better of it. He pushed past me. A smell of lavender and goose fat surrounded him. What was that? Perfume? Pomade? But before my mind could come up with an answer, my attention was dragged towards the Cardinal who had picked up that morning's requests for work as if they belonged to him and was now riffling through them with furious determination.

'Here!' he said, pointing to a request for the Triumph of Bacchus with a heavily jointed finger. 'It was the last one in the pile.'

'But there is n-n-no mention of the Duke's n-n-name on . . .'

'That's because it's been requested by his ambassador on the Duke's behalf. You idiot!' He glowered at me. 'The Duke is a man of the noblest birth, the best breeding. You don't expect a man of his birth to soil his hands in the business of buying commodities?' The hot air of frustrated superiority blew from the Cardinal's nostrils. I dared not answer. Pearls of sweat appeared across his forehead. I put my head down and waited for the blast. But it

230

did not come. Instead he turned around to face *La Donna Velata* and snorted out hot air once more.

'When the Duke asks for something, he gets it. You tell Raphael that. Or he'll be sorry.'

*

'*For maestro Raphael.*'

When a message arrived from the Vatican some days later Margarita was laughing at something Giulio had said while Raphael was walking round the workshop. The maestro continued to show signs of fatigue but surrounding himself with his apprentices never failed to bring a smile of deep satisfaction to his face. He tended them as a gardener would fresh young buds full of promise.

'It's for you, sir.'

Raphael looked up at the messenger and nodded. He rotated his wrists a little. A smile shone through a yawn. He was confident he knew what it would be.

'It will be another commission. After hearing about our designs for Bibbiena's *loggetta* I've heard that the Pope would like the workshop to decorate the loggia. Although I didn't expect it so soon. Open it, Pietro. Read it out. Perhaps you can work on this one.'

I opened it. Read it out loud. Then stopped. My eyes raced ahead. It wasn't a commission. This was a summons to a meeting to discuss Raphael's future nuptials with Maria da Bibbiena, the Cardinal's niece. At last. I handed it to Raphael.

'What is it?' Margarita ran over, still laughing at whatever it was that Giulio had said. She came up behind Raphael, stood on her tiptoes, and placed her chin on his shoulder. She looked at the letter. She stopped laughing. I'd had no idea she could read.

Chapter 32

'I don't want to go.' Margarita would not allow herself to be compromised. She would not give herself up to the pleasures of the flesh, and that was why she refused to accompany Raphael to a dinner held by Pope Leo X. 'I've heard about what happens at such dinners,' she said.

'That people eat fine food? Drink excellent wine? Listen to accomplished musicians? Watch entertaining diversions? Dance?'

'You know that's not what I mean.'

Francesca Ordeaschi had been instrumental in securing an invitation for Margarita to the Pope's dinner. The pretty young girl plucked from obscurity and the dank, dark alleyways of Venice had grown into one of the most powerful women in Rome. I for one would never have believed it possible. But now she could ask for favours, pull strings, and help those who had always been kind to her. Chigi still adored her. Pope Leo, like Pope Julius before him, adored Chigi's money. *Could Margarita Luti be invited to the dinner?* Why, of course she could.

Margarita had been surprised to receive the invitation. Raphael had been delighted. I don't think he knew where his relationship with Margarita was going but the atmosphere in Rome was more open than it had ever been to mixed couples and this was a sign that the woman he spent more time with than any other was accepted and for the moment he was happy with that. I was not. Yet I had faith in Margarita to do the wrong thing. She was a woman of her word. She said she would not accompany him to the dinner and I thanked God for that. But, to make sure, I whispered bawdy tales aplenty in her ear to keep the fires of her moral indignation burning.

The dinner was in honour of a group of clerics from northern Europe. Raphael had met Erasmus of Rotterdam when the Dutchman had visited Rome and had found him a deep thinker. He fully expected this latest band of religious scholars to offer just as much food for thought. He hoped this would win Margarita round.

'I know what goes on,' she said.

'So tell me?'

As I put together the drawings the maestro had finished for Chigi and rolled them up carefully I too waited to hear her repeat the scurrilous tales I'd told her.

'I've heard things. Scandalous things. But I can't say,' she said in a whisper.

'What do you mean, you can't say?'

'I just can't,' she said, instead voicing other objections, easier to express. 'It would be like throwing myself to the wolves and I know better than to do that. I know what they would say of me, those self-appointed arbiters of morality with an interest in promoting their own.'

The way cardinals appointed their nephews to seats of high office around the city was common knowledge and it was a practice I knew Margarita very much despised because of its unfairness. She'd told me often enough. There was now even a word for it – *nepotismo*. But this was no general complaint; this was a thinly veiled attack on Cardinal Bibbiena. He would be there, she knew it, plotting the union between his niece and Raphael while conspiring against Margarita herself. But even though this irked her, as it did Raphael, Cardinal Bibbiena's presence was not the stumbling block to her attendance at the papal dinner. Raphael grew suddenly serious. A look passed between them as if this was something far too deep to be discussed so lightly and so publicly. It would be saved for later.

Raphael glanced at me as he lifted the tone. 'Do tell me what these scandalous things are that you've heard. Both Pietro and I would love to hear about them.'

As if newly aware of my presence Margarita fell back into a superficial nervousness.

'I've heard things . . .' she said, glancing at me, 'that there are competitions, for men . . . for the number of times they, they, they . . . *break their lances.*'

The maestro bent double with laughter at the thought of what she meant. Margarita looked at me again. I smiled encouragement.

'Then that there are prostitutes who pick grapes up with . . . oh, I can't even say that. But it's shocking. All the people know it happens. You've heard this, Pietro, haven't you? Stand up for me here.' Margarita had taken on an indignant tone. I rolled up the drawings I had in my hand and looked at the floor, hoping she wasn't going to give me away.

'That was when the Pope was a Borgia,' Raphael explained, when he'd finished laughing. 'This one is a Medici. Far more civilised.' He winked at me. I felt the warmth in his eyes and I opened up immediately, like a flower before the sun.

I nodded. Margarita saw me.

'So will you come?' he asked her again.

'Yes,' was the reply.

*

Pope Leo X, unlike Pope Julius before him, had no qualms about being seen to dip deep into the coffers of the Church. God had granted him the Papacy and he intended to enjoy it to the full. The dinner to welcome the northern Europeans was, accordingly, a lavish affair. Colourful and ostentatious. Though there were none of the orgiastic scenes Margarita had feared, at least, none that were on public display. More's the pity because if there had been temptation of that sort it might have been enough to seduce the stone-hearted, pale-faced men in their dull-coloured frocks. Instead the excess was limited to food and wine, which they seemed to enjoy well enough at the time, as well as to matters of dress and ornament which, from the looks on their faces, they did not.

Cardinal Bibbiena had been present, and he smelt of that same mix of fat and lavender that I remembered from before. I noted earlier that Pope Leo had a similar smell. Strange.

I was not a guest. I was again one of the apprentices on duty to record the occasion. The usual lustre of such events was lacking, I noted, as I observed the assembled throng, due largely to the cold sensibilities of the guests from abroad. Nevertheless, my beautiful page-boy was here and did much to brighten the mood for me. The northern clerics in their dry, clipped accents discussed points of theology, the role of art in the glorification of God and became uncharacteristically animated about, of all things, the place of classical mythology in a Christian context. In Rome we saw classical and Christian as complementary, the one enriching the visual vocabulary of the other. How could we not as both were all around?

However, as I saw the small, pebble eyes of the northern clerics harden, I realised that they did not. I felt their iciness draw down around my heart and with it I feared the frost that threatened this artistic flowering of ours.

One of the Cardinal's assistants had picked up a fig, turned it round in distaste in his hands before discarding it and picking up a peach. His face relaxed at the sight and smell of the familiar fruit, running his fingers over its soft skin. He watched boys come back and forth to serve at the table, a strange yet distracted expression on his face. I watched him for a few moments. He seemed familiar. I tried to place him.

'Here, boy!' Bibbiena beckoned me over, hardly stopping his conversation with one of the pebble-eyed ones. 'Draw me,' he commanded. I drew him, though I had one eye on my page-boy who I was sure had one eye on me.

'Yes, he is engaged to be married to my niece, Maria.' He was talking about Raphael.

'Is that not your niece?' I heard the northern priest ask, his voice nodding approval. I looked over to see Margarita talking with Raphael, their heads touching, eyes loving.

'No. She's his whore.'

I shivered. Winter, I thought, as I caught the cleric's glacial stare, was most definitely on its way, and they were the ones who had brought the start of it. It promised to be harsh and cruel. My page-boy passed in front of the table. My eyes raced quickly over his ankles, calves, thighs, stopping eagerly on his buttocks. They were strong, muscular, the cheeks pulled in, taut, and tight at the sides. My heart beat with excitement at the sight of him.

One of the Cardinal's men was watching me, I was sure of it, the one I'd seen enjoying the peach, but I was too distracted to care. I only had eyes for this perfect youth. Giulio had nudged me earlier on and said he'd seen the boy with *Il Sodoma*. That did not put me off. In fact, he did remind me of one of that artist's figures.

Before I knew it the page-boy was standing at my side. 'Would you like me to fill your glass, *Signore*?' I could hear the blood rush in my ears, feel my skin become hot. Then came the throbbing.

His hand brushed mine. My loins were on fire.

My page-boy went to leave the room. He stopped at the door. Looked straight at me. Then was gone. I quickly finished my pencil sketch of the Cardinal and followed him out, unable to speak. It wasn't winter yet.

I remember Margarita calling out after me, 'Are you all right?' I think I staggered, but managed to nod my head in answer.

'Is he all right?' I heard her ask Giulio. But after that the blood kept pumping, making me too distracted to care what he said, what she thought.

Something was about to happen. My body was sure of it. I listened to my chest thumping, beating like a drum as I marched my way to war. There was no turning back now. Nothing could stop what had been started. I turned the corner, came face to face with my page-boy. He took my face into his hands, pulled it to him roughly. With his teeth he bit into my lips, with his hand he pushed open a door. I fell in behind him, as if chained.

In an instant I was stretched out on a couch, shirt open, hose down, neck back, eyes closed. My hands pushed hard on a head full of silken curls between my legs. I asked for more . . . more . . . more . . . And as I got it, so my soul threw itself against the fortress of my body, fluttering, flailing, flinging itself against its walls until finally breaching its earthbound defences and flying away on the wings of ecstasy. This was not how it had been with Clarice.

I don't know how long Margarita had been in the room. But when the page-boy and I were done I raised my head and saw the back of her head as she left.

Outside the door a man's voice spoke to her sharply. He wanted to come into the room. She wouldn't let him. 'I am assistant to Cardinal Bibbiena,' he said. My page-boy clutched a pendant that I had not noticed him wearing before. It was of Saint Sebastiano. A pendant. I froze at the sight of it.

Margarita slammed the door shut. I heard a scuffle.

'Move aside, wench. I have no interest in you.' My beautiful youth was shaking. I prayed that Margarita would not give us up.

'Unhand me, good sir,' she shouted. 'Is there anyone there?' she called down the corridor. 'I think the Cardinal's assistant here is in need of some assistance himself! Help! Guards, help us.' No guards came but Margarita had done enough.

Heavy feet pounded one way. Light footsteps tripped off in the other.

'If he finds me, here, with you . . .' I placed a finger on my frightened boy's lips. 'He's gone,' I said, 'but we must hurry back in case he should return.'

'The name's Fabio.' *Poor Fabio*, I thought as I looked at his pendant.

'He gave that to you?' I asked.

'I didn't want it,' Fabio said, a tremor in his voice. 'He forced it on me. Take it, please!'

Something about what he said, even the way he said it, seemed familiar. I'd heard those very words before, though I couldn't think where. As I plumbed the depths of my memory I searched for the answer, and there, emerging from the years, I could make out a face. Yes, I had heard those words before. And they were Luca's. Luca. Feelings of regret-tinged longing enveloped me.

'Please,' Fabio said, his hand outstretched, bringing me back to the present.

I did not take Luca's pendant when I had the chance. How different life might have been if I had. Well, I was determined I would not be making the same mistake again.

I seized Fabio's pendant and thrust it into a pocket for fear of it branding my skin. It was I who trembled now, but I knew I'd done the right thing. Fabio left first. I followed. When I entered the room the eyes of the Cardinal's assistant were raging and cruel. I don't know why I'd not noticed them before. They fixed themselves upon Fabio, now clearing the tables. The poor boy had the look of a hunted animal about him. I watched the face of the man tracking him. Those eyes, I'd seen them before; I was sure of it. Luca's face came back to me again. It was as if my memory was trying to tell me something. But what?

Then I had it! Luca! I'd seen those eyes when I rescued Luca. It was him. The Cardinal's assistant. He was the one who'd placed the pendant of St Stefano around Luca's neck that night. He was the one I'd frightened off. He was a dangerous man. More dangerous than I'd imagined. I looked away, but it was too late. I had already been caught. I felt the pendant scorching the insides of my pocket. I remembered Luca. And the other boys who'd been dragged out of the Tiber. All like me. All dead. All wearing similar pendants to the one in my possession. The Cardinal's assistant was a killer. And I was a marked man.

Chapter 33

The wedding that I believed would never happen all those years ago was about to take place. Pope Julius had been fond of Chigi and Francesca, while Pope Leo adored them. Indeed, it was *il Papa* himself who was going to officiate over the ceremony and marry them.

'It has to be finished before the wedding.' The date for the nuptials was set for 28th August 1519 and the decoration of the villa, though well underway, was still not finished. The designs had been completed long ago, all approved, and a host of artists had been working on the project for some time. Raphael had recently taken on yet more apprentices to meet the deadline. But even so, it was taking an eternity to get everything done.

Chigi was growing anxious, as I discovered one day on one of my now infrequent meetings with Bibbiena. I was sitting outside the Cardinal's office waiting to be called in when the impatient bridegroom thundered past me, opened the door and walked straight in. As he stood in the doorway, he paused for a moment then turned back to give me a withering look before disappearing inside.

*

Chigi's voice shook the walls.

'His mind's not on the job! I have no idea what to do about it! There's scaffolding everywhere and the sheets are down but the ceilings and the walls have big patches still to be done. It's causing chaos in the villa. The children are tripping over his things. And there's arsenic lying about. Francesca's worried it's not going to be finished by 28th August. He promises me he'll turn up. I see him first thing in the morning. The next minute I hear he's gone off site. Something has to be done about it!'

The door opened.

'Pietro.' I entered the Cardinal's office.

'Agostino here tells me Raphael is not sufficiently focused on the villa . . . that he is distracted . . . diminished . . . by something . . . or someone. Please, as an esteemed member of his workshop, would you please explain what is going on.'

His eyes told me what he wanted me to say, who he wanted me to blame.

'It's t-t-t-true that he sometimes goes off site . . . along w-w-with . . .' The Cardinal looked at Chigi, the self-satisfied smile of a man who knows what is going to be said next on his face. 'With Giovanni,' I spat out. 'They l-like to visit the T-temple of Titus . . . to find n-n-new details to add to *Signore* Chigi's rooms.'

The banker said nothing for a while.

'All very commendable, if true,' said the Cardinal, bristling. 'But has it not occurred to you, Agostino, that the baker's girl might be the real reason why Raphael steals away so often? Tell him, Pietro, tell him the truth.'

As a man driven by passion, and whose entire villa was intended as a temple to love, I would have been wasting my breath if I'd told Chigi the real truth – that the maestro's absence was driven by his desire for perfection. It was far easier, and personally more beneficial, not to mention lucrative, to repeat the truth according to Bibbiena.

'So, Margarita is the problem,' Chigi said when I'd finished.

What Bibbiena didn't realise, judging by the look of victory on his face, was that Chigi also saw her as the solution.

*

'How long do you think this room will take to finish?' he shouted up to Raphael on one of the days he was there. The maestro was lying high up on the scaffolding boards painting his sea nymph Galatea. As a lover from a story taken from Ovid's Metamorphoses, Raphael had made countless preparatory drawings of her and had decided to show her triumphant, hair flowing behind, draped in a red robe. Though not resembling Margarita in every particular, I could see he had imbued the sea nymph with her spirit and I wondered if she had perhaps modelled for him. Galatea had the shape of her, or so it seemed to me.

Raphael didn't answer Chigi, so absorbed was he by the task. 'Fetch me the miniver brushes please, Pietro.'

'I see you're suffering, Raphael,' he continued to shout up. 'Why don't you move in here? You will have no distractions then.'

'Thank you,' Raphael said to me. 'Could you mix me pigment to lighten the skin?'

The maestro focused on the ceiling. He'd blocked off all Chigi's interruptions, no matter how well meaning.

'Move her in too. Margarita. If you like.'

Raphael still didn't answer.

'Have her as your live-in mistress then we'll both be satisfied.' The banker laughed at his own joke.

'Arghh!' Flesh-coloured paint spattered Chigi's pale russet hair. 'It doesn't have anything nasty in it?' he cried out. 'Like arsenic?' And with that he was gone.

*

'Do you honestly think that I would?'

When Raphael asked Margarita to move in with him few people who knew her expected her to say yes. I alone was not surprised when several weeks before the Chigi wedding she did.

She had asked to speak to me some days before. I had never seen her so distressed.

'His art comes first,' she began, her hands folded in her lap. She said no more for a while though I observed a slight quiver in her lips. 'I would never get in the way of his work.'

'No.' I nodded in acknowledgement of the fact.

'Never,' she repeated.

She got up as if trying to free herself of her thoughts. She paced before me, unsettled, steadfastly looking to the floor.

'Margarita,' I said, reaching out to take one of her hands in mine. 'What is it?'

'Nothing.' Her lower lip trembled some more.

'You can tell me.' I waited. Her eyes looked into mine as though searching my soul. 'You can tell me,' I repeated in a whisper. I did not look away. She had protected me from discovery by the Cardinal's assistant, kept my secret about Fabio. I could keep hers. After all she had done for me I resolved that I would do this one small thing for her.

'Something is happening to me.' Her eyes welled up. 'And I don't know what to do.' The tears trickled down. And with them she poured out her heart.

'I won't live at Chigi's with him.'

This was the firm Margarita I knew.

'But, Pietro . . .' She stumbled as if what she had to say was too huge an obstacle to surmount. 'I . . .'

'Yes?' I asked.

'I . . .' she tried again.

'Margarita?'

'But, Pietro, what if I lose him? I can't live without him.' The words fell out of her mouth like a fast-flowing stream. 'The hours that I'm not with him seem to stretch out before me. And when I am not with him I am no longer myself. I catch myself sighing, crying, feel myself dying . . . when there is nothing the matter with me. It is as if I have been struck down by an affliction so grave it could snuff out my life at any moment.'

Her eyes sought succour within mine.

'The truth of it, Pietro, is that I am sick . . . sick with love, and I don't know what to do about it.'

It made me think that moving into Chigi's temple of love was not going to ease the situation but I kept that thought to myself. At the same time, my heart swelled with a certain amount of pride to think that Margarita had chosen me as her confessor.

'I can't sleep. Eating has no appeal for me.'

My mind conjured up a laughing Margarita, sitting next to Raphael and eating fruit and cheese together only the day before. She'd had a voracious appetite then. As if reading my mind, she added, 'When he's not by my side.' That I understood. A feeling of empathy ran through me.

I very nearly said, 'Me too,' because I did understand, and as Margarita's words expressed my own inner truth my own heart went out to her.

In that moment the person I was the most jealous of was the person I understood more than any other. We shared the same love. Raphael. I'd believed I was over him. Listening to Margarita talk of him this way I saw that I was not.

'When he's away from me I am consumed by the fear that I might never see him again. There have been days when I've felt as though I was dying. Dying with longing for him. What is this madness?'

By the end of the week Margarita had agreed to move into Chigi's villa. And I had encouraged her.

Chapter 34

'I pity that girl!' Clarice told anybody who would listen to her. 'She might be the one Raphael desires *at the moment*. But it always ends badly for girls like her. She's got no future. Not with someone as well connected as Raphael. Society doesn't like that sort of thing. Rich, well born and talented with . . . poor. No, society doesn't like that all. Oh, how I pity that girl! That poor, poor girl.'

But the fact remained that Raphael did desire Margarita and this alone made Clarice furious, in spite of her protestations of pity. But at least her sticks and stones, clods of mud, and cartfuls of muck would get the chance to be thrown, slung, and shovelled at Margarita now that the silly girl had attached her colours to Raphael so brazenly. There would be no turning back for the baker's daughter from Trastevere now, only a precipitous fall. It was I who had advised her to follow her heart. Did I hope it would destroy her? My own heart was torn; my head was confused. Feelings of loyalty towards the poor girl vied with those of jealousy and resentment.

'I am housed in my own room,' she insisted whenever she saw me. But it mattered little how respectable her living arrangements were; I could see how tormented she was by this new situation. Besides, nobody would believe her and she knew it. And it only compounded the problem when she added, somewhat embarrassed, 'I am here as *Signorina* Ordeaschi's chaperone.' She was three children too late for that and Margarita's plump-cheeked, round-bellied ward looked like she was well on the way to producing a fourth. Chigi had moved his young Venetian in some time ago and openly accepted the bastards she had borne him. And a chaperone? The citizens of Rome would show Margarita no mercy for insulting their intelligence.

Raphael, by contrast, looked at peace. Chigi allowed him to work unencumbered by requests while the woman who was his inspiration was ever at hand.

There were only two black clouds that appeared to mar the otherwise blue sky that was Raphael's soul at that time, both blown in by Cardinal Bibbiena. The first appeared immediately after a meeting with the Cardinal, not long after Margarita had moved in. The Cardinal had spoken to Raphael again about the commission that had been outstanding for some time, the one for the Duke of Ferrara. The second came the day after. This time the Cardinal had sent him sad news. His niece, Maria, Raphael's betrothed, had died suddenly.

The maestro approached me, the death note still in his hand. 'I need you to make sure Margarita is looked after for a day or two,' he said to me, his arm heavy around my shoulder. 'I will be expected to attend the funeral and in truth Margarita will want me to.'

As he pulled away, loud, heavy footsteps clattered across the marble floor. A slap accompanied by a guffaw split the air. 'Just heard the news. You're a lucky devil!' It was Chigi. Raphael did not reply. He left to express his condolences to the dead girl's uncle.

When he returned I knew he would be forlorn. I would have expected nothing less. He hadn't loved her but he mourned the passing of an innocent life. Margarita did too. She ran to him when she saw him again and sobbed. 'What have we done? That poor girl!' But it should have been herself she was crying over, as all of Rome would soon start pointing the finger of blame at her for *that poor girl*'s death. And Cardinal Bibbiena had already begun.

Chapter 35

It was 28th August 1519, the feast day of St Augustine, the day Agostino Chigi had chosen for his wedding to Francesca Ordeaschi. As part of Raphael's workshop I had been at Chigi's grand villa working right up to the 27th putting finishing touches to some of the frescoes. Frescoes dedicated to love. Beautiful, beautiful frescoes. The love they were dedicated to was that between the hard-living, rich fifty-two-year-old banker and the poor young woman he'd brought back from Venice some years back. But when you're the Pope's banker you can paint your own story, making it magnificent, wonderful, divine, or more accurately pay for the best artists to do it for you. And when you're the Pope's banker you can even get the Pope to conduct the nuptials. Nothing is impossible, I realised then, for the man who holds the purse strings.

And so Pope Leo X, dressed in purple, married the happy couple on that blisteringly hot day in August.

It was a lavish affair and the travesty of a ceremony I left for other artists present to observe and record. I myself spent most of the time, to begin with at least, scrutinising Margarita. If a banker could get the Pope to give his blessing to a union between his fifty-two-year-old self and a young girl, lowborn, and who'd given him four children (if you counted the one she

248

was carrying), there was hope for the maestro and his love. The pair would have known it. Agostino and Francesca had been the laughing stock of much of Roman society. Until it was time for their wedding invitations to go out. Then everybody wanted one.

I can honestly say that Margarita was the only person I knew who never made jokes about Francesca behind her back and on the day of her friend's wedding I watched her carefully. She was one of the few guests genuinely moved. But there was more than simple happiness for the newlyweds in her response. As I watched her wipe a tear away, I could read the hope smeared all over her face. And as she hoped so I despaired. I no longer wanted to see her destroyed yet neither was I in any mood to anticipate a lifelong union between the maestro and this girl so beneath him. The heat was oppressive and I was starting to feel faint. Now the ceremony was over, I decided it was time to start doing what I'd been invited here to do: draw and record to take my mind off the very real possibility of another mismatched bride and groom.

The guests were an interesting array of the city's finest and represented every powerful element of Roman society, from feuding families to disgruntled cardinals. Vain creatures mostly, used to sitting for portraits and having their best sides immortalised in paint. There were some friends scattered around the room, sharing in the couple's happiness, but more I would say were enemies. And I could see too that Chigi knew how to keep his enemies if not sweet then at least distracted. Cardinal Bibbiena caught my eye. Two servant girls flanked him, one ready to top up his goblet, the other prepared to offer him tasty morsels, which he seemed more than happy with from the expression on his face as one of the girls, eye-wateringly buxom, leant over him.

I made a little sketch of him looking uncharacteristically jolly, more as an amusement for myself than anything else. I was beginning to warm to my task. Chigi really had put on a most magnificent feast. And I could only congratulate him on knowing how to get the most ferocious of men to crack a smile. I added a few deft pencil strokes around Bibbiena's eyes. I looked forward to making another sketch of him later when even more fine food and wine would have slipped down his already engorged throat. It would be one for my secret collection to share later with the likes of Giulio.

'Pietro!' Raphael approached and gave me a slap on the back.

He looked at my drawings. I hastily placed the one of Bibbiena under the pile of paper, inadvertently revealing the one I'd drawn of Raphael himself viewed from the side. He held it up to look at. 'Oh how I wish I was on your side of the picture,' he said, looking up from it and casting his painterly eye around the room.

'And I yours,' I replied. I forced myself to laugh to make it sound like a joke but even as I said it I knew that it wasn't. There was something about being at the wedding as part of Raphael's workshop that made me feel little more than a servant. A hired hand. And to see Margarita, a baker's daughter, gliding round as if she was born to this pomp and luxury made me smart all the more. But, of course, she wasn't gliding round, nor did she feel relaxed in these circumstances in this company. I knew her well enough to know that. Yet it served my wayward reasoning to believe it so at the time. Poor Margarita. But Raphael worshipped her. And the plainer his feelings, the greater my jealousy. As for my desire for Raphael, at Chigi's wedding I was finding it hard to keep it under control.

I was already hot but as Raphael looked back down at the sketch I'd done of him I felt as though my head was going to burst into flame. 'Mmm.' He continued looking and said nothing. My eyes clouded as perspiration forced its way into them. I tried to wipe them with my sweat-covered hand. 'Mmm,' he said again, his tone lifting.

'The anatomy beneath is particularly well observed, Pietro. Remarkable sensitivity.'

'Raphael!' Chigi called him over. He had no choice but to go.

'How I wish I could stay here with you.' He put out a hand and caught the sleeve of my shirt and in that moment I believed him.

'Over here!' He beckoned a servant to him as he went. 'Get those young artists something to cool themselves down.' He gestured back to where I was sitting with a group of apprentices. I waited to catch his eye. It didn't meet mine. 'Let me,' I heard Margarita's voice say. 'I'd like to take them some wine.'

I sat there drawing; it helped me empty my mind, noting down compositions before guests got up, moved around, changed places. I walked around to identify dishes, some of which I'd never heard of never mind seen before. A servant about one or two years older than I was, no more, walked in front of me, obstructing my view. He lit the sweet-smelling beeswax candles on the table, though the sun still shone bright outside. I raised my eyes to the lush stucco garlands around the room, decorated with suggestively shaped fruits and vegetables. Little birds had been worked into them. *Uccello*, I sighed to myself. Though I could never understand why a *little bird* signified something erotic, the thought that it did was enough to set my imagination alight. My eyes dropped back to the boy.

He was long and slender and his movements were lithe and almost pretty. As he passed by again, this time turning his face towards me, he smoothed his thigh. He drew my gaze downwards with what I saw were elegant fingers. I looked back up to his face. His eyes and hair were dark brown, while his lips glistened like deep pink fruits against an olive skin. I drank some of the wine Margarita had brought over for me. The boy came past again. Closer this time. I imagined him to resemble Raphael. My pulse raced a little. I could smell the heat if not of his body then certainly of mine. Mixed with the contents of the goblet it was intoxicating. He looked like a god in the flickering candlelight, my god, while the sheen on his body promised more earthly pleasures. His hands, ears, throat, back of his neck. Deliciously moist. A promise of ripe, yielding flesh.

I looked behind me, momentarily distracted by the sound of the cascading fountain in the garden. My knees weakened. I looked at pomegranates strewn on the tables, cut in half and bursting with seeds. I was hungry. I looked at my young god. He looked back at me. He disappeared out of the room. I followed him.

*

'Why, you do look pleased with yourself!' Giulio was waiting for me when I came back into the room fifteen minutes later.

'I had to eat. Ravenous.'

Giulio laughed. There was something in the way I spoke the words that made them sound vulgar. 'What was her name? If only I'd known I could have come and drawn you.' Giulio had a respectable number of wedding sketches, well observed and finely drawn, beside him, but his interest in drawing men and women engaged in various sexual positions was never far from the forefront of his mind. And he was always on the lookout for opportunities to master his technique in capturing the human form in various, undressed poses. 'That's supposing it was with a girl . . .'

I turned my face away. My liaison with Clarice some time back had put paid to some rumours but not all. It had been a while.

'Now there's a couple I'd like to see! Don't mind mixing it up a little in the interests of variety.'

I followed his mocking finger to see Margarita and the blushing bride deep in wine-soaked conversation together. I gave a shuddering laugh, thankful the finger of ridicule was no longer pointing towards me. The bride had taken a shoe off and was currently showing Margarita the gold florin placed in there to bring wealth and fecundity. 'She's already got more than her fair share of both,' Giulio snorted. The young women were close. Margarita had been appointed chaperone to the bride-to-be after all. But there was something more that bound them. Both were from poor backgrounds, both felt out of place. To be in such lavish surroundings suited neither of them – I could see that.

And it wasn't fair. I looked at Raphael, rightly celebrated for his God-given talent. I looked at Margarita. Whore.

Though of course she wasn't.

My feelings for Margarita were confused, vacillating wildly between affection and a dislike so strong that at times I believed I hated her. You can tell me she saved my life; you can tell me she was one of the few people who saw the good in me. But believe me, there's no need, because all this I know already. But at Chigi's wedding, knowing all that I owed her made me despise her even more. She was good, kind, generous. And that evening she seemed so happy, hopeful, blessed. And I dreaded that what she was hoping for might come true. How could it not? In a world that was fair she deserved it. And even in an unfair world, such as the one we were living in, logic dictated that it should be so.

The impossible had happened in allowing the blessed union between Chigi and Francesca, and with it a precedent had been established. Pope Leo X was a relaxed ruler, his court tolerant. The bringing together of Raphael and Margarita in the eyes of the Lord and his representative here on earth was inevitable.

I was still glowing after my fifteen minutes of transcendental joy though the deadening, bony fingers of jealousy were furiously trying to extinguish any finer feeling it might have ignited within me. And I still hadn't responded to Giulio's leery remark about Francesca and Margarita. Mistaking my silence for disapproval he went out into the garden. 'In the dark, outside, far more fertile ground for elicit couplings . . .' he whispered, a sleazy edge to his voice.

I went over towards Cardinal Bibbiena. He still had the smell of lavender and fat about him. (Ointment for his piles, I'd discovered, while working for the Pope's personal physician recently, who prepared vats of the stuff.) His cheeks, nose, and robes all glowed with the same warm red. He throbbed with colour and his usual dour personality had all but disappeared. The two girls still flanked him.

'Agostino's calling me over,' Francesca said apologetically.

'He's your husband.' Margarita and Francesca both gasped, then laughed. 'Go on, go to him! Don't worry about me. Look, here's Pietro. He'll protect me,' she said, extending a hand to me while glancing at the Cardinal. 'Pietro's like a little brother to me!'

As Francesca walked off, giddy with wine and disbelief at her own good fortune, so the Cardinal tried to get up out of his seat.

'Oh, do excuse me!' Politely, Margarita squeezed between the Cardinal and the servant girl.

Impolitely, he sneered back. 'Going, are you? Good riddance!'

'Excuse me?' Margarita said, indignant.

'You heard me. You'd make a damned fine serving girl,' he slurred and gestured to the girls who'd been his personal hand-maidens all day. The Cardinal smiled, his head wobbled, then he started to dribble out of the corner of his mouth. 'Your problem is that you don't know your place.'

I watched Margarita. I hoped she wouldn't hold back. She wasn't afraid; that I knew. And if she let Bibbiena have it, which she could do so gloriously, it wouldn't help her cause. She was already the gossip of all Rome.

Instead she displayed restraint, no doubt out of respect for his recently deceased niece. '*Monsignore*, I know it is pointless to argue with you. Not because you are right but because I'm certain you won't be able to recall any of it in the morning.'

Whoops and cheers came from outside. Loud crashes and splashes filled the air. I turned my head in time to make out silver plates travelling in an arc and disappearing into the Tiber that flowed alongside the villa. 'Whoa!' Many of the other guests pushed past to get a better look at this extravagant discarding of precious tableware, a dazzling prelude to the fireworks up next. Margarita took this as her chance to extricate herself from the difficult predicament she'd found herself in.

'Please excuse me, dear Cardinal. I really would like to go and see some real fireworks outside to celebrate the marriage of my

254

dear friends Francesca and Agostino. I hope you manage to stand up without falling over.'

And with that she walked outside, calm, with her head held high, though inside I imagined her to be shaking like delicate blossom desperately holding on to the tree. 'Enjoy this, because it won't last,' Bibbiena called after her. 'Change is coming,' he said, slumping down into his seat. 'A wind colder than anything we've ever known here in Rome is on its way to us and it's blowing its way down from the north.'

'Get his litter ready,' I whispered to one of the servants. The Cardinal had hit that point in the evening where he was talking nonsense. 'It's time to take him back to the Vatican.'

Chapter 36

The Chigi villa had been finished in time for the wedding and had been hailed by everyone (with the exception of Sebastiano and Michelangelo) as a success. I, along with Giulio, Giovanni and a few other apprentices, had been asked to Raphael's home early one morning in October. He'd wanted to pass on his congratulations to us personally. He had a small studio there on the second floor at the back of the property as well as a larger one on the top floor. We were in the smaller studio and it was there that he also revealed to us his plans for the coming months. The list of works he'd accepted on behalf of the workshop was endless.

'Many are still at the planning stage,' he said, presenting his desk strewn with sketches, 'but we also have the new loggia at the Vatican to complete.' Excitement twinkled in his eyes. If he was ready for the challenge of so much work then so were we, his loyal assistants. But then, throughout the rest of the day, he was called away, to respond to messages, listen to urgent requests, make notes, and take measurements. By the time it came for us to leave, Raphael had only just returned. He looked weary. And old. And it worried me.

We went to his home to work for the rest of the week and the pattern was the same. We were able to get down to the designing and sketching while Raphael was weighed down by work-related troubles of one sort or another. And requests and correspondence punctuated his day, distracting him from what he wanted to do – his art.

He was being reduced to a businessman.

Doors slammed. Messengers came and went. Dogs barked. Tradesmen shouted. Life in all its indifference buzzed in through open windows while we immersed ourselves in our work. And then, we would look up to find the daylight had seeped away and discover the flickering candles lit. After the fifth day it was Giulio who suggested we go to a tavern together.

'To the tavern, lads!'

I started to tidy the materials away and made sure the empty plates of food and half-drained jugs (neither of which I could remember having touched though a greasy stain on my work clothes said to the contrary) were stacked up at a safe distance to the side.

'Raphael?' I asked.

'Try upstairs top floor.'

The house was now calm, the streets outside quiet, the only sound a distressed cat, and the occasional raised voice ricocheting between the buildings. The staircase in Raphael's house was dark. It crossed my mind that I should have taken a candle but by the time I thought this I could make out the light under the closed studio door and so there seemed little point. I would soon be there. I raised my fist ready to knock. But something stopped me. I held my breath. I placed my ear against the door. Furniture scraping across the floor scratched my ear. What sounded like cloth being shaken accompanied it.

'Yes, there were many women before you.' It was Raphael. My knuckles, poised to knock, held off to hear his confession and the lovers' tiff that would surely ensue.

'I saw them as my due. I saw you as my due, my sweet, virtuous pearl. But as I knew you better so you opened my heart . . .

You walked inside . . . You have remained . . . You have taught me a lesson no one else could – that love, when it comes, accepts no boundaries . . . It breaks down the walls society has thrown up . . . Worth comes from the pearl . . . not the grit that surrounds it.'

So not a lovers' tiff, I told myself, though judging from the pauses it seemed the maestro was taking his due to me. I would knock and stop this trifling.

'I will petition Pope Leo tomorrow.' Raphael's words turned me to stone. No. I had to be wrong. He couldn't be saying what I thought he was.

'He will agree, won't he?' Margarita said.

My blood ran cold. I dropped my hand. And listened.

'Come,' Raphael said, 'Let me wrap this cloth round your head like a turban. And let me attach this pearl to it. A pearl for my pearl.'

Margarita laughed.

'Oh, *la mia fornarina*, I love you. And you *will* be my wife.'

Margarita did not respond in words but she was breathing so hard I could hear it through the thickness of the heavy door that divided us.

Speak, speak, I thought, fearing the alternative.

Unfortunately, from what I could make out she managed to combine both.

'I . . . am . . . so happy . . .' Heavy panting entwined itself around her words. Cloth met cloth. Lips met lips . . . Sounds painted disturbing pictures in my mind. I couldn't knock now. I retreated back down the stairs. I stumbled, knocking over a small bronze statue displayed in a niche. It made the noise heavy metal makes when striking stone. But it didn't matter. Raphael and Margarita were too busy making their own discordant music to be disturbed by my dull thuds.

*

He walked into the tavern alone one hour later. We'd left a message with his servant telling him where we were. His beautiful eyes shone with tenderness while the smile on his face was almost triumphant. He seemed less troubled than he had done for days. He laughed and chatted with Giulio, and the pair ate and drank with relish in the glow of the candlelight. But I did not listen to their conversation, nor join in their feasting. I felt as if a black cloud had passed in front of the sun. All colour had vanished from my world and I was left in shadow.

Chapter 37

There was going to be no wedding.

The situation for Margarita was bad. Very bad. In fact it was desperate.

I was working alone in the top studio in Raphael's villa when she sought me out and turned to me for advice and consolation.

'I am done for, Pietro.'

'No, it's not so.'

'Yes, Pietro, I am. My life is ruined.'

She walked to the far side of the studio, a strange sense of urgency in her step, and she fiddled with a cloth carelessly draped over a picture. She coughed nervously and made sure it enveloped every part of the work most deliberately, before allowing her shoulders to relax a little and walking back towards me.

We talked a while, I bringing up innocent gossip, all the while trying to lighten the mood, but it was no use. The sorrow in her soul spread out from her and covered all around her in its mist. She should have made her excuses to me and left Raphael's home, gone back to her father, seen if Francesca was able to help her. But she was trapped and broken.

'To get to the top of Fortune's wheel, so close to Heaven!' (I missed a breath at her words.) 'I should have known the fall would be great from such a height.' (I imagined the delicious agony of the descent.) When she finished speaking, she got up and walked out onto the loggia. She leant down over it. As she did so her skirt and petticoat rose up in waves to show her pretty ankles. She was standing on the tips of her toes, as if trying to escape from the burden that kept her lodged in this place, her face looking down into the abyss below. One arm wrapped itself tight around one of the columns, another stretched downwards. The folds of her skirt flapped in the wind like the delicately coloured wings of a butterfly. The warm air caught in the fabric once more making it seem as if she were about to flit and flutter up and down, along the streets, around the people, until finally disappearing out of sight.

Instead she sank backwards with a gasp.

'The Pope has said no.'

That I knew already. When cardinals and popes are called on to pay the price for their sins, it falls on the people to pay the debt. It was ever thus.

The political climate had changed, brought on by our brothers in the north. It was the Pope and his court that had caused offence to their austere sensibilities but it was Margarita who would pay the price. She was to experience the full brunt of the chill wind that ensued.

The wedding was now an impossibility. Margarita thought herself ridiculous for ever having thought it could have been anything else.

For the next few days the gods blocked out the sun to convey their sorrow. The sky turned first grey then black and the clouds cried on and on, raining its grief down upon the city in torrents. Giovanni wore a face like thunder while even Giulio had stopped making his usual lewd jokes. The news that the Vatican would not support a union between their favourite artist and a baker's daughter was crushing. Decisive.

Only Raphael seemed unchanged. I took this as confirmation

that Margarita was but a convenience, and one that he would soon be rid of. Margarita had been a distraction and a means to break with Maria da Bibbiena. That the sickly girl had facilitated the break herself by dying prematurely meant Raphael had no further need of his baker's daughter. Soon Raphael would be wearing the Clarices of this world around his neck like fur capes once again and we would at last deserve our reputation as the wildest workshop in Rome. I was convinced of it.

It was a Friday and the heavens had been pouring down for three days. No one had mentioned a word about what had happened when the Pope had turned Raphael's request down. Margarita had not shown her face at the workshop. And if Elena, Raphael's housekeeper, was to be believed, she hadn't been seen at Raphael's house on the Via dei Coronari either. Although I couldn't wait for a return to our heady days of freedom, which I was sure were around the corner, I did not want to seem callous. I would have to go to see Margarita in the small rooms she kept in Trastevere. I waited for a break in the clouds and went to pay a visit to the recently expectant bride, now the newly fallen woman.

I knocked on the door, worried about the distraught sight that would surely greet me when it opened. I gnawed the tips of my fingers and shuffled from side to side. I suffered the guilt of the coward about to face a friend whose tragic plight I'd longed for. I appeared duly crestfallen. Though, when the door swung back, I noted that Margarita did not. She filled the doorway with a haze of joy, immediately followed by surprise at the sight of me. Her eyes burned brightly as she put her hands over her mouth and dropped like a puppet unable to support her own weight.

'Margarita.' I invested my voice with the sound of pity. And then, after a few forced responses, compassion flowed from me, gurgling as naturally as a mountain spring. My eyes wide, beseeching. My arms warm, embracing.

'The weather's atrocious!' I said.

'Oh! I hadn't noticed,' she chirruped. 'Well, it isn't anymore.

You've clearly brought the sunshine with you, Pietro.' Her small hands enfolded mine. 'Come in! Come in!'

I followed her into a tiny room. She closed the heavy wooden door behind us.

'I knew you'd come!'

I watched her, waiting for the pleasure at my appearance to melt away and reveal the heartbreak within. Her fingers played by her side while the most secretive of smiles traced itself across her face as if responding to the invisible stroke of a feather. Her eyes flickered to her sewing basket. I looked at her. She looked down. This didn't look like heartbreak to me. Feelings of anxiety started to stir deep within.

'Sit, please, Pietro.'

Her eyes drew mine to hers while her hands pushed the basket away to the side. Whatever it was she was sewing the drapes of her skirt now concealed it like a curtain.

'You seem happy,' I said.

'Why would I not be?' she replied.

I scoured the room looking for some clue to explain her mood. There on the table was a jug full of foliage. Myrtle, quince and thyme. My heart started to thump. Then, almost hidden in the shadow of the leaves lay two velvet pouches. I'd missed them at first. The deep black of the velvet merged into the darkness of the wood upon which they rested. But the instant I saw them I recognised what they were.

I felt suddenly ill.

Either I was witness to the delusions of a lovesick bride who had been abandoned, her dying hopes burning brightly before going out forever. Or these weren't delusions.

I was torn, unable to decide which was worse.

I swallowed hard. I had to know.

'What are you going to do with them? The rings?'

The quiet, secretive smile on Margarita's lips erupted into an unfettered expression of delight that covered every part of her face. At the mention of 'the rings' she flew to take them up in her hands. She held them to her breast and cradled them there a while, the light in her eyes still managing to shine out through the folds in a face that could only spell out joy. I looked at the basket now left exposed at the side of her chair. Embroidery needles, ribbon, thread, all wrapped round a pair of scissors. I was disappointed not to find anything more.

'Here! Before I reveal anything else, I want you to have this.' She got up and thrust a silver charm in my hand attached to a fine chain. It was a *cimaruta*.

'It's brought me more good fortune than I ever thought possible on this earth and now I would like to pass it on to you. There is no one who deserves it more.'

'*Grazie!*' I looked at it with feigned delight concealing my disdain. I put the crude trinket in my pocket. 'Now, what has fortune delivered to you that is so sublime that you have no further need of this most precious *cimaruta*?' I was back on the trail.

'He's not told you yet!' she declared in a delirium-drenched voice; I sensed the deluge of despair heading my way. So much for the *cimaruta*, bringer of good luck. I shuffled in my seat. She returned to hers after first very deliberately placing the velvet pouches back on the table in the exact spot as they were before.

'N-n-not told me what?' I stammered, afraid that what was good fortune for her was bad fortune for me.

'Here. Let me show you.' She leant to the side and picked up her needlework, unrolling the ribbon and holding it up for me to see. The ribbon was white and she'd obviously started embroidering what I could only guess was a piece for Raphael as she'd already finished the R and the a. Beyond that I had no idea why she was showing it to me. As she looked into my eyes, nodding, waiting, I could tell that it was clearly something of great significance. Though I couldn't for the life of me see what it was. I smiled but before she could explain the door opened. We both gave a start.

'Raphael!'

Raphael walked in, Giulio behind him.

'Giulio!' I gasped.

Margarita's eyes danced around once more. She quickly hid her hand behind her back and dropped the ribbon as soon as she could back into the sewing basket. I still had no idea what it was supposed to be, but whatever it was, having Raphael, or possibly Giulio, catch her with it in her hands made her coy in their presence.

*

Amor vincit omnia. Oh, how I hate Latin phrases masquerading as universal truths, popped out to excuse the most foolhardy of choices.

There would be a wedding.

Politics at court were what had made it impossible for the lovers to marry in public. But when love conquers everything it also always finds a way.

There would be a wedding.

'A *secret* wedding,' Raphael announced.

'*Amor vincit omnia*,' Giulio whispered in my ear with a sly tinge to his voice as if he had read my mind.

'And it is to be tonight,' Raphael announced.

I fell back off my rickety stool. No one noticed.

I got back up, looked at Raphael. He only had eyes for Margarita, and they were ablaze with the holy trinity of excitement, passion, and love. She looked back at him, impatient to be anointed. I turned away. The intimacy was too much to bear though the sight of it had done its work: it had thrown me into my deluge of despair. Raphael's love for Margarita was so pure, so deep, that he was prepared to sacrifice himself for it, for her. He loved her. And I could do nothing about it.

Giulio did not want to. He, it seemed, had always been happy about the couple, and as he listened to Raphael and ran an

265

appraising eye over the curves beneath Margarita's clothes, sounds of appreciation gurgled out of him as though he were a fountain of happiness and delight.

'You will be stopped, surely,' I said, trying to sound like the voice of reason.

Margarita laughed at me. Raphael nudged me playfully.

'I have arranged with a priest to conduct the ceremony at a private chapel tonight.'

'P-p-p-p-priest? Which p-p-p-priest?' I stuttered out.

Raphael placed a warm hand on my shoulder. My whole body screamed at his touch. I wanted to hold on to his hand and never let it go. 'That is to remain a secret,' he said, releasing me. His hand went to find Margarita's. Her hand went to find his. My hand plunged into the pocket where I'd thrust the *cimaruta*. I gave a little shiver.

*

I had an urge to rush to the Vatican to inform Cardinal Bibbiena. But I feared getting caught. Besides, I really had nothing to tell. I had been given the task of gathering more myrtle, quince, and thyme. Margarita hadn't found enough and it was Raphael who had requested these symbols of matrimony, no doubt to grace the chapel and add weight to the marriage ceremony. Consequently, I would find an abundance, for him.

The storms had disappeared, and though the ground was still soft the sun had soaked up all signs of rain. The air was deliciously cool and fresh and the foliage I was looking for seemed to beckon me. It looked luscious and green, plump and fertile. I found myself walking along the streets of Rome, my arms laden with matrimonial symbolism. But as I passed by the Vatican my thoughts turned to Cardinal Bibbiena once again. If he knew, he would put a stop to this charade of a wedding. But he did not know. Because I hadn't told him. I couldn't. To call on the

Cardinal would surely destroy Margarita, and, as I breathed in the freshly picked leaves, I knew that I did not want that. Though my thoughts writhed like maggots, not even they had any desire to spread that much rot. There had to be another way.

Who could stop Margarita? She listened to no one, not even her father, but he was my only chance. Once I'd dropped off the greenery I marched towards Trastevere. The plebeian character wouldn't, couldn't let me down. I could not tell the man where this abominable wedding would take place but, if I was as good a judge of character as I thought, that would not matter.

*

I went into the baker's shop.

'S-S-S-*Signore* Luti!' Of all the times for words to fail me. His round, pink cheeks plumped up like pillows, covering up his eyes.

'Margarita,' I spat out. 'She's getting married. To Raphael. Tonight.' There. I'd told him. Then I fled. His ambition would do the rest. I estimated he would be at his daughter's, or Raphael's, within the hour, brokering a deal for himself. Either way, he would disrupt the wedding.

Chapter 38

The union between Raphael and Margarita could not be stopped. Francesco Luti had not appeared. Fate was poised to take its course. I had no choice but to do as Raphael had asked and engage a driver and carriage to escort Margarita to the chapel.

When I arrived at her door she was waiting. The light outside was starting to fade, the sky changing from bright blue to deep purple. As she stepped into the street, a dark blue velvet cape covering her from head to toe, she became one with the air, heavy with colour. No one would have known it enveloped a bride. The voluminous folds of her cape concealed every sign; her hood, pulled forward, concealed every feature. I helped her into the carriage. The driver looked back at her. A sliver of pale silk escaped from beneath blue velvet as she climbed up. 'Where are we going, *Signore*?' he asked me.

'To the very end of the road,' Margarita replied.

When we alighted I followed her. Her breath was butterfly light, her footsteps urgent. She flew past the shops and houses. I ran to keep up. I pursued her round a corner, and there, at the end of the street, was a small chapel. Her feet quickened, her cape swayed, the white of her dress frothed up with excitement. She pushed her way in through the heavy wooden door. She saw Raphael. She ran to him. He ran to greet her. She pulled back her hood. A net threaded with tiny pearls covered her hair. A gossamer veil trailed behind it. Her lips quivered. Raphael kissed them. And then the pair embraced as though their lives depended on it.

I waited for the despair that had been lapping around my ankles to submerge me completely. The marriage that I had fought against had come to pass; Raphael so clearly loved Margarita with all his heart. Yet, as I beheld them, something very strange and unexpected happened. The mantle of jealousy that I had been wearing for so very long was lifted momentarily from my shoulders.

'You make me happy,' he told her. Eyes shone with rapture, hands sought hands and I joined Giulio as we followed the couple towards a priest standing at the end of the aisle. The flames of altar candles burned brightly.

I looked at Margarita, no longer in her cloak of deepest blue. Now, in her dress of white bound by a golden girdle, she pulled the white mist of her veil forward. I listened to the priest's singsong delivery of the ceremony, watched the exchanging of the rings, then felt hot breath on the side of my neck. 'They're now man and wife.' I turned to see Giulio grinning at me.

The heavy entrance door slammed shut. I looked back to see who had come in but there was no one.

'Come. Let us go home.' Home. Margarita blushed with pleasure as Raphael uttered the word and helped her into the carriage. 'Giulio, Pietro, come. Join us.' We climbed in and sat opposite them. Now, newly wed, the pair only had eyes for each other. Giulio watched with an unhealthy interest as their hands fluttered and heads touched. I looked away, my eyes preferring to settle on a Roman arch in the distance. My ears were granted no such escape.

'I would like to give a painting as my wedding gift to you, *la mia fornarina*,' Raphael said.

'I've also made something for you,' she replied. 'But I'll show you later,' she added, lowering her voice. Their words crackled in the air with an elemental power that caused Giulio to shudder as he sat on the seat next to me. It was not what they said but the way they said it, full of desire. I felt Giulio's excitement as his thigh pushed into mine. I kept my eyes fixed on the arch.

I was grateful to be out of the carriage and when we walked through the door of the house on Via dei Coronari a round of merry applause rippled round the hall. Relief, the sounds of approval, and even the joy I'd experienced at the marriage ceremony, all combined to give me a feeling of deep satisfaction. And while this feeling lasted everything seemed beautiful. I marvelled as Raphael's valet and cook wore excited smiles and bobbed up and down, bowing, curtseying and taking cloaks and jackets.

I was overjoyed to see that one of Raphael's dearest friends was here, Bindo Altoviti from Florence. Even the sight of Agostino and Francesca Chigi moved me. That most gentle of men and closest of Raphael's friends, Baldassare Castiglione, was present too and I looked at his shining eyes with wonder as though they were stars. I also recognised Pietro Bembo. The great humanist scholar had been a dear friend to Raphael, and Raphael to him, nursing him when he was ill. To remember such kindness brought tears to my eyes. Yes, I had been touched by a deep satisfaction that came close to euphoria.

'To the happy couple!' We drank a toast and made our way to the dining room. Sweet-smelling beeswax candles flooded the room in fragrance and light and the foliage I'd been sent out to gather earlier on twinkled like emeralds. I looked at Raphael and Margarita. They had achieved what I had thought was impossible. Married indeed. For the briefest of moments, the sleeping monster that was my jealousy started to stir deep within. It lifted its head, insults lining up like soldiers behind it. But it was no use. No sooner roused than it was crushed by finer feelings.

Raphael smiled at me, and when I saw the hope blaze in his eyes, its delicate thread became one with the rich tapestry that my newfound state of euphoria had already woven on this most unexpected of days. Joy, love, happiness, and now hope: I wondered at life's precious threads. Together they seemed strong. They kept the monster of my jealousy in abeyance – for a little while.

I cast my eyes around the table. Clearly more people knew about the wedding than I'd thought. It crossed my mind that it may have been one of them who had crept in to the church before.

I counted the guests. There were twelve. My place was next to Giulio and four places away from Agostino Chigi. I marvelled that I would be sharing such an intimate table with the richest man in Rome and I wondered at the illustrious friends I had beaten to earn a seat here. But that still left one seat unclaimed. And it was next to me. Who was it for? Who had not turned up?

There was a faint banging on the main door followed by the sounds of servants moving round in the hall. The laughter in the dining hall fell off slightly. The banging on the door came again. This time angry, urgent. Agostino's voice boomed out, requesting popular tunes for the musicians to play. He was not to be distracted from his fun. Background voices followed. Soon we were deaf to anything other than our own enjoyment though I saw that Raphael had one eye fixed keenly on the dining hall door.

The servant Ludovico came in and made his way towards his master. He carried a letter on a silver salver, bent forward, whispered a message in his ear.

'Is it another message for you from the rich man's ambassador?' Margarita asked him, her voice low and worry on her face.

'He says it's most urgent,' Ludovico whispered.

'Tsk!' Raphael said, throwing the message down.

'Commission, Raphael?' Castiglione asked.

'More a threat,' came the reply. 'But now is not the time to think about that. Come my new wife, *la mia fornarina*, let's rejoice! First a toast. To absent friends and family!' he said.

'To absent friends and family!' we all replied. Margarita toasted the empty space next to me. And after that, Raphael pulled Margarita to her feet, wiping away the concern that had started to creep across her face so that very soon all there was space for was joy.

I watched Ludovico close the dining hall door after himself, a dark look marring his features, while we ate, drank, and were merry as if this were our last night on earth.

*

There was to be no honeymoon for the secret newlyweds. No rest for the maestro, none for his apprentices. The night before the wedding Raphael had announced that he would be away from the studio for a day, but assured them that he would be there for business, as normal, the day after. Only Giulio, Giovanni, and I knew the reason for this absence, but it did not take the others long to work it out for themselves. The wedding may have been a secret, and those present had been made to swear an oath to keep it so, but the fact Raphael and Margarita were married in the biblical sense was impossible to hide, and Giulio's titillating speculations were doing nothing to help. Two had become one.

'I'll wager the maestro won't show up for hours.' He laughed, his voice hoarse from the previous evening's excesses. 'We'll be lucky if we see him before the middle of the afternoon,' he joked. But he couldn't have been more wrong. Though my head pounded and the poison I'd poured into my body couldn't make up its mind by which orifice to exit, Raphael, unbeknownst to the rest of us, was already in his office, poring over his work.

As I sat and listened to Giulio, unaware that the maestro was engrossed in a myriad of artistic endeavours on the other side of the wall, I winced as I recalled my drunken journey home the night before. Giulio had gone one way; I'd gone another. Neither had been a clever move judging from the state of us.

*

'A heavenly host of cardinals are asking to see the maestro. They say they have an appointment.' As Giulio made his announcement so Raphael appeared at his door, revealing a bench covered with papers and what looked like illustrated manuscripts. The entire workshop fell silent. All eyes turned towards the man who had been painting salacious images of the maestro and his new wife with his colourful tongue ever since he'd arrived that morning. He must have heard it all. Giulio's raised eyebrow declared that he didn't care if the maestro had caught what he'd said, while the pulse at the corner of his right eye whispered that he did.

'Cardinals, welcome. Let me show you the designs we've been working on.' Raphael allowed an amused smile, intended for Giulio, to sweep over his lips as he ushered the three red cloaks into his office. He extended his hand towards them. He was not wearing his wedding ring.

'If they are similar in theme and tone to those we've seen for the Pope's loggia so far,' the tallest of the cardinals said, 'then we shall be more than happy with them.' The door closed behind them.

Raphael had been working on drawings for the Pope's loggia from first light to last for weeks. The commission was huge, and heralded a drastic departure for the workshop. No more nymphs, satyrs, gods and goddesses. Instead the remit was strict – to depict stories from the Bible, from Genesis to the Last Supper. Cupid and Psyche, Venus and Mars had no place in this new northern European sensibility that was starting to permeate the whole of Rome. Biblical art was what we had to turn our brushes to if we wanted to survive and Raphael was prepared to do whatever was necessary.

But if his will to succeed was strong, his drive for perfection was stronger still. He would not be constrained. The artists of antiquity had so much still to teach him. The northern European mind might condemn the ancient world as pagan, but Raphael could not keep away. He returned again and again to the Temple of Titus. Because thin-lipped clerics said ancient art was immoral that did not make it so. There was something eternal and sublime there and in such perfection so God would always be. The cardinals could tell him what to do but not how to do it.

*

Then one day the doors of the workshop burst open and crashed against the walls. Two of the apprentices that Raphael had taken out with him that morning were standing there, wild-eyed, red-faced, and spewing fear, spreading panic. '*The maestro!*' '*He's collapsed!*' '*He's fallen sick!*' '*He can't die!*' I slapped the young apprentice who'd said this last one. Giulio pulled me away and told me to get the boys some water.

'Calm yourselves, boys. That's right. Breathe.' Giulio sat the two of them down. 'Now, tell us what's happened?'

'It's the maestro!'

'I know that.' Giulio was patient. 'What about him?'

'Collapsed. Had to be laid flat on the plank and pulled up to the surface. Skin was all grey.'

Giulio said nothing for a while. His shoulders slumped. He sat down on a stool.

'I'm confused, lads. So what's happening now? Giovanni's with him? A physician?'

'Yes, but no . . . but yes, Giovanni is with him . . . . and he sent us to tell you they were on their way back.'

Giulio pushed his stool back and unfolded himself back to standing, visibly relieved.

'They're walking here?' he checked.

The boys nodded.

'Then there's no need to worry, lads. A restorative drink or two later will put the colour back into his cheeks. Now let's get back to work. To catch us all idling, now that would upset him.'

By the time Raphael made it back with Giovanni it was dark

outside. The two men entered. They were in the middle of a disagreement.

'You need to rest. I will go down without you tomorrow.' Giovanni's gruff voice was frayed with tenderness.

'No. No. I won't hear of it,' Raphael replied.

'It wouldn't do for you to fall ill again.'

'I felt dizzy for a moment, that was all,' Raphael protested. 'I have to carry on with the sketches. It's a wasted life I fear, Giovanni, not illness, not even death. I will see you here tomorrow. The same time as this morning.' His eyes clouded over for a moment and Giulio and I watched him, stunned into silence, as he staggered to a chair. Giulio would not be insisting he accompany us to the tavern tonight.

'I think I need to retire early,' he said to us, 'just this once.'

Giulio took himself off to the tavern for that restorative drink alone while Giovanni and I walked the maestro home. He rested on us. He seemed too light for a fully grown man.

'Until tomorrow, maestro,' we said.

'Yes, *garzoni*. Until tomorrow.'

As the front door closed, we heard feet skip down the stairs and Margarita's soft voice reaching out for Raphael. 'Husband?' she said, and the strings of jealousy pulled tight around my heart.

Chapter 39

Work on the loggia at the Vatican was going well. Pope Leo was pleased with Raphael's design and his assistants' execution, not least because its biblical subject pleased his cardinals who were growing ever more northern in inclination by the day. And there was still much to do.

Giulio had much to say on the subject. 'Soon we'll all be made to go round in drab clothes, to appreciate the divine symmetry of the human body will be a sin, and there will be a law against laughter!' He laughed defiantly and slapped me on the back. Raphael was late. It was easy to attribute it to his recently married status and Giulio did. 'He's painting Margarita again,' he said with a wink. 'I know I would.'

But I wasn't so sure, after yesterday. Neither was Giovanni, who, that morning, had been waiting for Raphael and wrestling with his conscience. He was planning to stop the maestro from going back underground; he was anticipating a struggle. He came over and cuffed Giulio round the head. 'That's enough of your smutty euphemisms,' he barked. But once started Giulio wouldn't stop.

'Painting Margarita? Ha! Now there's a painting I'd like to get my hands on. There'd be a market for that, I can tell you.'

Giovanni and I drifted away, neither wanting to talk about

what had happened to the maestro the day before. As if not to name the dark truth we had both witnessed would mean that it didn't exist. Naïve fools that we were. Giulio, intent on wringing every drop of juice out of his joke, continued to laugh, working on his drawing for *The Last Supper*.

At that moment the maestro walked in. He still looked pale, drawn. 'Tired out in the service of Venus,' Giulio mouthed over at us, adding for me, 'too much f-f-f-f . . .' but I turned away. An old joke. The atmosphere in the workshop was sombre, the only laughter Giulio's. All eyes were on Raphael. He was pointing at Giulio's drawing. He was animated, enthusiastic. But he looked small. The shining, beautiful man I'd met twelve years ago was gone.

*

Later that day Margarita paid Raphael an unexpected visit. He had gone to study the ancient frescoes again; Giovanni had been unable to stop him. His new wife was cross.

'There's such a change in him,' she exclaimed. And as I looked at her, the beaded net she wore on her head signalled a change in her too. My aesthetic senses were not best pleased with this stylistic departure. Though the net was elegant, it confined Margarita's beautiful hair. I cast my eye over her dress. *Stop it,* I told myself as I heard her say repeatedly, 'I told him not to go. I told him.' The alarm in her voice reminded me there were more important matters upon which to expend my energies than dissecting her new wardrobe.

She made her way over to me.

'Have you noticed anything about him? Anything strange? Different?' Her tone was hushed, concerned. 'I packed food for him. Did he take it?' Her voice was strained. 'Did he seem tired? More tired than usual?' She sounded desperate.

She swept a hand across her forehead. Her skin was dotted with beads of perspiration despite it being January. She looked flushed. She mentioned feeling a little sick. I told her to go. There was nothing she, or I, could do at present. Raphael had gone to study the ruins.

'And has he received any more . . .' She paused, as if choosing her words carefully. 'Have any more . . . *requests* . . . appeared from . . . the ambassador?' Her voice dipped at the end as if swallowed by the chasm of her own fear.

I recollected that there had been two, possibly three, but I hadn't thought a great deal about them. That I couldn't put my hand on either pained her greatly. She lowered her eyelids. Tear-tipped, her lashes shone like jewels. I would have liked to know what was making the maestro's . . . wife (there, I said it) worry so. Raphael was the most celebrated artist in the entire world. He had no one to be afraid of. Though, at the back of my mind, reasons were piling up to make me afraid for him.

*

I went to open the workshop door. Someone was struggling to come in.

'Maestro?' Raphael had returned. 'Where's Giovanni?' I asked.

'The tavern,' he answered, a faint smile on his dry lips.

'Did I hear you say you wanted to go to the tavern?' Giulio shouted over. 'Because I do too. But there's something I need to ask you first.' He came over to Raphael, while giving me the nod that told me it was time for me to check all the windows were closed.

As I passed the maestro I looked him in the eye, hoping to see the man I knew there. Instead it was as if I was peering behind the still-intact façade of a ruined building; though the external walls were still standing, very little remained inside. Time and work were hollowing him out. I was looking at a shell. 'I think I'll go home and go to bed,' he replied to Giulio.

Not even Giulio looked for the innuendo in this.

'I'll be here bright and early in the morning,' he said in a weak, scratchy voice. We could hear his cruel cough as he made his way along the street.

Chapter 40

'It's cold enough in here to freeze your nose off,' Giulio said to me the next morning as we opened up the studio together. He laughed as if sharing a secret joke with himself. I did not respond. The *joke* was not that secret and it was not that funny. Though he was right about one thing – it was as cold as death.

Unwilling to take my jacket off, I went to the back of the studio where I noticed two large windows gaping open. I had closed them the evening before. A pain shot up my temples. I winced. I must have left them open. I went to push them to but before I could I saw something move out of the corner of my eye. Not quick, but sure, and slow. So slow that I wanted to pretend that it wasn't there. I went to close the windows once more, but this time I heard three equally sure, equally slow hoots. I moved away from the windows, leaving them ajar. My heart was now beating fast. I looked.

There, perched on the top of an easel, was an owl, with brown, round, blinking eyes. An owl. Fate's feathered messenger. Ancient Romans saw owls as omens of impending disaster. Hearing the hoot of an owl indicated an imminent death. Hadn't Julius Caesar heard the hoot of an owl before his demise? And I'd heard this owl hoot three times. I went to cry for Giulio but no sound came out.

I clutched at my throat. My eyes stared in horror and disbelief. The owl swivelled its head from side to side, then blinked at me some more. It repeated its three sure hoots.

Where was Giulio? Couldn't he hear the creature?

The owl spread its majestic wings. I could not move. I watched it swoop, out through the window, saw it vanish in the cold, morning light.

I rushed to the windows and closed them. The spell was broken. I found my voice. 'Giulio!' I cried. 'Did you see that?'

'See what?' he replied, no hint of mischief in his eyes.

I blinked. Good, I told myself. Perhaps I hadn't seen it, heard it, after all. Perhaps the owl had never been there. Though something deep within told me that it had. I took my jacket off, put on my apron, and got down to work.

The rest of the workshop trickled in. Two hours later and only the maestro himself was still to appear. He had not made it in bright and early after all. We continued to work. And wait. We watched the door. Messengers came and went. Errand boys arrived, bearing pigments. Models slipped in. Apprentices slipped out. The time for the maestro to be late had passed. No one said a word. Not even Giulio. The atmosphere was oppressive. More hours passed. Nobody dared move. It was getting to the point where we would have to send word to find out where, and possibly how, he was. And all the while the owl remained perched on an easel at the back of my mind, giving its three hoots. Fate had sent a message. Death was coming. Was it for me? Such superstitious nonsense, I told myself as my fingers felt around for the *cimaruta* in my pocket.

The door flew open. And there, in the doorway, stood Margarita. Her face was ashen and eyes red-ringed. The very sight of her struck fear into my heart. She ran to me.

'Raphael?' I asked. In my mind the owl spread out his majestic wings and gave three hoots. It had started.

Margarita nodded, holding back the tears, her face in a grimace of despair.

'I need herbs . . . to make a poultice . . . There's a woman, a healer I know. I must find her. He will be fine. He has to be fine.' She paced. Her eyes darted round the room, her breathing quick, her hands clammy. She wiped them against her dress repeatedly but to no avail.

'Is he well?' I asked.

'Of course he is,' she snapped, pushing her palms still deeper into the folds of her skirt until they disappeared completely. The grimace on her face tightened. The tears were beginning to sting – I could tell from the red rims that struggled to keep them in. She would not be able to do so for much longer. 'Well.' She spat the word out. She lifted her hands up as if she didn't know what to do with them; she sent a pot full of brushes crashing to the floor. 'He is well. Well, I tell you.'

Giulio peered up from his drawing, and, unaware of her distress, came over to ask Margarita where the maestro was.

'Where is he? Worn him out?'

I waited for a torrent of abuse to cascade down upon Giulio's head. Instead, when Margarita opened her mouth, she was unable to utter any sound. Words stuck in her throat. Hot tears spilled down her face, scorching her cheeks. Giulio realised his mistake. He went to console her but he was too late. She had already fled.

The owl flapped its wings within my imagination. My heart pounded against the walls of my chest with dread. I feared for Raphael. I felt him doubly in danger – from whatever malady had struck him down, as well as from the slipshod ways of the backstreet healer his new wife was presumably now looking for.

Fate had delivered its message to me, the owl its sinister messenger. It was for me to stop it. That had to be it. I had been chosen. Only I could save Raphael. And I knew how to do it. If the maestro was ill he required the best treatment. I would go to see Bibbiena.

'What's up with her?' Giulio called out. I went over to where he was working. Always an excellent draughtsman, his drawings done so far for *The Last Supper* were among the best I'd ever seen, beautifully outlined and with such depth and understanding of character that you would imagine his pencil tip had pierced the skin of the person and found its way right to their very soul. Raphael had always recognised his talent. That's why he'd given Giulio the preparatory drawings for this particular scene for the loggia.

It was no hardship for me to make my way over to Giulio's workbench and tell him his drawings were the best I'd ever seen him do. I studied each figure that he had now placed around the long table and remarked that he'd drawn every character except one. 'After all these years of painting Last Suppers and still you've not found yourself a suitable Judas. But the rest. The work of a master,' I said to him.

'What are you up to?' he asked.

I gave him a smile. 'The work of a master,' I repeated.

'I want to draw you, Pietro.'

Though I wanted to get this exchange with Giulio over and done with as quickly as possible, his matter-of-fact manner still had the power to thrill and frighten me. It anchored me to the spot.

'You have the face of a . . .' He stood in front of me and cupped his hands around my jaw. Excitement prickled my skin like a rash at his touch. 'Yes, you do. You have the face I'm looking for. The innocent face of a skilful traitor. I could watch you commit a crime and still question my own eyes,' he said. 'Ha! What it must be to have a face that says one thing and thinks another.'

It amazed me that people often missed the significance of the words that came out of their mouths. But as I felt guilt colour my temples it seemed that I hadn't quite achieved complete mastery over my duplicitous features quite yet.

'Stop now, Giulio. Margarita has just told me the m-m-m-maestro is not well.'

Concern and fear swept across his mocking features as he studied my face. 'So that's what was upsetting her. Unwell, you say?' Suddenly serious. 'In what way?'

'Tired. In need of rest,' I replied.

My answer satisfied him. Giulio was the type of man who did not like to accept that someone he cared for was ill. I'd seen him dismiss the incontestable proof that Raphael's health was failing before. To think that all Raphael needed was to catch up on his sleep made sense to him. He nodded and returned to his painting. I went to track down Bibbiena.

*

Everybody knew that cardinals and popes employed the best physicians. They were well trained to deal with many poisons, researched the latest treatments for dealing with that dreadful disease the French had brought into the country, and they'd done wonders for many a pope's piles. As far as I, and anyone else that had come into contact with Raphael over the past few years were concerned, what ailed Raphael more than anything was overwork. He was exhausted, and had been for some time, and the best people to deal with that were those who attended the most important men in the city – and not some illiterate healer who pounded together a little rosemary and thyme.

I informed Bibbiena, and, as I'd hoped, he dispatched a team of physicians to look after the maestro immediately. By the time I went to visit the patient not one hour later I expected to find him sitting up in bed with paper and pen in his hands sketching the men who had come to make him better.

Sadly, that was not the scene that awaited me, although it took more than an hour to find out what was.

The problems started from the moment I arrived at the maestro's door.

Guards now stood outside. I went to go inside. They blocked my way.

'Who are you?'

I told them. I stepped forward. They pushed me back.

'What is your business?'

'To see Master Raphael.' I stepped forward again. They pushed me once more, this time with force. I reeled backwards, rubbing my arms and looking at them with confused resentment. They seemed set to turn their weapons on me. Apprehension slipped its fingers around my neck. I went to speak but no sound came out.

My mind searched for answers. Then I had one. Bibbiena. Only he could have deployed these guards here. Though why I was less sure of.

I stepped forward. The guards bristled.

'I-I-I-I am here b-b-b-by order of C-C-Cardinal Bibbiena,' I declared, nervousness getting the better of me. One of them gave a cruel smile, the other craned his neck as if he couldn't decipher what I'd said. The fear in my throat had strangled my voice, caused me to stutter. I coughed quickly and repeated, louder and deeper this time, 'I am here . . . by order . . . of . . . Cardinal Bibbiena.' This time the two men did hear me. They glanced at one another, nodded, then stood aside.

I hurried past them. Once within, the door slammed shut behind me. I rested, my back against the oak, and waited for the relief to come. It did not. There was something wrong; I could smell it. My eyes searched the gloom of the hall and there, slumped on the settle, I saw two figures, draped like rag dolls. Scrawny, scruffy, lifeless. I walked towards them with trepidation. As I got closer so they raised their faces up, slowly. It was the red rings of sorrow around their eyes that I recognised first, and then, piece by piece, my mind looked beyond the vision of heartbreak before me to work out that these apparitions were Raphael's servants Elena and Ludovico. I made out Elena's apron, followed by the tell-tale unruly lock that was forever escaping from her otherwise well-coiffed hair. As for Ludovico I would know his red and black striped hose anywhere, surprisingly jaunty for a servant, while the scar on his cheek was his alone. It was them.

I stopped dead in my tracks at the realisation. This now spectral pair looked at me with fear. They had the same haunted look in their eyes I'd seen in Margarita's hours earlier. And now they had an air of prisoners in their own home and place of work. Elena stood up, a basket of her mistress's clothes at her feet.

'Where's Raphael?'

Words animated by fear tumbled over each other. They told me what had happened, how Raphael had tried to get up that morning, collapsed, how they had helped Margarita carry him back to bed. She had gone to seek help while they had taken it in turns to cool his forehead with wet rags. There'd been no sign of Margarita since she'd left, distressed, that morning. But an army of cardinals and physicians had descended on the house just over one hour ago.

'It's like we've been invaded,' Ludovico muttered, his voice low for fear of being heard.

'And the brutes pulled us away from the maestro, dear, sweet man that he is . . . Interrogated us, they did, all about Margarita. Oh, that poor girl. How I worry for her.' I heard the loyalty and love in their voices.

'I pray she gets help!'

'I pray they let her back in!'

Two guards marched by, escorting two priests. Elena and Ludovico fell silent. Elena's bottom lip trembled. Ludovico's left eye twitched. I'd only wanted the best physicians for the maestro, not a small army to keep Margarita out and strike fear in the hearts of these two loyal servants. An icy chill made me shudder. Had I done the right thing? The owl blinked in my mind. If the Cardinal's physicians saved Raphael then I had.

*

The fierce-looking guard standing outside Raphael's bedroom moved aside for me. I looked around the sick room. This occupation of the maestro's personal space seemed wrong. The bedchamber, though large, seemed small, peopled as it was by at least ten sinister figures, several of great bulk. All trace of Margarita had been removed, already, and as I observed the sly devils hovering in the darkness, I felt unnerved. I had a sense that they were waiting for him to weaken so that they could fly in and take the spoils. I told myself I was being ridiculous.

My eyes went to Raphael. Barely visible through the wall of physicians, my great master appeared small. Sick. Lying in his own bed. In the home that he'd built. Yet I'd had to push past someone else's guards to get in here. It felt wrong. And it was my fault. Why were guards placed at every entrance into the house? Who were they intending to keep out? What was Bibbiena thinking? I felt uncomfortable; I knew the answers.

The chink in the wall of physicians closed. I could see Raphael no more. I stepped back and looked around, my eyes now accustomed to the gloom. The men of God and medicine looked at me with suspicion as I did them. Yet at least they were here, I told myself, here to tend his body and his soul.

Moans, low and animal, came from the other side of the physicians attending Raphael. He sounded very sick. It was fortuitous that I went to Bibbiena when I did, I told myself.

I could not get close to the maestro though I waited hours for the chance. Time did what time does in moments such as these. Sometimes I willed it to rush by, at others I wanted it to stop. I sat on a chair positioned against a wall and breathed in the increasingly stale, rank air scented by the disgusting smell of disease. My eyes fought against fatigue, my head jerked back against sleep. I searched for answers in the shadows. Once or twice I imagined I saw the owl lurking there, in the darkest crevices of the room. But then I would rub my eyes, and tell myself I was imagining it.

More low groans came from the other side of the men caring for Raphael. It was dispiriting. Then came a word, a name.

'Margarita . . . Margarita . . .'

Never did I think that her name would cause such an upsurge of hope to spring in my soul.

'Margarita . . .' There it went again. My maestro was awake.

I heard a disturbance on the other side of the door, voices remonstrating with the guards placed on the other side. My fountain of hope overflowed. Could it be her? The door opened and closed. It was Giulio and Giovanni. No sign of Margarita. My fellows came forward and embraced me, pulling me to them so close I felt the pounding of their hearts. All three of us now stared at the impenetrable wall packed tighter than ever around the maestro. Small candles flickered their amber light at the corners of our eyes. We said nothing, saw nothing, but the sounds of death tortured our souls.

A ringed finger pointed us to the door. Giulio went to resist. Giovanni placed a hand on his friend's shoulder and shook his head. Now was not the time. We made our way down to the kitchen and slumped around Elena's large oak table. We were silent, chatty; despairing, hopeful; crying, laughing, all the while waiting for news. Why did we not see there was something wrong? Why did we not do something about it before? And how come that bastard Bibbiena had posted his guards on all the doors? It was Giulio who'd asked that last question, and he looked at me, confused. My face told him I had nothing to do with it. I had achieved complete mastery over my duplicitous features after all.

We waited: for Margarita to push her way in past the armed guards; for Raphael to walk into the room and tell us to get back to the workshop; for a physician to announce that all was well; for news, any news. We waited. For hours. When it was clear no news was coming, we made our way back up the staircase. But Bibbiena's guards barred our way into the maestro's room. Giulio moved in closer to show them a drawing he'd taken out of his pocket. Their eyes creased with lewd appreciation. The older of the two guards accepted Giulio's offering, folding it away inside his jacket. Giulio patted the younger one on the shoulder and gave him a look that said he'd get one to him soon.

The faint hum of a Latin incantation started up from the other side of the door. Two clerics appeared out of nowhere and rushed into the room. We went in after them. Giulio gave the guards a wink as we passed them by.

With the door now closed behind us we were plunged in candlelit darkness once more. The smell was heavy and unpleasant, as were the words that now weighed down the atmosphere.

'. . . sin . . . soul . . . repentance . . . forgiveness . . .' The words flapped around the room from cleric to cleric, waking those assembled from their waiting state.

But what of forgiveness? What was Raphael's sin? I thought to myself. Dirge-like laments and cautionary exhortations played like grim music in the background. I tried to get away from the dreary sound. I moved towards two physician's assistants.

'He is tired of the chase.'

'What chase?'

'The hunt.'

'What hunt?'

'Of that girl.'

'What girl?'

'The one that's lowborn.'

'Oh her!'

'He's given hundreds of Madonnas her face . . .'

'Sacrilege!'

Giulio nudged me. 'I hope they never cop an eyeful of Madonna's face with *her* naked body,' he whispered in my ear. He gave a knowing laugh, although I had no idea why. I would not become party to the joke until later. 'Let's hope they never see the maestro's latest painting,' he added.

Bewildered, I went to speak with the physician who was now standing in the shadows.

'What ails the maestro?' I enquired, my voice hushed.

The physician's face showed signs of fever as sweat ran down his forehead, his damp, grey hair stuck to his temples.

'Acute fever. General lassitude. Pains in the abdomen, sometimes chest. Intermittent vomiting.' He wiped his brow with the back of his sleeve.

'The cause?' I asked.

'It could be due to a number of factors. Fatigue. Master Giulio over there tells me he's been burning the candle at both ends. Then again, the initial vomiting suggests that this might be the body's way of eliminating any poison from his system. Age, but then he's not that old. The weather . . . um . . . Then again, he could be suffering from an infection. Do you know, has he been to any of the marshy areas of the city of late? Or maybe out of the city?' The physician, like most of his profession, had eyes to see the symptoms, but, though affable enough, he was useless in identifying the cause or nailing down the illness.

A stern-looking priest came to his aid. He had a body that slid like a snake and the head of a carrion crow eager to peck at its prey. 'The cause,' he said as he ran claw-like fingers through his black feather hair. 'I *know* the cause.' He poked his beak of a nose around in the air and sucked in his breath. The hollows underneath his eyes and under his cheekbones became bottomless pits of nothingness in the tenebrous light. 'The cause without doubt is . . .' I waited.

'Excessive copulation.'

It was then that I recognised him: Cardinal Bibbiena's assistant.

'Don't I know you?' he said. His black eyes tore into mine looking to devour my soul. The owl at the back of my mind gave three hoots. Perhaps fate's messenger was telling me the death I was seeking to avoid was mine after all.

I knew then that I could say nothing. I slipped my hand in my pocket. I froze with fear – my fingers had found the pendant I'd taken from Fabio. I'd put it there when I'd got dressed. I'd made up my mind to get rid of it at last, but in all the madness

I'd quite forgotten. If it had made me feel like a marked man before, it made me feel doubly so now as I stood face to face with the Cardinal's man.

*

Raphael moaned. The man with eyes like bottomless pits released me from his stare. He watched with grim interest while the physicians bled the maestro 'to release the poisons'. After a short time he left the room.

Relieved, I concentrated on the maestro. I prayed the bleeding would work and imagined my prayers answered when Raphael woke up. I was by his side. He called for Margarita again, not quite delirious, not quite lucid. I imagined I heard her reply 'Raphael', but I told myself I had to be mistaken.

'Here, sir, please drink this water.' I held the cup to his lips. He did not recognise me.

'Where is she?' he asked.

'Who?' a physician asked.

'My Margarita! My wife. *La mia fornarina.*' Raphael's voice was weak, distant.

'What's that he's saying?' the physician asked.

'I don't know . . . can't make it out . . . Something about the girl called Margarita. His baker's daughter. Keeps saying she's his wife, or some such nonsense,' another physician replied, pushing me aside.

'I need her. Margarita. Margarita.' I watched the maestro. His eyes shone with love. A smile cut through the pain. It was as if she was there. He held out his arms to an imaginary figure behind me.

'*La mia fornarina,*' he sighed.

I went outside the room. I couldn't bear to watch.

Where was Margarita? I too wanted to know.

'Ludovico, any sign of her?'

Ludovico told me what I knew already: that Bibbiena had put

a guard on every door and window and given strict instructions to keep her out.

'But she's not stopped trying to get in to see the master, sir,' he told me. 'It's heart-breaking to hear her.' I nodded and walked away. So I had heard her from within Raphael's bedchamber.

I had no wish to hear any more.

I looked around for the Cardinal's man. When I was satisfied he was not around, I descended the main staircase, and paced up and down the corridor that led into the entrance hall. Guards were posted inside the door. Outside too. All to keep a girl out. I heard distant banging. It had to be her.

Raphael was gravely ill. Rome's best physicians were caring for him. I'd imagined that was sufficient. But what if I was wrong and the girl was the only person who could reach the maestro? If anyone could give him the will to live, she could. I paced backwards and forwards some more. I was afraid for the maestro, I was afraid for myself. I imagined owls, pendants, evil eyes.

Elena ran after me. 'Come, sir. Come to the kitchen. You need to eat, drink. Please.' She pulled on my shirt sleeve. I followed her, helpless to resist.

She pushed me down into a chair, placed a cup of wine into my hand. I looked at it. The liquid was shaking and rising up like waves breaking the surface of a sea. For a second I wondered what strange drink was this Elena had given me. I put it down on the table in fright only to realise that the commotion was not within the wine but in me. I lifted my hands before my eyes. They were trembling.

'Drink,' Elena ordered. I heard the banging once more. Elena's hand shook. 'Oh, that poor girl! Can't you do anything to help her?' I still had the pendant to get rid of. I would have to do that later. I put on my cloak. Getting out proved as hard as getting in, but I managed it somehow.

I heard Margarita before I saw her.

'Let me see him! You have to let me see him!'

Two guards, on the inside, opened the door. Two guards, on the outside, grabbed me and pulled me into the street. They'd returned to blocking the way in before I'd got to my feet.

'Take that witch away,' a guard snarled at me. 'For her sake.'

I placed an arm around Margarita's shoulders. She crumpled at my touch. She allowed me to lead her away. When at a safe distance from the house she thrust a bag of herbs into my stomach.

'Give him these. He has to take these. Get Elena to put them in water. It will make my love feel better. You'll see. Take them now.'

I hid them under my cloak and promised, promised to do whatever she wanted me to. She broke down with gratitude. I looked at her and I felt no sympathy. My heart was too full of its own suffering to have any space for hers. She did not look well, and as I thought this I found myself wishing that it was Margarita and not Raphael who was lying in bed sick. I blamed her.

'Thank you,' she said. She looked at me. The agony in her eyes mirrored my own. I cursed fate for placing me here to share her anguish. Me. Of all the people. Fate. Far more cruel than I could ever be. Yet here I was, to share the deepest of pains with a woman who at this moment in time I hated. Why did I hate this dear, sweet, loving creature? My mind was a maelstrom of petty jealousies and grudges that had accumulated over the years. They had slowly drifted to the bottom of my memory but, with Raphael gravely ill, they rose up in eddying swirls, making me dizzy, making me nauseous.

I hated her because she had brought him to this even if she hadn't intended to. I hated her because she was poor and he was rich. I hated her because she had taken his life down a path that he would never have found if he hadn't met her. I hated her because I knew that he loved her. I hated her because I knew that her presence and her presence alone was the only thing that would soothe Raphael. And I hated her because I could never tell her how I truly felt. I, more than anyone, knew how stinging were the cuts that were lacerating her soul: they were lacerating mine too.

I let her sob into my cloak until I felt her go weak in my arms. I kissed the top of her head as my heart ached with confusion.

'Promise?' she whispered.

'I promise,' I told her as she walked away.

When I went back inside some time later, my reason had returned. It was Margarita Raphael needed, not her bag of useless herbs. I threw them down on the table in the corner of the hallway. I bounded back up the stairs and crept into the bedchamber. Raphael seemed recovered. And he recognised me. He pulled me to him and I put my ear to his mouth.

'I haven't long to live,' he said.

His words disturbed me but he appeared recovered to my eyes. The fever had subsided, and now he could talk. I congratulated one of the physicians. But then the sickness came again. Followed by the delirium. Soon a nightmarish pattern set in. I would not leave the house again. I knew I had to stay. Giulio did too.

For three days the waves of illness enveloped him. Pushing him to life, then dragging him to death. Push – pull, push – pull. We stayed, in the bedchamber, in the kitchen, in the hall, sleeping on chairs, floors, eating half-heartedly, and drinking when Elena reminded us to. The memories of that time are not the clearest of my life.

Yet what was, is and always will be clear from those days were the requests Raphael made of both myself and Giulio. He revived with the receding of a wave. He talked quickly. He seemed lucid. Demanded to speak to us both and it was then that he whispered his requests.

'*La fornarina . . . la mia fornarina . . .* my painting . . . of her . . . please, Pietro, you must get it . . . It is for her eyes only . . . And the ring, Giulio, the ruby ring . . . please, find it . . . Give it to her . . . and the money . . .' The effort was tiring him but he would not stop until he had secured a future for Margarita.

'Is that clear?' he asked when he'd finished.

'Yes, Raphael.'

'Do you understand?' he insisted.

'Yes, Raphael.'

'Swear to me this will be done.'

'We swear, Raphael.'

'Please, go now.'

Giulio and I left the room. He went to find the wedding rings and see to the financial arrangements in the study. I went to Raphael's studio on the top floor to fetch *La Donna Velata*. *La Fornarina* was the title of the portrait Sebastiano had painted of Margarita years ago. *La Donna Velata* was Raphael's version and a lesson to the Venetian in how to paint. The fever must have confused him.

I opened the studio door. Cardinal Bibbiena was already inside.

'Pietro!'

I wished he hadn't seen me but it was too late now. As he turned around, he stepped aside to reveal a painting of Margarita. *La Donna Velata* it was not, but it was very much Raphael's baker's daughter. *La mia fornarina*. I understood now. Giulio's nudge of complicity came back to me at his mention of a Madonna's face with Margarita's body – he'd already seen this painting before me.

The Cardinal covered the painting back up as quickly as he could. But it was too late. Though I'd not been able to take it all in, I'd seen enough. Margarita wore only a turban on her head fixed by a pearl brooch, and a veil as delicate as gossamer that revealed the yielding softness of her body beneath. The image was undeniably tender in its intimacy, and although I'd only caught sight of it for the briefest of moments, I confess that it moved me.

*

I've told you already that what was and wasn't acceptable had been changing in Rome for a while. Corruption had always been an issue, but because those most guilty were the arbiters of holy goodness themselves, very little was done about it. I've often wondered who knew about the dark deeds of the Cardinal's man – though I imagine his sins went beyond the pale even for those he hid behind. But on a lighter note, the holders and defenders of the Catholic church, while delivering a good sermon, could also put on the most amazing party. A blind eye was generally turned to most carnal sins, not least because many of the cardinals partook of them liberally.

Oh yes, there would be a token trial here, and a new law there, but generally most sins were tolerated. Or bought off. What was the point of buying and selling a good relic, or a boxful of indulgences, if you couldn't get away with a little sexual excess every now and again?

But then the Catholics of the North started to interfere. Cold, sexless figures. Sticklers for rules and completely lacking in life and colour. Even their artists, though technically brilliant, often produced work so ugly . . . well, that's a matter of opinion, and, as an Italian I'm biased. Suffice to say, there's a difference between us. I suppose Rome should have known change was in the offing when Erasmus of Rotterdam left the city accusing the Papacy of excess and hypocrisy. The Sumptuary Laws, until then rarely enforced and only when a particular guard had it in for you, started to be implemented with new rigour.

But it was when Martin Luther, a professor of moral philosophy from Germany, nailed his *Ninety-Five Arguments* to the door of a church in Wittenberg, that the die was well and truly cast. The power of indulgences in Rome plummeted. Codes of morality, usually only paid lip service to, were now applied, and *seen* to be applied, at every level of society. Money wouldn't do it, not completely, anymore. And art could not glorify it. Action was called for.

As I looked at Cardinal Bibbiena I understood: a scapegoat was needed, and it served his purposes for it to be Margarita.

Bibbiena studied my face. 'Rome isn't what it was. If word gets out about this immoral painting,' he warned me, 'it will destroy the workshop.' He paused to assess the effect his words had had upon me. 'It will destroy *you*,' he said, his mouth so close to me I could feel the wet heat of his breath on my neck as he moved forward to hiss in my ear.

As I left the studio he held up the key to the door. Bibbiena had the only one. I would not be able to get in so easily again. A well of profound sadness bore its way within me. I had let Raphael down.

*

When Giulio and I came back into the maestro's room the air was sour and thick. The candles seemed weaker, while quiet sobs hid in the drapery that shrouded the room. Friends had been informed and they now paraded through. Agostino. Bindo Altoviti. Baldassare Castiglione. Most could not bear to stay in the room. The end was near, though I could not believe it. I was still convinced the death foretold was to be mine. All the signs were there, though the Cardinal's dark-eyed assistant was nowhere to be seen.

Giulio had succeeded in locating the jewels and the money; I had failed in securing the painting.

I hovered by the bed, guilty. Raphael's lids flickered open. Recognition flashed within his eyes though the muscles in his face were too weak to do anything other than reveal his pain. He raised a hand. His veins cried out, like the roots of a tree clawing to hold on to the earth when uprooted. He opened his mouth but no words came out. Decay was its only message. I wanted to withdraw but his eyes were pleading. I knew what they wanted me to do: help the woman he loved. 'Yes,' I whispered. 'Yes,' I said again. Life fluttered beneath his eyelids. As he slipped into unconsciousness so tears fluttered beneath mine. I wiped them away on my shirt sleeve.

*

The fever set in for the last time. It was savage, ugly, though at times the physician's attempts to intervene seemed worse. And when his chest rattled, spitting out the last traces of Raphael's life, sobs broke out around the bed most volubly. Three days after he fell ill the curtains in his room flapped, the window blew wide open, and a brown-feathered owl spread its wings and flew out and up to the heavens. No one saw it, only me.

The tired physicians could do no more to bring Raphael back.

I looked at him. All trace of pain had vanished. His face was beautiful and young again.

The sweetest man that I had ever known was dead.

When his body had given up the fight it was almost a relief. That time can run in two directions when a man is on the point of dying was something that I learned while at Raphael's deathbed. That a person can want opposite things, feel opposite emotions, at the same time was another lesson. Relief entered my body when Raphael grew calm, getting ready to leave this life forever. I would no longer have to see his pain because he would no longer feel it. But anguish tortured my senses too, full of bitterness that a beautiful life was soon to be snuffed out. My longing for him would scorch me for all eternity. The man that I had loved for so long would never ruffle my hair, laugh at my jokes nor help with my work again.

Like tongues of flame on a burning lake news of Raphael's death rampaged round Rome, raging and roaring. Tears rolled in artists' workshops and private villas, in grand churches and ducal palaces. Hot, burning tears. Chigi, Bibbiena, Pope Leo X. Not even wealth, injured pride and power could escape. Yes, even Bibbiena felt the loss.

But the most agonising grief of all was that experienced by a lowborn young girl as she screamed silently into the floury overalls of her father in another part of the city.

Chapter 41

Grief – I didn't know that was what you called love when you'd lost it. I didn't know it burned a hole deeper than the size of love it replaced. I did now. I did not sleep or eat for days. I recalled Margarita when she confessed her love for Raphael to me before she went to stay with him at Chigi's villa. She'd felt the same to be away from him. What was she going to feel now?

But it didn't pay to linger on such things. She'd be all right, I told myself. Raphael had asked Giulio and me to make arrangements for her and make arrangements for her we would.

There would be a large amount of money, enough to make her a woman of independent means, enough to buy a home for her father, enough to buy a home for her sister if she wanted. Perhaps together they could even buy a little estate in the countryside. Giulio had passed on the money to me to get to her. Then there were the jewels Raphael had wanted her to have. Giulio would get them to her. Then there was the painting. The one Raphael had wanted me to give to her. The one the Cardinal had discovered.

I would never be able to give it to her now, no matter what I'd promised.

I'd worked out where to find her. I'd been wrong about Francesco Luti. He was a loving father, unlike mine. That he was

299

looking after her did not surprise me. I planned to go and pay them both a visit, and settle matters, as soon as I felt stronger. But before I could I needed to find some solace myself, and I found that in the arms of Cardinal Bibbiena's young page.

*

Rumours were whistling along the back alleys and corridors of power alike. Rumours about the much-loved Raphael. They blew one way. *He had a secret wife. A secret family. She was a poor girl, a Madonna of the people.* They blew the other way. *He had a concubine. She pulled him down.* You know the sort of thing.

Rumours. Depending on the direction of the wind, they could blow anywhere. And if you were the one doing the blowing, or could afford for others to do it for you, the rumours could blow any way you liked. And Cardinal Bibbiena, a man of shrewd intelligence, knew this more than most. He'd had much of the wind knocked out of him after Raphael's dealings with his niece. But the artist's death had done much to restore what had been lost. Bibbiena knew the truth, as did I. But the truth was not what was needed here, and besides, nobody was greatly interested in hearing it.

'*They say she was a whore. A gold-digging one at that. I have a friend who told me the priests had to make Raphael give her up on his death bed to save his immortal soul.*'

Unfortunately I had been the unwitting *friend*, Bibbiena's young page the eager gossip.

'*Lust, far more deadly than any illness. They say it twisted his heart, sucked the very lifeblood from him . . . as did that whore of his.*'

That was what people wanted to hear: a tragic tale of a great man brought down by human weakness and a worthless woman, and my perfidious, loose-lipped lover had been more than happy to refashion my words for his eager audience. I never told him Margarita and Raphael were married.

*

300

I received a message to meet the Cardinal at Raphael's home on the Via dei Coronari on the Saturday. I picked up Fabio's pendant as I went out. I would show it to the Cardinal and tell him of my suspicions about his assistant.

When I arrived at Raphael's, Elena let me in. 'Does the Cardinal have any of his men with him?' I checked.

'No, he's alone,' she answered without looking up.

'You can wait for Cardinal Bibbiena here,' she said to me, wincing as if sucking something sour. 'He's here more now than when our dear Raphael was alive,' she tutted as she led me to the large entrance hall. 'Now if you'll excuse me.'

I'd not been here since . . . I looked around the familiar space. It echoed with the loneliness I felt. I stood up and went up the staircase to the bedroom. I trembled before the closed door. My breathing grew shallow, my head faint. I shoved my way in.

Once inside I was relieved to note the smell of sickness had disappeared. My eyes traced the light squeezing in around the edges of the closed shutters. I stood there, unable to move. The light, I needed the light. I stumbled to the windows, pushed them open. The day flooded in, gushing and gurgling over me, making me feel awake and alive once more.

I cast my eyes around the room. It too had come to life. I noticed that Elena had made up the bed, placing the cushion Margarita had embroidered in pride of place. She had even brought down a pot full of pencils and scrolls of paper ready to be used. Signs of love and art signalled a past, present, and future for the loving couple. It all seemed so familiar – the way it was meant to be. Except now Raphael was dead, and Margarita was banished. I looked at the cushion. It tugged at my conscience. And that was the bed from where Raphael made me promise to look after the girl who'd embroidered it.

'*Raphael!*' I cried out loud, overwhelmed by his loss. I put my hand out against the wall to stop myself from falling. I closed my eyes. My body struggled to remain steady and waited for the feeling to pass.

The door opened. So did my new eyes. But they had come too late.

'So this is where you are.' It was the Cardinal. He presented his ring. As I stooped to kiss it, he waved the key to Raphael's private studio before my face. 'Here. Take it. Lead the way.' I did as I was told, ascending the stairs, my reluctant legs heavy and slow. The Cardinal panted, equally slow but in no way reluctant, behind me. I put the key in the lock, tried to turn it. The lock resisted. I rattled it around, tried again, to no avail.

The Cardinal blew through his nose as he shoved me to one side. 'Allow me,' he said, snatching the key from my fingers and forcing the lock open in one movement. The rebuke I anticipated did not come; self-satisfaction brought with it magnanimity. He smiled at me as at a lesser mortal. He slipped the key into a purse attached to his belt, but not before locking us in.

He lumbered towards the painting of Margarita. A cloth had been draped over it untidily. Bibbiena pulled it neatly to cover the entire surface.

The Cardinal's neck was nearly as red as his robe, his breath fighting with his words to break out. He was panting again, though I was confused as to why. I stood, waited, saying nothing. I saw Marsilio Ficino's *Vinculum Mundi*. How was it Raphael had once described it to me? *The beautiful book about love that binds all of God's creations together, where classical beliefs and Christianity come together in joyful union.* The Cardinal took a step to the side. Dried leaves crackled and disintegrated into dust beneath his feet. I looked in horror at the foliage I myself had gathered to celebrate the wedding of Raphael and Margarita. It now littered the room. The wedding. It belonged to another time. As did Ficino's book.

The Cardinal picked it up as if weighing its worth in his hands. 'You knew.'

I said nothing.

'You knew,' Bibbiena said again.

302

'The woman in this painting,' he tugged on the cloth without removing it, '*killed* Raphael.'

I said nothing.

'With her wantonness she seduced him.' His breathing quickened, the colour rose from his neck to his face. It was as if his entire being was being licked by the flames of hellfire. He took the corner of the cloth in one hand and tapped the side of the painting with the other. Then, with all the panache and flair of a magician, he whipped the cloth away. I looked at the painting for only the second time. I said nothing. Because I couldn't. The greenery now desiccated on the floor was alive in the painting before me. It gleamed with the promise of a happy and fruitful married life.

So many details I'd missed before I drank in now. The square-cut ruby ring that Raphael had given to Margarita was there for all to see, glinting on the third finger of the painted Margarita's left hand. And yes, I gasped with recognition, there, painted around her arm was the ribbon I'd once caught her embroidering some months back. It had 'Raphael of Urbino' upon it. If the woman in the painting had killed Raphael, she had been no whore and he would have wanted his sweet death. But she did not kill him. I'd witnessed his death.

'A fine painting . . . of a whore.'

An intimate painting of a much-cherished wife, my thoughts corrected him, though I said nothing.

I looked at her eyes: warm, sensual, and so alive it was as if she might see into my soul. I looked to the floor in shame.

'It needs finishing.'

It was finished but I did not disagree.

'A little going over of the hands . . . in particular the ring, you can paint that out . . . and perhaps all this greenery we could paint over . . . and the ribbon . . . ah!' Bibbiena moved his hands with a flourish over the sections of the painting he wished to be *finished*.

'The ribbon. Aaaah. The ribbon. I've been thinking about

303

that. Perhaps we could leave it. A gift from the great artist to his courtesan. To show his generosity and her . . . well . . .' He swept his hand in the air again. 'To show that he's paid for her,' Bibbiena said of the girl who refused to be bought.

'We can get it done and sell it. Perhaps put it on display somewhere *public* for a while. To celebrate Raphael's genius – there are some magical touches here – and to help keep the workshop ticking over at this most financially difficult of times. What do you think, Pietro?'

I thought of Margarita. This was her painting, a wedding gift from a husband to his wife. And it was *la fornarina*, the painting that, while on his deathbed, Raphael had asked us to secure. In truth, I should never have seen it, nor would have done if Raphael had lived. Giulio was the only other person who had, and I was guessing that was because he'd sneaked a sly peek at it. He had a lively interest in couplings, marital and otherwise. All things sensual intrigued him. He would have been interested in seeing how Raphael expressed desire in paint.

Dark thoughts swooped above my head, circling then diving, their sharp claws tearing into my skin. Pearls of sweat broke out across my forehead as I imagined Margarita's agony at the thought that everybody would see this most personal and loving of works. I have no doubt Bibbiena envisaged the same agony, as a sadistic smile twisted his lips revealing yellowing teeth in fleshy gums. At last, he could elevate his private grudge against Margarita to the level of public condemnation with a painting.

I put a hand in my pocket and pulled out a handkerchief to wipe my brow. The pendant I'd hoped to show the Cardinal dropped onto the floor. I went to tell him my suspicions about his assistant but the moment I saw his face I realised it was pointless. He froze at the sight of the accursed object as it hit the marble: he knew about his assistant already. He coughed while I picked it up. Although shaken, Bibbiena would not be put off.

'I do hope you understand the importance of what I'm asking

you to do. If this gets out . . .' He pointed to the ring and the foliage. '. . . It will mean the end of the workshop.' He was so calm as he spoke. Perhaps I was mistaken in thinking he recognised the pendant. 'Many cardinals will take their commissions elsewhere. Some may even use it as an excuse not to settle up, which, I believe, will leave the workshop in a parlous state . . . It's the fault of this new northern sensibility that has come over the city.'

He paced the floor for a while as if deep in thought. 'Talking of which, we might have to make a few more serious changes . . . I'm thinking of sending one of my men to Rotterdam, or Wittenberg, to offer a palm leaf to those most critical of Rome.'

I rolled the pendant round in my hand as he told me he might send the man I feared more than death itself away. He kept his eyes focused on the painting – away from me. 'The sooner you finish this painting the sooner I will be able to arrange such secondments. So you see, it pays to get on. This painting reveals too much about Raphael's whoring and we can't be seen to tolerate immorality in our artists. The survival of the workshop depends on it. Besides, make a good job of it and I may have some commissions for you to consider.'

I warmed to his words. Sensible. Practical. Margarita was a survivor, I told myself. Besides, she would have the money, and this was only a painting. People would soon forget about it. And the Cardinal's man would be dispatched to a northern city and leave me in peace. If this was bribery it was well timed, and I laughed at myself, to think that I was afraid of a pendant.

As we left, Bibbiena patted me on the back. 'Has anyone else seen this painting?'

'I don't think so. Only Giulio.'

'Splendid!' the Cardinal spluttered, alarmed that someone else knew the truth about Raphael and Margarita. 'He must help finish it too.'

*

'You knew.' When Cardinal Bibbiena spoke these two words to me I never did understand if he meant I knew about the wedding or if I knew that Margarita was a whore who'd destroyed Raphael. I surmise that as an intelligent man he intended for his words to be deliberately ambiguous. He was a political beast after all who knew the efficacy of the vague expression. And my guess was that he cared about the wedding only in as much as it could tarnish his reputation. As for thinking Margarita had killed Raphael off with her amorous exploits, the Cardinal knew better than that: he had placed himself in the path of many whores over the years and was still standing. But there was no way he was going to allow the truth to get in the way of a compelling story; I was soon to observe his brilliance when it came to rewriting the past.

I stepped backwards. I heard the dry leaves crackle beneath my feet. I remembered the wedding. How I'd wanted to stop it. It seemed like a dream that belonged to a far more innocent time than the one I found myself inhabiting now. My sweet master was gone forever. And I looked upon my days of scheming against Margarita as what they were – ridiculous, pointless. The Cardinal patted me on the shoulder. There would be no going back now. Scheming was about to become political.

Raphael died on Good Friday, 1520, and his funeral was conducted with all the pomp and ceremony you would expect for Rome's most celebrated artist. Pope Leo X himself shed tears of sorrow at the passing of this prince among men and the great and the good came out to bid him farewell. Cardinal Bibbiena was pleased. He was the power behind the throne and the funeral, and when he'd decided that Raphael's marble sarcophagus should be interred with that of his niece Maria, no one said a word against it. Raphael would be entombed forever with his betrothed in the Pantheon and history would look back and say, 'It was fitting so.'

Yet anyone who had known Raphael knew the truth. Of course, the apprentices in Raphael's workshop gossiped and griped for a while. 'She was a good girl,' 'I liked her,' 'She brought out the best,'

'Bibbiena's a liar,' 'Saying it's true doesn't make it so,' 'He can't buy the truth.' But he could and he did. That was, is, and always will be the way with people of privilege and power. And the voices that clamoured against what was being peddled as fact had neither the means nor the authority to make any difference. After all, who would believe them? And who would care if a driver of a carriage said he'd taken Margarita to the church to get married, or mind that a jeweller had once made a ruby ring for a famous artist? Besides, apprentices might moan but they'd be foolish to speak out when the might and wealth of a cardinal could bring them all down and their entire workshop as well.

That was the problem. Their – and our – future depended on Bibbiena. That's why Bibbiena could write history any way he wanted. And part of me believed that he had no choice but to do what he was doing.

That's why Giulio did nothing to stop it. And neither did I. For a while.

*

Once I'd found out Margarita's father was there for her I told myself there was no hurry. She would be all right. I intended to keep my promise to Raphael. Giulio would get the jewels to Margarita and I would pass on the money. Eventually. But, for now, I had to secure the future of the workshop. Many livelihoods depended on it. It was not in our interests to make Raphael and Margarita's marriage public knowledge, even though that would be the honest thing to do. Society would not like it. And it would tarnish the reputation of us all. The Vatican would refuse to pay us for work completed and new commissions would cease.

It seems strange to think that a marriage should be deemed such a sin, and that a marriage based on love between an artist and a baker's daughter should be viewed as an outrage. But that was the situation. A new order was emerging. That was why the couple had kept their union a secret. That was why Giulio and I had to paint over the evidence in oils.

The day Bibbiena locked us in Raphael's top studio in his house on Via dei Coronari to cover up the truth was a day both of us would rather forget. I can't remember now which one of us painted over the ring and which the marital foliage. All I know is that we did it.

But before this act of barbarism was committed we both did something Raphael had always stressed was important and respectful to do. *When asked to paint over someone else's work, always remember to make a copy of it yourself.* That's what we did. We sketched as lovingly as we could then rolled up the evidence, hiding what we'd done so as not to get caught by Bibbiena. Later, when I'd finished it, I gave mine to Margarita. I can only imagine what Giulio did with his. Some adulterated form of it might well have ended up in *i modi*, his book of sexual positions, for all I know. Regardless of where it ended up, I remember that he took great care over it.

Nevertheless, I took the task set by the Cardinal seriously, and I would be lying if I said that some part of me wasn't flattered to have a hand in it. And I believed Bibbiena would reward my loyalty and my talent, as well as send his dastardly man far away.

Giulio was under no such illusion, nor was he running from the Cardinal's man.

'He's written a play – the Cardinal,' he said, as he studied the naked Margarita.

'Bibbiena?'

'The very one.'

His brush hovered over the curve of her breast.

'He's not so very upright,' Giulio said, his finger running over the copy he'd made on the table to the side.

'His play . . . it's full of *keyholes*.' He looked at me with raised eyebrows. '*Keyholes* that need lots of *oiling*.' He made a suggestive gesture with his paintbrush as he plunged it in the lock shape made by his thumb and forefinger.

'Oh,' I said. I would have laughed at this not so very long ago, but now, it angered me.

'He's an oily piece of work,' he said. 'Not trustworthy. Don't get me wrong, I'm partial to keyholes myself. But then I've never made a secret of the fact.'

'He cares about the workshop,' I said in his defence, trying to steer us away from keyholes.

'That hypocrite?'

'He cares about art,' I went on.

Giulio took a brush and worked the skin of Margarita's hand, the one that I'd just been working on, and carefully removed the excess paint I'd applied. He gave a wry smile. 'Does he really?'

Bibbiena's key fumbled around in the lock behind us. I looked for the copies we had made, made sure they were out of sight. Giulio smirked. I grimaced. The Cardinal unlocked the door and stood in front of the picture we'd been working on for hours. It was now a different painting. I watched him as he looked at it. A semblance of a conscience fought for life inside my breast.

'Exquisite,' the Cardinal said.

My conscience was dead.

Chapter 42

It was time to track Margarita down and give her the money. I was about to try to pay off the girl I more than anyone knew was the girl who never could be bought.

But she would have to be. There was no other choice.

*

I last went to Francesco Luti's shortly after Raphael's death. That's where I would go again. I knew Margarita wouldn't be there this time – Francesca, Agostino Chigi's wife, had recently told me she'd taken herself off to the convent of San Apollonia – but I thought a visit to her father would help me salve my conscience. Raphael's money was dragging me down and I needed to get rid of it as soon as possible if I was ever going to be able to sleep again at night. If Margarita could not be paid off, I felt sure her father would oblige and take the money off my hands.

'She's not here.'

'I know. It's you I'm looking for.'

'Oh.'

'I have something for her.'

'She said you might have.'

'It's a lot of money. It will buy her a life. Will you take it for her?'

'She won't want it.'

'She will.'

'She won't.'

I offered the money to him.

'No thank you.'

It was a sorry day when I couldn't give money away to Francesco Luti. Where he'd picked up morals, until recently discarded rather loosely around him, I wasn't really sure. The man surprised me. Said it meant the world to see his strong, clever daughter get married in church on her wedding day. I recalled the shadowy figure at the back of the church. Wished he'd had the courage to come to celebrate with her. Yes, the baker surprised me with his outpouring of fatherly love. But I had no desire to see his fine feeling now. Filthy lucre, that's what his sort liked. He'd sell his own mother, and daughter, for a purse of gold.

But he didn't.

I was not as good a judge of character as I had supposed.

'Here, son, you can't leave without some bread . . . You've been a good friend to my girl. I can't thank you enough for that.'

By the time I left the bakery the sky had clouded over. Birds waited on a nearby roof. They screeched their displeasure at me.

It was time for me to try to give the money to Margarita herself. I prayed to God that she would see sense and take it. As I walked to the convent I went over all the betrayals I'd committed against the girl.

I'd lied to her, been jealous of her, deceived her.

What choice did I have? I whispered as the rain started to fall.

I'd supported Bibbiena's every petty word and deed. Spied for him.

What choice did I have?

I'd helped him to repaint the truth.

What choice did I have? I murmured to myself as an old woman bumped into me, a ragged scarf pulled round her head.

She gave no answer, though I saw a look of judgement in her eyes. I tore my face away to see a rat scuttle away and disappear into the shadows. A wind started up. Whether it was that which pulled and pushed me or whether it was my conflicting mind I couldn't really say. Only my heart was certain which way to go.

By the time I'd reached the convent the wind had dropped though the streets were still empty. I stood outside, took a deep breath then, bang, bang, bang. I hammered on the forbidding door breaking the uneasy silence.

As I watched it, large and wooden, open slowly, I felt friendless and alone. I glimpsed the abyss beyond and knew I had to face it. I waited for it to consume me.

*

Margarita. Guilt gnawed away at me while I waited to see her.

It engulfed me completely when she appeared. She walked to where I was standing, slowly, as though in pain, her skin pale against the dark habit she wore. In one hand she held a small box – Giulio must have been here before me, I realised with a pang of jealousy – and she held it close to her heart. I unfurled the copy I'd made of the painting Raphael had given her as a wedding present and thrust it towards her.

At the sight of it her bones turned to water; she flung her arms around her body as if to support it. 'No!' she cried, and the box she'd been holding as if she valued it more than life itself clattered to the floor. She collapsed in a heap against the wall, where she stayed, eyes closed, head lowered, as if waiting for her strength to return. Her arms remained like straps across her body.

Her reaction alarmed me. It did not augur well. Should I attend to her? Or pick up her jewel box? I thought it was the money I was going to have trouble persuading her to accept. What if she refused to take the copy I'd made of La Fornarina as well? In an instant I had decided. I glanced over at her – her eyes were closed. I opened the box, placed the money on top of the jewels, closed it back up. I would carry out Raphael's last wishes. She *would* take the money.

'Margarita?'

Her eyes flickered open as I called out her name. She gave a nod of acceptance. Her shock at seeing my copy of *La Fornarina* had been replaced by reason. It was her painting, or so she believed, and she would have it. Raphael had painted it for her and it was meant for their eyes only. The certain knowledge that I had seen it too made her cheeks flush crimson.

'Forgive me, Pietro . . . and thank you,' she said. She could not look me in the eye as she held out a hand to take it. Guilt fluttered around my head like a butterfly. When it landed I crushed it dead.

'Here. Take this too.' I pressed the box into the hand she still had crossed over herself. She jerked back suddenly as if I had been a little too insistent.

'Be careful, Pietro!' she cried. 'You'll hurt . . . me. But thank you,' she said, choosing to take the box in the hand that already held the rolled-up painting. I stood back. Something was wrong. But I banished the thought. My work was done here: I had given her both the painting and the money. My heart gave a leap. I had fulfilled my promise to Raphael.

It struck me then that this might be the last time I ever saw her. I wanted to embrace her. I sensed I could not. She was fragile. Precious. Like a glass ornament I was now too afraid to touch for fear of it shattering in my hands. All of a sudden an impulse came over me. I needed to give her something to remember me by. She had given me her good luck charm, the *cimaruta* I wore under my shirt constantly. The only thing I had on me was the pendant of St Sebastiano in my pocket. Better to give her nothing than to give her that, I told myself. But if I did, I reasoned, I would be rid of it and her lasting memory of me would be that I was generous. My fingers hesitated while they grappled with my conscience. Before I could stop myself I was placing the pendant around her neck.

'Here. Have this as a memento.'

Her delicate features replied with a grateful smile. 'Now you must go,' she whispered. Raising the hand she'd kept conspicuously free, she stroked my face for the last time. 'Goodbye, Pietro. My one true friend.'

'Goodbye,' I said.

Her fingers fell from my cheek and her face elongated to sadness as she pulled away. My feet dragged. I stopped when I got to the door. The guilt I'd believed I'd crushed to death came back to life.

What choice did I have? I cried.

I turned to look at her.

She stood there, crying without tears, a picture of desolation. *What choice did I have?* I said to myself one last time.

Her small hand ran over the curve of her stomach once more. She cupped it with a tenderness that troubled me; instinct told me there was something significant in her gesture.

As I walked away from the convent I quickened my step, walking fast, faster, running, relieved to be heading back into the world. Rain was starting to fall. I needed to make it to back to my late master's house. To tell Elena and Ludovico that Margarita had accepted the money. To add a last stroke or two to Raphael's painting of Margarita to please the Cardinal.

As the rain fell down upon my head I hoped that he would like what I had done – Cardinal Bibbiena.

Chapter 43

'Every ass thinks himself worthy to stand with the king's horses!' I hadn't heard that saying in years. It used to be one of my father's favourites. As I stood outside my late, beloved Raphael's workshop I wondered who Cardinal Bibbiena was laughing at. 'As for Raphael's *fornarina*,' he continued, 'we can see what she is.' Though the painting was still not completely finished it was clear that the Cardinal had not been able to wait. He was already rewriting history. And I had helped him.

I am sorry. And still I would have continued to do so.

It was only because he'd insulted my vanity and forced me to see it for what it was that I changed direction. But I now knew what he thought of me as an artist. I, more than most, deserved to hear no good of myself. And the Cardinal did not disappoint on that score.

Much of what he said of me I have not included in these pages. Still, his betrayal (poetically just, I know), made me see I had a choice. I always did. No matter how much I railed against fate, I'd done bad things against Margarita knowingly, and seen bad things done to her by others while saying nothing. I'd never spoken up for her. That was the choice I'd made. Now was the time for me to choose differently.

That night I slept most fitfully, my dreams washing up all of my treacherous deeds from the impenetrable depths of the seabed of my memory and leaving them on the beach to dry out in the sun for all to observe. On waking, I thought I saw the owl I had seen before Raphael's death pass from my dream to reality. I rubbed my eyes. When I opened them again it was gone. But this time its presence had elicited no fear within my breast. Instead it had left a repository of hope within my heart. Now was the time for me to make the right choice, and write the story, the true story about a talented young artist who fell in love with a humble baker's daughter. I was determined to do so. For a while.

But then the money Bibbiena paid me kept coming in and Margarita's refusal to see Giulio, who persisted in trying to see her every few weeks, assured me I shouldn't even bother. And the years slipped by. Six to be exact. I knew what the right choice was, reminded by the now recurring dream, but it was easier not to make it. Margarita had the money. She was fine. Probably.

Then I received a letter.

San Apollonia Convent, 19th April 1526

My dearest Pietro,

    ~~I will be dead by the time you read this letter~~ *The end of this life is nigh for me and though it fills my heart with joy to know I will be with my beloved Raphael soon, my leaving this world is bittersweet. These last six years have not been the agony I feared. In many ways they have been a joy.*

    I have a child, you see, Rubina, who reminds me of her father every day and brings such sweet purpose to my life. There was a time ~~when I wanted to leave this~~ *when I would have seen death as a blessed release, I would have been grateful for its aggressive approach,* ~~its rapid invasion arrival in my body little by little.~~ *but no longer. I have fought and resisted with every fibre in my body so as to keep it at bay. Of late,*

*the nuns who are caring for me tell me I'm losing the battle.
I don't have long.*

*~~Forgive my directness but~~ I want you to look after Rubina.
My good, honest friend, I have loved you and seen you as a
brother, I know how loyal you were to Raphael, and how you
have tried to be so to me. The nuns told me how a young artist
repeatedly attempted to see me over the years and I thank you
for that. Forgive me that I did not have the courage to accept
your visits. It seemed better that way.*

*I want you to look after Rubina. I know I have written
that already, but apart from saying goodbye and thanking
you for the loyalty and friendship you showed me, that is the
reason for this letter – Rubina. Are you surprised? Yes, I have
a daughter, Raphael's daughter, and it is to you alone that I
can entrust our most precious jewel.*

*I send the money that I have never touched for you to buy
that vineyard in the countryside you talked of owning once.
There, I remembered. The box that is with it also contains our
wedding rings, Raphael's and mine, as well as the pendant
of Saint Sebastiano you gave to me as a keepsake the last
time we met. But I have struggled against the darkness long
enough. I am tiring and need to keep the strength to hold
my one perfect creation in my arms once more. It is time for
me to say goodbye. The nuns have gone to fetch Rubina. She
will be here, waiting for you when you come. I know you will
be kind to her.*

Your ever-loving Margarita

Margarita and Raphael had a daughter. I thought back to the
nausea when she came to the workshop in January. I'd noticed
she was feeling sick, but as she'd come to check on Raphael I'd
thought it was worry that had made her so. Then the day I went
to see her for the last time at the convent came back to me – the

317

signs that she was with child were all there and I'd missed them. A daughter.

Shock, love, shame, anger, I felt them all. My sin was clear to me now. While heaven had wheeled its glories out for me to behold I had kept my eyes firmly fixed on the mud beneath my feet and there I'd wallowed, mired in jealousy and lies. Margarita believed to the very end in my honesty, testament to her integrity, and yet I had not even tried to see her again. That was Giulio. Oh, how her faith in me was misplaced.

I looked back over the letter with its crossings-out: the rushed outpourings of a woman who was running out of time. The vineyard. Of all the things for her to remember. I'd forgotten about it. I was moved, my conscience, with a hide as tough as old leather boots as a rule, crackled with the first signs of life as her words unlocked doors in my heart that I had thought locked forever. But to think that she believed I might look after her child. No. I put the letter down. She trusted me. She'd always trusted me.

Well, more fool her.

I looked up old Francesco. He was Margarita's father after all. He could go and collect this Rubina. But I quickly discovered that wasn't going to happen. He'd shut up shop late 1520. Local gossip had it that he'd died of a broken heart. Rubina would not be looked after by him.

Next I tried to track down the Luti sister I'd never met. Discovered I never would. She'd left Rome with her husband's family to go and live in the mountains. No one knew which ones. Rubina would not be looked after by her aunt.

I couldn't think of who else to ask. In the meantime the child was still at the convent and the money for her care had been delivered to me. And the box. I opened it: inside were rings, pearls, brooches, and buried beneath them all was the Saint Sebastiano pendant. My weak flesh, as confused as my mind, shivered. My body was as cold as death, yet covered in sweat as I pushed away memories of mutilated bodies and dark, scorching eyes. The pendant was cursed. And I had given it to Margarita. Was that why she'd died?

My head said no while the quickness of my breathing showed that my body said otherwise. I snatched the vile object up and pushed it down deep into the bottom of a pocket. I could bear to look at it no more. I rushed outside and wandered the streets. I had much to think about.

Soon my mind was back with the child.

She would be better off staying in the convent. That was the only solution. I would tell the child's story, I reasoned with myself. That way, one day, a day when I was dead and gone, she would be able to find out what really happened between her mother and her father. Until then, she would be better off staying with the nuns.

Unable to keep my hands off the pendant, I turned it round between forefinger and thumb over and over again as my conscience, still sluggish, struggled to find the right thing to do. Distracted, I bumped into someone I had not seen for six years. I was miles away. I wished the man I'd walked into had been.

My hand flew to the accursed pendant, gripping it in terror. It was him. The Cardinal's man. He was back.

The moment he saw me, his eyes – sharp as arrows – pierced my skin. I fled. I had to get rid of the pendant. I passed beggars, arms outstretched. Should I give the accursed piece to one of them? My conscience, newly roused, whispered no.

I quickened my pace to keep up with the rapid beating of my heart, my head bursting with confusion. I weaved my way down alleys, around corners, pushing through walls of people, on and on, my head turning back constantly to check the Cardinal's man wasn't following me, my fingers pulling roughly at my collar as I struggled for breath. A hand clamped itself around my arm, stopping me dead. The drumming of my heart was louder than ever.

'You dropped this.' A kind-eyed stranger's hand held up the *cimaruta* Margarita had given to me. I reached out for it in desperate gratitude and held it in my free hand. It had been my

319

portafortuna – my lucky charm – for such a long time, while I realised all too well that the pendant of Saint Sebastiano did nothing but attract *il malocchio* – the evil eye – to its wearer. I knew what I had to do. The best place for this poisoned chalice, not just for myself but for everyone, was the bottom of the Tiber. I rushed to the riverbank and threw it out over the water as far as I could and waited for the splash.

A moment, that was all it took, and then it was gone. I would never get to wear it again; it would not hang around some poor man's neck; nor would it lie at the bottom of an innocent young girl's jewellery box. The burden weighing heavy on my chest had been lifted, and as I looked up at the clear blue sky I could have sworn I felt the first flutterings of hope within my heart.

Before I knew where I was, a nun was walking towards me in the shade and light of the cloisters. I had found my way to the convent to see about Margarita's daughter. I would make arrangements with her, the nun, I told myself, for the girl to be kept on here. What good would I be as the child's carer?

'*Signore* Pietro?' A small voice called me by my name. I don't know why but it took me by surprise. But not as much as what happened next. I looked down and saw, peering out from behind the folds of the nun's dark habit, familiar, kind brown eyes. They smiled up at me, their warmth as comforting as the sun. Like her father's. Everything changed in that moment. This was Raphael's daughter. Strange and wonderful to think how something as insubstantial as a look could have the power to navigate the course of a life and lead it to the right path.

She put her little hand in mine, reminding me I was still holding the *cimaruta*.

'Here,' I said, placing it round her neck. 'This belongs to you.'

And that was how I met dear sweet Rubina, her mother's very special jewel, with her father's eyes. I had no choice but to choose her. She was my past and my punishment. When I looked at her I remembered the love her parents had shown me and why I had not deserved it. But she was also my future, my redemption. I would care for her and atone for my sins. I would tell the truth and pray for salvation, and do all I could to protect her.

*

And so I retired to a vineyard, far from Rome, Rubina in tow. I would not blame you if you thought I'd left the city to escape the Cardinal's assistant. However, love was the greater reason. For Rubina's parents. For Rubina. Truth was another. I needed space and time to tell it. And so far love and truth have been forgiving of me.

My life has been sweeter than I deserve, my days taken up with tending the vines while listening to the laughs of a happy child playing with a puppy, before I sit down of an evening, while she sleeps peacefully in her bed, to record her history.

Night after night, I have purified myself with tears, remembering Raphael. Yet it is over the girl whose reputation I wilfully destroyed that I have cried the most. I confess I did bad things against her knowingly. Like Judas I deceived her for thirty pieces of silver. She believed in honour, in virtue, in self-respect. I was desperate to take them away from her. I failed, I realise, whenever I commit the next part of her story to paper, whether as the artist's model, the baker's daughter, the friend, the girl Raphael fell in love with, the woman in the painting, the bride, Rubina's mother. I carry her identities deep within, each one a beacon of truth in the darkness that is, or I dare to hope, was, my soul. I know it is too late, to bring her back to life, but I can restore the shine to a reputation that I, and others, sought to tarnish.

Margarita was blameless. She loved and was loved, and her only crime was to have been lowborn and that is no crime at all.

There. I've come to the end of my tale. My eyes are misting up. I've never liked goodbyes. I will miss revisiting the maestro and his woman in the painting.

But Rubina is calling me. I must have stayed up all night to finish. 'Coming, Rubina!' She's calling me to light and to life. I have no choice but to go to her.

Historical Note

Although inspired by a true story the facts narrated and the characters represented in this novel are fictitious.

Key paintings in the novel

La Fornarina, a portrait of the baker's daughter, by Sebastiano Luciani (now known as Sebastiano del Piombo) 1512, the Uffizi, Florence

La Donna Velata, a portrait of the baker's daughter, Margarita Luti, by Raphael, 1514, Pitti Palace, Rome

La Fornarina, a nude portrait of Margarita Luti, by Raphael, 1519, Villa Barberini, Rome

Acknowledgements

For the story I am indebted to the following:

Giorgio Vasari, whose **Lives of the Artists** gave me the push I needed, after seeing Raphael's La Fornarina, to write about the woman in the painting, the baker's daughter, Margarita Luti. According to Vasari, one evening the great artist indulged in pleasure with her 'more than his usual excess', only to return home 'in a violent fever' from which he died. Ever after, historians, artists and writers, from Balzac to Picasso, have vilified Margarita Luti as Woman, who, with her lascivious ways, robbed the world of a great genius.

Vasari created a myth: that Raphael died from too much sex, and Margarita was to blame. My eyebrow arches as much now as it ever did whenever I think of this. I had no choice but to pick over the bones of history to discover a story that would exonerate her. So, thank you Giorgio for rousing me to action.

Nabokov for drawing my attention to the feud between Sebastiano and Raphael and suggesting the baker's daughter was at the root of it. This added a much-needed tension to the relationship between the three of them.

Maurizio Bernadelli Curuz, and the article in The Guardian, June 2005, where I read about the art historian's X-ray analysis of Raphael's La Fornarina. It revealed Margarita wearing a ruby wedding ring, surrounded by myrtle and quince. These symbols of matrimony had been painted over shortly after Raphael's death.

For making it from idea to publication I extend my heartfelt gratitude to:

The **HQDigital** team for making this possible.

The very special **Abigail Fenton** who helped me whip my narrator into shape and showed me unfailing support, kindness, not to mention patience during the editing process. She has been a beacon of positivity throughout.

Dear Reader,

We hope you enjoyed reading this book. If you did, we'd be so appreciative if you left a review. It really helps us and the author to bring more books like this to you.

Here at HQ Digital we are dedicated to publishing fiction that will keep you turning the pages into the early hours. Don't want to miss a thing? To find out more about our books, promotions, discover exclusive content and enter competitions you can keep in touch in the following ways:

JOIN OUR COMMUNITY:

Sign up to our new email newsletter: hyperurl.co/hqnewsletter

Read our new blog www.hqstories.co.uk

🐦 : https://twitter.com/HQDigitalUK

📘 : www.facebook.com/HQStories

BUDDING WRITER?

We're also looking for authors to join the HQ Digital family!

Find out more here:

https://www.hqstories.co.uk/want-to-write-for-us/

Thanks for reading, from the HQ Digital team

Keep reading for an excerpt
from *A Forbidden Love* . . .

PROLOGUE

March 1940, Malaga

Luis de los Rios ran out of the university building onto the Avenida de Cervantes, black jacket in one hand, tan leather folder in the other. The porter called after him, 'Running late today, Señor?' But the unlikely academic had already been swallowed up by the bushes on the other side of the road.

He was on the Paseo del Parque, a long pathway shaded by trees that ran between the harbour and Malaga's old town. Every Friday morning between ten and eleven Luis walked up and down it. Always on the same day, always at the same hour. He never taught then. He'd insisted it be written into his contract. No one knew why. And today he was running late.

At 9.50 a.m. a student had turned up at his door. Luis' instinct had been to brush him aside but the better part of him had won out. He'd sat back, listened to the boy. Or tried to. He'd looked at his watch – 9.52 – and rolled his eyes. Looked at his watch again: 9.57. He thrummed his fingers loudly on the desk. Why was he not able to focus on anything the boy was saying? By seven minutes past ten Luis had had enough. The wooden chair he'd been sitting on went crashing to the floor. 'I must go,' he'd said, running to the door, hurtling along the corridor and flying out of the building. And wishing he'd listened to his instinct in the first place.

It was ten minutes past ten by the time Luis set foot on the path in the park. Lined by tall plane and palm trees, it felt like a cool, dark, cavernous cathedral and it calmed him instantly. He blinked. His eyes adjusted to make out strips of light and shade on the path beneath his feet. He looked upwards. The sun shot through the green ceiling above. He blinked again. His eyes focused further. He saw people as they walked back and forth under the high, fringed canopies, an optical illusion of unbroken movements bathed in radiance.

Was she here?

He was later than usual – 'but not too late,' he said to himself.

He proceeded to walk along the path. Purpose pumped through his veins. His skin tingled, senses crackled, as parakeets flew through the air, their plumage igniting into a vivid green. Their fiery wings blazed a trail into his soul, lifting him on his way.

He went past the old men, acknowledging them as he passed, just as he did every week; nodded to the widows, and the young women who shared their grief. They were here, survivors all, leading a semblance of a normal life, just as he was, refusing to let the past destroy them. They milled around, sat on benches, talked about the weather. Luis winced, moved by the dignity of the everyday in the face of a memory of the horror they all shared: civil war. A nation could not recover from it easily.

Yet if innocence had gone forever, hope had not. That's why he was here, making his way to a clandestine meeting, the details of which he'd written in a note and handed to a girl over four years ago.

He didn't even know if she'd read it.

Meeting place: *the Antonio Muñoz Degrain monument, Parque de Malaga*

Time: *10–11 a.m.*

Day: *Friday*

I'll wait for you.

Luis sat on a bench and looked at his watch: 10.45. He thought back to the last time he'd seen her. He'd pushed her away. He'd had to. It was time for her to go. But he had given her the letter. She had it. He hoped she'd read it.

He leant back against a bench and cast another glance down at his watch. 10.55. Time to start making his way back to the university. He'd always been a good timekeeper. A smile broke out across his face as he remembered that the girl he loved had not. He ran his fingers through his hair, resigned to the fact he'd not found her. This time.

He went to pick up his jacket and folder when the screech of a parakeet overhead distracted him. Threat or warning, either way it was too late. The brilliantly coloured bird had already left its dull coloured deposit on the shoulder of his crisp, white shirt.

'Filthy beast!'

An old gypsy woman dressed in tattered clothes, a black shawl wrapped around her wiry grey hair, smiled at him through cata-ract-misted eyes. 'Supposed to be lucky,' she laughed at him. In the haze of her fading sight Luis had something of the angel about him. To Luis, she looked like a fat, old bird, too large and heavy for the tree above, sat as she was on a nest made of cloth, her skirts billowing up all around. He watched as she plunged her hand in amongst the many layers that surrounded her. She pulled out a dull-coloured patch with frayed edges and waved it at him.

For want of anything better to clean himself up with, Luis accepted her tattered offering. He rubbed away at his shirt as quickly as he could, his head nodding in the gypsy woman's direction, grateful that all that was left of the parakeet's slimy gift was a suspicious, damp stain on his left shoulder. She flashed her crucifix at him in response with a smile that made her eyes disappear. But now he really had to go. He walked swiftly back along the dry, dusty path, shouting back his thanks.

He'd very nearly packed all the emotions he'd allowed to spill out over this last hour back into the neat compartments he'd allotted them in his mind when he lurched backwards, pulled back by a familiar voice. 'Don't run off now, Paloma!' A little girl, swift as a comet, hurtled past him, her flaming hair dragging his eyes along with her. When the speeding ball of fire screeched to a halt back along the path, not far from the Antonio Muñoz Degrain monument, Luis' heart missed a beat.

The child clung on to a young woman with long, dark hair.

It was her. It was Maria.

Chapter 1

'What are you going to do when you grow up?' It was a clear spring day in 1936 and Maria lay back under the gnarled, black branches of the olive tree and looked up at the Andalucian sky above: vivid blue, and as cloudless as the future she saw for herself. She and her friend Paloma often sought shade and solace in this grove, under this tree, far away from the dust and heat of the village. And here they would dream.

'When I grow up, I'm going to . . .' Paloma began. She flicked out her fingers in frustration, brushing Maria's own. 'Oh, I don't know!' she cried in answer to the older girl's question – but she did. She would grow up to do the same as her mother, and her mother's mother before her. A husband would be found for her, she would have children, and both she and her husband would work up on the landowner's estate. That was the way it was; that was the way it had always been. Paloma's fate was as set as if written in the stars. It was only Maria who saw a future full of possibilities for her friend as she gazed into the bright, limitless sky above. And Paloma loved her for it.

Instinctively she turned on her side to wrap her limbs around Maria's. Legs, arms, fingers interlaced, a tangle as fixed and as complex as the roots of the olive tree beneath.

The girls' skins squelched, mollusc-like, as Maria pulled herself away. Pushing herself up to sitting, she propped her back up against the solid trunk of the tree.

She looked at Paloma, cheek squashed against forearm. The skin, usually so plump and firm, gathered in folds and pushed her left eye closed. It struck Maria that in that moment her friend took after her mother Cecilia, whose skin cascaded in folds all over her body; ill-fitting, stretched and worn out, through overuse no doubt. Maria's father would often sing the woman's praises – how she fed her children well, repaired their clothes, kept a spotless home, worked hard – but the fact remained that Paloma's mother was irritable, illiterate and limited. There. Maria had thought it again. Guilt ran a feather over her skin, causing her to shiver. Perhaps she'd judged Paloma's mother too harshly – her father was always telling her so – but the fact remained: if she didn't show Paloma there was another way to live, a future other than the one she saw mapped out for herself, then her dear, sweet-natured friend would slowly but surely turn into a beast of burden, just like poor old Cecilia.

And Maria wouldn't be able to live with herself if she allowed that to happen.

'Sit up,' she snapped. 'So, what do you want to do when you grow up?' She would have a response.

Paloma rubbed her eyes and sighed.

'If you don't answer I'll have to ask somebody else.' Maria's voice was sharp and vaguely menacing. Her eyes scanned the olive grove for possible candidates. They alighted upon a herd of goats resting under a nearby tree. She recognised her own stupidity.

Thankfully Paloma did not.

'No, it's fine. I'll play,' the gentle soul said, her tone one of quiet resignation. Two years younger than Maria, she always felt grateful the older girl had chosen her and not her sister Lola to confide in. Lola was sixteen, the same age as Maria. It would have made sense for the two older girls to be close. But they weren't.

Never had been. They were fond enough of each other, and the fact that they were opposites in every single way was not, in itself, insurmountable. But that Paloma was so easy to be with, so innocent and good-natured, made her a perfect companion. Lola's little sister had become the little sister that Maria had always wanted. She could love and protect her, and teach her about all the great and good things in life. Lola, on the other hand, came fully formed with a tongue as sharp as a knife.

Paloma brought her chin to nestle in the curve between her knees, her black hair still curled up flat with perspiration around her face. A stray lock misbehaved and draped itself like a dark rope against the deep pink of a cheek that was soft and plump once more. If Cecilia had ever looked like this Maria could not imagine it. She leant over towards her friend and pushed the dark unruly coil back with tenderness and waited for an answer.

'Well,' Paloma began, unsure how to proceed. To get married was the pinnacle of her life, and the thought of a wedding with an abundance of flowers, food, finery, and all the froth that went with it, had started to fill many a quiet moment. But to admit this, Paloma knew, would displease her friend. She waited for guidance.

'Will you have children?' Maria asked.

'Y-yes,' Paloma answered. 'Once I'm married.'

'Why?' Maria asked.

'Why? Why what?'

'Why would you get married before having children?'

Paloma's dark brown eyes widened; Maria's creased with satisfaction. 'In fact,' Maria ventured, emboldened by the surprise in Paloma's eyes, 'why would you get married . . . *at all*?' Her young friend's already wide eyes turned into the fullest of moons.

The evening before, Señor Suarez, the village teacher who used to work in Madrid and still had family and friends in the capital, had come to eat with Maria and her father, Doctor Alvaro.

The winds of change were blowing and whistling their sinewy path around Spain and though they'd barely touched Fuentes de

Andalucía in any significant way, the more travelled citizens, of which Señor Suarez was one, often brought back stories from the outside world whenever they returned to the sleepy little village. Suarez was teacher, philosopher, and general do-er of good deeds (mostly political), and a frequent dinner guest at Maria's home where the precarious state of the government and how to best help workers in the area were his topics of choice. But last night, as he had smiled over at Maria and realised for the first time that she was a young woman, his conversation had taken a new turn.

'You know, in Madrid, and I hear it's the same in Malaga, things are so very different for women now. They have more freedom. More choice.' He'd looked over at Doctor Alvaro who'd nodded for him to continue. Suarez had already told them that night about a growing vegetarian movement in the capital. Nothing his friend had to say, Alvaro thought to himself as he chewed on a particularly gristly bit of sausage, could be more challenging for both he and his daughter to swallow than that.

But then again.

'A woman no longer has to get married if she wants to live with a man.'

The doctor had choked on the wine he'd just poured into his mouth. He'd expected talk of work opportunities, education . . . not co-habitation. But he was open-minded, fair, forward-thinking; he knew his good friend to be so too. 'Please, carry on,' he'd spluttered, waving his hands around as he struggled to keep his eyebrows from arching.

'And it's true that some women no longer want to have children.'

This time it had been Maria who'd choked, though her father's eyebrows, try as he might to stop them, now leapt up to meet his fast receding hairline. This was a strange conversation indeed. Fascinating and embarrassing for Maria in equal measure. The teacher's words had slapped her full in the face like a wave, waking her from her romantic dreams; as they receded, she'd taken in their meaning.

'To have or not to have children, women see it as their right, their right to choose. Times are changing.' And with that Se or Suarez had coughed most dramatically, prompting the doctor to slap him hastily and heartily on the back while pointing his daughter towards the door with his eyes.

Maria hovered around the old oak table, topping up wine glasses and clearing away dishes as if she hadn't noticed.

'How's the reading programme going up at El Cortijo del Bosque?' Doctor Alvaro asked his friend.

El Cortijo del Bosque was the name of the local estate owned by Don Felipe, principal employer in the area. Work on his estate was agricultural. His workers were paid a pittance. Don Felipe himself was fabulously wealthy. And that was how it had been for centuries.

But things weren't only changing in Madrid.

In February 1936 the left-wing coalition, known as *el Frente Popular*, had won the general election in Spain. This had allowed the good doctor and teacher to push through much needed reforms in Fuentes de Andalucía in general, and up at El Cortijo del Bosque in particular. In the early months of the year both had worked tirelessly to secure better pay and conditions for the estate's workers, Suarez at the negotiating table, Alvaro behind the scenes. Guido, the estate manager, represented his employer's interests, at times most savagely. But, snarl as he might, there was little he could do against what was legal; he had the will, but not the right, to resist.

Don Felipe, the landowner, was furious of course: with Guido and with the useless lumps of flesh who worked his land and whom he thought less of than his bulls and horses. As for Suarez and Alvaro, if Guido had ever mentioned them to him he certainly didn't care enough about them to waste his energy remembering their names; they were men of no consequence. No, he was too busy shouting abuse at Manuel Azaňa, the new prime minister, along with the motley collection of left-wing degenerates that made up the government, to take any notice of them. Don Felipe despaired. Even his beloved Falangist party, a party that believed in the true greatness of Spain, in the monarchy, the Catholic Church and centuries of tradition, was coming under attack.

Don Felipe's Spain, the Spain he knew and loved, was disappearing.

He had no choice but to whisk his family off to their second home in Biarritz.

And thus Suarez had no choice but to seize the moment and take education to the workers so that at the next round of negotiations they would be able to help themselves. That was what he was doing presently up at El Cortijo del Bosque. And Guido could do nothing to prevent it, no matter what orders his master barked at him from the south of France. But progress was slow.

'The truth is we need more teachers,' Suarez had confessed.

'The truth is very few people in the village can read,' Alvaro had replied. The sound of a creaking door disturbed him. His eyes had shot round like a searchlight at the top of a watch tower. There, standing in the kitchen doorway, a copy of *Don Quixote* clutched to her body, was his daughter.

'*You* can do it,' he'd said, knowing she'd been listening to them and confident that she would relish the chance. She'd nodded, pulling back her chair to re-join them. But before her skirt could touch the rush seat her father's voice had scooped her back up and pushed her out of the room and towards the staircase. 'Now bed, my girl!'

'But if I'm to help out surely I need to . . .'

'Bed!'

That night Maria hadn't minded that her attempts to stay up late had failed. She had gone to bed happy and excited. Happy that she would be helping Señor Suarez with the reading programme, excited at what he'd told her about women in Madrid. All night ideas of choice and freedom had stampeded around in her head looking for somewhere to live.

By morning they'd found a home. The teacher's words were now her own.

And so that was how Maria was here, under her favourite olive tree, about to take a familiar game in a new direction. Starting to feel sticky, she shook her hair, generating at most a slight, warm breeze. She cast a 'brace yourself' look in Paloma's direction: her friend was about to become the testing ground for her very own liberal education project.

She repeated, as word-perfectly as she could, what Señor Suarez had said about women, children and marriage the night before. She lingered on the phrase 'right to choose'.

Paloma said nothing. Maria continued.

'Señor Suarez—' Maria slipped in his name because Paloma liked him '—said that women in Madrid have more . . .' The older girl paused before opening her arms out wide and shouting out 'freedom.' She could not have drawn any more attention to the word if she'd underlined it and decorated it with a bright red ribbon.

Paloma fell back against the tree.

'Well, you could get married, if you want to,' Maria backtracked. 'But you don't have to. That's what I'm saying. Things are changing. Gone are the days when parents start planning a wedding the moment a boy looks at a girl.' Paloma breathed heavily out through her nose as if by the expulsion of air alone she could find room in her head for this shocking revelation. That she dropped her head to one side suggested that she'd failed. It was far too heavy a load for her fourteen-year-old brain to manage. She looked questioningly at Maria and rubbed the back of her head as if it were a magic lamp. A light flickered in her eyes.

'It's true,' Maria insisted. 'According to Señor Suarez, women are having babies and they aren't even married. In Madrid. Even Malaga!' Paloma screwed up her nose then let out a snort. Madrid and Malaga were both as alien to her as the moon and every bit as inaccessible. 'And some women in the city don't even want to have children. At all. Not ever,' Maria continued. 'That's what Se or Suarez says. They'd much rather have *a career*.'

The older girl looked up at the sky and hid herself there a while, a smile of satisfaction on her lips. She'd delivered what she told herself was her *coup de grâce* (a phrase she'd learnt quite recently after having found it in some book or other, and she congratulated herself on having found an opportunity to use it, even if it was inside her own head). She'd chased away all thoughts of husbands and playing children from this game of theirs.

Paloma scrunched up her eyes to scrutinise her friend more closely. Was she teasing? Admittedly, Paloma had trouble imagining a husband for herself. As she went over the list of local prospective suitors she could not deny that they were unappealing. She shuddered as she had them parade across the stage of her mind one by one. Maria liked to re-christen them, as pirates, or book characters, to make them more exciting for her friend, but even that didn't seem to be working for Paloma at this moment in time. Perhaps, if she were lucky, she might find a husband who came from another village. Or a nearby town. She pulled herself together. She would have a husband, one day, of that she was certain. But there was no point making herself distressed by going through all candidates just yet. As for children, of course, she sighed with relief, on safer and more comforting ground, she most certainly would have them.

Maria must want them too, surely, Paloma thought to herself. *'That girl has no sense of family!' 'She's always been such a selfish girl!'* Her mother's unfair criticisms of her friend ricocheted around the confines of Paloma's own mind. Maria was an only child. She had no mother. Cecilia always used one or other fact as an accusation whenever Maria did anything she didn't agree with. Although she did not like the damning place that her mother's reasoning led her to, Paloma found her own thoughts heading in the same direction today. She knew better than to articulate them. Instead, she would enter into the spirit of the discussion.

'If you don't want to get married, or have children, then what does it mean to be a girl?' Paloma wriggled with what she told herself was justifiable indignation as she asked Maria the question. Maria gnawed on her thumbnail. She hadn't expected rebellion. 'What indeed!' she said, dodging the bullet. She sat back and looked up at the infinite blue of the sky yet again. 'All I know,' she replied at last, 'is that I don't want to tie myself to any man.' She stood up and brushed the earth from her clothes. And with that she drew the game to a close.

But Paloma hadn't finished.

'I don't believe you!' she retorted, still indignant. 'You're in love with Ricar.'

'Oh, don't be so silly!' said Maria. 'And if you're talking about Richard, it has a *ch* and a *d* in it. And it would help if you could learn how to pronounce his name. Properly. In English.' And with that she walked away and headed back to the village.

'What's love got to do with it anyway?' she called back over her shoulder.

If you enjoyed *The Woman in the Painting*, then why not try another sweeping historical novel from HQ Digital?

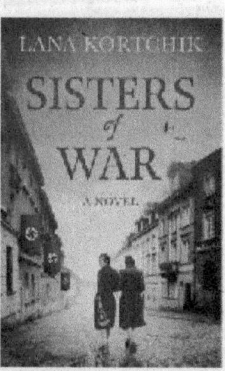